THE BEAST OF THE CAMARGUE

Xavier-Marie Bonnot

THE BEAST
OF THE CAMARGUE

Translated from the French by
Ian Monk

MACLEHOSE PRESS
QUERCUS · LONDON

First published in Great Britain in 2009 by

MacLehose Press
An imprint of Quercus
21 Bloomsbury Square
London
WC1A 2NS

The Beast of the Camargue by Xavier-Marie Bonnot © Editions L'Ecailler du sud,
Published with original French title: *La Bête du Marais*
The Beast of the Camargue is published by arrangement with L'Ecailler du sud,
care of Agence litteraire Pierre Astier & Associés
ALL RIGHTS RESERVED

English Translation Copyright © 2009 by Ian Monk

A CIP catalogue reference for this book is available
from the British Library

ISBN 978 1 906694 10 4 (HB)
ISBN 978 1 906694 11 1 (TPB)

Printed and ... es plc

To my father, who first told me the story
of the Tarasque when I was his little boy.

AUTHOR'S NOTE AND ACKNOWLEDGEMENTS

The characters and situations in this novel are the product of my imagination, and are not based on reality.

Some sections will probably bring a smile to the lips of specialists in prehistory or members of the Marseille murder squad. I have intentionally altered places, transformed research laboratories, shifted around hospitals, upturned hierarchies and metamorphosed the murder squad's offices. I have also taken liberties with a number of official procedures.

Without asking a single word of permission . . .

My sincere thanks go first to Maurice Georges and Jérôme Harlay, two friends who spent many hours correcting this text and who have enriched it with their always pertinent remarks. My gratitude also to Michel Emerit, formerly professor of animal ecology at the University of Montpellier and correspondent for the Museum of Natural History, who was of great assistance thanks to his knowledge of the environment of the Camargue, and the documentation he supplied about its flora and fauna.

TRANSLATOR'S NOTE

In the original French, a large amount of Marseille slang is used. No attempt has been made to imitate its probably inimitable presence.

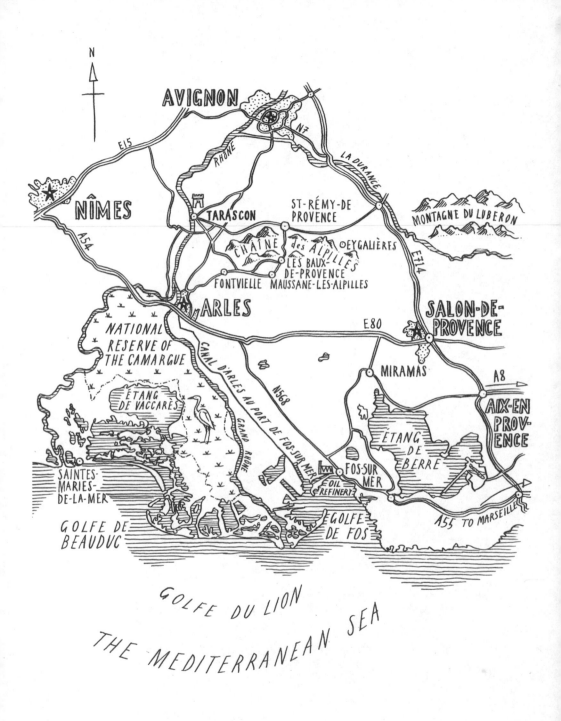

. . . Alabre
De sang uman e de cadabre,
Dins nòsti bos e nòsti vabre
Un moustren, un fléu di diéu, barruolo . . . Agués pieta!

La bèsti a la co d'un coulobre,
A d'iue mai rouge qu'un cinobre;
Sus l'esquino a d'escaumo e d'àsti que fan pòu!
D'un gros lioun porto lou mourre
E sièis pèd d'ome pèr miés courre;
Dins sa cafourne, souto un mourre
Que domino lou Rose, emporto ço que pòu.

. . . Thirsty
For human blood and corpses
In our woods and our ravines
Roams a monster, a scourge of the gods . . . Have mercy!

The beast has a dragon's tail
And eyes redder than cinnabar;
On its back, its scales and spikes are terrifying!
It has the muzzle of a great lion,
And six human feet, to run faster;
Into its cavern, under a rock
Overlooking the Rhône, it carries all it can.

Frédéric Mistral, *Mireille*

1.

Last night, the mistral had stopped suddenly, just after nightfall. There had then been a moment of delirium, the bars had turned into bodegas full of heady music, gleaming faces and sleepless eyes.

The police patrols cruised around in second gear, laid back and bored to tears. A few brawls broke out between gypsies, Arabs and gorillas from the town hall outside a gaudy fairground. But the national police force turned a blind eye – no treading on the toes of the boys from the municipal brigade.

The last crackers had exploded far away, in the hidden nooks and crannies of the town, before the sun came up: the last fireworks of a party that weariness had now put to bed.

That morning, liquid heat poured down from the sky.

The man was lying on the riverbank, in the foetal position, arms wrapped round his knees. He opened his eyes and, through his twitching eyelids, saw the white shape of the towers of the castle above him, melting into the saturated light.

The man was drenched in sweat, his raven hair stuck to his forehead like strips of cardboard. In the distance he could hear vague noises, presumably the last party animals stumbling home. But he very soon changed his mind: it was the baying of an angry crowd that was echoing off the walls of the fortress.

The clamour made his head spin. He closed his eyes again.

The man had hardly slept for three days. Three days of solitude. A taste of acid bile twisted his lips and flared his nostrils. The pastis he had drunk had now worn off. Time to get going.

He sat up. In front of him, the Rhône flowed calmly by. A few crooked roots scratched at the placid surface like monsters, as though trying to hold back the river's regal progress. He tried to stand, but then realised that his legs would not hold him for a while, so he lay back on the warm, dry grass and stared at the powerful branches of the acacia that clawed at the sky above him.

It was time to think, to go over the past three days.

On the first day, as soon as the sun rose over the Camargue, he had started watching out for white spoonbills, spending hours hidden like a crocodile in the rock samphire across the marshland, a few metres from the Redon lagoon.

He had been waiting for months for the spoonbills, since March, when thousands of grey mullet gather in the placid waters of the delta, within easy swimming distance of the empty beaches, still shivering with cold; the time of year when the cormorants and herons come to gorge themselves on the surface fish.

For some time he had been studying the habits of spoonbills, and the places where they came to rest on their way back from Africa. This was often at the foot of clumps of tamarisks. He wanted to be able to observe them in the dawn's golden light, but spoonbills are capricious as well as rare. That year, he had had to make do with the gluttonous antics of the cormorants and herons.

That morning, those large birds had still not appeared. He had waited until noon before finally deciding to change his vantage point and heading further west, towards the Capelière nature reserve. He had exchanged a few words with the keeper. Chitchat, nothing more.

During the afternoon, he wandered around for some time, his loaded camera in one hand and his binoculars in the other, stopping now and then to observe.

He had walked to the ends of the earth. Then the first spoonbill appeared, immaculate, stretching its long neck through the reeds, at the edge of the marsh. A second came to rest on a half-submerged tree trunk, in the middle of the dark waters. The ground, cracked in places and spongy in others, led away towards the setting sun, the flat horizon and the sea, which the mistral was furrowing.

The spoonbills had then flown back into their mysterious habitat, and night fell on the tip of the Camargue. In the distance, beyond the straight lines of the marshland, the flames of the great Fos oil terminal rose red into the dark sky, like proud banners. At one in the morning, he went back to his car and drove home, further north in Provence.

Day two was the day of the beast.

He had decided not to take his car and to hitchhike instead. He had waited a good hour for a friendly driver to pick him up at the Tarascon exit. It was a solitary tourist, an Englishman burned by the wicked sun, who had said, in perfect French:

"I've been living in Mouriès for three years now."

"Really?" he had replied, pretending to take an interest in his driver. "I come from Eygalières."

"I'm going to Marseille today . . . taking the boat to Corsica," the Englishman went on, waving a hand through the hot air towards an imaginary sea.

"You have a good journey," he had said, for want of anything better.

The Englishman's Land-Rover, an old model, about as comfortable as a church pew, made one hell of a din. By the time they reached the turning that led to the Thibert farmhouse he had fallen into a sort of torpor, before pointing to a lay-by on the long straight stretch of Route Nationale 568, between Arles and Martigues.

"You can drop me off there."

The Englishman braked abruptly, without asking any questions. The man got out and waited for the Land-Rover to fade into the distance. Then he slipped off through a barrier of reeds, careful to avoid their long leaves, which were as sharp as razors.

He walked straight on, like a bush hunter, across the huge flat expanse covered with scrawny grass and partitioned in squares by barbed wire: an hour's walk, perhaps more. Behind him, in the distance, rose the dark crests of the Alpilles hills and the peak of Les Opiès, bleached by the sun's last gleams.

Far off, in the direction of the rank of cypresses, the sheep of Méril farm were just visible. Not pausing for a moment, he leaped over a fence and found himself in the middle of some heifers, presumably belonging to the Castaldi herd. He walked straight on, keeping close enough to the pitch-black calves so as not to be spotted by chance passers-by, but far enough away so as not to spook them. A couple of times, his gaze met their empty eyes.

But he knew them too well to be afraid.

The day was fading by the time he reached Départementale 35, which marked the eastern border of Vigueirat national park, just a few kilometres away from Thibert's farm. He decided to spend the night on that strip of the Camargue. The end of the day was luminous, as thousands of stars came out over Provence. Before nightfall, he was back at the beach and had crept through the ruddy clumps of samphire, without being noticed. Then he waited, as he usually did, flat on his stomach among the pink sea daffodils, white sand camomile and yellow sandy everlastings.

Then he sang, and the beast came. He told it of the Festival marvels and then took his leave.

When darkness fell on sea and land, he unrolled his sleeping bag in a warm hollow of a dune, sheltered from the wind. He slept for a few hours. In the depth of his sleep, he toyed with his craziest dream: to liberate the beast on the Festival of Saint Martha.

On the night of July 29.

He would talk about it with the master. But, in any case, he didn't give a damn for his advice. The monster listened only to him.

The Rhône flowed on, heavy with late spring rain. Beneath the walls of King René's Castle, some children had climbed onto a little promontory over the green waters of the river by clinging to the ivy that snaked its way along the rocks.

The man had completely recovered his spirits. He stood up, slung his jacket over his shoulder and walked towards the cries of the crowd.

It was Monday, June 30. The third day.

The last bull race had just finished, and with it, the grand festival of la Tarasque.

2.

The bell of the Opéra Municipal of Marseille echoed brightly from the gallery stairway to the marble of the main function room. It stopped abruptly when Michel de Palma burst into the Reyer Hall. Félix Merlino, the ancient cloakroom attendant, patted down the few locks of curly hair which still fringed his gleaming scalp.

"Ah, Michel! You're the last!"

Merlino grimaced, making his massive chin rise and his pale lips droop.

"Hello, Féli, has it started?"

"Oh yes, it's started! For the last time this year. Come on, Baron, get a move on . . ."

The Baron. Commandant Michel de Palma's nickname. The idea had come from Jean-Louis Maistre, his blood-brother on the *Brigade Criminelle*, who had started calling him that one evening, as a joke after a few too many drinks. He thought it suited the "de" of his surname, his slender build and melancholy aristocratic manner.

The Baron pushed open the padded doors that led to the first balcony, paused for a moment, then glanced around at the audience, as he had always done ever since his father had initiated him into serious theatre when he was still a little boy.

The auditorium was bathed in velvet, and crammed from the first row of stalls up to the gods. The air was laden with sour breath, musky perfumes and the dust of face powder. From the orchestra rose a riot of trills, scales and snatches of melody twisting around each other like superheated atoms. De Palma spotted Capitaine Anne Moracchini of the *Criminelle* and nodded to her discreetly. He was at least an hour late. In the ten years that they had been working together in the *Police Judiciaire*, this was the first time that he had invited her to the opera; at the very last moment, too, because this was the final performance of *La Bohème* that season.

Darkness had fallen when he sat down beside her.

The first few minutes passed by. Moracchini seemed totally wrapped up in the music, which trembled in the air around them. Then the old man in the gods who for years had been coughing at the start of each performance suddenly stopped. An electric sigh ran through the opera house and silence descended.

Rodolfo walked towards the front of the stage:

> *"Che gelida manina*
> *Se la lasci riscaldar*
> *Cercar che giova? Al buio non si trova."*

Instead of looking at Mimi, Rodolfo never took his eyes off the conductor and stood on tiptoe each time he hit the middle register and compressed his diaphragm.

> *"Chi son? Sono un poeta.*
> *Che fascio, scrivo . . ."*

In the end, Rodolfo didn't do too badly for an end-of-season show, but de Palma felt disappointed. Under the cover of the applause, he crept out of the auditorium. In the Reyer Hall, Félix Merlino was pacing up and down, lowering his heels in slow motion so as not to make the parquet creak.

De Palma turned on his mobile. Two messages had been left that day, Saturday, July 5. The first had arrived at 7.58 p.m., just before he had entered the opera house, and the second at 8.37 p.m., presumably while Rodolfo had been sounding off in his garret in Montmartre.

"Good evening, Commandant de Palma. Maître Chandeler speaking. I'm a lawyer. The person who gave me your number would prefer to remain anonymous, but I'm taking the liberty of calling you. We don't know each other, but I should very much like to meet you so as to discuss a case . . . as soon as possible would be best, if that's alright with you. Say Monday the 7th? See you very soon, I hope."

It was a male voice that made its nasal consonants sing slightly, both deep and smooth at the same time. The second message was also from Chandeler, leaving a different mobile number and begging him not to give it to anyone else.

Félix Merlino came up to the Baron and pointed at the phone.

"Turn that thing off at once. If ever I hear the damn thing ring, I'll . . ."

"Don't fret, Féli. In any case, there's no need to worry considering the warblers on stage this evening."

"You should have heard the first cast. Then you'd have really heard something . . ."

"Oh really? Because this lot sound like the mistral rattling the shutters in my ex-mother-in-law's house."

"That's right! It's a disaster tonight."

"But they're still applauding . . ."

"People clap anything these days. Not like before . . . You remember?"

De Palma raised his eyes to the ceiling and waved his right hand over his shoulder in a sign of shared nostalgia with Merlino.

"When things were as bad as tonight, they even had to call in the police sometimes to calm the audience down!"

Félix Merlino shook his head and, with his foot, swept away a scrap of lace which must have been torn off a gown.

"We haven't seen you for ages, Michel. The other day I was talking to the pianist Jean-Yves, you know, the singing coach, and he asked after you . . ."

"You know I had a bad accident?"

"I read about it in the paper. But you look better now."

De Palma did not reply, but looked at the square tiles of the parquet. Applause could be heard coming from the auditorium, muffled by the padded doors. Merlino walked reverently over to the varnished doors of the dress circle and opened them in the manner of a sacristan with a cathedral doorway.

Anne Moracchini tapped de Palma on the shoulder.

"Well, for a night at the opera it was quite a success!"

"I'm sorry, Anne. I did try to get seats for . . ."

She looked at his mobile and pulled a wry face.

The police capitaine was wearing a black pencil skirt that revealed her knees, and a silk purple top onto which her dark hair tumbled down. Her legs were clad in sheer stockings that clung to the curve that rose from her fine ankles to her knees. When his cheek brushed against hers, he recognised the peppery notes of Gicky, and felt a thrill.

"You left before the end! Didn't you like it? I thought it was really good," she said, laying a hand on his forearm.

He did not want to disappoint her on their first night at the opera together by telling her what he thought of the cast.

"Yes, yes, it was fine," he replied, with a wink at Merlino.

He had never seen her look so beautiful, so elegant. Usually she wore trainers or flat shoes, jeans, and a bomber jacket over a T-shirt or pullover, depending on the season. And of course the Manurhin revolver that she wore in the small of her back, to keep it inconspicuous.

"Come on, let's have a drink," said de Palma at last, rousing himself from this trance of admiration. He ordered two glasses of champagne and they went back to the main hall.

"It's marvellous here! All this art deco stuff. What's that on the ceiling?"

"A painting by Augustin Carrera, *Orpheus Charming the World* . . ."

"I sometimes wonder what the hell you're doing in the force," she said, with a sideways glance.

"So do I. But I have my reasons."

"I hope you do."

Moracchini gazed at the huge Carrera fresco, before examining the details of the metalwork and gilt masks along the cast-iron balconies. The Baron's mobile rang.

"Change that ring tone, Michel. It grates!"

"M. de Palma?"

He knew the voice at once.

"Speaking. One moment please."

The Baron sat down on a purple divan, set a little apart from the crowd.

"This is Yves Chandeler. I'm a lawyer."

De Palma paused for a moment, taking control.

"Yes?"

"Um . . . did you get my message?"

"I did."

"I hope I'm not disturbing you."

He did not like the way this plummy voice prolonged each open vowel it came across. It suggested a childhood spent in Marseille's best private schools, in a society that de Palma knew nothing about, but tended to despise.

Again, he imposed a moment's silence.

"Not at all."

"I'll get straight to the point. When can I see you?"

He felt like saying that people seldom asked him questions that were more like barely concealed orders, that he had no idea why this man was calling him and that he did not want to see anyone except Anne Moracchini. Instead he replied perfunctorily:

"Monday, 4 p.m. in your office? Does that suit you?"

"Today's Saturday so . . . yes, that will be perfect. I'm at 58 cours Pierre-Puget. I suppose you know where that is."

"Indeed, not a very original address for a lawyer."

"No, you're right. Next door to the high court!"

"See you on Monday, then."

He hung up without a goodbye. Moracchini walked over to him, holding her glass of champagne.

"I suppose that horrible ringing means that the interval's over? And are you planning to let me go back to seat number 35 all on my own?"

"No, Anne, certainly not!"

He slid a hand around her waist.

It was 2 a.m. when de Palma drew up in front of the little house Moracchini owned in Château-Gombert, at 28 chemin de la Fare, the last remainder of her marriage.

"How about a nightcap?"

The air was alive inside the car. She looked at him hard. He lowered the window for a breath of air.

"No, I'm going home . . . I need to sleep. I don't feel so good. In fact, I've . . ."

"You've got another of your migraines. Come here and I'll give you a massage."

She laid her long fingers on his temples and rubbed gently.

"What does your doctor say?"

"He says he doesn't know, like all the doctors!"

Moracchini continued her massage, tracing small circles above his eyebrows, then she withdrew her hands like a caress, took hold of his temples and squeezed them gently.

"Do you remember, Anne?"

"Yes, I do, but I don't want to talk about it . . ."

"Nowadays, I think about it less, but a month ago I kept on playing the film in my head like a loop from hell. Non-stop."

She pressed the top of his skull softly and raked through his hair with her nails.

"I can still see myself going into the Le Guen cave and reaching the bottom. I've never told anyone, but if you only knew how frightened I was. Guts in a knot, balls on the ground."*

"That's pretty . . ."

"So to speak."

He breathed deeply and shut his eyes.

"I can still see those marvellous paintings, how impressive they were. I can't describe how I felt, seeing the hands of prehistoric men. And then I saw her. And he was behind me. I turned . . ." De Palma's breathing speeded up. He closed his eyes and turned his head in a circle. "I can see myself spinning round on my left leg, and firing at him . . . Then he hit me smack on the forehead. It was like being struck by lightning."

"It's made you into a top cop, with a medal and accolades and

---

* De Palma is relating the conclusion of his previous investigation in *The First Fingerprint*.

10

all. Plus a good deal of jealousy. Well done. And I might add it's not done away with your charm."

"His strength was superhuman. I often think about that. My aim was straight, I can see myself lining it up . . . I'll never get it out of my mind that he managed to dodge a bullet. He had the reflexes of a great prehistoric hunter, I'm sure of it. He was stronger and quicker than a normal man. Compared with him, we're all degenerates."

"You're talking as if you admired him!"

"He dodged a .38 bullet! Lightning versus lightning. At incredible speeds. You can't help respecting something like that. Do you see?"

"What I see is that he's going to go down for life, and that it's thanks to you."

"You could also say that I missed him!"

"I've never said that."

"In any case, I didn't arrest him on my own."

"Thank you, from all the little cops like me, Michel."

Almost imperceptibly, she drew him against her breasts. He sensed that they were tense beneath the thin fabric. She stroked his forehead tenderly, just where the man who called himself "the Hunter" had hit him with his tomahawk.

"I'm going home, Anne."

"As you want, boss."

She moved her hands down to the nape of his neck, and met his mouth with lips swollen with desire.

Isabelle has just had her third child.

The Baron has received an invitation.

A pale blue card with a photo of the little fellow.

He is called Michel, just like him.

Isabelle wanted that. In memory of that firebrand policeman who crossed her path.

Isabelle has always been a friend to him.

And it is true that he has never let her down.

NEVER.

He has always prized the memory of the beautiful teenager he loved.

ALWAYS.

How could he ever forget her?
Isabelle wants Michel to be her third child's godfather.
He is not sure if he will accept.
But he is thinking about it. He's already refused twice.
She will end up thinking that he doesn't care about her any more.
Poor Isabelle.
If only she knew how much the Baron thinks about her.
Night and day.

Day and night.

The paper had yellowed with the years.

It was written in the muscular hand of Commissaire Boyer, the father of police headquarters. Boyer the magnificent, who made people grow up in a single burst.

De Palma was naked on his bed. He still had Anne's perfume on his lips. He could hear Boyer's voice: "Bring him to me. Bring him in. Right here. I want to see him before the big farewell. De Palma, you go to the crime scene with Maistre. I think she's still there. You'll see about all that with Marceau. I want your opinion. You young people sometimes have new ideas."

And Boyer the boss had written across the sheet of paper, with his big fat pencil, one end blue, the other red:

RAPE AND MURDER, in red.

And at the bottom, in blue: CASE UNSOLVED.

Name: Isabelle MERCIER.

Fair hair, 16 years old. 1m 63cm. 56 kilos.

28 rue des Prairies. 20th arrondissement.

Date of discovery of the body: 20 December, 1978, at 9.56 p.m.

Case followed by Inspectors de Palma, Marceau and Maistre.

"Case unsolved," the Baron repeated, smoothing the sheet between his thumb and index finger. The letters U.N.S.O.L.V.E.D. burned into his eyes.

"Bring him in!"

In his first notebook, the Baron had written: Isabelle Mercier. And that was all.

*

At the top of the page, Isabelle's photograph is stuck on with a paper-clip.

It is an identity shot.

Black and white.

Isabelle is sixteen.

She is smiling shyly.

Her hair makes two commas on her velvet cheeks.

Maistre and de Palma arrive at 28 rue des Prairies.

It is the first time that Boyer the Terrible has entrusted them with a case.

And this one seems to mean a lot to him.

Isabelle is lying on her stomach.

Jean-Claude Marceau is looking out of the window.

The official photographer is staring at her, the corners of his mouth trembling.

"Maistre and de Palma . . ."

"Hello, lads. The old man is throwing you in at the deep end. Take a look. I've never seen anything like it."

De Palma bends down.

He raises a lock of hair caught in the coagulated blood.

It is like a piece of caramel.

Beneath it, an eye stares at him dumbly.

An eye in the middle of nothing.

An eye without a face.

Jean-Claude turns round.

"To do that to a face, you really have to hit it hard. Fucking hard. Never seen anything like it, lads."

Jean-Louis Maistre has gone to throw up.

De Palma swallows back his saliva.

He wants to keep the horror inside him.

And the horror is inside him.

Never forget.

"Hello, Maistre?"

"Have you seen what time it is, you bugger?"

"She's back, Le Gros."

"Isabelle?"

"Yes."

"She's never been away . . ."

"I dreamed she sent me a card for the birth of her third child."

"That's funny, Baron. I had a dream just like that, too."

3.

La Capelière, two old buildings standing side by side, belonged to the *Société nationale de protection de la nature*. In 1979 this ancient property, hidden away among the tamarisks that skirted the lagoon of Le Vaccarès had become the information centre for the National Reserve of Camargue.

At the entrance, a notice on the ramshackle dry-stone wall displayed a pair of flamingos, face to face, and the acronym S.N.P.N. in the middle. The paint was wrinkled by the rising damp from the stagnant water, and baked into strips by the sun.

On the ground floor there was a small museum, the administrative offices and a laboratory. The first floor held a dormitory for students who were in residence, as well as the flat of the institution's head, Dr Christophe Texeira, a researcher and lecturer at the University of Provence. He was forty-five; his hair was speckled with grey and his face was dominated by his prominent chin and two dark eyes that kept in perpetual motion beneath his bushy eyebrows. His thick lips brought him great success with his female students. He seemed the happiest of men.

That evening, alone in the office that was also his laboratory, Christophe Texeira was finding it hard to concentrate: a report on the latest survey of the insects of the Reserve of Vigueirat, on the far side of the Rhône, had raised a tide of weariness inside him.

Texeira had come to the Camargue for its birds, but for the past two years he had been regularly asked to count its mosquitoes and spiders, not to mention the frogs and toads. That night, he was pacing up and down and occasionally glancing out of the window.

The moon was setting.

On the surface of the reed bed, the tips of the rushes were quivering in the lingering brightness. In the gusts of the salty breeze they intermeshed like lines of silver blades.

He peered through his binoculars, then slumped into his chair. What intrigued him that evening were the photographs laid out on his desk, beside the pink and green files of reports.

The pictures were magnificent.

A walker who had called by the previous weekend had managed to photograph some white spoonbills: two near Grenouillet and another which had strayed into the grass that runs between the canals towards Sambuc, near the stud farm at Loule.

It was incredible! This hiker had taken several pictures of these mythical birds while he, the head of the nature reserve and with a doctorate in biology, had hardly seen any on this side of the delta. Usually they gathered on the south bank of the Vaccarès, near La Gacholle. But not always.

"I'm looking for white spoonbills," the visitor had said.

"That will be difficult," Texeira had replied.

"They need to be told of love and marvels."

Marvels!

The man looked distinctly eccentric: shoulder-length black hair, smooth face, as stocky as a prop forward, with the air of someone who doesn't know what to do with all his muscles. What was more, he was dressed like something the cat had dragged in: Viet Cong sandals, a heavy wool sweater despite the heat, scuffed jeans and a patched-up haversack.

On the other hand, the Zeiss binoculars, the 200 mm narrow aperture zoom lens and the Nikon digital camera that hung around his neck made the biologist green with envy. Not to mention the pair of periscopic binoculars he glimpsed in the man's bag.

These rare photographs had arrived through the letter box of the S.N.P.N. and had been postmarked: Tarascon, July 1.

The biologist could not remember the walker's name, otherwise he would have telephoned to congratulate him.

In fact, had he ever got his name?

Texcira went into the entrance hall of the centre, turned on the lights and glanced at the bulky visitors' book on the table, beside the till.

Each page was divided into six columns, in which the visitors could note down the species they had observed, the places, dates and of course their names, and their addresses and jobs as optional extras.

On the page for Saturday, there were a good ten names, but they were just tourists, who had wanted to leave a trace of their visit and find something witty to say.

He looked at his watch again. It was nearly 1 p.m. He decided to get down to work and polish off the figures in his insect survey.

A few minutes later, he noticed that his new assistant had made yet another mistake: he came across a *Cassida viridis* and a *Cassida sanguinolenta*, two larvae, beside a *Polistes gallicus*, a variety of wasp. He would have to go back over the whole thing, label by label. He decided that it was high time to sleep on the problem and go up to his flat on the first floor.

As he closed the shutters in his bedroom, he noticed that the gate of the reserve was open. Grumbling, he pulled on his trousers and trainers, then went out into the grey night air.

He could have sworn he had closed the gate before going into his office. This gave him pause for thought: his memory was utterly infallible. He could see himself lifting the latch and could even remember thinking once again that he really should get it fixed because for some months now the accumulated rust had been making it ever harder to close.

So someone had entered the park after 7 p.m.

He decided to check, took the torch from the cupboard and set off down the path that ran alongside the Fournelet canal – the only practicable route for a visitor to this miniature bayou.

After five minutes spent weaving through creeks overgrown with ash trees and monstrous brambles, he came to a halt beside the observation hut of Les Aulnes, overlooking the swamp. He listened to the night air. At first, there was total silence, then, as the seconds crept by, the little sounds of nature swelled again.

A short while later, he felt everything stirring around him: there was a gentle slapping of stagnant water nearby, the scurry of tiny rapid feet among the clumps of rock samphire; no doubt a rodent fleeing some pressing danger.

Like a wild cat, he sprang up the wooden steps of the hut. The quiet waters gleamed like old silver beneath the moon. In the middle, a dead oak had slumped into the mud, poking its branches out of the filthy water like a drowning man waving for help. Up on its trunk, a little wader was sitting up for the night, surveying the glittering pond around it.

It took him a moment to realise that the song of the frogs had stopped. He was so used to their incessant racket that he hadn't been paying attention. But now, Texeira pricked up his ears: he could still hear them, further off, by the Vaccarès, but not in his immediate vicinity. Experience told him that some other presence was close.

Then he heard the sharp sound of footfalls and snapping reeds on the far side of the swamp, in the direction of the salt meadows. In fact they were coming from the old warden's hut, which lay about two hundred metres away, beyond the reed bed.

With all of his senses alerted, Texeira listened. The sounds of footsteps stopped. His first thought was of some big game, a wild boar perhaps, or a roebuck escaped from a hunting reserve, or else a bull which had managed – as they quite often did – to break through the barbed wire around the Loule estate.

But that would not explain the open gate! It must be a human presence, maybe the type of keen birdwatcher who came to take up position long before the sun rose over the marshes so as to admire the dawn ballet of the birds of the Camargue.

He went down from the observation hut, crossed the last few metres of the path beneath the trees, and stopped at the edge of the clump of samphire. At the far side, the bright walls of the shed and its pointed, churchlike roof stood out clearly against the dark grey of the tamarisks.

The sound of footfalls had started again, in fits and starts, as though someone were looking for something beside the reed bed, at the far side of the swamp.

Then came a splash and movement in the water.

18

And footsteps. Massive, weighty ones.

It reminded Texeira of the big game animals he had tracked in eastern Africa. He threw himself flat behind some samphire to get a better view.

Then a strange high voice, like a counter tenor, like a tinkle of crystal, arose from the surface of the stagnant water:

"*Lagadigadeu, la tarasco, lagadigadeu . . .*"

Then a second, more virile voice, as deep as an organ's bass notes, joined the first one, becoming a scream of terror ripping apart the shadows.

"*Laïssa passa la vieio masco . . . Laïssa passa que vaï dansa . . .*"*

The two voices mingled.

"*La tarasco dou casteu, la tarasco dou casteu . . .*"†

Then utter silence fell. Texeira emerged from his hiding place and aimed his torch in the direction of the voices. But he saw nothing. He searched through the darkness, playing the light across the black surface of the swamp. Nothing.

To build up his courage, he shouted: "I am Christophe Texeira, the head of the reserve. You're trespassing, and I'm asking you to leave now . . . Immediately! The joke isn't funny any more."

* "Let the old witch go by, let her go so she can dance . . ."
† "The Tarasque of the castle . . ."

4.

Monday, July 7.

De Palma rang the doorbell of Chandeler & Associés, 58 cours Pierre-Puget, just a stone's throw away from the high court, in a desirable residence guarded by a pair of brawny telamones.

A female voice husky with years of smoking emerged from the intercom.

"Chandeler & Associés, can I help you?"

"Michel de Palma. I have an appointment with Maître Chandeler."

"He's on the first floor. Come on up."

De Palma climbed slowly up the huge staircase flanked by cast-iron banisters that led up towards the light streaming in through a glass roof.

He knew Chandeler by name: a youngish lawyer specialising in the most lucrative cases, a squeaky-clean, US-style brief, whose clients included shipowners and thrusting promoters of the tourist business that was flourishing along the coasts of the city.

Earlier that year, in spring, Chandeler had been shaken up by two incorruptibles from the drugs squad during an investigation into one of his clients: a big name in the export–import business, a king of the container trade, who had finally been put away behind the bars of Baumette prison for smuggling cigarettes and cocaine. The drug squad reckoned that Chandeler had been in it up to his ears, but couldn't make it stick.

"Please do take a seat," said the voice from the intercom, a tall blonde secretary, painted like a Sicilian puppet, who pointed to a sofa upholstered in buffalo hide. "I'll tell Maître Chandeler that you're here."

Chandeler & Associés had huge premises, full of period furniture and collector's items: an eighteenth-century sedan-chair, antique ship's compasses, a few Ambrogiani paintings, a harbour scene of Algiers by Bascoulès.

All that wealth on display must have excited the boys from the drugs squad, who would still have in mind the several other famous lawyers who happened to have figured prominently in recent trials of underworld bosses.

From the hall, the Baron could hear plaintive telephones in the neighbouring offices, as well as deeper voices punctuated by the tap of a computer keyboard.

A huge man appeared through the double doors. In two strides, he was standing in front of the Baron and sketching a ferocious smile.

"Monsieur de Palma, I presume. I'm so pleased you're here," Chandeler said, shaking the policeman's hand with a vice-like grip.

"I was rather at a loose end today," the Baron replied, shrugging awkwardly.

"How lucky!"

Chandeler invited de Palma to sit, then flung himself down on a leather-upholstered armchair.

"First, allow me to thank you for agreeing to see me. I suppose you must be wondering what this is about?"

The Baron trained his eyes on the lawyer, who was now swivelling ninety-degree arcs back and forth on his chair, as though an axis ran through his body and up to the crown of his skull.

"So, why are we meeting?"

"It's rather delicate. Here it is. My client, Madame Steinert, believes that her husband has been murdered. Unfortunately, the police have concluded that he has simply gone away, and so of course there's nothing as yet they can do."

"And how long has her husband been gone?"

"Thirteen days."

"Is that all?"

"I see what you mean, but his wife, my client, is convinced that he is dead! She has good reason to think so: her husband is not in the habit of going off. He's not exactly footloose, if you see what I mean."

"Yes, I do see. But what I don't see is what I can do for you."

Chandeler stopped fidgeting. He placed his elbows on his desk and joined his hands in mid-air, as though about to pray.

"Well, the point is that my client is not just anybody. Have you heard of Steinert-Klug Metals?"

"No."

"Never mind. And does the name William Steinert mean anything to you?"

"No, I'm sorry."

"Evidently you do not read the papers!"

"You know as well as I do that hacks write a load of nonsense."

"But they do repeat things they've been told," Chandeler said, tightening the knot of his tie. "There was an article about his disappearance, as well as an article that drops me in the shit!"

De Palma sized up this lawyer, who met his gaze for a few seconds before looking down and starting to rummage around on his desk.

"Here," he said, handing him a press cutting. "William Steinert was one of the most powerful magnates of the German metal industry. Imagine what a fortune that means!"

"I can," de Palma said, nodding.

"And this is the man who has disappeared. Of course, his family would like the investigations to be carried out as discreetly as possible for the time being."

De Palma put the cutting down on the desk without reading it, and instead glanced at the blue file that lay in front of Chandeler. He read, upside down: "William Steinert Case. SK Metal." Nothing else.

"I see you're already calling it a case. What makes you think that he hasn't just dropped out of sight for a few days, as people like that often do?"

"I'd so like to agree with you. But I think that what we have here is at best an accident or a kidnapping, and at worst a murder."

De Palma uncrossed his legs and rubbed his chin.

"O.K., Chandeler. There's plenty of money in the family. Millions, if I get your drift."

The lawyer nodded and swivelled again on his chair.

"They can afford whatever they want. Including the best services that the French police force has to offer."

Chandeler leaned heavily on his elbows and clasped his hands together.

"I can easily imagine what you're thinking," he said, flashing de Palma a smile. "But I must say that you now belong to the police aristocracy, given that the hacks you despise so much have been talking about you for so long. I have even heard that you are to be decorated shortly."

De Palma raised a hand, as though chasing away such flattery.

"And then, surprising as it may seem, there are very few private detectives who know the region really well, its criminal culture, the underworld, that sort of thing . . . and you know all that like the back of your hand. To be quite honest, I was the one who suggested you. I only knew of you from the media and your reputation at the high court. So I know that you're a brilliant officer, even if you don't like being mentioned in such terms! You have a career full of big cases and high-profile prosecutions. Most important, you go all the way. You have the courage to do that. And it's you who knows the local underworld best. All of your former colleagues agree about that. And I think that the underworld is involved in this business. There you have it."

"What makes you think I'll be interested in this case?"

"Nothing. It's just that my client . . ."

"I don't follow you."

"Of course, you will be paid for what I'm asking you to do. And, believe me, you won't regret it."

"And you know perfectly well that I can't accept! I may be on sick leave, but I'm still on the force and intend to stay there till I retire."

"I know, I know . . . all I'm asking for is a few days' spare time. In any case, the affair will become public knowledge in a few weeks' time. We won't be able to keep it secret as long as we should like to. This article has done us considerable harm. I don't know where their information came from . . . Well, never mind."

"What do you mean?"

"What I mean is, officially, or at least up until today, William Steinert has gone off on a little jaunt to the tropics. But you know as well as I do that there's no fooling people in a scene like this one. Last Friday, questions were already being asked. When this article comes to the right people's attention, I hate to think what will happen. At the next board meeting, the wolves will be baring their teeth. I suppose I am making myself clear?"

"Loud and clear. But once again, I don't see what I can do to help."

"What I want you to grasp is that I'm ready to do all I can so that, in a week's time, the theory of a kidnapping can be ruled out."

"So what you want to know is whether a ransom is in the offing or not."

The lawyer tightened his lips and nodded.

"And perhaps you'd also like to know if Steinert is still alive?"

"You are reading me like a book! So, yes, we quite understand one another, M. de Palma."

"I still haven't said yes."

Chandeler clenched his jaws several times and focused on a point in front of him.

"Do you know where he disappeared?"

"In Tarascon."

De Palma smiled: the emperor of the machine tool disappearing in the town of Tartarin . . .

"I know, it might seem funny to you, but that's how it is. William Steinert hasn't been heard from since June 24."

For the Baron, Tarascon was an unlikely name and place, with a castle adorned with beautiful towers and spanking new arrow slits. The home of the true-blue Provençals, in the heart of their eternal land, a white town at the top of the vast Rhône delta.

"His wife wasn't worried for the first few days. In those circles, people don't see each other all the time. But then she made some phone calls to Germany, and then to his Paris office, and she had to face the truth: her husband had indeed vanished somewhere between his office in Tarascon and the farmhouse where they live a few kilometres away, between the villages of Maussane and Eygalières."

Maussane: part of the golden triangle of Provence, the home of snobs, fading artists, and natives proud of their stuffy traditions. Everything that the Baron most detested.

"So what do you think, M. de Palma?"

He took a deep breath then curled his lip sceptically.

"I think that you suspect someone, or some organisation, and that you don't know how to contact them . . . I mean, you don't want to contact them. That's why you thought of me and were given my phone number. Probably by some retired old bastard who keeps going on about what a great cop he used to be. How he arrested gangland bosses . . . never mind.

"And it's true that there are not many private detectives in this town, and I'm one of the last policemen able to recite the local mafia's phone book without getting a number wrong. I've taken liberties with official procedures, but the times required it. The old bastards you know aren't up to date. They are a murder or two in arrears. And that's what matters! I can tell you quicker than anyone else when someone in the mob catches a cold or steps out of line. It's a hobby of mine. Some people bet on horses, I keep up with all the files on serious crime. Which means that I've got my informers out there and can find out quite a lot."

Chandeler coughed slightly and fiddled with the Steinert file. De Palma laid his palm on the lawyer's desk.

"Chandeler, you know that I know a lot about the underworld, but I've always stayed as straight as a die. Both feet in the gutter, but straight. I'll be able to write a book about it when I'm an old bastard too . . . Just like all the old coppers who think that they've served some purpose on earth."

"I can see that there's no getting round you . . ."

"I'm sorry, Monsieur, but policemen like me aren't there to help men like you . . ."

"What do you mean by that?"

"I don't like your furniture, or your secretary, or your shoes . . ."

Chandeler took the blow manfully. He stayed sitting, completely understanding the barely veiled threat that had just been made.

"I'm sorry, M. de Palma, I thought that we could reach an understanding. Never mind."

De Palma stood up and stretched, without taking his eyes off the lawyer.

"If you should change your mind, de Palma, don't hesitate to call me, even late in the evening. I suppose you have made a note of my mobile number!"

When he pushed open the door of the La Rivière bookshop in the middle of Tarascon, he pretended not to notice the bookseller who was smiling broadly at him. She was pretty, with her milk-white teeth and big shy eyes.

He went over to the Provence section, which took up all the space beside the window and which thus provided a view of the Bar des Amis, on the other side of the rue de la Mairie.

He took down a huge coffee table book that covered Provence from Palaeolithic times to the present, taking in the glory of Rome as well as all its major and minor conflicts, its parades and traditional flim-flam. It contained some beautiful photos: Arlésiennes in their ancient costumes, the fields of lavender around Sénanque Abbey, gypsies on the pilgrimage to Saintes-Maries-de-la-Mer, white manes and long bracket-shaped horns in the Camargue half drowned by salty water, rare birds . . . But no white spoonbills. What a shame.

Over the road, the owner of the Bar des Amis went out onto the pavement and waved his large hairy arms about as if to chase the unhealthy air of his premises from his tarry lungs.

The man replaced the book, then looked for another title on the shelves, without taking his eyes off the comings and goings across the street.

"Are you looking for anything in particular, sir?"

"Um, no," he said, still staring at his objective. "It's for a present. And I haven't made up my mind yet."

"Maybe I could help you?"

"No, don't worry. Thanks anyway."

The pretty bookseller gave him a thin smile and disappeared among the shelves of paperbacks.

Then he saw the person he was looking for. Christian Rey was going into the bar. A second man, whom he had never seen before, arrived less than a minute later. He was tall, with a swaying gait and grey hair. He might well be no more than a normal customer.

"Can I take this please?" the man asked the bookseller, handing her *Mémoires et récits* by Frédéric Mistral.

"Do you need it gift-wrapped?"

"No, no, I'm in a bit of a hurry in fact," he said, giving her the exact amount.

He placed the book at the bottom of his bag and went out. The first tourists had now appeared. He walked fast, turned down the first alley to the right and stopped in a doorway, as though following a pre-rehearsed route, then from his bag he took a cotton jacket and a baseball cap. He added a pair of light sunglasses and took out his Nikon with the 200 mm lens.

He retraced his steps and stopped for a moment to examine his appearance in the chemist's window: his disguise looked convincing enough to confuse any potential witnesses. Whatever happened, he would be the man in a cap with sunglasses and a camera – a commonplace sight in the streets of Tarascon in midsummer.

A minute later, he went into the Bar des Amis and ordered a beer at the counter by pointing at the tap of Leffe. That way, he would be the man in the cap who did not even speak French.

The owner, a big Corsican with a grey complexion and smiling eyes, set the beer down and went on shining the zinc bar in silence, occasionally glancing at the television screen, which was showing highlights from that year's football championship.

All at once, Christian Rey emerged from the back room like a shadow, accompanied by the man with grey hair. The two exchanged a few words. As they did so, he paid and left the bar.

Rey and the man with grey hair . . . this was something new. But, it did not disturb him, and did not unduly complicate the mission he had set himself. Maybe he would have to eliminate Grey Hair too? It did not matter much. One more or one fewer. He took a couple of photographs in front of the bar, as Rey turned left, and Grey Hair right.

Then he had to change once again, quickly at the corner of rue de la Mairie. He knew that Rey was cunning, and he did not want to take any risks. He took off his jacket and glasses and put on a red polo shirt.

Rey stopped at Chez François, then opposite the town hall at Le Narval, and finally at the Bar de la Fontaine, not far from the ramparts of King René's Castle. Each time, the scenario was the same: he went inside, shook a few hands, then came out again a few minutes later with a package concealed in a supermarket bag. And each time, the man took some photographs.

Rey then headed for the castle car park and got into his Kompressor convertible. The man watched as he drove off, and only stopped looking when he took the bridge that crosses the Rhône towards Beaucaire.

The morning had been well spent. He now knew exactly where he would capture Christian Rey.

Then he would take him to see the beast.

It was time.

5.

De Palma saw her as he passed the war memorial commemorating the dead of the wars in the Far East. She was standing on the other side of Corniche Kennedy, looking out to sea from the bridge of white stones that arches above the stream in the valley of Les Auffes.

From that distance, he couldn't make out her face, but she looked beautiful and blonde, with a slender figure. Probably a foreigner making the most of the last light of day to take a photograph of the sea.

Just like thousands of other tourists.

But the woman had neither a camera nor a camcorder, just a black bag slung over her shoulder. And she seemed to be observing him.

De Palma stopped for a moment and leaned on the cast-iron railing in front of the war memorial. Rain was on the way. At the far side of the port, the housing estates of the northern suburbs were fading into the dingy nightfall.

A customs boat emerged from the Passe Sainte-Marie, slipping across the calm sea. The customs officers 'had recently decided to dismantle the cigarette-smuggling networks, so they were pulling in all the boats that came from North Africa. Instinctively, de Palma glanced to his left and, through the grey light, could make out the *El Djezaïr* in the distance as it slid calmly between the Château d'If and the Frioul archipelago.

The din of cars along the harbour road rose above the railings then spread out across the sea. De Palma stopped in front of the Grand Bleu bar, looked inside and signalled to the waiter to serve him a beer on the terrace outside.

He sat down facing the sea, turning his back on the roar of the traffic. A migraine was starting up. He closed his eyes and breathed deeply, as if to open the jaws of a vice.

"Good evening, M. de Palma."

He opened his eyes. A violent rush of adrenalin pinned him to his chair. The creature he had seen near the war memorial was standing in front of him. It was Isabelle Mercier, with her almond eyes.

For a few seconds, de Palma wondered if he wasn't suffering from one of his now familiar hallucinations. His hands shook slightly. He hid them beneath the table.

"Forgive me for introducing myself in such an abrupt manner . . . My name is Ingrid Steinert."

After his appointment with Chandeler, he had supposed that this business of the German billionaire was well and truly over. But he took Ingrid Steinert's proffered hand, and its soft touch made him feel ill at ease.

"Good evening, Mme Steinert . . . please, do sit down. Can I offer you a drink?"

She was wearing a huge diamond ring on her middle finger. The sort of luxurious gem that can be seen either in jewellers' windows on place Vendôme in Paris, or among the hauls from famous burglaries.

"Mmm . . ." she said, pursing her lips. "I'd really like a pastis . . ."

Mme Steinert trained her eyes on the Baron. Her resemblance to Isabelle Mercier was striking. She had large eyes of a pure blue that fondled whatever they looked at. Big blue eyes that shifted to turquoise when her mood suddenly changed.

She produced from her bag a cigarette case of leather and gold and opened it delicately.

"Cigarette?"

"No thanks, I've quit."

He saw in her eyes that he was failing to conceal his discomfort. He cleared his throat, and his curiosity was drawn by the wedding ring on Ingrid Steinert's finger, which matched her diamond and her earrings. An absolute fortune.

"What can I do for you, Madame Steinert?"

30

Her eyes clouded over, and she ran the tips of her elegant fingers through her hair. De Palma realised that he had upset her, and immediately felt sorry about his brusqueness. He felt awkward, and she noticed.

"My lawyer met you and he told me that you refused to help me. So today I've come to see you myself."

"You haven't wasted time! You're not used to people refusing you, is that it?"

"You're quite right. But that's not why I'm here."

"How did you find me?"

"It wasn't hard," she said, and glanced at a man who stood across the avenue.

De Palma spotted the bodyguard, then another: two heavies, probably Germans, who were trying to blend in among the kids of Malmousque who were kicking a ball about.

"And you never go out without your two bruisers?"

"Not since my husband died. There are three of them, actually. It's the price I have to pay to feel safe."

De Palma swallowed a mouthful of beer, then slammed his glass down so hard that its contents shot over the rim and splashed her cigarette case.

"I'm sorry, Mme Steinert, but I'm going to have to repeat what I told your lawyer. I can't and won't do anything to help you."

She did not reply, but merely raised her glass of pastis to her lips, without taking her eyes off the Baron. A yacht was moving almost imperceptibly towards the old port, its main jib swollen by the dying wind. For the first time in months, de Palma felt a stab of fear. He observed Ingrid Steinert and realised that something was happening, a game that he couldn't control.

"Does it surprise you," she said mockingly, "that a woman should make contact directly?"

"It does, when it's a woman like you."

"Why?"

"Because you're extremely rich and you can pay for men like me just as you please, and not have to stir yourself!"

"You think so? Don't put yourself down! Money can't buy everything, and *Es ist höchste Zeit!* as we say in German – we're out of time."

She opened her cigarette case again. Her fingers were shaking slightly. She looked towards the islands.

"You have to help me, M. de Palma."

The tone of her voice had darkened. Her whole body was tense. De Palma felt sorry for her.

"You have heard of my husband, William Steinert, haven't you?"

"No, sorry, I haven't."

Ingrid Steinert's expression hardened, and her chin jutted out as though to stress her determination. She clasped her hands on the table. In the distance, the hills of L'Estaque were fading into the twilight. In Mourepiane, the lights from the gantries glittered on the ro-ro ships bound for North Africa or the Black Sea.

"My husband has been murdered," she said calmly. "And I want to find the person or persons who did it."

"Look, I understand how upset you must be, but I can't help you. Really I can't. I'm just not allowed to."

"You tell me what's allowed? The Tarascon police are shelving the case. So far as they're concerned, my husband has gone off somewhere and there's nothing they can do about it! No-one will believe me. What does it all mean?"

She kept her hands clasped tightly together, which gave even more strength to her bearing.

"All I can advise you to do is to go to the authorities, to the public prosecutor, and try to have them open an investigation. That's what Chandeler should have told you to do. The *Brigade Criminelle* in Marseille has some very good people, the Tarascon section too. I've an old friend I could phone up if you want. You could . . ."

"There are things that I can't tell you here. We'll have to meet again." Then she added: "If you want to, that is. And don't forget that money is no object."

De Palma remained silent for some time. His migraine was returning and he gently massaged his temples. Ingrid Steinert was observing his slightest reactions. He looked up and met her steady gaze.

"O.K., tomorrow, I'll try to get to know your husband's case."

The lights of the cargo boats heading for Corsica lit up one after the other. The wind had turned again, barely a breath of air.

"Thank you."

"Let's get this straight, I am promising you nothing."

A voice inside told him he'd just been snared by Ingrid Steinert. He wanted to say something spiteful, but swallowed it back. The woman in front of him wasn't just trying to clear up her husband's death. In fact, all through their conversation she had spoken his name just once, and hadn't shown the slightest sign of sadness. Anxiety, yes, but not sadness.

"Here's my card," she said. "It has all of my addresses and phone numbers, personal and professional. You can contact me whenever you want."

She smiled and raised her glass. He had the impression that she was about to propose a toast to their unlikely collaboration.

"Try the mobile numbers first," she said in a strangely muted voice. "They're the most reliable."

The moment she stood up, a Mercedes 500 with German number plates drew up at the pavement. De Palma had no idea how Ingrid had summoned her watchdogs. The driver got out and opened the door. She disappeared behind the smoked-glass windows.

A few sailing boats were roaming around the port of Marseille, propelled by their outboard motors. As it passed by the seawall, the *Danièle-Casanova* gave two blasts of its siren, filling the sky.

He strolled for a while in the little quartier of Malmousque before returning to his new acquisition: a vintage red and chrome Alfa Romeo Giulietta coupé, which he had haggled for with an old collector in Mazargues, a few days after coming out of hospital.

Ten minutes later, he found his legendary car where he had left it in traverse de la Cascade and, not for the first time, had to admit to himself that he was suffering from lapses of memory.

Reversing dangerously, he crossed traverse de la Cascade and turned onto Corniche Kennedy. The traffic was getting heavier, in fits and starts in some places and total gridlock in others. Most of the

Marseillais who worked in the middle of town went home to the southern suburbs by way of the Corniche.

The Giulietta was heating up. The Baron clenched his jaws, and kept an eye on the dashboard thermometer. His nerves were as taut as steel cables, no doubt because of going on the wagon. Since his accident, alcohol affected him physically as never before, hacking away at his nerve endings.

In the distance, at the far side of the harbour, the day's last ray of sunlight crossed the greyness hanging over Ile Maïre. It came like a sign from the elements: it was there, years before, that he had first kissed Marie, his ex-wife. Now and then, on days of nostalgia, he would stand in front of Maïre to count the waves. For some time the island's tip had been his navel, the centre of his existence, but now he was not so sure. He needed a new centre.

At the end of the Corniche, he drove around the statue of David and left the calm of the sea behind him. The long traces of the cars' brake lights drenched the view of Le Prado in blood red and created the impression that they were rising up to the hills of Saint-Loup. He slipped a C.D. into his walkman and put on his headphones: Mozart, or Boche music, as Jean-Louis Maistre used to say, who preferred the full and brassy melodies of the Italian masters.

"I'm the bird-catcher,
Ever joyful, hooray!
I'm known as a bird-catcher
By the young and old in all the land."

Mme Steinert's face settled in his mind, the sheerest fact, above the traffic jams, with its perfectly oval shape, straight nose and azure eyes that could pierce sheet metal.

Isabelle Mercier.

The real world up to its tricks again.

A cop at the end of his tether.

Dark thoughts his constant visitors.

A slight prickling made his brows crease. Another migraine. He chased away the images of the two women.

"I'm known as a bird-catcher
By the young and old in all the land.
If I wanted girls, I'd trap them by the dozen!"

He headed towards Rabateau, overtaking the entire rank of cars that seemed glued to the tarmac, before driving into the industrial estates around La Capelette.

"If all the girls were mine,
I'd barter them for sugar,
And all my sugar I would give
To the one I liked best."

In front of the half-demolished old sulphur plant, he avoided the mattresses and wrecked washing machines on the paving stones. Then he lowered the window to feel the air on his face; there was still that same electric smell as when he had been a boy, when he used to bring girls to these dead streets to fondle them, while his friends were at home groaning over Euclidean geometry.

When he got home, the Baron drew the curtains across the French window overlooking the gardens of the Résidence Paul Verlaine. Night was falling; the orange light of streetlamps spilling out across the grey and black bark of a tall sea pine.

Jean-Louis Maistre rang the doorbell. De Palma could not remember having invited him round.

"Sorry, Le Gros, my brains are jelly at the moment."

"No matter," Maistre said, sitting down on a chair. "Any news of your medal?"

"No, why?"

"Because it's supposed to be soon."

"I couldn't care less . . ."

"Come on, don't play the romantic cop. A bit of recognition never did anyone any harm!"

Maistre was the exact opposite of de Palma: short and stocky, with a bright face beneath a black mane of hair. Always ready to laugh at anything, even the dirtiest tricks. The two friends had met in the *Brigade Criminelle* at 36 quai des Orfèvres in Paris, the sanctum of the *Police Judiciaire*. Their friendship had been cemented during long evenings spent over packs of beer instead of their guns.

When the Baron returned to Marseille, Jean-Louis had followed him. Now he had a wife and children, and had abandoned the *Police Judiciaire* for the quieter pastures of the *Sécurité Publique*.

"Tell me, Le Gros, does the name William Steinert ring any bells?"

"You should move to a real police office, Baron, that way you'd be up to date – we know our stuff in the *Sécurité Publique*! We've got a missing person's alert for him. It arrived this morning. You do mean the German billionaire who lives in Provence?"

"That's him. Do you know anything else?"

"No, sir. Nothing apart from the notice dated today."

Maistre's face was covered with fine wrinkles announcing imminent old age, and tiny pink veins ran across his fleshy cheeks.

"Why are you interested in Steinert?"

"Good question! His wife has asked me to find him."

"Just like that?"

"Just like that!"

Maistre burst out laughing. He crossed his arms over his stomach.

"I wouldn't mind playing at private eye myself."

De Palma sighed.

"There's something that's bothering me."

"What's that?"

"She looks like Isabelle."

Maistre fell silent. He was thinking, trying to find the right thing to say. The Baron interpreted this silence as a sign of mistrust: his friend had doubts about his mental health.

"When will I see you next, Baron?"

"Dunno."

"How about next weekend? The children haven't gone on holiday yet. They'd love to see you."

"I'm fine for this weekend."

Maistre stood up, took a C.D. down from the shelf beside him and pretended to read the cover.

"Come to think of it, in fact it's the boys in Tarascon who are on the case at the moment. At least they're the ones who put out the alert. But I reckon it will all end up with the *Police Judiciaire*."

"Do you think Marceau is in the know?"

"I reckon so. He's always the one who deals with this kind of thing."

"How do you get on with him?"

"I haven't seen him for ages. But things were O.K. the last time I did. We had a good chat: two old-timers going down memory lane."

"It's odd that he should be mixed up in all this as well."

Maistre opened his eyes wide and shook his head.

"It's a coincidence, Michel. It's true that Marceau was with us when we got stuck with the Mercier case, but that's as far as it goes."

"He worked very hard on it . . ."

"We were three young officers from the same year at the police academy, and we happened to end up on a case that affected all of us. We were marked by Isabelle. Marceau maybe more than we think."

"You're right, Le Gros. I'll look him up in Tarascon."

"He'd like that."

The Baron ran his index finger along the line of C.D.s and picked out *The Court of the Crimson King*. He slid it into the player, poured himself a shot of Aberlour and slumped into the armchair.

"You're into pop music now?"

"You made me listen to it on stake-outs, don't you remember?"

"Like it was yesterday. We used to smoke the evidence as well."

Maistre pulled a face and knitted his eyebrows. He scratched the tip of his nose and shrugged.

"I think I've found a boat, Baron."

"For fishing?"

"Affirmative. It's a lad from Pointe-Rouge who's selling it."

"Then we'll go fishing with King Crimson on full blast."

At night in La Capelette, the factories stood in dark rectangular clusters, ruins of pitiless time.

It was in front of the huge wall of the pith helmet factory that the local boys used to fight with the lads from Pauline or Saint-Loup. With bicycle chains and hobnailed broom handles.

De Palma was generally the last to get into a fight, but he was also the most violent – a violence he had now locked up behind bars of alcohol and music, and, when he was young, doggerel verse as well.

The Marseille that the Baron knew could turn the sweetest children sour; it fed them neither folklore nor good intentions, but rather violence and the lure of money.

In La Capelette, the role models were the local gangsters, who drank in the Bar de l'Avenir under the bridge of the railway that ran through the neighbourhood and ended up in the municipal dump. The hard nuts of l'Avenir were the only ones with even a shred of prestige, a success that stuck like shit to a blanket. They all had Italian roots, but were proud to be from Marseille, despite the great white city's record of injustice.

The others, that seething mass of proles, worked like nobodies. After their shift was over the smartest of them used to go and rack their brains at the offices of the Communist Party, reforming the world with Stalinist slogans.

The Baron had been born in this area, but had never belonged to it. He was not raised with his feet treading sawdust in the bars or cafés, talking too loudly and waving his hands around the way the plebs do on T.V.

But when he bumped into a childhood friend in the street, who had been in and out of prison, he would greet him as a friend. Their eyes would meet, and commonplaces rained on the tarmac. Nothing more. The true Marseillais is a silent man.

6.

On Friday, July 11, at 5.50 a.m., a fine drizzle was blowing in from the bay.

From the dual carriageway overlooking the harbour, you could see the flickering yellow lamps on the bellies of freighters streaming with rain. Anne Moracchini and Daniel Romero were driving in silence, their mouths bitter from the day's first cup of coffee and their eyes still puffy with sleep.

Capitaine Moracchini, the only woman in the *Brigade Criminelle*, did not like the rain. It reminded her of her early years with the *Police Judiciaire* in Versailles.

"Daniel, did you remember the blotting paper?"

"Yes, Anne," Romero sighed. "It's in the bag."

Daniel Romero was wondering whether his boss's explosive mood was going to cool down, or if she was always like this when she went to grab a gangster while the milkman was still doing his rounds. He did not know that Moracchini could not bear rain, especially not at 6 a.m. when they were about to make a difficult arrest in a lane in the village of Saint-André. It was enough to make you think that criminals had a guardian angel out to ruin the best-laid plans.

"What's your aftershave, Daniel?"

"*Habit Rouge.*"

"Tomorrow morning, try *Pour un Homme* by Caron. It's just as virile and doesn't get up my nose so much."

Lieutenant Romero had just arrived on the brigade. With his good looks and relaxed, feline gait he looked perfect in his new part. He kept his cool in all circumstances, had a brain that still sparked and a true belief in his mission. He had been with the *Brigade Anti*

Criminalité, before taking the officers' exam and joining the *Criminelle* in Marseille – his deepest wish come true.

On the church square of Saint-André, Moracchini looked at the clock on the Xsara's dashboard.

"Jesus, what are the B.R.I. boys up to? They're not here yet! And it's six already!"

"Maybe they're lost?"

"That's not funny, Daniel . . ."

At the top of rue des Varces, a Mégane appeared, with its headlights off, followed by a 306.

"Just look at them," Moracchini said, mechanically checking her Manurhin. "Aren't they just wonderful?"

"They're on time, you can say that for them. On the dot of six . . ."

"Yeah," she said, spitting her chewing gum out of the window.

A third unmarked car drew up behind the Xsara.

"How many are we altogether, Anne?"

"Eleven . . ."

She got out and shook hands with Capitaine Bonniol, of the *Brigade de Recherches et d'Intervention.*

"It's there," she said, pointing at number 32, which was half erased.

It was a ramshackle maisonette, set back from the rest of the street. A rusty fence, mended with reinforcings for concrete, stood in front of a small garden of irises and scrubby rose bushes. To the left was a prefabricated garage, and at the far end the house itself, with its bedroom under the rafters; one of those prewar shacks put up by Italian labourers in one weekend, using materials nicked from building sites. A first step out of their shanty town.

Moracchini drew her 357, signalled to the B.R.I. hard cases to hang back and gave four violent kicks that almost demolished the door.

"This is the police, M. Casetti!" she shouted loud enough to crack her voice. "Open up!"

More kicks, then she nodded to her team-mate.

"This is the police." Daniel Romero, in a voice that was almost soft. "Come quietly, M. Casetti."

"Shall we break the door down, Anne?"

"Why not bring in the anti-terrorist squad and T.V. reporters while you're at it! Are you joking or what? We'll do it the old-fashioned way. He'll come down and open up like a good boy."

"My arse he will," said Bonniol.

At that moment, a light shone through the bedroom shutters. A shotgun barrel gleamed in the air.

"This is Capitaine Anne Moracchini, of the *Brigade Criminelle*. I have a judge's warrant... You know me, Jean-Luc... come on, open up!"

Events unfolded just as the two had imagined from the start. The door was pulled ajar, a figure appeared and a pair of eyes shone in the half-light. Romero kicked hard at the bottom of the door and Moracchini aimed her revolver at Casetti standing ashen-faced in his underpants.

"No messing now, Jean-Luc. And no sudden moves. Put your hands where we can see them and turn round."

Jean-Luc Casetti, a crook used to the routine, turned and offered his wrists to the police officer. Bonniol turned on the kitchen light, and a greenish glare came down from the neon on the ceiling.

"Not too tight, please," Casetti begged.

"Don't worry, Jean-Luc. We've been here before!" Moracchini grabbed hold of Casetti and sat him down on the kitchen table.

"We've got a warrant..."

Casetti shook his head and looked skyward.

"We're here because you're suspected of taking part in a raid on a security van. So, as of now – and it's ten past six – you're in police custody. If you want, you can see a lawyer, and also a doctor. How are you, no problems at the moment?"

"No, I'm fine."

Jean-Luc Casetti was short, with bright eyes that darted around in all directions. A gypsy called Bagdad de la Cayolle had fingered him as the gunman in the double murder of the Ferri couple. After two lean years in a post in Nice, the *Criminelle*'s new boss, François Delpiano, had jumped at the chance of solving his first big case in Marseille. But Moracchini was sure that the tip was a phoney. She had said as much to Delpiano, but he wouldn't listen. All he had agreed was to bring in Casetti for a hold-up, so as not to put the wind up the people who had taken out the contract on the couple.

"Casetti, the security van raider . . ."

"Please Inspector, not in front of the children. Don't say a word."

"No, Jean-Luc, I'm a Capitaine now!" Moracchini said, to cool things down a little.

A little girl wearing a blue-flowered dressing-gown over her bony shoulders and foam slippers on her feet was standing in the kitchen doorway.

"Hello," Moracchini said, as simply as possible, smiling at the wide-eyed girl.

"Hello, Madame."

"What's your name?"

"She's called Marion," Casetti butted in proudly.

"You had a son too, no? A big lad . . ."

"Christophe? He's in jail."

"Why?"

"Because he takes after his prick of a father."

"For a long stretch?"

"Ten years."

"Jesus, ten years, Jean-Luc! That's no life."

Despite her years on the force, it still riled her when a crook spoke so coolly about his family's troubles. The verdicts seemed to rain down on the Casetti family without ever teaching them anything. They went in and out of prison and seemed to accept these return trips between the free world and "inside" as if they were the terms of a contract. A contract often settled by a bullet.

"We're going to search the house, Jean-Luc. Have you got anything to tell me before we begin, and find it ourselves?"

"There's nothing here. Zilch," he said, gesturing at the corridor from which his wife had just emerged, with the family's latest addition in her arms.

"Here's our youngest – Pierre. He's just turned three."

Moracchini and Romero looked at each other in silence. Casetti's wife, her eyes still red with sleep, put her son down. The child immediately went over to his father and grabbed him by the handcuffs, beaming widely. Romero looked away.

"O.K., Jean-Luc. We're going to have you spit on some blotting paper, so as to take your genetic imprint. You know, your D.N.A. . . . Then you'll come along with us, and if you're clean you'll be back home tomorrow morning. O.K.?"

"Jesus, you turn up mob-handed with all that artillery! It's like the Napoleonic wars in here. That one over there's got a pumpgun loaded with buckshot, and you ask me if I'm O.K.?"

"That's right!" Madame Casetti almost screamed, raising her hand towards Bonniol. "The last time you turned up, there were just two of you. With that big copper, the one who was in the paper. What's his name again?"

"Commandant de Palma."

"Yes, him. He's a real man. He risks his life. Everyone knows that. He's got respect for people. No need to come with a squad. I've got nothing against you, Madame. I know you're on the level. But him" – she pointed at a guard from the B.R.I. – "aren't you ashamed of pointing a gun at children?"

Bonniol made to open his big mouth, but Moracchini glared at him.

Five years ago, on the orders of a nervy magistrate, she and de Palma had come to fetch Casetti on suspicion of murder, but nothing had come of it. Forty-eight hours later, they had taken back home "Casetti the Gangland Killer" as an inspired sub-editor had dubbed him.

"In fact, we nearly brought the T.V. cameras along," she said, to lower the pressure.

"That's all we need! The last time, for the lad, we had those local telly shitheads round. I thought it was just the new police procedure to film everything. Then two months later, they showed the boy on T.V., and everyone knew. Fuck the lot of them!"

Moracchini's mobile rang. She went out into the garden.

"Anne? It's Michel."

"What's up with you? Insomnia?"

"I'm not waking you up, am I?"

"Thanks for the kind thought. It's six thirty, and you'll never guess where I am."

"Go on."

"At Casetti's. Don't pretend you didn't know."

"For the Ferri murders? What a prick that magistrate is. Every time there's a hit he's going to send us to Casetti's!"

"No, this time it was the new boss."

"Delpiano! Good, now I feel better off on leave."

"What's more, we've picked him up on a Friday, which means we'll spend all weekend questioning him."

"That triple bastard."

"And I wanted to see you a little!"

One of the B.R.I. team came close, so she went out into the alley.

"O.K., so what's up? You're going to pop the question?"

"Um, no, but I'll have to think about it . . ."

"We're made for each other, Michel, but only after ten in the morning."

"I can imagine those nights of passion."

"Hmmmm . . ."

"Tell me, does the name Steinert mean anything to you?"

"You never change. I talk love to you, and you talk job. Who do you mean?"

"A guy who's disappeared. I found the case interesting and . . ."

"And you want me to ask around! O.K., Baron. But right now I'm going back to Casetti. Who told you that it was the Ferri murders?"

"I know everything, you should know that."

She went back into the house. Casetti had spat conscientiously onto the blotting paper that Romero had handed him – so conscientiously that the two from the *Criminelle* realised at once that he must be in the clear. Or at least over the Ferri affair. The rest was quite another story. De Palma had always suspected him of doing jobs for the one-armed-bandit racketeers. Before running his own amusement arcade, Casetti had been a top bank robber. Not the sort who screws up and gets pulled in by the *Brigade de Répression du Banditisme* every time he fails to make ends meet. But between that and becoming a gangland trigger man lay a gulf that a magistrate fresh in from Lyon was too quick to cross. The credo was to apply constant pressure on the big boys of organised crime. To dig for information constantly, whenever official procedures gave them enough leeway. The police might drag their heels, but the magistrate took himself very seriously.

Moracchini glanced at Casetti's daughter. She was born during his first spell out of prison. A child of the visiting room, which explained the great difference in age between her and her elder brother. The little girl had the look of a weary Madonna, despite the sparks that occasionally lit up her eyes.

"It's half-past seven. Are you going to school soon, Marion?"

"Go to school while you take my daddy to prison?"

"If it isn't him, he'll be home tomorrow."

"The last time, the magistrate put him in prison anyway! For my daddy, even when it's not him, it's still him!"

"Don't talk to the police like that," Casetti said. "They're doing their job."

At ten o'clock that same morning, de Palma was driving slowly along Route Nationale 568, north-westward from Marseille, in heavy rain. Visibility was down to about twenty metres, which did not improve his mood.

The thirty-year-old radio in the Alfa Romeo was crackling. De Palma took out his walkman, put on the headphones and swore when he realised that he had forgotten the box set he had bought the day before: a legendary version of the *Götterdämmerung* with Astrid Varnay and Wolfgang Windgassen, conducted by Clemens Krauss. He wanted to compare it with the ten other versions of *The Ring* he already owned.

So now he would have to be content with reflecting on the day he was going to spend far from Marseille. That night, he had made the decision to investigate the Steinert case. It had been neither the billionaire's wife's money, nor his unhealthy curiosity that had clinched the decision; but rather the simple fact that this woman looked like Isabelle Mercier. De Palma saw it as a sign, something that had risen up from the chaos in order to drive him forward. He was also intrigued by the fact that she had personally sought him out, after the blunt refusal he had made to Chandeler. Something in her story rang false, and de Palma could sense the turbulence in these big-money cases like a weather radar.

The rain redoubled, and he suddenly had the impression of being inside the belly of a snare drum during a parade on July 14, which made him slow down even more, and thus increased his irritation.

He hated this long road, as straight as an American freeway, punctuated with chip vendors, sellers of melons and other local produce, and whores in caravans who serviced truck drivers by the edge of meadows as flat as the sea.

Each time he took the R.N. 568 it was always for some shady affair: bar owners murdered by slot-machine racketeers, or some settling of scores among the gypsies of Arles and its outskirts. All he needed now was a migraine to ruin his day completely.

When he reached Tarascon, by now on Route Départementale 99, the rain stopped abruptly. He parked on rue du Viaduc in front of the commissariat, in one of the spaces reserved for police officers. Straight away the security guard, wrapped in his royal blue outfit, hurried over.

"De Palma, Marseille P.J.," he said, flashing his tricolour card. "I'm here to see Jean-Claude Marceau."

"Oh, right. Talk to my colleague then."

The second security guard behind the grille was not so bad: brunette, about twenty, with an angular build, an inviting smile and big dark worried-looking eyes. The first hint of charm on this gloomy morning.

"Capitaine Marceau? Yes, stay there; I'll see if he's free," she said, poring over her list of telephone numbers.

The hall of the commissariat smelled of stale tobacco and the sour breath of its hundreds of visitors. A winding staircase, pockmarked with chewing gum and cigarette burns, led up to the first floor, where the departments of investigation and public safety lay in a curving corridor with a low ceiling and brick walls. Voices broke out from behind the wall of the drug squad.

"On my mother's life, it wasn't me . . ."

"Fuck your mother, arsehole. We've been tailing you for six months. Can't you see yourself in the fucking photos?"

"On my mother's life . . ."

That morning, in the Cité des Rosoirs, the drugs squad of the *Service d'Investigation et de recherches de la sécurité publique* had nabbed a housing estate baron with 40 kilos of dope in the boot of his car, some of it in his son's cot and the rest in his wife's vanity case.

De Palma arrived at the door to the investigation rooms.

"Hide everything! The P.J.'s here!" a voice wrecked by filterless Gitanes yelled from behind the half-closed door.

De Palma shoved it open.

"Hi, Jean-Claude, sounds like things are heating up next door!"

"Really? It's never them, you know how they are . . ."

Marceau greeted the Baron with a hug and took a long look at him.

"Jesus, Michel de Palma. The Baron . . . you can't imagine how pleased I am to see you. It's been ages."

"You haven't changed."

"And you've still got just as much imagination! How are things?"

Jean-Claude Marceau was a year younger than de Palma, and had kept the look of an eternally melancholy teenager, into hard rock and dope. Of course he was into neither, just an excellent police officer who was now rotting in a small commissariat after a brilliant start to his career with de Palma and Maistre in Paris. It had all been down to a fit of nostalgia.

In the early 1990s, Marceau had decided to go back to Tarascon, his home town. He wanted to find his roots again, to unlock the Provence that lay deep inside his body and soul. He had started with the *Brigade de Répression du Banditisme* in Marseille, before asking to be transferred to the *Sécurité Publique*.

Through the partition, the din was growing louder.

"I've got out of touch with the drug squad," said de Palma, pointing at the wall with his thumb.

"We've got that guy by the short and curlies. His wife and two brothers-in-law are involved in smuggling and they've just coughed. Starting with 40 kilos this morning, we've now reached one ton. He's a wholesaler."

Marceau swivelled round his computer screen, which showed a black-and-white picture of a stairwell.

"This is a live webcam! You can see the stairs of a building in Les Rosoirs, just beside the other bastard's flat. And it can pivot, and zoom . . . Look!"

Marceau clicked his mouse and the camera moved.

"We hid it in an air vent. We're expecting another delivery any day. According to our grass, there'll be 150 kilos."

"You're rolling in it these days in the commissariats."

"What's more, it records the whole lot on D.V.D. – it picks out the places when there's movement. The highlights of these arseholes' lives."

Marceau occupied the current investigations office. In practice, he dealt with everything.

"You came here specially to see me?"

"No, I wanted your recipe for fake pastis."

"Come on then, out with it."

"William Steinert?"

Marceau pointed to the missing person's notice which was pinned to the wall.

"You're with missing persons now?"

"I want to do someone a favour. So they can clarify the situation. It isn't all that clear."

"Same old de Palma, still the big boss with the know-nothing air . . . You remind me of a hack I used to give stories to from time to time. He always used to play the ignoramus."

"Steinert disappeared on the 24th, is that right?"

"That's what his wife says . . . it's not the official account. But there is no official account."

"What do you know about it all?"

"He's loaded," Marceau said, opening his arms. "And he's been missing since at least June 24. I say that because no-one really knows. It could easily have been the 22nd or 23rd."

"Yeah, I suppose he's not the sort who goes home from work every evening at the same time. I can just picture all that money."

"Then multiply by ten and you're probably closer."

"Have you seen his wife?"

"Yes. She came here with two heavies and her lawyer."

"Chandeler?"

"That's right."

De Palma's expression suddenly changed. He stared at his fellow officer sadly.

"It's a striking resemblance, isn't it?"

"The case isn't closed for you either?"

"Not that one."

"And yet when you look at it, Michel, it's just a case like any other."

"Yeah."

A long silence fell in the room. From the neighbouring office, quiet sobs could be heard.

"O.K. I just wanted to know what you made of it. Then I'll call her, tell her the case is closed, and that's an end to it."

"Michel, the guy has disappeared, that's what I make of it. And nothing is going to be closed before he breaks surface again, dead or alive! The problem is that I can't do anything about it! If you only knew the amount of work that lands on me day after day: drugs, rapes, muggings, a fucker who's swindled his wife . . . it's all the time the jackpot! And I'm a jack of all trades, my friend!"

Next to Steinert's missing person's notice, there were some press cuttings covering the few good results achieved by the local police in Tarascon: mostly about drugs, smack sold by Tunisians from Beaucaire, who regularly got rumbled; there had also been a network of stolen car dealers, with faked number plates on identical models that were chopped by a gang in Paris before being passed on by gypsies during their pilgrimage to Saintes-Maries-de-la-Mer.

It was nothing to get excited about, but there were little signs of improvement in the area: for the older locals, a stylish house with a swimming pool in a Provençal village; for the younger, a dwelling of the same sort in an estate by the highway. It would always be better than council housing in Marseille, or worse, the Paris

49

suburbs . . . De Palma respected this sort of police work. He knew that it was as hard to arrest a middle-league drug dealer as it was a mad-dog killer.

"What's your feeling about the Steinert case?"

"There are two possibilities. Either he's dead, or he's off galli-vanting for a few days. There'd be nothing surprising there, with this kind of customer. In the latter case, we don't give a shit. In the former, we wait to find the body and the cause of death. That's all."

"You're right, Capitaine. In fact, you can't get any righter. But apart from that, do you know anything about our client?"

"Yes, a couple of things . . ." Marceau slid his right hand beneath a file and produced a packet of filterless Gauloises. "I know that he's been buying up land left, right and centre, and not everybody likes that. I also know that he's often been seen in the company of local personalities."

"What sort?"

"The sort that have been under investigation for decades . . ."

"For example?"

"Mayors, deputies, a couple of well-known Greens . . . but only the sort who have friends among the magistrates."

"That doesn't mean anything!"

"Of course not, but you asked me what I knew. So I'm telling you!"

Marceau's grey eyes were sparkling.

"Talking of pastis, I think it's time."

"And you leave your magic camera on all day?"

"Twenty-four-seven, my friend. This is real police work here."

"That's what Maistre says too, since he started work with the *Sécurité*."

"How's Le Gros doing?"

"He's fine."

Outside, now that the rain had stopped, a peppery smell was creeping through the white streets of the old town.

Marceau drew de Palma through the maze of paved sidestreets that glittered in the blue light. The shopkeepers were taking back out their revolving displays of postcards, until the next shower arrived. On place de la Mairie, the owner of the café/tobacconist was sticking his nose outside to inspect the sky, while drawing on a cigarette gripped between thumb and index finger.

The two officers sat down on the terrace of the Guardian, a discreet bar between two plane trees, just opposite King René's Castle. Marceau surveyed the area several times, before leaning closer to de Palma.

"Michel, in fact there is something that's been bothering me about this business."

"I'm listening."

"Those public figures I mentioned. All of us have already seen or heard their names somewhere, in police reports or files, during phone taps or else in real estate deals. There aren't many of them, but they are the ones who pull the strings around here. This isn't Marseille, you know, everything comes out sooner or later."

"O.K., O.K., but I don't see what's so surprising about a businessman like him hanging out with their sort."

"Steinert isn't from around here . . . How can I put it, people here . . ."

"I see, I see . . ."

"He's bound to have upset some of the local big boys. In his neck of the woods, by Maussane, there are some big landowners who are well known for their shady deals . . . and the price of land has shot up, these last few years, if you see what I mean."

"So you think he's been whacked, one way or another?"

"I don't think anything for the moment. These are just possibilities that shouldn't be ruled out. You can't imagine what's at stake financially in little rustic villages round here!"

From the way Marceau slumped back into his wicker chair, de Palma understood that the confidences were now over. Maybe he did not in fact know anything else. In any case, the time had now come to pay a call at the Steinert residence.

Marceau read his mind.

"I thought you were still convalescing, Michel . . ."

"I am, more or less . . ."

"Wait till you're given the case before getting your hands dirty."

"Given the case! I'll never be given this case. No, I'm just out for a little information, that's all. I couldn't give a damn about the rest of it."

"Since when have you been coming out to Tarascon about cases you couldn't give a damn about?"

De Palma looked up towards the walls of King René's Castle. On the ramparts, a few tiny tourists were waving energetically at anyone who chanced to look up at them. Instinctively, the policeman waved back.

Christian Rey had no time to react, or to do anything at all. Stuck in traffic on the far side of the pont de Beaucaire, he saw a man coming towards him and soon spotted the automatic concealed under his T-shirt. The man asked him to unlock the door, then he sat down on the rear seat.

"Give me the gun you keep in the glove compartment," he barked, pressing the barrel of the automatic into the nape of Rey's neck.

He did so, handing over his snub-nosed Smith and Wesson.

"Good. Now turn round and head for Marseille."

"Look, I don't know who you are, but I swear to you that I never touched Nono!"

The man slapped his neck.

"Who mentioned Nono, you lump of afterbirth?"

"Fuck . . ."

"From now on, keep it shut."

They left Tarascon heading south, and turned onto the R.N. 568. At the Mas-Thibert junction, the man told him to stop and park behind an abandoned caravan, which must have been used for some years by a whore.

The sea breeze whistled gently in the cypresses, rolling dried grass and strips of greasy kitchen roll along with it. There was a smell of warm car oil, hay and melting tarmac.

"Now get out and put your hands on the bonnet."

With a violent kick, the man spread his captive's legs.

"Hands behind your back!"

"But . . ."

"I told you to shut up. Stick your conk on the bonnet and put your hands behind your back."

Trembling, Rey did so. He almost felt reassured when he felt handcuffs being closed round his wrists.

They got into another, smaller car and drove on endlessly along the tracks and roadways of the delta. Rey realised that the man was trying to disorientate him in this maze of byways.

At the tip of the delta, they turned back towards Arles and the sea, crossing the Salin-de-Giraud and passing alongside the huge mounds of white salt that rose up towards the blue sky like chalk pyramids.

They came to a halt on a lane that swerved between clumps of saltwort, lost among the samphire at the end of this world of wind and salt. The man put a blindfold over Rey's eyes and tied it tightly around the back of his head.

"Now walk."

They went on for some time. To Rey, it seemed like hours, first on a hard, flat surface, then across a reed bed and finally through a swamp with water up to their waists.

Rey supposed that they were heading more towards the interior of the delta, through an incomprehensible mass of marshland and wild vegetation. At the beginning, there was a smell of sea air, laden with hints of marine plants and oxygen. Then came the stenches of saline earth and stagnating swamps, warm with sun and maceration.

The driveway of La Balme farmhouse was lined with old free stones and described a large S through groves of olive trees. It was an ancient property in the foothills of the Alpilles, with a fine solitary dwelling for the owners and large buildings for the farm workers.

De Palma had had to scour the region to find it. In Mouries, he was told to take the road to Les Baux, but then he had driven too far. So two bends before the entrance to the village he had turned back and asked the way once more from a labourer who was tinkering with the motor of a chainsaw in the shade of an olive tree. The man, as knotty as the tree he was threatening with his saw, shot him a suspicious look.

"La Balme? Go straight down towards Maussane, then turn left onto R.D. 78." The man gestured broadly, the better to indicate the direction. "Then, after about two kilometres, you'll see three pine trees, three tall ones that is – round here we call them the Fairy Pines. Then take the track that leads towards the mountain. You can't miss it."

"Thank you very much."

"Don't mention it," the man mumbled, leaning back over his chainsaw.

From the Fairy Pines, a few metres off R.D. 78, the Steinert place looked like something from Tuscany. A few sunbeams broke through the ceiling of the sky which was muffled in darkness, and cut the gloom with broad, gilded shafts.

The property covered over 100 hectares, smoothly sloping down at first, then rising gently up towards the buildings that stood with their backs to the Alpilles. This solid earth, with stones as large as fists, had been constantly ploughed through the centuries; it was never sticky or black, and rose in dust beneath the stifling sun.

The homestead of the farm was thirty metres long by fifteen wide, and stood at right angles to the outbuildings. Four huge plane trees framed a fountain and stretched their pollarded branches over what used to be the stables.

From a distance, the sight was impressive, but only the turquoise rectangle of a swimming pool almost as large as the stables suggested that the owners had greater means than the soil would usually support.

As it happened, the Steinert family had maintained most of the buildings in their original functions: the barn door was open on a giant tractor, parked like a crab in its hole; next to it there was a vine tractor, which looked like a scale model with its narrow chassis.

De Palma parked his car beneath a plane tree. To his right, he could see the pool, which was a good twenty metres long, and, beyond it, a green artificial tennis court complete with changing rooms.

Further on, where a green meadow stretched as far as the first white rocks of the Alpilles, three horses were killing time by chasing off the flies that pestered them.

There was no gate or fence. And apparently no bodyguards. If the farmhouse was under surveillance, then it was highly discreet.

Ingrid Steinert was in the midst of three groups sitting around like obedient schoolchildren at small tables on a vast paved patio half covered over by climbing vines and flowering wisteria.

The lady of the manor was radiant, passing from one group to the other, making her light dress swirl with its Provençal motifs. Each group was gathered in front of small phials full of olive oil. The various members were holding tasting glasses and scribbling on notepads.

When she noticed de Palma, Madame Steinert did not look surprised. She gave him a formal smile and graciously beckoned him to join her.

"We're defining the new collection of our oils," she said, shaking his hand energetically. "We taste them again and again. They're last year's oils."

"You're . . . you're tasting oil?"

"Of course . . . it should be savoured like a fine wine! In fact, let me introduce you to Eric Bartel, one of France's greatest wine experts."

Bartel, a little fellow with a turned-up nose, barely glanced at de Palma before he grimaced and bent back over his glass.

"We taste each variety so as to decide which one we're going to send to the miller, and which ones we're going to dilute and flavour, such as Salonenque, Lucques or Grossane, and then sell in bottles. A lot of it goes abroad, especially to the U.K. and Germany."

Bartel suddenly came alive. He wriggled on his seat, his eyes flashing.

"This one is more mature," he said, raising his glass in front of his animated eyes. "It has notes of toast and hints of rosemary. Just enough, no more. It's extremely fine . . . And beautiful, just beautiful."

He twisted his glass, while the other tasters adopted serious expressions and confirmed the chief expert's diagnosis.

"We're aiming to get an *appellation d'origine controlée*," Ingrid said. "That would bring us some sizeable business opportunities."

De Palma felt about as relaxed as a young actor struck by amnesia.

Madame Steinert went over to him, laid a hand on his forearm and said softly:

"I think that we have a lot of things to talk about. If you have the time, of course. As a matter of fact, I was expecting you."

She turned back towards the tasters, delivered a few remarks, cutting the air with a swipe of her right hand, and arranged to meet them later that afternoon to continue their deliberations. She then beckoned discreetly to de Palma to follow her indoors.

The farmhouse living room was huge and worn by time. Four narrow windows looked out over the terrace and, in the distance, rows of olive trees.

"My husband never altered anything," she said, with a sweeping gesture. "At least, not in this part of the house. He was rather mystical . . . He used to say that we shouldn't change the old ways. Hence the lack of luxury. Simplicity, always more simplicity. Practically the whole place is the same, apart from the few rooms I dealt with myself and decorated as I wanted."

The whitewashed walls were hung with a hunting rifle, a set of battered copper saucepans and a few paintings, presumably by Provençal artists, which slumbered in the darkness alongside a couple of abstract canvases. These were the only touches of wealth in this decidedly peasant décor.

"William finally agreed to putting up these pictures, after years of arguing . . . As you might imagine, there were no works of art here originally. People just worked and had no leisure time at all."

"But you also have a tennis court, horses and a swimming pool!"

"Oh, you noticed?" she said with a broad smile. "But it was I who wanted them, not my husband. Although he did take a dip sometimes, when it was really hot."

The entire place created an odd impression. Why had Steinert left everything as it was? Why hadn't he wanted to leave his stamp on it?

De Palma could not help thinking about the former owners. How long had the same family lived in this farmhouse? There were probably still some descendants.

She disappeared for a moment, then came back with a massive

photograph album, which she put down on the table before inviting him to sit down beside her.

"I'd like to show you some pictures of my husband. I think it might help you to get to know him better."

She opened the first page of the album delicately, as though it were an ancient grimoire. De Palma leaned forward and saw a typical marriage photograph: William Steinert, wearing a pearl grey morning jacket, stood to the left, a top hat in the crook of his right arm, and a rather carnivorous grin on his face; to the right, Ingrid, wearing a diadem set with diamonds, and holding a bouquet in her left hand, was pouting at the photographer. The whole thing looked highly conventional.

The second shot she lingered over was a portrait of a young Steinert, with a John Lennon haircut from before the hippy era. He looked like a nice young man, and his long pointed nose gave him a sad and blasé look, which might have seemed pessimistic or melancholy, but which de Palma judged as revealing an excitable, fiery nature.

"This is my favourite photo," she said, placing her open hand on the portrait.

For the first time, he noticed that she had extremely long fingers, with trimmed nails perfectly lacquered with transparent varnish.

"It's absolutely him. That blend of strength and melancholy, and you can see the intelligence in his eyes."

"It's funny, he doesn't look German at all."

"*Provenzale* . . . How true. He almost looks Provençal."

She showed him more photographs of Steinert, posing amid the machinery in a factory in Munich. He was born in 1942 and had inherited a majority holding in Klug-Steinert Metal, one of the largest tool manufacturers in Germany.

"A year ago, my husband handed over most of his responsibilities to his younger brother, Karl Steinert. You can see him here, in this family portrait. He has the same forename as his grandfather, the founder of the company. William had the same name as his great-grandfather . . ."

"How old is Karl Steinert?"

"Forty-eight."

"Ten years younger than his brother."

"That's right. But the youngest brother is Georg, who was born in 1962. He's an eternal Bohemian, and revels in it."

With an agitated gesture, she turned over the page.

"Between Karl and Georg there's Isabella, who's forty-two. She was artistic when she was young and started out a career as an actress. But now she deals with part of the family business."

She gave a scornful look and sat back.

"She never comes here . . . I mean, very rarely. She has an office in Paris and looks after the watchmaking business – Klug Steinert also makes mechanisms for brands of luxury watches, like the one you are wearing, M. de Palma."

"Is Karl married?"

"Yes, to the family's worst enemy. She's French and comes from an aristocratic family. Her name's Ann-Sophie de Bingen. Quite a ring to it, no? I find it *wirklich lächerlich* . . . absolutely ridiculous."

"What, the aristocracy?"

"No, I mean . . . never mind, M. de Palma. What about your name . . . ?"

"I'm from an old Italian family. But my grandfather was just a plain seaman in the merchant navy. My father too . . . And I'm just a plain policeman."

"I didn't mean to offend you, I do apologise."

A ray of sunshine lit up the room. Through the window, two rows of olive trees were just visible as they disappeared into this fresh stream of light.

"Forgive my asking you this, but your accent . . . I mean, you don't have a German accent!"

"My mother's French, and I've spent much of my life in France, in Paris. A good family and a good education . . ."

Her fingers were drumming on the table. She opened her cigarette case, took one out and turned it between her thumb and index finger.

"And how do you find life in Provence?"

She lit the cigarette and flexed her mouth, which for the first time made her look unrefined.

"You can ask me that again some other time."

"Sorry, but I'm a police officer, not a confidant. I'm trying to understand certain things."

De Palma stood up abruptly and walked over to the window. The garage door was open, revealing a brand-new black Mercedes, a metallic grey 4×4 B.M.W. and the latest Porsche convertible, also grey. They all had Bouches-du-Rhône number plates.

"Is there a car missing?"

"Yes, the one my husband used every day. A Range Rover."

"Do you know its registration number?"

"It's 8526 VM 13."

She knew it off by heart, which de Palma found unusual for a woman, especially for a woman of that class.

"I have to leave you now, M. de Palma. The tasters' meeting will be over in a few minutes' time, and we have to make our choices by this evening."

They went out onto the patio and strolled towards the tennis court and swimming pool. A damp, slightly sour smell hung in the air. A tractor appeared at the far end of the drive, pulling a huge chrome-plated tank.

"By the way, why did you go to see the police in Tarascon instead of the local gendarmerie?"

"Because the last time I saw my husband was in Tarascon, not far from his office. In fact, I just followed Chandeler's advice. He doesn't have much time for the gendarmes."

"His office?"

"Yes, he has a huge one, just by the theatre. I was going to suggest showing it to you, if it isn't too late."

"I don't think that's essential. I . . ."

"You don't believe me when I say he's dead, do you? I suppose I don't seem sad enough for you . . ." she said, drawing out her words.

He ignored her remark.

"William doesn't sound very German. It's more of an English name."

"Yes, in German it's Wilhelm . . . My mother-in-law was English."

She moved closer to him.

"We should talk about your payment. I thought that a sum of . . ."

"I don't want anything, Mme Steinert."

He spoke so firmly she was left speechless.

A sound of tinkling bells echoed off the walls of the barn. In the hills just above the farmhouse, a shepherd was leading his flock to pasture, shouting incomprehensible instructions to his dog.

"Look, M. de Palma, my meeting will be over at about six o'clock. We could meet at seven in front of the theatre in Tarascon. If you agree, of course . . ."

"I . . . alright."

The shepherd came to a halt. De Palma could have sworn that he was observing them.

"So you have neighbours?"

"That's Eugène Bérard, an old shepherd. You wouldn't guess it from looking at him, but he's ninety-two and he's a poet, a real, very traditional Provençal poet."

De Palma took his eyes off the hills and went over to his car. On the way, he noticed a huge rectangular container carved from limestone. He stopped to look at what he first supposed was an old water trough.

"What is this thing?"

"It's a genuine Roman sarcophagus. My husband discovered it in the Downlands."

"The what?"

"Some fields we own on the other side of the main road. Nothing of any real interest, apart from their size. About thirty hectares, if you include the woods and hills. We grow a bit of lavender there, that's all."

By the Fairy Pines, de Palma turned left then drove towards Eygalières, away from Maussane. He went far enough to be out of sight from any curious eyes in the farmhouse and parked his car in a hollow in the road.

In front of him was a tiny valley, dug out by wind and rain storms, a mineral chaos in which only green scented grasses, a few stubborn mastic trees and oaks could survive.

He plunged into this network of pathways and corridors that usually ended in limestone gulches, overhung with rock faces pitted with skulls of stone, their empty eye-sockets staring out to the void.

From the far side of one such block, de Palma could hear the bells of Bérard's sheep, but the echo stopped him placing them exactly. He clambered over a large ledge overgrown with brambles and at last emerged from the canyon. An arid slope dotted with charred tree trunks led up to the foothills of the Alpilles.

Suddenly, a sharp whistle and a booming voice echoed off the rock face. De Palma spun round, with the feeling that someone was playing a trick on him.

"*Matelot, toque lei.*"

He saw nothing and could hear only the rhythm of the bells that was speeding up as though on an infernal merry-go-round.

"*Toque lei.*"

De Palma turned round once more and, two metres further down, saw a huge mongrel dog, its fur ruffled by the vegetation, and its canines bared.

"Matelot, it's a friend," the voice said.

The dog started wagging its tail, and the shepherd emerged at last from behind a bush. He was a short man, gnarled by the years, and wore an ancient black hat, with a ribbed velvet waistcoat of the same colour over a grey shirt. Beneath his aquiline nose, his thin, almost white lips were quivering, dropping down in a half-moon over a slightly protruding chin. His extraordinarily bright, jade eyes danced below bushy eyebrows, constantly shifting from his flock to de Palma.

"Good day to you, M. Bérard."

Bérard gave no reply, but just stared intently at the police officer, leaning his knotty hands on the top of his stick.

"So she told you my name, did she?"

"You mean Mme Steinert, I suppose . . . there's no hiding anything from you, at least! You're highly observant."

"Good lord no, I can scarcely see anything any more . . . not at my age."

"Well enough to have watched me just now."

Bérard turned towards his sheep which, driven by some whim or another, suddenly formed a file and vanished behind a rock.

"*Matelot, toque lei, aqui, ah . . . Aqui.*"

"Did everything burn here?"

"Yes, three years back. Some business about hunting, and rivalry between federations. That's the fashion around here, they burn everything down if you won't toe the line."

The shepherd sat down and his stare became calm, almost engaging. He took off his hat to reveal steel-grey hair which was still curly above his broad, deeply wrinkled forehead.

"How many head do you have?" De Palma asked, gazing round in the direction of the flock.

Bérard plucked a piece of yellow grass and chewed it.

"Good lord, almost none. Forty-odd. But only old ewes. The young ones are up in the mountain pastures with my grandson."

The animals came back, driven once again by some unfathomable instinct, and continued to graze, in time and hurriedly. The sound of tearing grass rose up between the two men.

"In the old days, there used to be lots of flocks in the area, but now there's no money in it. Except down there, on the plain of La Crau. But not up here in the hills . . . Anyway, they all think of nothing but making oil."

Bérard stared down at the Steinerts' fields of olive trees. From there, the property looked huge.

"It's because the land's got expensive. Young people can't afford to start out here nowadays."

"How much does a farm like La Balme cost?"

Bérard looked at his stick with a cunning air.

"There's a farm on sale like this one, with its land and machines, over by Mouriès . . . Say a price, just to see."

"No idea."

"Over a billion, young fellow."

"You mean in centimes . . .?"

"Yes, in old francs!"

"Who can afford such a place?"

"Some Americans are interested. But the youngsters are trying to organise something with the local authorities so that they can turn it into a cooperative."

"What about the Steinerts?"

Bérard looked at the Baron for a few seconds, knitting his eyebrows, then he turned back towards La Balme.

"That's not the same. William was a real man, a master, with fine manners. I taught him how to prune olive trees and many other things about the land. I'm going to miss him."

Bérard licked his lips with his pointed tongue and swayed gently back and forth. Then he nervously slashed at the grass in front of him with the tip of his stick.

"Why do you say that William was a good man? What about his family?"

"They're not the same. No-one knows his wife, and she never speaks to anyone. His brothers are worse. Poor old William! And poor old me, I'm all alone now."

"All alone?"

"Some things you can't talk about . . ."

"Why are you so sure that he's dead?"

Bérard stood up and walked towards his sheep. De Palma followed him.

"Everything to do with La Balme is cursed."

"Why do you say that?"

"There are evil stones, from the old days . . ."

"Evil stones?"

"Goodbye, Monsieur. My sheep are waiting for me."

The old man vanished into the scrub, just as he had arrived, followed by his sheep, with his huge dog bringing up the rear.

Going back down into the valley, the light changed, becoming greyer and more uniform. The bushes in the rugged rocks looked darker. As he walked, de Palma had the feeling that he could hear a voice. He stopped and listened. It was like a complaint, an ancient vibrato recitation in a language unknown to him, words arising from some mysterious place he could not locate, from behind one of those countless rocks:

> "... *Alabre*
> *De sang uman e de cadabre,*
> *Dins nòsti bos e nòsti vabre*
> *Un moustren, un fléu di diéu, barruolo ... Agués pieta!*"*

Anne Moracchini had taken advantage of the perfect calm that reigned in the offices of the brigade to look through some files. At 6.15 p.m. she called de Palma on his mobile.

"Michel, I've got some info about your fellow, William Steinert."

"Go ahead, but don't ask me to take notes. I'm driving and it's starting to pour again. I can't wait to get back to Marseille."

"I dropped in on the S.T.I.C.,† and they have him on file. Nothing much, just some business about financing a political party ..."

"Was he convicted?"

"Just formally questioned, by the boys in Tarascon."

"Which party?"

"Jacques Chirac's R.P.R."

"Really? I would have imagined him more as centre left, the champagne socialist type, someone who cares about paupers like you and me."

"Hang on a minute, that doesn't mean he was *in* the R.P.R. What's more he's German. Anyway, it was all based on phone tapping and town hall rumours. The sort of thing that smells decidedly fishy."

Suddenly arriving at a roundabout that he had forgotten existed, de Palma had to brake abruptly. To his right, a brand-new sign indicated the Abbaye de Montmajour and Fontvieille. A truck from a cellulose factory on the banks of the Rhône was concealing the exit for Tarascon. He drove all the way round the roundabout, now breathing heavily into his telephone.

"Are you still there Michel?"

"Shit, I nearly took the road to Montmajour!"

---

* " . . . Thirsty
  for human blood and corpses,
  In our woods and our ravines
  Roams a monster, a scourge of the gods . . . Have mercy!"
† Service de Traitement de l'Information Criminelle.

64

"It's for holidaymakers . . . So, as I was saying, he was questioned for corruption."

"O.K., I'm not deaf! So what had our dear William done?"

"Nothing at all, apparently, he was completely cleared!"

"Hmm. Listen, don't worry about all that, I'm going to see what I can find out today, and then I'll let it drop. Maybe he's the sort of man who vanishes like that, only to reappear a few days later."

"You think so?"

"It's possible. He might be a billionaire who likes to treat himself to a little adventure from time to time. He could be sunbathing in the Caribbean while I'm getting drenched in Provence."

"Whatever, Michel, you should still get some rest."

"Yes, *chérie*, I know. What happened with Casetti by the way?"

"He's here, in Daniel's office. We're waiting for the D.N.A. tests to come back from Nantes. He'll be home tonight or tomorrow morning. That's all. See you later, Commandant."

The clock-tower of Saint Martha's church was ringing the angelus when Ingrid Steinert got out of her B.M.W. in front of the Tarascon theatre and adjusted the strap of her sandal.

From the far end of the street, de Palma was watching her. As she approached him, he observed the mane of dishevelled hair that fell over her bare shoulders.

"Excuse me," she said contritely. "I'm a little bit late."

She had changed her clothes, and was now wearing a yellow cotton dress that fluttered over her body. She had also removed her big diamond and now just a fine gold chain hung around her neck while discreet earrings were hidden by her blonde hair.

When she was just a metre away from him, he smelled the perfume that she was wearing on her neck. At that moment, the policeman's head was about as much in order as a jigsaw violently shaken in its box.

"Let's go," she proclaimed, with a hint of anxiety in her voice.

William Steinert's office was on the second floor of an old nineteenth-century building. She produced a huge set of keys and, as she went over to the door, he could not help admiring the hem of her dress as it swung against her sumptuous legs.

The door was reinforced, as were both sides of the walls, enough to keep out the most determined of burglars.

"I think it's the round key, the yellow one."

"Really? If you say so."

"There's maybe an alarm. You should be careful."

"We'll see."

She eventually found the right key, which was indeed the one that de Palma had suggested.

"It's the first time I've been here . . . It's very upsetting. Please, go in first. I'm feeling rather apprehensive."

She pronounced the final word with a slight accent, rolling the "r" and aspirating the "h". De Palma noticed this tiny detail at once. He stopped on the threshold and groped for the light switch.

No alarm went off, even though William Steinert had furnished his office with the latest in security equipment. The detective at once deduced that either the industrialist had forgotten to switch it on – which seemed strange for someone who took such precautions – or else somebody had disconnected it and couldn't put it back into action. Why not Ingrid Steinert herself? But that didn't square with the emotion that showed in her gaze.

"Does your husband employ a cleaner, or anyone else who looks after his office for him?"

"I don't know."

"You'll have to find out."

Steinert's office was in fact a large flat, presumably dating back to the same period as the theatre, and it was made up of three huge rooms that communicated directly one into the other, without a corridor. The ceilings were unusually high, with decorative mould-ings, like Bavarian cream cakes.

The owner could not have opened the windows for some time: a smell of scented tobacco and accumulated dust filled every nook of the first room, which served as a hall, and was furnished with a coffee-table and four old-fashioned upholstered chairs to take up the space.

Why this furniture? Was it a waiting-room? Did Steinert receive clients in this office?

She crossed the room without stopping. She was worried and seemed to be looking for something in particular.

The second room was very much more spacious. The two high windows and the shutters were closed, and also reinforced. The dying yellow gleam of evening filtered through the blinds. Ingrid turned on the light.

It was a library, with genuine rococo shelves in massive walnut, each shelf crammed to bursting with books, some displaying their spines, others piled up anyhow. The fine layer of dust that covered them showed that they had not been touched for some time, presumably since Steinert's disappearance.

"My husband used to read a lot," she said with emotion. "My God, all these books . . ."

For the first time, de Palma sensed that she felt sad when she thought about her husband.

He glanced at the spines of the books. Steinert did not seem to have arranged his books by subject, or by author, and still less in alphabetical order. Many of them were in German.

On the shelves facing the windows, the books were arranged more neatly, a sign that they had been considered more important, or maybe read less often than the others. However, the layer of dust was thinner than elsewhere.

The Baron's lips formed the titles on the worn covers: *Le musée de sorciers* by Grillot de Givry; *Sciences occultes et magie pratique*; *Les admirables et merveilleux secrets du grand et du petit Albert*; *Le matin des magiciens* by Pauwels and Bergier; *Les arts divinatoires*; *Orthodoxie maçonnique* followed by *La maçonnerie occulte et de la tradition hermétique* by Jean-Marie Ragon; *La science des mages* by Papus . . .

De Palma gingerly took down the *Traité de l'apparition des esprits*, a tome written by Noël Taillepied and published in Paris by Guillaume Bichon in 1587. Although knowing nothing of the occult arts, he realised that this must be a very rare work, most probably owned only by initiates.

"Your husband seems very interested in the occult!"

"I didn't know that. But I can see that most of the books here in

German are on the same subject. Do you know much about it yourself?"

"Far from it," he said, opening *Les états multiples de l'être* by René Guénon, the most renowned French mystic of the nineteenth century. "Some of these books seem extremely general, and not a high level, while others are far more specialised. This one, for example."

De Palma was thinking hard. Every time he discovered something, it felt as though he were sinking deeper into molten tar, with nothing to stop this slow and progressive suffocation.

The third room was William Steinert's actual office. Expensive paintings on the walls: a Léger, a De Staël, a couple of Bascoulès . . .

What a strange combination, de Palma thought. There was nothing symbolic in all this. But he understood the point of the alarm. On a shelf, there were several statues of Greek gods, which he was incapable of identifying, and two bulky Egyptian ushabtis, funerary figures, standing on a metal mounting; all of this must have been worth a fortune.

On the table lay a disordered pile of manuscript notes, mostly concerning Provençal myths and legends. On one page, Steinert had jotted down in his very fine, neat hand details about the mythical monsters found in the region of Tarascon.

The Drac, an amphibious dragon, used to spirit away big-breasted washerwomen to feed its young . . . Less interesting than the Tarasque, the heroine of Tarascon became a star of regionalist marketing . . . A hideous beast that consumed everything in its path . . . Tamed by Saint Martha shortly after Christ's death. See monuments and abbey.

"Your husband writes?"

"Yes, he loved writing. Part of the reason why he'd partly retired from business was to devote more time to his passion."

"A book about the myths and legends of Provence . . ."

"I didn't know that."

De Palma went round the office once again, examining the pictures. He lingered in front of a Bascoulès canvas, a scene of boats being loaded in the port of Oran. For a moment, he had the impression that the tugs were busy pushing at the huge black hulls of the freighters of the Paquet company, while blowing columns of smoke into the burning sky.

He went back into the library and examined every surface. Mentally, he photographed the exact layout of the furniture and of various books that seemed important to him, then he returned to the office to do likewise. He noticed that there was no computer or telephone. But there was a telephone socket on the wall.

"Curious for a man of such importance. I don't see him casting a laptop around and only using his mobile . . . Still less, doing without the Internet."

He took a long look at the office. The placing of the notes didn't look natural. The pen lay well to the left, while Steinert was definitely right-handed, you could tell from his handwriting. Things had been moved about and then wiped clean.

Beside the pen, there was a feather measuring a good thirty centimetres, which was thin and extraordinarily white. De Palma picked it up carefully, stared at it for a moment, then put it back down where it had been.

"I don't think that our visit has taught us anything of significance, apart from getting to know your husband's character better. And first of all, that he was hiding some things from you."

Ingrid did not reply, and felt ill at ease. Was it because of the presence of this police officer in her husband's personal space, she wondered. Was it the discovery that he had hidden whole aspects of his life from her? She remembered that once, after the theatre, her husband had invited her to visit his den, but she had refused, saying that she felt too tired. It had been one of the few occasions when they had made love late into the night. She felt swamped by emotion and decided to bring this visit to an end.

De Palma waited for her to go back into the hall before unbolting the shutters and the office window and blocking them with two wads of paper – in case he had to come back, without coming in through the front door . . .

"Did your husband have any enemies?"

"Of course. In his position, you always have enemies!"

He noticed a hammer on the desk, of the sort used by auctioneers, with a black handle and ivory head. It had a rare beauty and looked very old. He picked it up and made to hit out at something in mid-air.

"I mean people capable of taking his life . . . Had he received any threats? Was he worried the last time you saw him?"

"I'll think about those questions, M. de Palma."

He knew from the tone of her voice that she was lying. But as yet he did not know to what extent or for what reason.

As they left, de Palma told her that it was standard procedure to carry out a neighbour inquiry. But it would not be done by him, and for two reasons: first because he wasn't allowed to, and second because he thought it wiser not to make things public. A neighbourhood inquiry would happen, or it wouldn't. But he sensed that in the end it would serve no purpose.

On the R.N. 568, he drove straight towards the big refineries at Fos. Two clouds darker than night had risen in the distance, above the flares of the oil terminal.

Several questions beset him. Why had Madame Steinert gone out of her way to show him her family photographs and her husband's office? Why just those two things? Why not the rest of the farmhouse? And the family?

Why did she always talk about her husband in the past tense, as though she was sure he was dead? She could just as easily have said nothing to him at all. So what was going on? He would take care not to ask her these questions for some time.

Third point: he was almost certain that Steinert had a computer and that it had been removed from his office. Was this for no particular reason, or because someone wanted to get at his hard drive? Maybe Steinert had removed certain objects himself, because of some threat or fear?

When he got home, he phoned Moracchini.

"Good evening, my lovely. Where are you at with your hold-up?"

70

"We've just got the D.N.A. results. They're negative. But Delpiano wants us to squeeze him anyway. I don't like that."

"You'll always be a sentimental girl."

"It's because of his kids that it gets to me. I don't give a damn about him . . ."

"So what about me, in all this?"

"What? You're not going jealous on me, are you?"

"I'm asking you to dinner this evening."

"I can't, commandant . . ."

"You put your suspect inside for the night, then tell Delpiano that you've got a migraine and come and eat with me."

"Michel, you know perfectly well that I can't do that."

He hung up and gazed round his three-room flat. His ex-wife, Marie, had left with the walnut bookcase she had inherited from her mother, who had had it from her own mother, and so on for generations. As a result, the Baron's criminology books were now piled up on the carpet in two stacks a metre high. On top of one was *Précis d'analyse criminelle*, and on the other *Crime et psychiatrie*, which he must have read a good twenty times.

In place of the bookcase and sofa, which had also disappeared in the divorce, two big rectangular patches divided the space like archaeological remains. They were just about all that was left of ten years of marriage. Two rectangular marks and a few poorly framed photos.

Only the C.D.s and unobtainable vinyl had been given new shelves. Dozens and dozens of bootlegs of opera greats sung in marvellous theatres: Del Monaco and Callas in Verona in a superheated *Aïda*, Flagstad and Melchior in a forgotten *Tristan* . . . Then the collector's albums of the Stones bought in London in his carefree youth; all of Muddy Waters which he had brought back from the States; Jimi Hendrix . . . they all meant as much to him as his .45, the legendary piece concealed behind the boxed sets of the Beatles and of Rossini, whom he disliked and never listened to.

He slipped Strauss's last *lieder* into his C.D. player and sat down in front of it, his eyes fixed on the crystal display. Tomova-Sintow's vibrato flowed over his tired skin. He remembered that Marie had given him this record on a wedding anniversary. He could picture her with her brilliant smile revealing her extraordinarily white teeth, as she waved the little package at the end of her long fingers. That night, they had made love several times, and she had admitted that she had not used any form of contraception for a month. But nothing happened. The child de Palma wanted and dreaded had not arrived. He would never arrive.

He lay down on the carpet, his hands clasped behind his neck, and fell asleep before the third *lied*, his mouth bitter with alcohol, with a deep crease down his forehead, alongside a faint scar shaped like a question mark.

A scar that hours of surgery had reduced.

A few months before, the Baron had been disfigured, his fine features split open.

Luckily for him, his nose had not been totally demolished and the bone of his forehead had mended. For the rest, the surgeon had removed strips of skin from his backside and stitched him back together patiently, over several hours, like an old granny patching some workaday jeans.

Looks wise, things had not turned out too badly: a remodelled nose that took a few years off him, and a scar ringed with pale purple streaks on his forehead which made him look dangerous when he scowled.

Inside, it was a different story. Migraines that wouldn't stop any more and that made him fear the worst of his demons, crude blood-red snapshots of agonies that came back more and more.

In Le Guen's cave, he had been afraid, with this fear he could no longer expel from inside him. It was a fear that invaded the hazy zone of his awareness, the zone he hardly ever dared to enter. If the Baron had never thought about revenge, it was no doubt to avoid transgressing his own prohibitions, gambling with his own taboos. The incubation time for revenge was far too long. He was a man of anger and storms, not a sneaky obsessive with no statute of psychic limitations.

In the middle of the night, a nightmare caught de Palma in the depths of sleep.

15 September 1982. 9.30 a.m.

The first anonymous call. A raucous voice.

A supermarket bag hung from a green oak on the hill of Notre Dame. Inside the bag, a head.

The neck has been severed just under the chin.

He and Maistre examine it: there is a trace of sperm on the forehead, like a diabolical unction, the signature of Sylvain Ferracci, or the "Dustman", as a hack on Paris-Match *called him.*

11 a.m. A second call.

A woman's voice. The trail will now begin.

In a dustbin in Rabatau, some clothes: a woman's severe houndstooth suit, flesh-coloured stockings stained with blood.

12 a.m. A third call.

A child's voice.

Behind it, "Us and Them" by Pink Floyd.

On the jetty of La Pointe Rouge, the torso and legs. The belly has been opened from the pubis to the sternum.

A whirlpool.

Maistre, the crack shot, withdraws a Beretta from the armoury.

He weighs the clip in his hand and slips it into the butt.

De Palma watches him stroke the automatic's black breech.

He is a certified marksman and can bring a man down firing blind at twenty metres.

Maistre wants to get this over with. His eyes are red with fatigue and misery, and his brains a grenade with the pin pulled out.

De Palma hardly feels any better.

If they catch sight of Ferracci, he's a dead man.

Everything happens so fast.

A street corner, a chase.

A cellar.

De Palma sticks the barrel of his gun into the Dustman's mouth and shuts his eyes.

He's going to press the trigger.

He will if this creep doesn't stop screaming.

Maistre approaches.

De Palma's whole body is trembling.

Slowly, his friend withdraws the barrel of the Manurhin from the predator's mouth.

Streaks of light enter the Baron's head, they hit him, again and again.

Thick blood runs down over his eyes.

It's Marie's head in the bag.

No, it's Isabelle–Ingrid who's winking at him.

An obscene peekaboo from the hereafter dark dreams.

He got up, swallowed two aspirins and stood in front of the bathroom mirror.

He looked long and hard at his face, made younger by the summer sun and the knife of the surgeon who had spent half a day refashioning his features. He pushed back his hair and examined the scar at the top of his forehead. Then he leaned closer to the mirror and looked at his nose, the only part of his face he had ever liked.

His nose had changed, and now looked like something moulded out of plastic: it was an intruder in the picture, a part of himself torn away from him for ever. He lowered his eyes and splashed water over his face, as if to purify himself.

7.

At 6 a.m., Christophe Texeira left his office in La Capelière. He wanted to be at his observation post before sunrise and, most of all, to make himself scarce as soon as the first tourists showed up.

The day before, he had told Nathalie, his new assistant, that he would be out for most of the morning.

"How am I supposed to cope with all those groups and families?" she had protested timidly. "Do you realise?"

"You give them their tickets then escort them to the start of the green track. Then let them get on with it. Anyway, they aren't at risk. If there's an emergency, call me on my mobile. I won't be far away. I'll be in the reed hut, just by the samphire meadow, the place I showed you yesterday."

Nathalie had adopted a sulky look which rather appealed to Texeira.

"I hope the ghost in the hut doesn't gobble you up."

"No, he only moves at night."

The two of them had discussed at length the voices he had heard in the night. Nathalie had made fun of him at first, then they had ended up deciding that the world was full of waifs and strays and that there was nothing they could do about it. There was no peace to be had anywhere, not even in the marshes of the Camargue.

There was no point sending for the gendarmes from Le Sambuc.

That morning, the biologist made his way rapidly along the straight path that led to the hut. The grassland and nearby marshes were silent. Only the *oup-oup-oup* of a hoopoe could be heard across that brown vastness.

The heat of the previous day still weighed down on the baked ground.

When Texeira reached the edges of the marsh, he noticed that the cracks in the earth had widened again. Some greenish samphire, impervious to thirst, still survived in that tiny Sahara.

Panting, he put down his bag, checked that his mobile was off, then took out his Zeiss binoculars and Reflex camera and hung them round his neck in case a rare bird happened to pass by.

A mauve gleam spread over the flat, salty waters. The level of the marshes had fallen again in the heat wave. He heard a faint noise: a little egret, completely white, emerged from the reed bed and advanced into the pond in search of its first meal of the day, making little plops with every step.

This bird was not very rare at that time of year, but he still took two photographs, pleased with this first encounter. The thought of the tourist who had sent him those shots of spoonbills crossed his mind.

The light was changing fast; the salt marsh was turning pink. In less than an hour, the sun would start its torrid trajectory, indifferent to nature's torments.

Texeira picked up his bag and strode towards the reed hut, with its whitewashed walls, in the only clump of trees on the reserve at the far end of the little canal.

He stopped twice to observe a redshank that seemed to be following him along the other side of the canal. He knew this nesting pair. His former assistant had pointed them out to him last spring, before going to join the team in Vigueirat. This specimen didn't look afraid, it must have got used to tourists and other lovers of high-class bird life.

Once at the hut, he put his bag onto a table half consumed by earwigs, took out his thermos and poured himself some coffee.

The window provided a discreet view over the entire marsh. He raised his binoculars and made a slow panoramic scan of its greenish waters. Nothing. Just plain solitude, slightly disturbed by a soft morning wind that ruffled the occasional tufts of reeds.

He would have to wait, perhaps for an hour, for the insects to come out of their hide-outs and offer themselves to the neighbourhood's gourmet beaks. Making the most of the calm, he placed his

Zeiss on a tripod. Just at that instant, a black stork, an extremely rare bird, landed thirty metres from the hut, just below the haggard tree that had been sinking slowly into the swamp since time immemorial.

The large bird was so close that he could hear the heavy beat of its wings stirring the humid air. He did not have time to grab his Nikon before the stork flew off again, ponderously, towards the east.

Its sudden departure surprised him. He had been so careful not to make a sound.

Two squadrons of rooks landed behind a tamarisk and started squabbling over what was presumably a scrap of carrion lying there. The rooks' verbal jousting was disturbing his morning observations. He had to put a stop to it.

In less than two minutes, he had covered the distance. The rooks flew off to the far side of the marsh. At first he saw nothing unusual, and looked for their feast for some time among the twisted roots, wary of the deepish mud around the area.

Near the tree, there was nothing to be seen, but looking up he noticed a round shape, like an old leather football, just emerging from the water about three metres in front of him, out of reach.

He went back to the hut, fetched a long herdsman's pole and returned to the scene.

It took same effort not to sink into the muddy slime. The stick glanced off the surface of the object, so he tried to get at it from beneath and the pole caught onto what he took to be a bit of bone or a piece of a large bird's wing. Then, slowly, he dragged the thing back towards the edge.

At first, its weight surprised him. It wasn't a bird, but perhaps it was some big game animal, a boar maybe, which had drowned in the marsh.

Suddenly the object turned over in the water, in a peculiar slow motion. Texeira tried to step backwards, but the warm mud sucked at his boots and kept him glued to the bank.

A nervous shudder captured him, before he finally dragged himself free.

The stringy weeds receded and the face of a man appeared, swollen, with empty eye-sockets and jutting teeth, as though smiling at his terrible end.

At 2.30 p.m., the offices of the Tarascon gendarmerie were deserted. All that could be heard was the purring of computers awaiting the next rounds of questioning.

Marceau was alone, busy typing out the final report of an unpleasant case: a man who had been stabbed to death outside a bar by a gypsy after some row about slot machines. He had reached his final sentence when Commissaire Larousse rushed in, his tie askew, with a haggard look and rumpled hair.

"Marceau, I've just had a call from the boys in Le Sambuc. They've fished a dead man out of the marsh. It might well be our guy, what's his name again . . . ?"

"Steinert, William . . . Could be."

"O.K., I'm coming with you. Give me a couple of minutes and we'll take your car. Mine's had it."

Marceau had always been fascinated by the way his boss could suddenly shift gear in response to events: but it had to be worth his while, he had to feel certain.

Conclusion: it really was Steinert who was floating somewhere in the Camargue surrounded by a squad of gendarmes in combat dress.

When the two officers parked on R.D. 36b, the sun was a white ball dancing over the Vaccarès lagoon. The air tasted of rusty metal, laden with rancid mud and the scent of hyacinths.

Marceau already felt nauseous.

Capitaine Nicolaï shook hands with his two colleagues.

"Hello, Larousse. It's Steinert alright."

Nicolaï was a real military type, with a three-braided kepi screwed onto a shaved head, and a paratrooper's badge pinned to his camouflage jacket. It was all a bit over the top. He had a piercing stare, cheeks hollowed by the strains of combat and a jutting nose like a Gothic hero, which made him seem stern all the time.

"How do you know that?"

"Gendarmes know their job," said Nicolaï, working his smile.

"Give us a break, Capitaine," Marceau butted in. "That's just state prosecutor bullshit."

Larousse twisted his mouth into a grimace, which might mean any number of things that his men still had problems working out. He squeezed his nose between his thumb and index finger. Marceau had already noticed during other investigations that this implied that he was worried.

"As a matter of fact, the prosecutor is already on the scene, gentlemen. Come with me."

"If that's an order," said Larousse, shifting in the damp heat.

The gendarmes had done a decent job: there was a taped-off safety area, with technicians in waterproof body suits, down on their knees examining the marshland with scrupulous attention. Plus an inflatable dinghy, divers, a helicopter . . .

The prosecutor was standing beside the red tape that sealed off the area, talking to Colonel Audouard, the gendarmerie commander, who had come especially from Marseille to supervise the forensic teams.

Larousse coughed gently when he spotted the prosecutor, adjusted his tie and walked over with his hand extended.

"I came as soon as I got your message, sir. This is Capitaine Marceau. He took Mme Steinert's statement."

"Very good, Commissaire. I was talking with the Colonel here while waiting for you, and I told him of my wish to have your unit deal with the case. After all, you've practically started working on it already! What do you think?"

"I think that will be fine. We . . . we still have enough men available. I would even suggest appointing Marceau as chief investigating officer."

"O.K. No objections, Colonel?"

"None. It will allow me to put more men onto the Vidal case in the Var."

"Good, for once the gendarmerie have no complaints . . . I must leave you now, gentlemen. Forgive me if I remind you of a few extremely important points. I don't want any journalists poking around, either from the T.V. or the press. Given the identity of the victim, I don't want to take any chances. I shall be paying close attention to the case, and I won't conceal the fact that the chief state prosecutor rang me up earlier to have a word about the matter."

The prosecutor raised his hand and pointed a finger skyward.

"There's no need to tell professionals like you that the Steinert family has a long arm. And when I say long, I do mean long . . ."

He paused for a moment and rolled his eyes behind his square glasses. The policeman and the gendarme both nodded.

"Commissaire Larousse, all I can do now is to wish you luck. And let's all just hope that it was simply an unfortunate accident."

Larousse and Marceau were unsure how to interpret this final point but, knowing the prosecutor, they took it as a covert order.

"There's a spare seat in the helicopter, sir," the colonel quickly added, with a broad smile. "If you want, it's all yours."

Larousse watched the blue lark rise into the sky, and could not help saying to Marceau, through clenched teeth:

"What a tosser that prosecutor is. As soon as he sees a blue uniform he goes weak at the knees. It's as if they turn him on."

"That's normal enough. His father was a gendarme."

"Well, you certainly are in the know. I thought he was more into gay S&M."

"Anyway, we can really thank him for this case. Any more rotten and you die!"

"Come on, let's go and see our customer."

Before he uncovered the corpse, the gendarme who was guarding the bodybag said to Marceau:

"I warn you, it's not a pretty sight."

"Really?" he replied. "Thanks, it's the very first time I've seen a stiff . . ."

The gendarme swiftly unzipped the bag and pushed its two halves apart.

William Steinert's face was swollen, and still splattered with mud and little brown weeds; a liquid that looked like white dribble was oozing from between his teeth.

The small carnivores of the marsh had already started devouring the tenderest parts: the lips, parts of the cheeks and the eyes had already vanished. But Steinert was still recognisable.

Marceau bent over the body. The smell of decomposition was unbearable, and there was a stink of lukewarm sludge.

"The back of the neck and head don't seem to have been touched. There are no traces of a struggle on his hands, and no broken fingers. On the abdomen, there are no apparent wounds. Nothing to speak off on a superficial level. Neither on the back nor on the legs. The stomach is bloated. He must have drunk quite a lot of water."

"I think he must have drowned," the gendarme said.

Marceau did not answer, but looked towards the marsh. A few bubbles rose from the silt and burst on the surface.

"Where was the body?"

"Right here, in front of us. According to Christophe Texeira, he was about three metres away from the edge. In fact, the pole used to drag him in is just that length, so he could even have been nearer."

"Who pulled the body up onto the bank?"

"Some colleagues."

"And who put it in the bag?"

"Some colleagues."

"And where's the forensics report?"

"Um, there isn't one for the moment."

"Great, that makes three foul-ups in one. You've beaten your own record, lads. Congratulations. Where are his belongings?"

"We found a rucksack with a wallet, purse, car keys, cash . . . the usual stuff you find in a bag. Then there was some photographic equipment, binoculars and a folding spade."

"A folding spade?"

"Yes, like the ones commandos carry. But we're not sure if it was actually his. We'll have to check the fingerprints, if there are any. In fact, we found it by the hut. If you come with me, I can show you everything."

"Later, later."

"Can I close the bag again?"

"O.K., and put him on ice at once. He stinks like hell."

Marceau moved away from the group and called de Palma on his mobile. The Baron answered at once.

"We've got him, Michel."

"Who, Steinert?"

"Yeah, in the marshes, just by a dump called La Capelière, in the Camargue. Stone dead, and in an advanced state already."

"How long?"

"About a fortnight, I reckon. That also fits with the dates."

"Thanks for telling me so soon . . ."

"Listen, Michel, I only heard an hour ago. Ever since then, I've had Larousse on my back, so sorry if I couldn't call you in secret. We also had to deal with the gendarmerie."

"Don't worry, my boy!"

"I've got the case."

"Why you? That's the gendarmes' patch!"

"It's a funny business. The prosecutor was out here in person earlier."

The Baron whistled.

"Speak to you later, Michel. We'll have to inform the widow. I'll go as soon as they give me the green light."

A 4×4 B.M.W. appeared on the road, followed by a cloud of dust.

"It looks like I won't have to bother, Michel. I'll bet you anything you like that she's just showed up. Thanks again, the gendarmerie."

The B.M.W. drew up next to the group of vehicles and Ingrid Steinert got out, along with a man in a suit and tie, presumably the family's lawyer. A brigadier went over to her. They exchanged a few words, then shook hands. Jean-Claude Marceau's expression changed, and the veins in his neck tensed slightly. He frowned, took a step forward, but Nicolaï held him back.

"Leave it, Jean-Claude. Let the brigadier handle the widow. He's used to it. We'll see about her later."

Marceau went back to the body and tried to imagine its last moments of life in the slime of this outlandish place.

From what the gendarme had told him, the body had had its back to the bank, as if it had fallen into the water head first.

"That's one hypothesis," the officer said to himself. "But I don't see why he would have thrown himself flat on his face into this shitty pond. There's no reason at all. Unless the body moved over time . . . But there's no current in this marsh. Unless it was the wind. Or some animal."

He looked for traces in the earth and mud beside the bank, but all he found was a mass of boot and shoe prints, presumably left by the investigators. Nothing else. He walked over to the clump of reeds, parted a few canes and noticed that a couple were broken.

"A man did this. And longer ago than yesterday . . ."

Marceau kneeled down amongst the reeds. The earth here was particularly dry and cracked in places, even though barely a metre from the marsh.

He thought of Boyer, the guru of the force back in Paris: "Move outside the problem, lads. Go and stick your nose where no-one else would stick it. Even at random. Widen the circle. There's bound to be something. Remember Locard's exchange principle. They always leave something behind and always go away with something."

Just as he was about to rejoin Larousse, he saw the print of a shoe, deeply encrusted in the dry earth. He spread his fingers wide in the hollow of the print and saw that it measured almost two spans long. It was a fairly big man's shoe and he must have been running, to judge by the deep impact of the heel and the smearing at the toe.

Marceau had done enough mountaineering and hiking to recognise at once a Vibram sole, as used on a large number of walking boots. He followed the direction of the step and noticed a second, half-formed print, as if the walker had been perched on the tip of one foot. It was almost outside the reeds, close to Steinert's supposed place of death.

Marceau went back along the path and found two more prints on the way to the hut. The way they were pointing showed that they came from the hut.

"He walked this way without stopping," he murmured to himself. "Otherwise somewhere or other there would be two prints practically side by side. He walked, then he jumped into the water. As though he was running away from something. Try turning that into an accident!"

He called to the gendarme and asked to see William Steinert's shoes. They had Vibram soles. Of the right size.

"Mme Steinert has just identified her husband's body," Nicolaï said. "I spoke to her for a few seconds. It looks like she's getting over the shock."

"Yes," said Marceau vaguely, still lost in his thoughts.

"She's just gone, look."

"She gets over things quickly, you're right. I'll go and see her soon."

Commissaire Larousse arrived, flapping his arms and staring into space.

"Finished, Marceau?"

"Nearly, boss."

"Stop calling me 'boss'. We went to the academy together."

"Yes, but I'm not a Commissaire Divisionnaire."

"Commissaire or not, I'm still getting devoured by mosquitoes. Found anything?"

"Nothing at all. Anyway, we got here when the party was already over."

"I talked with widow Steinert. She's extremely beautiful and a pain in the arse. She could make trouble. She wanted me to know that she knows people who know people. I wouldn't have minded leaving this business to the gendarmes. To be honest, with just a few days to go before the holidays, it looks decidedly iffy to me."

When the two policemen left the Camargue, the sun was beginning to ripple its twilight colours across the surfaces of the ponds: the pale pink of the horizon, the gold of the reeds burned by its beams, the dark grey of the endless Vaccarès.

A hint of coolness settled on the sleeping waters.

Marceau had just dropped Larousse by his Golf when his mobile rang.

"You don't waste time, Michel. How did you guess I was in my car?"

"Turn round and you'll see."

De Palma was standing a few metres away, in front of the Tarascon commissariat.

"You're back for a breath of Provençal air?"

"I was looking up an old colleague . . . Can we talk for a few minutes?"

"Let's take a stroll around the block. I need some fresh air."

They walked for some time without saying a word. The roads in the centre of Tarascon were lit by reddish streetlights.

"Do you know what this street used to be called, Michel?"

"No idea."

"The rue des Juifs. There used to be a Jewish ghetto here."

"They can't have had much fun in the days when the pope lived in Avignon," de Palma remarked.

"Unhappily, the worst was yet to come."

They passed some tourists, the heels of their camel-leather sandals clacking on the still-warm paving stones: a couple of old English-women, their noses raised, scrutinising the façades.

On place de la Mairie, they ordered two double whiskies. Marceau knocked his glass back in one and ordered another.

They swapped small talk. Marceau looked rather on his guard, as though the thread of their friendship had not stood up to the frictions of life and the horrors of their profession.

Marceau sank his second glass just like the first. He was a man who rarely displayed his inner troubles, and this trait had always impressed the Baron; he seemed to stow away the worst things he experienced in his career on the force in some part of himself that was insensible to emotions, like an attic where people store what they no longer want to see and will end up throwing out.

But this was merely a front. De Palma knew how deeply violence affected him and how he had to work on himself so as not to look troubled. He knew about Marceau's real need to regain his inner calm.

They paid and strolled off again through the night towards the Rhône.

"Still, there were a couple of things that bothered me just now." Marceau was speaking in a monotone.

"There were traces of footsteps. Tomorrow I'll go and take moulds with a boy from the lab. They lead from the hut and head straight to the place where Steinert was found. I don't know why, but they looked really odd to me . . . The kind of thing that looks as though it can't have got there by chance."

"Why do you say that? Lots of people visit the place."

"Yes, but not the edge of a stinking marsh!"

"You mentioned a hut . . ."

"Yes, it's just nearby. That's where the spade was found."

"What spade?"

"The gendarmes think it was Steinert's, but they're not sure. Anyway, that's not hugely important, or not for the moment."

Lit by the town lights, King René's Castle stood out as an imposing white mass in the darkness of the night. At the foot of the ramparts, some kids were playing football.

"We'll have to wait till tomorrow to get a clearer idea. Did Ingrid Steinert phone you?"

"Yes, just now."

"Well?"

De Palma breathed out long and hard to drive off the enveloping heat. The ball came to rest at his feet. He kicked it back and heard a distant thank you.

"It was as if she felt nothing and wanted to declare war on the entire world, she is so utterly convinced that her husband was murdered."

"For now, apart from a few footprints, it looks like a drowning. We'll see after the autopsy tomorrow."

"It's funny all the same . . ."

"You find this funny?"

"The shepherd I told you about . . . he said that La Balme farmhouse was cursed."

"If you start believing all the stories told by old peasants in

Provence, you won't get very far. They're all completely crazy out there."

There was a hint of hostility in Marceau's voice, mixed with a growing curiosity which he was failing to conceal.

"We'll go and see later, if the autopsy doesn't last too long. What's more, I'm going to have to see the director of the reserve, Christophe Texeira. He's the one who found the body."

Marceau shook his head, as though trying to chase away an unpleasant mental picture.

"Then I'll try and find out a bit more about our William."

"How?"

"For once, I might be in luck. I've got an old school friend who didn't go the same way as me. He had a brilliant university career and ended up as a big businessman round here. Sometimes, when I need to find out about the local rich kids, I go and see him. He knows a thing or two."

Marceau headed off again towards the Rhône. From afar, in the direction of Saint Martha's church, T.V. sets could be heard, filling the air with the last programmes of the evening.

"You'd better wait for the results of the autopsy before doing anything, Michel. In my opinion, the forensic surgeon is going to say that he drowned in forty centimetres of water and the prosecutor will close the case."

Marceau was staring at the wall of the house across the street. He seemed hypnotised by a rectangle of light and the murmur of the street.

"It sounds like you're dying to close this café."

"If we keep on delving, we'll come up with a pile of shit. Just wait for the press to get hold of the story, and you'll see."

"The press is in the know already, Jean-Claude, you must realise that."

"How the hell should I know that?"

The Baron gestured vaguely. It crossed his mind that it might well be Marceau himself who had tipped off a local Tarascon hack about this disappearance.

*

When he got back into his car, at about 1 a.m., summer lightning was brightening the darkness. De Palma looked for a C.D. in the glove compartment and realised once again that he had forgotten his discs.

Wearily, he pressed his temples between his fingers to ease a nascent headache.

8.

Billionaire's body found in marshland in the Camargue
The body of William Steinert, 57, has been found by a scientist in the nature reserve of La Capelière, in the Camargue. The man, a wealthy German industrialist, lived for most of the year in his farmhouse near Maussane. His love for the land of Mistral and Daudet . . .

De Palma folded *La Provence* in four and tossed it irritably onto the living-room table.

The article about Steinert was brief and said nothing particularly precise; neither the gendarmes nor Marceau had given any information to the local news hound.

A photograph to the left of the article showed Steinert amid a jungle of milling machines and lathes. The caption read:

In the 1960s, William Steinert became one of the top German machine-tool magnates.

De Palma rubbed his chin and glanced at the photograph. His morning stubble was itchy and an unpleasant taste of coffee clung to his palate. He went into the bathroom and examined himself in the mirror. The wrinkles around his face seemed to have been dug deeper by a malicious designer who had pressed hard with his pen during the night.

He cleaned his teeth, gargled for a long time then spent a quarter of an hour in a scalding shower.

At 10 a.m., he got a call from Ingrid Steinert. She asked him to come and see her as soon as possible, but he dodged her invitation by claiming a doctor's appointment. That would give him time to wait and see what the results of the autopsy turned up.

He put on some jeans and his last clean T-shirt, and telephoned Yvan Clergue, his contact among Marseille's most powerful financiers.

"Michel, my old mate, how are you?"

"Not so good. I still get these damned pains in the head."

As usual, his friend was in a hurry. He went straight to the point.

"How can I help you, Michel?"

"How about lunch? We could . . ."

"I'll stop you right there. I'm off to Tokyo in an hour's time."

"I just wanted to ask you something."

"Go ahead. I'm on my own, my secretary's out."

"Do you know a man called William Steinert?"

"He was in *La Provence* this morning. Of course I know him."

"Joking apart, do you know anything about him?"

"A big wheel, a real captain of industry – 'they don't make his sort any more.' But as far as he was concerned, business was secondary. Just to pay the rent, as it were. What mattered to him was creativity. I'm just giving you an idea of his personality. He was rich, and when I say rich I mean immensely rich. A family fortune and so on and so forth. But he wasn't at all into being a celebrity or being stuck in a rich man's ghetto."

De Palma rummaged for his notepad and pen.

"I met him once, maybe twice. I can't remember exactly. He was a true enthusiast. Not the sort of person you often meet in our field. People said that he was capable of talking to you for hours on end about something quite different from what you came to see him for."

"What was he doing here in Provence? Business?"

"Not at all! At least not to my knowledge. I think he had a farmhouse, but I'm not sure where."

"Near Maussane."

"Maybe. In industry, he was highly respected. He was primarily an engineer, the sort who was able to roll up his sleeves and literally go back to the drawing board . . ."

"What I don't understand is why the two of you met."

"I was waiting for that. Here I am, talking to you about the poetry of industry, and you stay the copper right to the end! O.K., to put it briefly, I was contacted by some financier colleagues to look into starting up a leisure park. That was two years ago. They wanted to open a sort of Provençal-style Disneyland. If I remember correctly, the people involved were the Tarascon town hall, the *département*, region, local villages and so on and so forth . . . But it never got further than the planning stage."

"And so?"

"And so Steinert was involved . . . I don't know why exactly, but he was involved. Anyway, when they organised a drinks party over a model for the park, he came along. But when it came to the subject in hand, he was rather cold, hostile even."

"Hostile?"

"These are only hazy memories, but I think he was against the idea."

"So why go to this party?"

"That's just what I'm wondering about now . . ."

De Palma clamped the receiver between cheek and shoulder and poured himself some coffee.

"I see. And what happened then?"

"As a matter of fact, I don't really know. I heard that they then started prospecting around the Camargue. But I didn't get involved because it was a real hornets' nest."

"Why do you say that?"

"As if you didn't know. Imagine a huge leisure park in the middle of Provence, then imagine all the wolves coming out of the woods!"

"Yes, I see. Can you give me any names?"

Clergue was about to speak, then fell silent. De Palma could hear his secretary's voice before his friend placed his hand over the receiver.

"No, I can't help you any more there! Look at the local authorities I mentioned. Especially in Marseille. There aren't that many politicians over there. They're all from the same family, if you get my drift."

"Loud and clear. Thanks, my friend. Next time, lunch is on me."

"No problem, Michel. *Ciao.*"

Clergue had said "all from the same family", which translated as "freemasons". There was nothing unusual about local businessmen or politicians belonging to the masons. De Palma had even found a hammer, a Masonic artefact, on Steinert's desk.

Oddly enough, what intrigued him the most about all this was Steinert's attitude during the drinks party to launch the project. Clergue had said cold and hostile. But that did not square with the image he had of the German billionaire. He tried to piece together a scenario based on the few elements at his disposal, but nothing fitted.

At 11.30 a.m., he arrived at the front desk of the archives of the Marseille Chamber of Commerce. The director, an indolent forty-something, welcomed him by looking at his watch.

"Do you have a reference number or something?"

"No, but I do have this."

The Baron produced his police identity card.

"That hardly solves the problem of the reference. But I'll see what I can do."

Michel watched him disappear behind the shelves. The air conditioning was cool and through the building's large windows you could see La Bourse shopping mall and the remains of ancient Massalia.

The archivist returned with a spiral-bound folder of forty pages.

"Here you are. That's all I can find for now. The rest of it is closed because it's industrial property. I don't even really have the right to give you this," he added, waggling the folder.

"Listen, my friend, I can always come back with a warrant from the judge. But I wouldn't want to bother him about such a trifling matter. All I want to do is check a couple of things."

De Palma removed the brochure from the archivist's grip.

The Big South
The first leisure park where culture is a pleasure

The title was printed over a series of photographs of white beaches, Camargue landscapes at sunrise, and historic sites, overprinted with the outline of the castle of Tarascon, a portrait of Taven the witch, and a depiction of the Tarasque that took up a good part of the image.

De Palma glanced through the first pages, which were mainly taken up with words of introduction from each of the politicians involved in the project: the presidents of the departmental and regional councils, the mayors of Maussane, Tarascon, Arles . . .

On the second page, the authors had written a note outlining their plan and their ambitions to found "an alternative" to Disneyland:

> . . . The accent will be placed on ludic and cultural activities that will plunge the visitor interactively and transgenerationally into the heritage of Provence, and more generally into the cultures of the lands of the northern Mediterranean.
>
> As regards Provence, we have selected certain strong cultural markers: a reconstruction of Le Guen's cave (a prehistoric site beneath the sea), Greek remains, Roman antiquities, literature (Mistral, Daudet . . .), and, of course, various aspects of the particularly rich legendary heritage of Provence: the Golden Goat, Taven the Witch and the Tarasque seem to us to be especially interesting subjects for the creation of a theme park . . .
>
> With this in mind, a study will be carried out so as to select the mascot for The Big South. So far, Taven the Witch and the Tarasque have been chosen as focal points for activities in the park.

The company in charge of the feasibility study was S.O.D.E.G.I.M. (*Société d'étude et de gestion immobilière*), whose C.E.O. was a Philippe Borland. De Palma jotted down his name and his company's on his notepad. Then he flicked through the rest of the brochure, skipping the details of the financial set-up, since they were too complicated to be analysed rapidly.

On page 21, he came across a more detailed description of the ludic and cultural activities: they had planned a legendary journey, rather like a ghost train, with a reconstruction of Taven the Witch's den, a rather complicated merry-go-round consecrated to the

Tarasque, and presented as the linchpin of the show; and a criss-crossing of roller-coasters with a "super splash" in a pool set in the middle of the park.

On his notepad, de Palma wrote in block capitals: TARASQUE. Then he looked for what interested him most: the planned site for the project. The idea was to set it up in a triangle between Maussane, Les Baux and Fontvieille. Just where Steinert owned land. A lot of land.

On the next page, there was a surveyor's plan and map showing the various holdings. De Palma pointed at the photocopier behind the counter.

"Could you copy this page for me?"

"Sorry, sir, but that isn't allowed."

"Look, one more time, we won't quarrel, you'll just copy it for me and no-one will be any the wiser. After that I'll leave you in peace."

The archivist glanced at his watch, then placed page 29 on the Xerox glass.

At 12 p.m., the Baron double-parked his Alfa Romeo in front of a kebab shop on avenue de la République. He ordered a doner and chips, with cream sauce, tomatoes, onions and lettuce. His mobile rang.

"Michel? It's Marceau. The autopsy leaves no room for doubt: death by drowning."

"He drowned!"

"Yeah. They've been at it since seven this morning, and it's just what I expected."

"Who performed it?"

"Mattei, as usual."

De Palma trusted Mattei's verdicts completely.

"I think the case will be closed any time now," Marceau said, "and there's nothing I can do about it. There's no evidence at all."

"There are your footprints!"

"Are you joking? Are you expecting me to go down on my knees in front of the prosecutor and tell him that I've found some traces of boot-marks in the dry mud in the Camargue? Wake up, Michel!"

"Did you get moulds made?"

"Yes, this morning. There's a team of technicians on hand. So it will be the last time we have to drag our feet over to that stinking place!"

De Palma tried to concentrate. The case was going to be out of the police's hands before long. He was torn between his desire to believe in the forensic scientist's conclusions and his own instincts.

"I'm going back to the commissariat to see what's going on. How about you, Michel?"

"I don't know. Maybe I'll go and see Ingrid Steinert, a courtesy call."

"Did she call you this morning?"

"Yes."

"So, see you later. I hope she won't stir things up for us. She'll have to accept that there's nothing more that I can do."

After the Fairy Pines, the air shimmered as if emerging from a wood stove; the trees were cracking under the blaze of the sun.

De Palma looked at the photocopy of the surveyor's plan from the Chamber of Commerce. He climbed a hillock that overlooked the whole of the valley, then orientated the chart.

To the east lay La Balme farmhouse, its buildings rippling in the noon day sun. Then, standing out against the pure blue sky, the white lines of the chalk hills of the Alpilles contrasted with the brown, scrub-covered mounds and rust-red slopes that led to the legendary cliffs and viewpoints.

The Baron turned south, in the direction of the Camargue, and observed the plain. He selected a few landmarks from the map and noticed that, broadly speaking, the planned site for the park occupied what Mme Steinert had called the "Downlands": woods of little agricultural interest, close to the main roads and far enough away from La Balme farmhouse so as not to disturb the billionaire's seclusion.

Why had Clergue mentioned Steinert's hostility?

It was one of those places soaked in history, where people have been living since time began, fragile sites which have become retreats for billionaires and snobs of all descriptions, loaded with money and pride. The smallest plot of land could fetch a fortune. So de Palma supposed that an amusement park, which was bound to attract a lower-class clientele, would not have appealed to most of the people who had chosen to live in this luxurious ghetto.

Along the road between Aix and Tarascon, thousands of cypresses were swaying heavily in the thick air. De Palma thought he could hear the din of Marius's Roman legions.

Then his mind went back to William Steinert, a man from the north and its winters of snow and greyness, a descendant of the very Teutons who Marius had cut to ribbons not far from the Via Domitia.

Steinert was the sort of billionaire that Michel would have liked to have known. He himself knew next to nothing about the Provence next door to his native Marseille, nothing except for a familiarity with its murder cases, the memory of a school trip to Saint Rémy Museum on the far side of the Alpilles, and the name of Marius, the saviour of Rome who gave independence to Marsiho, here at the foot of these modest peaks.

The name of Marius had long dwelt in the Baron's imagination; he could still clearly remember his primary school teacher showing him the image of the soldier's trophies, engraved in the stone of Saint Rémy.

The promoters of the future park must have thought of making Marius into one of the heroes of their tourist amusements. And they had already chosen the Tarasque of Tarascon as the mascot of "The Big South". As he got back into his Giulietta, it seemed to de Palma that this was not such a bad business idea. He could imagine shelves full of cuddly Tarasques in the stores as souvenirs . . . the Tarasque and the Tarasquettes . . . two thousand years of oral tradition transformed into bar codes. He also sensed that this monster of the marshes had not cropped up in this investigation by chance. Everyone was interested in it, and this was starting to worry him.

Mme Steinert was alone on the patio. He felt he was looking again at Isabelle Mercier, as she had been in the Super 8 films that her father had loaned to the police.

She did not stand up when he closed his car door and gave her a clumsy wave.

"At least you'll believe me now," she called out, in a tinny voice. "I'm really sorry."

She lowered her head, her face disappearing behind the golden veil of her hair.

"The hardest thing of all was seeing him, recognising him even when he was – what is the word? *Verstümmelt*! Completely disfigured . . . It was . . . *Unerträglich*, unbearable."

She jerked her head back to toss her hair over her shoulders and spoke without emotion, as though she were reciting a text, focusing as she did so on a piece of Provençal cloth that presumably came from one of her new collections.

"I've been trying to wipe that image since this morning . . ."

"If you'd like me to leave," de Palma murmured, "I can always come back tomorrow, or another day . . ."

"Stay, take a seat. I've sent everyone home today. Even the three 'thugs' as you call them, who take care of my safety. I didn't want to see anyone. Except for you. How odd."

She gazed at the Baron. Her eyes, usually azure, had turned turquoise, making them look hugely empty. He coughed so as to avoid having to say anything.

"Have you heard the results of the autopsy?" she said, without taking her eyes off him.

"Yes, and I think they can be trusted. The forensic surgeon is the best I know. No doubt about it."

"And you? What do you think?"

De Palma sat down in front of her.

"I think there's no reason to look any further. It was just an accident. A stupid one, as all accidents are. If he had been murdered, the pathologists would have found something."

She kept on gazing at him, but her expression had changed. It had become familiar, even teasing.

"You don't believe a word you've just said, but I'm not blaming you. Not at all. It's simply some problems between different police authorities, and hierarchies, something like that, that are worrying you or holding you back. But you know full well that my husband didn't drown in fifty centimetres of water, or was it eighty . . ."

"You know, sometimes . . ."

"My husband was the best swimmer in his year at the engineering school in Munich. He was one metre ninety tall."

De Palma lowered his gaze and allowed a silence to settle between them.

The facts were there and he could not deny them. No one could deny them.

The sky gleamed like blue silk. It suddenly seemed to him that the stink of the swamp was sticking to his skin like a wet shirt, along with a smell of fish sauce and rotting seaweed.

He looked back up towards her.

The wind had blown a lock of her hair over the corner of her mouth, just where he had noticed two beauty spots. She looked dreamy, as though asking herself questions before providing the answers.

"You know, we'd been out of love for ages . . ." she said, drawing out her words. "Not long after our wedding, he started to become strange. He read peculiar books, and had passions not readily shared with a young woman. He was much older than me. Our marriage was a mistake that I made, but I still had enormous affection for him. And respect, too. Immense respect . . . it's more a friend I've lost than a husband."

She pointed towards the property then glanced around, as though trying to take it all in in a single sweep.

"It's for him that I'm going to stay here, and that I won't touch anything for now. His soul is still here. At night, I can sense him roving around the buildings and up there on the hills. He loved the hills so much. Have you read *Wuthering Heights*?"

"Heathcliff and Cathy . . ."

"It was his favourite novel. He could talk about it for hours . . . hours on end."

De Palma felt as if he had just been bled dry. At that moment, he no longer knew who he was exactly, or what he was supposed to be doing there. Some dark force held him close to this woman.

She stood up and went into the kitchen, then returned with two bottles of apple juice and a jug of cold water on an olive-wood tray.

"I'm being a terrible hostess. You must be thirsty?"

"A little, I must admit."

"Have you eaten?"

"No, but I don't want to abuse your hospitality."

"You're a strange man, M. de Palma. It's as if you're afraid of me, or else you mistrust me. I'm a woman like any other woman. All I'm doing is fighting to know the truth about my husband's death. And it will be known, believe me."

"Indeed," said de Palma, feeling vexed.

"Don't get angry."

He swallowed his glass of apple juice and poured himself another at once. Ingrid watched him, missing none of his gestures, which duly increased his irritation.

"I must explain something very important to you if you want to understand my husband."

She breathed deeply, her chest swelling as if she wanted to draw out of herself something that had been weighing on her for far too many years.

"You must understand that my husband's father was here, during the German occupation."

She stared at the swaying lines of olive trees, as though memories that were not her own had come to haunt her.

"And when I say he was here," she went on, tapping the table with the nail of her index finger, "I mean here, in this farmhouse."

She fell silent for a moment. A warm breeze, scented with pine and scrub, blew down from the Alpilles and subsided beneath the huge plane trees.

"It was my father-in-law who dug up the sarcophagus you saw over there. And many other things, too. I suppose that you must now be beginning to understand the particular associations that connected my husband with this place. I want you to understand that he was not like the other rich residents who live around here!"

The questions clamoured at de Palma. What role had William Steinert's father played during the war? If he was in the Nazi party . . . Why had he, a great industrialist, buried himself in this hole?

She guessed what he was thinking, and did not wait to be asked.

"At the start, the industrialist wasn't him. It was his elder brother, who died during the Dresden bombing in 1945. As there were only two children, my father-in-law took over the business. But he was no manager. He had trained to be an archaeologist and got his doctorate in 1939. In the spring of that year, just before war broke out."

"But . . . how did he end up here?"

"The Nazis sent him to this region because during the two years before war broke out, he'd spent his winters here, studying old stones."

"So it was him who carried out the dig in the 'Downlands'. Then, in 1939, he was obviously forced to leave France. But soon afterwards the Nazis sent him back. It must have been good propaganda for them. And let me tell you that he was clearly very well received by the people in the village since he came back on a number of occasions after the war. One of the few Boches not to be seen as the devil incarnate."

"When did he die?"

"In 1980. He was seventy-six. He's buried in a discreet grave in the cemetery of Eygalières."

She sat up in her chair and poured herself a glass of water. Her expression seemed less stern. De Palma noticed that the vengeful expression he had observed on arriving at the farmhouse had vanished. The colour of her eyes had changed again.

"Of course, I'd rather you didn't mention all this to anyone. It's *unter dem Siegel des Verschwiegenheit*, a well-kept secret in these parts, and no-one mentions Karl Steinert. When my husband bought the lot in the graveyard, he had his father's remains transferred there with the greatest discretion. He had the necessary money. So I'm counting on your discretion too."

She placed her hand delicately on de Palma's forearm; instinctively, he laid his hand on hers.

*

For the past three days, Rey hadn't drunk a drop of water or had anything to eat.

For three days, he had been in a black hole, left there by the man he had taken at first for a policeman. The only thing Rey had managed to keep was a vague notion of time. In his prison, he could feel the variations of temperature when the sun rose or set.

That was all he knew about the outside world.

Despite the darkness, his eyes were burning in their sockets. His tongue was thick and hard with thirst, and his hands were shaking.

The day before, when he had had his first visions, he had thought he had come down with a fever. Then the visions had gone, the same way they had come. It must have been his thirst playing tricks.

First, he had seen his mother, with her nasty little eyes, saying to him in her sour voice: "Your father won't come back, your father won't come back . . . son of a bitch."

Then he had walked down a long corridor leading to a round room. In the centre was an armchair with its back to him. He knew this room well. A hand as dry as dead wood emerged from the chair and beckoned him to come over. He approached slowly, with fear in his guts, his mouth twisted in disgust, before walking around it. Father Morand was sitting there, his weak neck propped up on a mauve cushion and twisted like a loin of veal. The man of God stared at him with his wicked eyes: "Come and kiss me, my son. Only you can kiss like that . . . Nearer, yes, like that . . ."

He had woken up and chased away this image of his boarding school with a blast of insults bellowed into the night. He had howled like an animal for some time, then his howling had dwindled into a groan, from which two syllables occasionally emerged: "Pa . . . Pa."

Then sleep had overtaken him by surprise, suddenly, as if an invisible hand in the shadows had injected him with morphine.

The final image that he had retained of the outside world was of a hut with a thatched roof, in the middle of a marsh. He was incapable of saying where it was.

The man had taken off the blindfold near some rushes, then made him walk on, with a .45 dug in his back. They had crossed the reed bed along an unseen path before emerging onto a dry marsh, with stars of salt spangling its mud. On the far side, he had made out a hut, half concealed by some poplars and ash trees.

And then, there had been a heavy blow on his head. Everything had wavered and turned white, just like when he used to shoot up.

After that, he had found himself in darkness and had felt round the cellar where he was being kept prisoner, like a mole sniffing out the nooks and crannies of its little underground world. He had also yelled out.

How long now? He was no longer sure. But he could remember yelling during the first two days. No-one had come. He had heard nothing, and it was this utter silence that was now driving him crazy. He could cope with the darkness, but this almost total absence of sound was unsettling him and affecting him physically.

The temperature was rising. Soon his body was going to be covered with a layer of salt water, that seeped out inexorably from every pore of his exhausted skin, and his thirst would grow even more unbearable. He wondered how many days he had left to live: two, or maybe three.

Maybe less.

From what he had read about survival, Rey knew that you couldn't last long without water. He knew that madness would take hold of him and not let go until his body had dried up like a corpse in the sun.

He had counted the days. Tomorrow it would be Tuesday, July 29. The festival of Saint Martha.

He almost smiled. It brought back old memories. The snapshots of his childhood and the pleasures of his life as a man before it had all fallen apart and he had ended up underground.

He scratched his face several times as if to punish himself for all his errors.

The mayor of Eygalières was still on duty when de Palma requested an appointment with him from his secretary, a chubby brunette with false nails that turned the tips of her fingers into claws.

"And you are Monsieur . . . ?"

102

"De Palma, I'm a journalist."

"O.K., I think he'll see you when he's through. He shouldn't be long."

The Baron walked over to a revolving display decked with brochures about the town and browsed through some of them.

"Has M. Simian been mayor for long?"

The secretary looked up from her register and gave him a challenging look.

"This is his fifth term of office, and I think he'll be standing again."

"So he's popular here!"

"Very," she said nodding her head and whistling. "He gets re-elected every time, with a landslide."

"Is he right or left wing?"

The secretary swayed her hand.

"In the centre, more like. But officially the right, the U.M.P."

The office door opened. The mayor was a small man, balding, with bifocal glasses perched on the tip of his nose. He held out his hand to de Palma and looked him straight in the eye.

"My secretary tells me that you're a journalist?"

"Yes, I'm freelance. At the moment I'm working with *Villages* magazine, we're doing a report about the mayors of small towns in Provence which have become the country retreats of the rich."

"Then you've come to the right place! But I must point out that the rich people you're talking about are extremely discreet, and rely on me to maintain that discretion."

"Don't worry, that's not what it's about."

Simian walked round his desk, sat down in his chair and opened his arms to invite de Palma to take a seat too.

"So? I'm listening."

"We're trying to see how it works out for the local people, those who want to stay here and can't afford a single patch of land any more. How do they cope?"

"For me that's a constant problem. I am a farmer's son myself, and my father used to be mayor of Eygalières . . . what I mean is that we've seen how things have changed. I must admit that there's not much the town hall can do. Land is bought and sold at the prices agreed on by the various parties. It's the law of the market."

"But you could issue some decrees about how the land is to be used, or something like that?"

"Yes, but that wouldn't change the property prices."

The mayor discoursed on various aspects of the problem. De Palma simply took notes while waiting to get to the heart of the matter. The man in front of him was clearly a wild old bird, an expert at sounding sincere.

"Have you heard anything about plans for a leisure park in the region?"

"Not a thing. Who told you about that?"

"Someone who said they worked for S.O.D.E.G.I.M., I can't remember their name."

"Never heard of it. You must be misinformed."

The Baron searched through his notebook.

"Here it is: Philippe Borland . . . he's the chairman of S.O.D.E.G.I.M."

The mayor twisted his mouth to express his ignorance. Then he stood up and walked over to the map of the district on the wall.

"We have zones that can or cannot be built on, for various reasons, as you know. I try to keep a harmony between the residential areas and the more traditional rural environment. And I must tell you that it's a peculiarly difficult balancing act."

He pointed at various plots of land and circled his finger around them.

"The people who live here have considerable means . . ."

"By the way, one of your residents has just passed on! Did you see the papers?"

"William Steinert? Yes, I read about him. It's sad."

"Did you know him?"

The mayor's attitude changed. Clearly the question upset him.

"We had very little to do with him. He was very discreet. Like all the big landowners we have here."

Anne Moracchini had discovered in police records that William Steinert had been questioned about the illegal funding of the local

104

right-wing party, though the case had subsequently been dropped. But it did mean that Steinert must have known the mayor of Eygalières, as well as the other politicians in the area.

"A colleague told me that he owned half the district."

"Half would be an exaggeration. Let's just say that he owned a lot of land."

"Indeed," de Palma said, looking at the map. He placed his index finger on the Downlands. "And what's this zone here?"

The mayor took off his glasses and nibbled one of the side-pieces.

"It's called the Downlands. It's woodland. We need a bit of greenery."

"An old boy in the village told me that there are Greek or Roman remains there. Is that true?"

"No, it's not! That's just an old story, nothing more."

"And can this land be built on?"

"I . . . I'd have to check the zoning regulations. There might be some available plots there. I can't remember. You know, our district is quite large!"

Simian put his glasses back on and looked at his watch.

"There is a small problem, Monsieur Simian . . . you tell me that you've never heard of S.O.D.E.G.I.M., but I know that you were contacted by this development company, just over a year ago . . ."

The mayor went back to his desk and tapped his nose several times.

"Indeed. I did hear about that project. But, as you surely must realise, the town hall of Eygalières cannot take part in a . . . an amusement park. You should go and see the people in Maussane. The land is there, in fact."

"But it would be a good thing for the district, wouldn't it?"

The mayor looked once more at his watch and stood up, his hands pressed on his desk.

"I'm sorry, M. de Palma, but I have a meeting with the inter-municipal steering committee. I shall have to leave you."

The dark waters of the Rhône merged with the night. From Beaucaire bridge, beyond King René's Castle, the restless tips of the trees sketched out a shadowy silhouette.

De Palma left his Giulietta in the castle car park. Before going out into the darkness, he waited for a municipal police patrol to disappear behind the church of Saint Martha. He walked for some time through the streets of Tarascon, drinking in the atmosphere of the old town centre with its inevitable pots of flowers at each corner and its paving stones polished by the tourists' heels.

When he was just a few metres away from the theatre, he stopped and listened to the sounds of the evening. Most of the inhabitants were at home in front of the evening's film or talk show.

A few tourists were still wandering around. Two of them, apparently Dutch, were standing in front of the baroque façade of the theatre. A salvo of flashes lit the darkness.

He waited for a while, pretending to read the theatre's programme: they were performing *Mireille* with some star unknown to him.

As soon as the tourists had vanished into the humid night, he walked towards the door of Steinert's building. He gave a last glance around, then climbed up the drainpipe that ran down from a neighbouring house.

Trying to make as little noise as possible, he arrived on a terrace roof made of old tiles and crouched down for a moment to get his breath back. His temples were pounding and he wiped his forehead with a nervous gesture. He was thirsty; *like a carpet slipper in your mouth*, as Maistre put it.

Slowly, he stood up. No-one could have seen him.

He crept forward like a cat, being careful not to disturb the terracotta tiles. After a few metres, he arrived below the window of Steinert's office. The hardest part was still to come. He had to hand himself upwards, open the window, get a foothold and find his way inside.

For the first time in his life, he paid homage to the skills of the *Groupe d'Intervention* of the national police force. He decided to proceed a stage at a time.

He leaped up, gripped on with one hand and opened the shutters with the other. Then he slumped back onto the roof, exhausted by his efforts.

Now for the window. During his visit with Mme Steinert, he had wedged it open with a piece of paper folded in four, so there should be no problems.

He waited to get his breath back, braced himself again, slid one elbow over the sill, then the second, and pushed the doors open with a sudden jerk of his head, making them bang against the inner walls of the office. The noise alerted a neighbourhood dog, which started howling into the night.

With a single leap, de Palma vanished into Steinert's office and then closed the shutters and window behind him.

Once inside, he flopped into the armchair and gathered his wits. His shirt was soaked with sweat and stuck to his back. He had scratched his forearm against the roughcast on the wall and cut one of his fingers while climbing up the drainpipe. It was nothing to be proud of.

Gently, he slipped on his surgeon's gloves, took out his Maglite and, without moving from the chair, played the beam methodically around the room, metre by metre.

Nothing had been touched, or at least nothing that he had mentally photographed during his first visit. There was still that dominant fragrance of fine tobacco, tinged with honey; presumably a special pipe blend.

De Palma got out his notebook and jotted down this detail, then went into the library to examine each shelf thoroughly.

Among the dozens of books about the occult sciences, his attention was drawn to some files that were yellow with age, bound in thick cardboard and tied up with blue ribbons. He took down three of them and laid them on the central table.

He opened the first folder. One by one, he turned over the pages, which were covered by a very fine, very regular handwriting with occasional sketches of vases appended with captions.

Some of the captions were in French: Massaliots, Mouriès, canopic jar, aquamanila . . . and after each one there was a date: 525, 480 . . .

The second file also dealt with vases from Mouriès, while the third was about bronzes and contained a large number of drawings.

He went back into the office and checked all of the surfaces that might hold fingerprints. Nothing. Which meant that someone had wiped everything off after their visit.

"Not very smart," he thought to himself. It was better to wear gloves rather than clean everything up. This was an amateur job . . . They should have realised that a place like this should at least contain its owner's dabs.

He returned to the library and checked the other surfaces. Nothing. The only conclusion he could draw from all this was that someone skilled enough to open a reinforced door had then wiped the whole place behind him. Why?

"Unless the person in question had the keys," he thought. "That would be quite a different story . . ."

Going back into the office, he sat down in Steinert's chair and leaned back. A migraine was on its way, no doubt triggered by the exertions he had just made. He massaged his temples for some time and at last took in the scale of what he had done.

But, in fact, it was not the first time that he had broken into someone's place, and presumably not the last. He closed his eyes as though to evade his guilty conscience.

When he opened them again, he at once saw three objects on Steinert's desk: a white feather, the ebony and ivory hammer and a large pen of the Omas brand. This rarity lay beside a pile of notes, photographs of sculptures and reproductions of ancient engravings. He picked up the pen and turned it round under his eyes. Not a single fingerprint on this either.

"Things are looking more professional," he mumbled. To make sure, he dismantled the bakelite handle of a drawer with his Swiss army knife and checked inside. Nothing. The cleaner had clearly not missed a thing.

"Someone came here, certainly several times . . . then came back to remove all the fingerprints and any clues he might have left behind. Someone who doesn't want to be traced . . ."

De Palma picked up the hammer and tapped it several times on his palm. "But it's not necessarily Steinert's murderer." He put it back and began to examine the papers, which had to be Steinert's. They were written in perfect French:

The oldest and most horrible representation of terror is a man-

eating monster, called the Tarasque by the Provençals.

There are countless depictions of the Tarasque in paintings, sculptures and drawings: the most impressive example is without doubt the 140-centimetre sculpture in the Musée Lapidaire in Avignon.

It is an expression of what the Salluvii, or more precisely the Cavari, found most terrifying.

The Tarasque is depicted holding two severed bearded heads in its lion's claws, while devouring a human torso in its mouth. It would seem that the Greeks, who were widely present in the region of Tarascon, were inspired to make such a representation of horror by various barbarian customs: head hunting etc. For these Greeks, it would also seem that the civilised world stopped at the summit of the Alpilles . . .

The British scholar Moore saw in it the murderous aspect of the gods and compared the Tarasque to other man-eating monsters that can be found in Ireland and throughout Northern Europe (cf. Crom, the idol struck down by Saint Patrick).

According to art historians, this tradition seems to have been initially Italian, essentially Etruscan, and then Greek. It can thus be supposed that the monster followed the routes of colonisation. In my opinion, the myth's origin lies in the sedentarisation of mankind during the Neolithic period.

Previously, the natural world that surrounded hunter-gatherers was magical (cf. the depictions in painted caves). With the emergence of notions of ownership, the Neolithic farmers began to experience fears of the future: worries about drought, or extreme weather . . . They answered the questions that tormented them by inventing gods and monsters . . . These forces of chaos could be tamed only by being depicted, and no doubt by being offered human sacrifices to satisfy their appetite . . .

The text ran on for another three pages. He set it down and glanced at the photographs. There was an old picture of a flagon with the caption: "Bronze from Durenberg, Austria, with monster devouring a human head." There were also amateur shots of the papier-mâché

Tarasque that the inhabitants of Tarascon paraded in the streets during the town's festivities, and a picture of a stone monster eating a man, reproductions of other sculptures on the same theme . . . after that he found ten sheets of paper, the first of which was headed in the right-hand corner by a title written in black felt-pen:

Heracles, the civilising hero of Provence.

Then some notes:

His life was a series of senseless murders . . . [There followed a list of massacres carried out by Heracles]. *In the Crau, he stoned to death the monster Albion (personification of the Albigues of Upper Provence) and Lusis (eponym of the Ligures). BUT* [word underlined in red] *a civilising aspect:*
  – *he forbade human sacrifice*
  – *by killing the thousand-armed Lysis, he overcame the dangers of the Rhône, thus making it navigable*
  – *he taught weaving*
  – *he taught house building*
  – *he taught how to organise a city*
  – *etc* . . .
Cf. the release of the cosmic cattle [two words underlined in red]. *The guardian corresponds to the forces of chaos, the cattle to life* . . . *By freeing the red, divine kine from Geryon's control, Heracles effects a change in his nature: he abandons brute force and becomes a civilising hero* . . . *WORLD HARMONY.*

And, at the foot of the page:

See the digs in Maussane and Mouriès. Especially, Art strt/37-10B and Art strt/38-11A.

Finally, written in large letters he read:

DOWNLANDS.

De Palma lingered for a while over that last sentence. It presumably indicated two library reference numbers – the last thing Steinert had noted before his death. He noted them carefully, and beside them wrote the names of the Tarasque and Heracles and underlined them twice.

It was two in the morning. He decided to search William Steinert's den with a fine-tooth comb, like a forensic scientist. This took him longer than he expected, but he was careful to miss nothing.

At three thirty, he leaned out of the window, checked that no-one could see him and let himself slide down the wall until his elbows were resting on the sill.

Just as he was about to brace himself to close the first shutter, he heard a faint metallic click that he recognised immediately. It was the safety catch being taken off an automatic, somewhere in the darkness.

In an instant, he turned round and saw a figure on the opposite pavement taking aim at him. He only just had time to drop down onto the roof before he heard the "plop" of a silencer. Intense pain held him pinned to the tiles. Instinctively, he curled up in the darkness to get out of the sniper's sight.

His entire body was shaking, each of his muscles twitching uncontrollably. This was not the first time that he had been fired at, but it still took some time to collect himself.

Then he analysed the situation.

Someone had just shot him.

Using an automatic with a silencer.

The bullet had hit his right shoulder, that was all.

The person knew where he was.

The person must have followed him from La Balme farmhouse, or even before.

Perhaps he'd had orders to follow him.

He touched his wound and found that the bullet had just left a shallow graze. He took out a paper handkerchief and pressed it onto the gash. He closed his eyes as his fingers made contact with the sticky blood.

This was the second time in less than a year that someone had tried to kill him.

"It's amateur work . . ." he said to himself. "The guy's a bastard, but not a professional one. Otherwise he would have waited for me to come down the drainpipe and taken me out without any problem."

He let fifteen minutes go by and listened to the night. All he could hear was a T.V. set somewhere up above him and some more distant music.

A car drove by. He went over to the edge of the roof and looked down into the street, his face pressed against the tiles. It was empty.

Suddenly, loud voices and laughter echoed off the walls; apparently a group of young people were leaving a party in the building across the street. De Palma made the most of the situation and threw himself down onto the pavement, his Bodyguard pressed against his chest.

When he hit the ground, he rolled over to take cover behind a delivery van, just as he had learned during his commando training course in the army. Then he stood up, pretended to be getting out of the van and stayed as close as possible to the group . . .

An hour later, he parked on a lay-by on the R.N. 568 in the middle of the vast plain of La Crau. His hands gripping the wheel, he stared into space. Far, very far in the distance glowed the flames of Fos-sur-Mer.

9.

The weather had been stifling all day. At the end of the afternoon, as the temperature went down, a light wind had risen out to sea, stirring the air as gently as a fan.

De Palma was leaning on his balcony rail and sipping a beer. He had spent the morning at the emergency admissions of the La Timone hospital, waiting for a houseman to sew up his shoulder. Nine stitches.

The doctor had been skilful and hadn't asked too many questions. De Palma had simply told him that he had torn his shoulder on a car-park fence while getting out of his vehicle.

The telephone rang. It was Jean-Louis Maistre reminding him that they had arranged to meet at the yachting harbour of Pointe-Rouge.

De Palma put on a light jacket, slipped his Bodyguard into its holster and also took the .45 that he kept hidden behind a pile of C.D.s. He checked the clip and slipped the automatic behind his back. Then he changed his mind and replaced it, telling himself that he would not let paranoia get to him yet.

In any case, the Bodyguard with its six .38 special rounds was good enough to deal with the most desperate situations.

Half an hour later, Maistre and de Palma were strolling along the quays of Pointe-Rouge.

In the shipyard of Plaisance Plus, a whole row of hulls stood on a set of huge shelves, waiting for a lick of paint. There were also small speedboats and a fishing vessel half corroded by the sea. A workman in blue overalls started up a sander. Maistre had to shout:

"I think it's here, Michel. He said the fourth ring after the electricity meter. I think he must have meant that one."

A dilapidated boat was bobbing up and down on the sluggish swell. Maistre gave it a long affectionate look, then walked slowly towards it, like a child encountering his wildest dreams made real.

"Yes, this is the one, Michel. There's a bit of wood missing from its bow."

De Palma stared blankly in the opposite direction.

"Hey, Michel, are you listening to me or daydreaming? Don't forget that we're here to look at a boat, not just for a stroll on the quays."

"Sorry, I was miles away."

Maistre pulled on the mooring rope to bring the boat nearer, then clumsily clambered aboard.

"You coming, Michel?"

The manager of Rouge Plaisance, a ship chandler, came out at once, wiping his hands on an oily rag.

"Excuse me, gentlemen. But do you know this boat's owner?"

De Palma gave him a chilly look.

"We've got an appointment with him. He's late."

"And why do you want to see him?"

"We want to buy his boat."

"What, is it for sale?"

De Palma remained silent. The man from Rouge Plaisance turned on his heel and went back into his store.

"O.K., Jean-Louis, is your comedian going to show up or isn't he?"

Maistre came back onto the quay, still staring at the object of his dreams.

"I don't get it, Michel. We've talked about buying a boat a hundred times. You agreed to it and now you've got cold feet."

"I've not got cold feet."

"If you could only see yourself, you'd scare away a sea snake. Just think about the boat and going sailing in her."

"We haven't bought it yet."

"And if our man doesn't show, we certainly won't be able to."

Maistre's mobile rang. It was the boat's owner to cancel the meeting. He had decided to keep the boat for his son.

"Fuck him," Maistre said as he hung up. "The bugger's called it off."

"It doesn't matter, Jean-Louis. We'll find another one."

"Sure, but I could just picture myself in this one already. Behind Maïre making soup, just like two and two make four."

"That's for later."

"Yeah . . . but when I think of all these boats that just stand here idle, it really gets me down . . ."

"I'm deep in shit, Jean-Louis."

Maistre looked his friend up and down, while searching for something in his pockets.

"What's going on?"

"A nasty business. Something serious happened to me yesterday evening. I mean, last night."

Maistre opened a packet of cigarettes, removed one, lit it and dragged on it nervously, swaying on his feet.

"What happened is that someone shot me . . ."

Maistre closed his eyes, exhaled loudly and stared at the boats that were rocking gently in the port. After a long silence, de Palma added in a flat voice:

"I was coming out of Steinert's office, and someone took a shot at me. I've got a fine scar on my left shoulder. I had it stitched up this morning."

In a fury, Maistre threw his barely started cigarette onto the ground and stamped on it.

"Nothing serious, just a scratch. But . . . I was scared out of my wits, Jean-Louis . . ."

Maistre sniffed and looked his friend straight in the eye.

"And can I ask what the fuck you were doing in the middle of the night in Steinert's office? I thought I heard he was dead!"

"I wanted to . . ."

Maistre wanted to shout, but he spoke quietly, through clenched teeth.

"Don't tell me you broke in, then the landlord or someone took you for a burglar in the heat of the moment!"

"Something like that."

"Jesus, I was sure of it. Now, out with it all."

"I got into Steinert's office through the window, and when I came out someone was waiting for me on the pavement opposite and tried to whack me. Now you know everything."

"And that's all? And you tell me this, just like that? In Pointe-Rouge! You should have called me at once!"

"I must admit that didn't occur to me."

"And all because of this investigation you're undertaking into this sodding billionaire, even though everyone says he drowned in twenty centimetres of stinking water!"

"You've got it, Le Gros."

Maistre produced a second cigarette and stuck it in his mouth without lighting it.

"And don't tell me that all this proves you're right, Baron. I don't want to hear it."

The sun disappeared behind the harbour wall of Pointe-Rouge, so that the sea turned violet and tinged with pink on the surf around the rocks. At the end of the jetty, a boy was playing with a puppy. Maistre stopped and finally lit his cigarette.

"I'm sorry, Le Gros."

"What's there to be sorry about? Some fucker is out to whack you. The problem is that he won't let it drop. Have you got that into your sorry head?"

"I . . ."

"And if that's so, he's there ahead of us. Have you got a description?"

"No. Just an automatic with a silencer."

"Classic. But not with a silencer. I don't want to give you the wind up, but this sounds like a contract."

"I don't think so. If it had been, he would have waited for me to reach the street. That would have been easy."

"Get your car and come back and stay at my place. Then we'll see."

"Not this evening."

"Drop it, Michel."

"Not this evening, I've got an appointment."

"Go fuck yourself, Baron. One day, you'll be beyond anyone's help."

He tried to make his words sound as forceful as possible, but the

116

Baron had already taken out his car keys. He was no longer listening. His face was set.

The Majestic was at the corner of boulevard Banon and traverse Casse, in the quartier Montolivet. It was a shabby bar that had seen its moments of glory in the days of the French Connection: it was there, over a formica table, that the smuggler, Constant Ribellu, and the greatest chemist of them all, Jo Cesari, had discussed the next shipments of heroin to New York and Italy. All under the observant eyes of the boys from the drug squad.

From behind the bar, Paul Brissonne was staring at the Baron. A worried furrow formed an S shape between his pale grey eyes.

"You should lay low for a while, boss. Otherwise they'll end up nailing you once and for all."

"Don't worry, Paulo. If he'd wanted to get me . . ."

Brissonne blinked several times, which for him was a sign that he felt nervous. Suddenly, he slammed his fat hand down on the counter, palm turned upwards.

"Don't talk shit, Michel. Some guy tails you without you noticing, then takes a potshot at you using a silencer . . . so this guy had really thought out what he was doing, no question."

De Palma took a swallow of his beer and drew imaginary forms in the condensation on the cold glass.

"But what I don't get is that he could have taken me down in the street!"

"Maybe he missed you on purpose! I mean, sorry to put it this way, but it's one of our guys. I've no idea who, but someone from our side of the fence. And if I ask around, I'll find out."

De Palma had known Paul Brissonne for ages. He had arrested him during a police round-up after a settling of old scores, one more in a long series of killings between rival clans. Brissonne was not part of any team or family, just a good fellow, half gypsy and half Italian, as dangerous as a big cat and at home in any kind of water, even the filthiest.

He was almost sixty but still very much alive. In Marseille it was said that he feared no-one. His record was perfect: the social services, borstal, the attempted murder of his own father, a good thirty hold-ups, Poissy prison and a few other stretches inside before coming back to the old port.

Brissonne had become de Palma's friendly informer during a spell in police custody. The gangster had been beaten up all day, and been passed to the Baron for questioning at around eight p.m. He was like a beast chained to the wall and had been thirsty for the past twenty-four hours. De Palma had ordered a crate of beer and the two of them had talked for several hours. The crook then laid out his life story like a bad poker hand, full of fishy runs and busted flushes. He described beatings and more beatings until the day when he had decided to stop taking it and punch before being punched.

That day, he had grabbed the man who claimed to be his father by the neck and squeezed with an iron grip. He would have killed him if the neighbour had not come by.

"I'm vicious, chief. If you only knew how vicious I am," he added in tears.

At the end of the night, the Baron had torn up his statement and typed out another, which Brissonne dictated to him. And at eight in the morning, Brissonne had left police headquarters with a debt of honour to the Baron.

"I'll ask around, Michel. By the way, if I find out who did it, do I ice him or not?"

"Don't touch him, Paulo. I want him for myself."

"Any ideas?"

"There's some real estate deal which is going to be signed around Eygalières and Maussane, down in Provence. Serious dosh . . . for an amusement park with all the trimmings. And maybe someone got in the way, a man called William Steinert. For now, that's all I know. They're burying Steinert tomorrow, and I'm going to be there."

"Do you want me to come with you, or send someone along?"

"No thanks, Paulo, but I'll keep my eyes peeled."

Brissonne clicked his signet rink on the zinc of the counter.

"It's only the boys from Aix who could take on a score like that . . . I know them. Last year Morini, Le Grand, wanted me to open a bar with him. It was going to be Lulu, the Chink and Paulo. Not forgetting Le Grand, of course. If it's them who've taken out the contract, I'll know by tomorrow. But it'll be bad news if it is. They're crazies up there."

"What about S.O.D.E.G.I.M., ever heard of it?"

"Fuck it, yes! You've hit the nail on the head. It's one of Morini's covers. He's got a guy called Philippe Borland to run it. They're involved in the buildings going up in the new suburbs around the port."

"Morini controls all that?"

"Yeah, I'm telling you, Le Grand is no slouch."

"What about this Borland?"

"Don't know him. He's never much in view. But that's normal for a figurehead."

With the back of his thumb, the thug massaged the white scar on his lower lip.

"No later than tomorrow. I'll call you around four."

"Thanks, Paulo."

"My pleasure."

"Come on, let's get some pizza."

"Have you seen the time? Are you mad, Baron?"

"There's Vincent's place. He's open late."

Brissonne took his .45 from under the bar and they went out into the night.

10.

William Steinert was buried early the next morning.

Ingrid had made it known that her husband had always wanted his funeral to be as private as possible: family members, a few people who had frequented the farmhouse, and no-one else.

A very simple farewell ceremony was conducted among the olive trees, with Steinert's body facing the Alpilles. Madame Steinert did not weep, and looked very dignified in a black silk dress with her hair tied back.

She read out a beautiful text which she had written for her husband the day before: a few simple words, which summed up their shared life, the year that they had loved each other, and then their rather solitary existence in Provence which he had made his second fatherland.

> *"Ich hatt' einen Kameraden,*
> *Einen bessern findst du nit,*
> *Er ging an meiner Seite*
> *In gleichem Schritt und Tritt."**

No-one noticed the tiny black figure, sitting on a bump of windswept rock. It was Bérard, the solitary shepherd in the middle of the hills and burned trees.

The old man, his head bare, had not taken out his flock that morning and was murmuring some verses by a distant relation, the Master of Maillane:

* *I had a friend, You will never find a better one, He walked by my side, step by step.* (Ludwig Uhland)

"O belli Santo, segnouresso
De la planura d'amresso,
Clafissès, quand vous plais, de pèis nòsti fielat;
Mui à lu soulo pecadouíro
Qu'à vostro porto se doulouiro,
O blànqui flour de la sansouiro,
*S'es de pas que ié fau, de pas emplissès-la."**

Steinert's body was then taken to the cemetery of Eygalières, where the industrialist would now sleep beside his father.

As the cortege passed in front of the chapel of Sainte-Sixte, at the entrance to the village, it halted for a minute. This was Mme Steinert's decision. She remembered that the first thing her husband had spoken to her about, when they had first met in Munich, was this simple chapel which had since become a symbol of Provence for tourists.

He had said: "Sometimes, I feel as if I had been born there. I don't know why, but I really feel at home . . . I belong to that land."

The procession then set off down the avenue lined with Florentine cypresses which led to the graveyard.

De Palma hung back, beside a plane tree a good ten metres from the Steinert burial vault. He watched as the little crowd gathered and he mentally photographed as many faces as possible. He looked for resemblances to the figure who had fired at him, and noticed that about a dozen people had similar builds.

There were a few village elders, who never missed a burial while awaiting their own. They stayed for a few moments, then vanished behind the tombstones.

The mayor of Eygalières also attended. He shook a few hands, then offered his condolences to the widow. They exchanged a few words and, from his expression, de Palma deduced that he knew her well. So Simian had lied to him.

---

* *"O beautiful, sovereign saints/Of the plain of bitterness,/You fill, when you so wish, our nets with fish;/But for the crowd of sinners/Who lament at your door,/O white flowers of our salt moors,/If it is peace they need, then fill them with peace!"* – Frédéric Mistral, *Mireille*, Canto XII.

Behind her stood two men, as stiff as church candles, whom de Palma had noticed at the farmhouse. One was about forty, and the other twenty-something; they were both Provençal, at first glance country people who were ill at ease in their black suits. The two of them looked as though they were on guard duty behind their mistress. They seemed so alike that de Palma would have sworn that they were father and son. The elder of them stared hard at the policeman, as you do at an intruder, or someone whose face and appearance you want to remember.

The close family, from Germany, stood in front of her. From the photographs he had seen, the detective recognised Karl, the younger brother, and his wife. To his right, stood the second brother, plus a few friends or cousins. He looked at them intently. Their grief was sincere, and he eliminated the family hypothesis completely. Nobody here could help him in any part of his investigation.

A prayer in German rose up, like a murmur from between the graves. He had the impression that the stones around him were shivering.

The prayer came to an end. The family and close friends formed a line to say a last farewell to William Steinert. De Palma waited for the widow to be alone before offering his condolences.

"That's curious," she said in a thin voice. "You look sad as well."

He did not answer and gazed into the blue of her eyes, washed pale with grief.

"Death always affects me. And today more than ever."

He waited for her reaction, and that of the two men behind her, but she seemed not to have heard.

"Come to the house. The custom is to get together and eat something in memory of the dead."

"I can't. I have to go back to Marseille this morning."

De Palma went over to the grave and stared at Steinert's coffin. He picked up a handful of earth and threw it down. As it fell on the pale oak, it set off a hollow echo.

He had just glimpsed the truth behind this murder, which he had so far refused to see.

*

At 3.50 p.m., the Baron's telephone flashed up a number withheld.

"Good day, my man. Can we meet?"

He recognised Paul Brissonne's voice.

"Whenever you want."

Brissonne sounded slightly strained, as though out of breath.

"As usual, then?"

"O.K., five o'clock."

De Palma thought for a moment about the boys from Aix. For some time now, they had been involved in all the deals from Nice to Marseille, including all of the small towns in between.

The man who ruled this empire was obese, a huge tub of lard: Marc Morini, a.k.a. Le Grand. He was a vicious thug de Palma had watched climbing since the end of the 1980s.

Le Grand had done time, just four years for pimping, and had escaped by the skin of his teeth from the killers of the Marseille clan as he emerged one night from The Funk House, a nightclub in Aix.

That was in 1995. The *Brigade Criminelle* had counted 69 bullet holes in the crime boss's car, mainly double zeroes, 9 mm rounds and the inevitable 11.43s.

Le Grand had had the presence of mind to lie flat in his Merco Coupé and drive blind before piling into the car of a tipsy student girl. In fact, he owed his life to his lieutenant, who had opened fire to cause a diversion before taking a burst from an Uzi in the chest.

When Laurent Le Gulvinec, the brigade's commander, had caught up with Le Grand in the pine forest, panting and with blood pouring from his forearm, the sun was rising over the steaming countryside.

The gang boss had stared at the cop like a child scared by the dark. He had pissed himself. This was a story that did the rounds of the dark corridors of the *Brigade Criminelle* for some time: "Le Grand had pissed his pants." But the story had gradually faded from memory as the pisser had risen in the ranks of the underworld. Nowadays, in criminal circles, not even the police dared to speak of it.

So there was nothing surprising about Marc Morini taking an interest in plans for an amusement park. He had put money into the new opportunities in Marseille: theme bars, rum dives, karaoke joints blazing with neon, techno clubs . . . So he was not about to go back to bourgeois jazz haunts in the centre of Aix. So it was natural that he wanted to expand a little, and the Provence of Mistral must have seemed to him to be the best investment in the world. Especially because Morini was a local boy, born in Tarascon and jailed for the first time in Arles.

De Palma took the sun-bleached R.N. 568. The road was littered with vegetable crates and melon packaging, left there by greengrocers' vans and blown by the wind.

On the horizon, the tarmac shimmered in the light laden with benzene and carbon monoxide. The huge storage tanks of the oil terminal were barely visible.

Paul Brissonne was sitting on a cube of limestone facing the wall of Crinas, in the only scrap of shade in old Marseille: the Centre Bourse, at the feet of the huge commercial exchange designed by some Vauban of the age of money. It vaguely resembled an enormous concrete hand with some fingers missing, laid on the four remaining walls of the Greek Phocea, Lacydon's old port. Now, the harbour lay between lawns browned by the sun and dog piss, not to mention turds and litter.

Beside Brissonne, an old Algerian was reading the latest edition of *Al Watan*, a sandal dangling off the tip of his foot.

The gangster was starting to feel that he wouldn't mind taking advantage of the air-conditioning in the Centre Bourse, if he had not been armed to the teeth.

The Baron's hand slapped his shoulder.

"Good day, Paulo. So you're contemplating the marvels of Greek Massalia?"

"This was a wasteland when I was a kid. But now, Jesus, it stinks of dog's piss . . ."

"Who knows, maybe it stank like that in Greek cities!"

"Let's go for a stroll."

They took a few steps across the huge paving stones of the Phocean roadway then came to a halt beside the harbour.

"Le Grand doesn't take kindly to you sticking your nose into Mme

Steinert's business, but he says that it wasn't him who sent round the boy with the silencer. It's not one of his guys. That's for sure."

"Can you arrange a meeting between me and 'Piss-pants'?"

"Who?"

"Piss-pants. That's what we used to call him at headquarters. Because, one fine morning, a friend of ours from the brigade found him in some woods near Aix with his pants wet."

Brissonne glanced round him.

"Don't fuck with him, Baron, because he could really take you for a ride, one of these days. Cop or not, Le Grand couldn't give a toss."

"All I want is a meeting."

"Every day, he goes to the Café des Deux Mondes, on place de l'Hôtel de Ville . . ."

"Thanks, Paulo."

"You're welcome."

"You're the big man, Paulo, not him."

When Brissonne looked up, de Palma had already vanished behind the Crinas wall.

11.

As he parked his Alfa Romeo alongside a mud-spattered Range Rover, de Palma glanced at the clock on the dashboard: 10 a.m. exactly. The time of his appointment with Texeira.

La Capelière was deserted, an odour of dried mud and dead weeds rising as the sun heated the air. Mosquitoes were dancing crazily over the reed beds. De Palma wiped his hand over his forehead, which was beaded with sweat, and headed straight for the museum.

Texeira was talking with the student who was in charge of welcoming the visitors; he turned round quickly as soon as the police officer came in.

"Step this way, M. de Palma," he said, over a vigorous hand shake. "Let's go into my office."

On entering the lab where Texeira worked, de Palma noticed the prevailing smell of alcohol. Several test-tubes full of water and containing the shoots of various plants had been placed on a draining board. Beside the microscope, tiny insects were soaking in flasks full of preserving fluid.

A number of species had been pinned onto a polystyrene strip, each with its label:

Scarabeus laticollis
Le Sambuc (dep13), 3/05/2003 CT rec

Texeira warmed to the Baron's interest in his work.

"They're the results of samples we took a few months ago . . . Scarabaeid beetles are very important animals for us, because they eat cattle dung. It's a good job they do, otherwise . . ."

"Your job is really fascinating!"

"My main subject is birds. But these days, it's the dung-beetles that are in the limelight. There are nearly 700 species of coprophages like them! There we are. We can't always do what we want."

De Palma simply shrugged to show his agreement. For the moment, he was trying to soak up the atmosphere, the smells and sounds of a universe totally alien to him, certain that he would uncover scraps of the truth in such a place.

"M. Texeira, did you know, in any way whatsoever, William Steinert, the man you found in the marsh?"

"I spoke to your colleague about that – I can't recall his name . . . Anyway, yes, I used to know Steinert during the time when he often used to come here."

De Palma bent over the microscope.

"And how did you get on?"

"Very well. Really. He often stayed for lunch."

"And you say that he hadn't been back for a while?"

"Not for about two years. He preferred birdwatching either round Méjanes way, or by the Fangassier and Grand Rascaillon lagoons. He said there were fewer tourists. And it's true that there's quite a crowd here in the summer."

"And what did he do when he used to come here?"

"Well, he arrived early in the morning, before sunrise, and he waited for nature to awaken. A bit like everyone who's a real enthusiast."

"And did you ever go with him?"

"No, I think the two of us preferred making our observations alone."

"When did you see him last?"

"Last winter, quite by chance at the market of Tarascon. We bumped into each other and exchanged a few words. He promised to come back and see me in the spring."

"Nothing else?"

Texeira looked at de Palma for some time, while jangling some keys in the pocket of his lab coat. He seemed suddenly to be on his guard, suspicious even. De Palma realised that he was not going to get everything he wanted to know out of the scientist that morning.

"I don't quite understand the reason for your visit, M. de Palma. I've already told all this to your colleague. What was his name . . . ?"

"Marceau."

"That's right."

"Don't worry, this is just a routine check," the Baron said, handing him his card. "If anything else comes to mind, call me on my mobile. Sometimes, days later, witnesses remember details . . . I'll just go and take a look at the scene, so as to wrap up the investigation."

Texeira examined his police card.

"I'll come with you, there are places that are better avoided. You could come back covered in mud from head to toe. Or even fall into quicksand."

"That's all I need!" the Baron said, opening the lab door.

They walked for some time between the ash trees and alders, which made the scene look like a mangrove swamp, as did the dead trees rotting slowly in creeks covered with pondweed and duckweed.

The muggy heat stilled everything, drawing a stench of decay from the canals and creeping brambles.

This path, christened "Nature and Observation", was a complex circuit, winding between pools and crossing some streams before reaching a vast expense of dried mud. Texeira stopped and pointed at a hut some fifty metres away.

"I was in that hut you can see over there, at the end of the scrub."

The hut was shaped roughly like a teepee, with low walls which must once have been white and a thatched conical roof that took up almost two-thirds of its height.

"The body was on the other side of the reeds, in the marsh."

"That morning, did you come exactly the same way to get here?"

"That's right . . ."

"And you didn't notice anything?"

"No, nothing. It was still dark."

The scrubland, partitioned into thousands of diamonds, was running a temperature and the samphires were curling themselves up as small as possible in their beds of parched mud. When they went inside the hut, de Palma felt as though he had burst into a lost paradise.

"The body was over there, by that clump of rushes. As I explained to your colleague, the first thing I saw were some rooks circling around in that direction. I thought at first that they'd found some carrion . . . Boars sometimes drown there. But I would never have imagined that it was a man."

De Palma gazed round the hut. He saw nothing that could tell him a thing about Steinert's death. He went back out into the heat and headed slowly for the place where the body had been found.

Dozens of footprints were set hard in the dried mud, presumably left by gendarmes and various onlookers.

"Great job," he murmured. "Now we can't make sense of it."

He walked several times around the grove, but found nothing. He hunkered down for a moment, as though to make contact with the past and reconstitute the scene as it must have happened. He searched for images, but none came.

"The body was lying in the water, is that right?"

"Just in front of where you are. It was face down."

De Palma stood up. Something did not fit.

Ingrid Steinert was right. Her husband could not have died with his nose in the slime of this stinking marsh by accident. Either he had been thrown into the water, or else he had thrown himself in. Texeira had drifted away, so he took the opportunity to call Marceau on his mobile. He got the answering machine. Then he tried Mattei, the forensic surgeon.

"Good day, Doctor Death, it's Michel."

"What's up, Baron? Are you asking me out to lunch?"

"No, I just wanted to know if you found any diatoms on Steinert."

"I did indeed, super-sleuth. And you aren't the first person to ask."

"Shit."

"What's the problem? You too would like him to have been murdered? Well he wasn't. He drowned."

"And that's all you found?"

"Yes, that's all. And it's already quite a lot."

"Nothing else."

Mattei sighed into the telephone.

"No, except for his adrenalin level . . . which had gone crazy . . . He'd pumped a ton of it into his heart before dying. I'll leave the conclusions up to you."

"O.K., doc, never mind. I'll drop by and see you some time."

"It'll be a pleasure, as always."

De Palma was still in the dark, but he was sure of two things: Steinert had drowned, hence the presence of diatoms, and he had been utterly terrified before he died, hence the high level of adrenalin.

And that was absolutely normal. The billionaire had been scared before his death.

He looked again at the stagnant waters. A few bubbles rose from the slime before popping on the surface. Further off, a fish leaped out of the water to plunge back down into the murky depths.

"M. Texeira, is there only a single path that leads to this hut?"

"No, there's at least one more, if you go round the other side of the reed bed. In fact, this track is circular, you can go all around it if you want. On the other hand, you can also get here over the grassland you can see over there . . . so long as you're not afraid of bulls."

De Palma turned around and behind a fence saw some dark forms that stood out against what was left of the greenery.

"Are those bulls really dangerous?"

"It's better to be careful . . ."

Texeira went back to his office. De Palma decided to go all the way round the circuit.

He crossed the rest of the scrubland, then walked beside the barbed wire along the meadows before reaching the edge of a drying marsh. A grey heron on the waters headed straight into the rushes as soon as it spotted him.

Right in the middle of the marsh, a turtle as big as a calabash was sunning itself on a log rotten with damp. He realised that it was the first time he had seen one in the wild and stopped for a moment to savour the spectacle.

The path continued into a sodden reed bed, and the heat enveloped him. The plants grew so close together that no-one could push their way through.

"If somebody carried Steinert here to drown him," he said to himself, "then he certainly didn't come this way. Given his size and weight, even the footpath wouldn't be wide enough. No, he came over what Texeira calls the grasslands."

When he got back to La Capelière, Texeira was talking with a group of tourists dressed in camouflage gear, with boots on their feet, and binoculars and zoom lenses hung around their necks. They had just come back from a morning's observation.

Texeira left them for a moment to speak to him.

"What else can I do for you, M. de Palma?"

"You've already done a great deal. Just a reminder: if you remember the slightest detail, anything at all, even if it seems of no interest to you, then please inform me."

"No, I don't think there's anything."

Texeira gave the impression of hiding something.

He might be lying, the Baron thought. If Steinert pumped up that much adrenalin, then he must have cried out before dying . . . or at least, that is a real possibility. And Texeira would have heard him from here . . .

"Really," he insisted, staring into his eyes. "Don't hesitate to call me."

Texeira came up to him, scratching the back of his neck.

"Well, there is one thing I didn't tell your colleagues."

"What's that?"

"One evening, I heard voices. People singing on the far side of the marsh."

"Is that unusual?"

"Extremely. It's the first time I've ever heard such a thing."

"And what were they saying, these voices?"

"Something in Provençal, or else Italian . . ."

"Do you remember any of the words?"

"Sorry, no . . ."

"It doesn't matter. When was that?"

"The night before Steinert died."

"And could you pinpoint where these voices were coming from?"

Texeira looked very embarrassed.

"From the far side of this reed bed."

"And what time was it?"

"About midnight."

"And was it far from the place where Steinert was found?"

Texeira shook his head and pursed his lips.

"No, not very far."

De Palma decided not to pursue his questions, and simply trust Texeira. He had hidden a few things to spare himself trouble. The Baron had seen it thousands of times. He just shrugged his shoulders.

"Oh well, it was probably just a coincidence, nothing more."

Instead of heading towards Tarascon, he turned left on leaving La Capelière and tried to drive around to the other side of the reserve.

He found himself on the road to Le Sambuc and noticed that both sides of the marshes of La Capelière were only accessible by foot. And even then you would have to scale the barbed wire and avoid the marshes and perhaps quicksand too.

To find a way through that succession of stagnant waters, clumps of white poplars and brambles, ghost trees and impenetrable reed beds, you would have to know the place like the back of your hand.

To go and howl at the night in such a location meant making a real effort. And probably more than that. He was now sure that William Steinert had drowned in the marshes after being terrified out of his wits.

At the end of the morning, he parked his car between two plane trees, beside the old army recruitment centre in Tarascon.

Five minutes later, he was in rue du Théâtre Municipal, just a few metres from Steinert's office. He let a municipal vehicle go by, then a driving-school car which seemed to be grazing on the sweltering paving stones as it crept along. He examined the scene around him closely, then leaped up the drainpipe which he had climbed two days before.

When he was back on the roof, the tiles burned his hands. He stood and walked on as far as the office's window-ledge.

He looked at the shutters: they had been carefully closed from inside. He bent down and looked down the street, trying to imagine the trajectory of the bullet that had hit him. It took him barely a minute to spot the tiny impact in the cement on the façade.

The bullet had ricocheted.

"Shit," he said to himself. "Why couldn't it have got stuck in the fucking cement?"

He looked around the tiles, but found nothing.

He tried to imagine the bullet's trajectory after the ricochet, then he headed towards the far end of the roof. There it was, clearly visible between two tiles. De Palma picked it up and put it in a plastic bag.

"You've just made your first mistake, idiot," he muttered between his teeth. "I wouldn't be in your shoes if this bullet tells me what it knows."

12.

On Tuesday morning in the ballistics department, de Palma gazed at the weapons on their pegs: quite a lot of .45s, CZs, a row of Herstals . . . He paused in front of a Walther P38, one of the favourite guns of the old-time gangsters, the ones who had fought in the war and stayed in business until the 1980s. He had even met a superstitious old boy from Le Panier who never went into a hold-up without his P38.

"It's a 9 mm. A good old number 9."

"What about the weapon?" the Baron asked.

Pierre Diaz looked up over his rectangular glasses, which were perched on the tip of his turned-up nose, leaned on the test barrel and looked resigned.

"Instead of saying 'Thanks Pierrot', you do my head in with stupid questions. Come on now, Michel!"

The Baron raised both hands in a sign of apology.

"It was a SIG, my friend. A SIG 29. A precision weapon, often used by marksmen who take part in competitions. I've got quite a few colleagues who go to clubs who use one. A nice gun."

"How do you know it's a SIG?"

"There are two very fine grooves, there, on the sides. All the SIG 29s do that. It's their signature!"

"Don't take me for an idiot, Pierrot. I know you're good, but don't push it too far. Without your machines, you're no better than me. A 9 mm is a 9 mm."

"In your opinion, Baron, does your gun talk, yes or no?" De Palma felt a wave of heat climb up from the tops of his thighs to his stomach. Diaz looked at him, pleased with the effect.

"It talks like a jackass, as a matter of fact. The barrel says it all: two grooves, and no more. This SIG has been used once before, for a hold-up." Diaz picked up the notebook that lay next to him. "I'm bored stiff at the moment . . . there's really fuck all to do," he cursed, staring at his cross-ruled notepad. "So, I found out a few things on the side. And here we go: the Ben Mansour case. The hold-up of a lousy Arab grocer's on rue de Lyon. Jesus, using a SIG on a corner store! You've either got no religion or you're a fucking idiot, take my word for it!"

"You're certain of this?"

Diaz whipped off his glasses.

"I'm not even going to answer that . . ."

He beckoned to de Palma to come and look at the screen of the comparator: on the right was the image of the projectile that he had collected on the roof in Tarascon; on the left, the comparison. The grooves were a perfect match. Diaz tapped on the top of the left-hand screen, where the words "Incriminated Bullet" flashed up.

"The guy who used this gun is a real jerkoff."

"Have you had the boys from criminal records round?"

"Yeah, but their computer is down, they've been waiting to have it changed since June, and now it's the end of July. So no records. No nothing, for that matter."

"Shit."

"So go back upstairs, you lazy sod . . ."

"Yeah."

"The best thing you can do is go and see Le Gulvinec. He was the one who looked into the Ben Mansour heist. He was on a crusade to put the whole lot of them in the slammer, all those little buggers from the northern estates who were holding up late-night grocery stores."

Diaz tapped the Baron's forearm.

"There's no more respect . . . they even shoot each other now."

"What can you do? They're allowed to be as dumb as we are!"

Anne Moracchini had put both feet up on her desk and was staring into space while chewing the end of her ballpoint.

"Hello, my lovely."

She stretched and offered the Baron her cheek.

"Well, what a surprise! The opera, a great night out, then zilch. Nice work, Michel!"

"I . . . I was up to my eyes in it. Plus, I did call you . . ."

She threw her pen onto the desk.

"Stop right there, Michel. People could get away with that before the invention of mobiles and electronic address books and all that. You're getting past it, my friend."

"I came to ask a favour."

"Fancy that!"

De Palma could hardly meet her eye. He felt like a shit. He had told her nothing, had not answered her calls and did not know how to talk to her.

"I'd like you to talk to Le Gulvinec."

"Why go through me? You afraid of him?"

"It's not that. But officially, I can't."

"Then try being unofficial."

"Anne, this is important."

"What's this all about, now? You turn up just like that, all of a jitter, like a schoolboy going to his first party, and then you ask me to do you a favour without even telling me why?"

De Palma pulled over a chair and sat down beside her.

"The other day, someone shot at me," he blurted out.

She immediately pulled her feet off the table and leaned towards her colleague.

"WHAT?"

"You heard me."

She ran a nervous hand through her hair and stood up.

"And now you tell me!"

At first, she looked at him tenderly, then her expression hardened. De Palma shook his head in surrender.

"I found the bullet and showed it to Diaz, he . . ."

"Just a second, Michel, just a second. You're telling me that you were shot, you found the bullet, you showed it to Diaz and . . ."

Moracchini was worried. She walked round the desk to sit down opposite the Baron.

"Michel, look at me. We've known each other for fifteen years. You're the only cop I admire in this fucking profession. You're the man who . . . Anyway, I think you've seriously lost the plot and you need a good head doctor plus a few months of R and R."

She let a long moment of silence go by, then moved close enough to touch him.

"Show me."

He uncovered his shoulder. A piece of lint with two strips of plaster made a white square on his brown skin. She placed a kiss delicately on the dressing.

"'The little kiss that cures everything', as my father used to say."

He realised that he had not felt the least touch of affection for days.

"I spoke to Maistre yesterday. We talked about you a lot, but he didn't mention that. There's male solidarity for you. How touching."

It was difficult for de Palma to hide his emotions. His temples had tightened and were pressing on his eyes. He wanted to hold Moracchini in his arms, even for a moment. But he stopped himself.

"Le Gulvinec isn't here at the moment," she added in a sombre voice. "He's on leave back in Brittany. Lucky him. It's baking here. A real scorcher."

De Palma rubbed at his forehead.

"What did Diaz tell you?"

"He said that the bullet came from a SIG and that the gun had already been used in a hold-up. He also told me that Le Gulvinec had caught the case. Young thugs from the north suburbs robbing the local Arab grocers."

"Why don't you call Maistre? It's his section, after all! If they're his local thugs, then he must know them. Also, he'd love you to call him. I bet he hasn't slept since you told him your story."

Daniel Romero came into the office and came up to the Baron.

"M. de Palma, I have been so much wanting to meet you!"

"So you're the new recruit?" De Palma said, shaking Romero's hand. "How's old Casetti?"

"Fine. Listen, I'm really pleased to . . . I mean, to get to know you, Michel. I've heard so much about you."

De Palma kept his eyes fixed on the floor. Romero caught Moracchini's eye.

"When I was in the B.A.C., Maistre was always telling us that there was only one good officer on the force . . . and it was you. The 36, the French Connection, the works."

"That's nice for the rest of us!" Moracchini said.

De Palma stood up, holding the small of his back as though nursing lumbago.

"Tell me, Daniel, what if I said the name Ben Mansour?"

Romero sat down, propped his chin in his hand, and flicked his lips with his index finger.

"Ben Mansour . . . Shit, that does ring a bell . . . But in the B.A.C. you see so many of them! Ben Mansour . . ."

"A grocer, on rue de Lyon."

"Ah right . . . a hold-up in a corner store. It was the gang from La Paternelle, with a few boys from Bassens. Arabs and gypsies who'd teamed up."

Romero was waving his hand in the air.

"Seriously mean bastards, I can tell you. They'd put a bullet in you for the slightest reason. In Ben Mansour's place, they shot up the bottles of plonk. Poor old bastard."

"Is he still alive?"

"No. He died shortly afterwards, just like that. It was really sad."

"And then?"

"Some bigshot in your office took over the case. We gave him everything we'd found out, but it didn't do any good."

"Why do you say that?"

"Well, in the B.A.C. you know no-one can spell their own names!"

"Leave it out, Daniel, don't start that crap."

"The man in the *Criminelle* . . . I can't remember his name, something weird, with a Breton ring . . . anyway, he never got back to us."

"Le Gulvinec. He's a good cop. When was all this?"

Romero looked up at the ceiling and wrung his hands, as though to rack his memory.

"1988. In the winter and spring. I'm sure about that. The year my daughter was born."

De Palma studied Romero for a while. He was in very good shape. An athlete's physique and square features, which suggested a straight character, but with considerable abilities beneath his rather rugged look.

"We questioned one of those bastards once. It was some years later, in 1991 or thereabouts. A little routine I.D. check at the McDonalds drive-in on the roundabout, and who do we come across? Jérôme Lornec."

"The gypsy?"

"Spot on. In an Audi A6 and everything. The bugger was straight. With his papers, and all. But he wasn't insured. And that was enough to drag him down to the station. The fucker was furious."

Moracchini was tense, concentrating on what her new colleague was saying.

"The problem with people like Lornec is that they have an answer to everything."

"What happened?"

"We knew he was involved, because we chased them once. They'd just done a grocery in the town centre, the one next to the station, when you go down . . ."

"Rue de la Grande Armée", said Moracchini.

"That's it. So we went down boulevard des Dames then the dual carriageway towards L'Estaque. We caught up with them near the petrol station. A real race! All of us were breaking two twenty, with them in front with their foot down, driving like crazy! And they could have kept going! But then they turned off towards Saint-Henri, and so we were sure to nab them."

Romero was gesticulating wildly, his left hand imitating the getaway car, and his right the pursuers.

"First roundabout, by Saumaty, they go straight across. Second, they mount the pavement. For a couple of seconds, they stop . . . Jesus, I had the window open . . . I remember it as if it was yesterday, it was poor old Jacky who was behind the wheel . . . Believe it or not, I emptied my clip. Six 38s in the driver's door. Jesus fucking Christ!"

Romero stood up, gripped by a sudden excitement.

"My whole clip, it had never happened to me before."

"I remember that business. Maistre told me about it. He misses you, you know."

"Poor old Maistre, he had a lot of reporting to do about those six 38s. Me too, for that matter."

"And what about Lornec?"

"Jesus, you don't let up! Lornec was the driver. I put one in his shoulder."

Romero slapped his left side.

"We found out because we heard tell that they were looking for a nurse later that night. At the time, they weren't too careful with mobiles. But that's over now!"

"What about the motor?"

"We found it at the bottom of Plan d'Aou. Classic."

Moracchini tidied away a file that was lying on her desk, making as much noise as possible.

"And Lornec?" said de Palma. "What happened when you nabbed him at McDonald's?"

"I got him to take off his shirt, and bingo! He had a lovely scar on his left shoulder."

"Nice one," said de Palma with a whistle.

"That day, I cracked. I stood right in front of the fucker and said: 'I'm the one who got you in the shoulder. The next time, it'll be one in your head.'"

Romero sat down, lost in his memories.

"All he answered was: 'I don't understand a word you're saying.' End of story."

"And what became of Lornec?"

Moracchini closed the cupboard door, making a sound of buckled sheet metal.

"He does odd jobs," she said. "He's a big boy these days. In fact, he's just out of prison. He did a year for gun possession. Apparently, security vans are his thing."

"That doesn't surprise me. I told you, they were a gang of real bastards. You should see the boys in records to check if there's anything new."

"You haven't got any other names?"

"No, none," Romero said, gazing at de Palma as though he wanted to question him in turn.

"I've found a bullet that comes from a gun used in a hold-up by that gang. The Ben Mansour case."

Romero literally jumped backwards.

"Fuck me! Show!"

The Baron stuck his hand in his jeans pocket, removed the plastic bag and placed it daintily on the table. Moracchini looked at him sharply.

"I shouldn't think it was them . . . after all this time. They must have passed on the piece, though it's surprising they didn't junk it."

"Not that surprising. Such things happen. Especially with gangs like that. They aren't great thinkers. They aren't about to take a PhD in logic, if you see what I mean."

"So, if I'm getting it right, you're back on the team?"

"Soon, soon. A month from today."

Romero was longing to ask where the bullet came from, he could sense it.

"That bullet almost killed me a few days ago."

Moracchini looked daggers at the Baron. Romero didn't know what to say. A few seconds later, he walked out of the office.

"I'll have to check. But I reckon I know how to get hold of your Lornec," Moracchini said.

She walked over to the Baron. He realised that she needed to hold him, to feel him against her. He hugged her waist and nestled his face in the hollow of her breasts. They stayed like that until the ringing of the telephone parted them.

Casetti looked around in all directions when he saw Moracchini draw up beside him and lower the window of her Xsara.

"Jean-Luc, I dropped by at your place, and your wife told me that you'd taken the car. So I drove round the block, and here I am. Can we talk for a minute?"

The gangster glanced at his rear-view mirror.

"I'm alone, Jeannot, so don't worry. I just want to ask you for some information. You're not scared of a woman, are you?"

"Follow me, I don't want to be taken for a grass."

"O.K., except you follow me."

She drove towards L'Estaque along the coast road, keeping Casetti's Volvo in her mirror. Once they had reached the village, she took the chemin de Cézanne up towards the hills that overlooked the whole of the port of Marseille, with its huge sea wall, the Sainte-Marie pass and further away the white heights of the city.

Glancing around him, Casetti got out of his car. Moracchini checked her clip, undid the leather strap of her holster and walked over towards him.

"I'm here as a friend, Jean-Luc. There's nothing to fear."

"Don't worry about me."

"I'm trying to connect Lornec and Le Grand. Do you know how?"

The gangster swayed from one foot to the other, his hands stuck deep into his jeans pockets.

"Le Grand you say?"

"Don't pretend you don't know. Morini!"

"Lornec is at home, in Les Tourettes, you know where! But for Morini, it's more complicated . . ."

Casetti was panting as though he had just performed some feat of acrobatics.

"Does he carry a gun for Le Grand?"

"Who, Lornec?"

"No, the Pope!"

"People say a lot of things . . . anyway, what I've heard is that Le Grand spreads the good word whenever he can."

"He's a saint!"

For the first time, he looked straight at her.

"I swear it, he always spreads the good word."

"And it's best to listen."

"I think so."

She shifted so that she was looking at him in profile. In the underworld there are things that aren't said face to face.

"I closed the case yesterday. But I'd advise you to change your mobile. Understand? Change it at once."

"Thank you, Madame."

"And if you hear about a SIG 9 mm lying around there, you phone me, O.K.?"

"O.K., Madame. I'll ask around for you, but don't think I'm turning into a grass. This is just returning a favour."

She lowered her head and whispered:

"And if you want my advice, drop Le Grand. It's starting to smell bad for him."

She turned on her heel and went back to her car. By radio, she notified Mélina, the centre of all Marseille's police, of her whereabouts just in case Casetti changed his mind and lost his cool.

Lornec was sitting on a low wall outside a building. He looked to be rehearsing his prison career to a couple of teenagers who were hanging on his words.

"What shall we do, Jean-Louis? Jump him?"

Maistre dropped his binoculars onto his stomach.

"This is a gypsy camp, my old mate. You can't barge in just like that! We'll go round the block and in from the other side. After that, let me handle it."

Maistre started up the unmarked Clio and drove round Les Tourettes: two rows of shacks lined with the wrecks of cars, standing back from the coast road, between Saint-André and L'Estaque.

The Clio pitched across the bumps on the only road. Maistre stopped in front of the second house and got out. A little old man, bearded and wrinkled like a piece of old fruit, raised the curtain over the entrance and shook the officer's hand. They exchanged a few words, then Maistre returned to the Clio.

"It's O.K. We're expected."

Lornec had not moved. He stood up and waved away the teenagers when he saw the Clio approaching.

"Jérôme Lornec?"

"That's me."

"I'm Commandant Maistre of the north section and this is Commandant de Palma of the *Brigade Criminelle*. Can we ask you a couple of questions?"

"Anything you want, boss!"

Lornec was more than 1.80 metres tall, lean and wiry. His face was pockmarked, his hair black, and his green eyes flashed with energy. He kept tensing the muscles of his jaw while he gazed from one policeman to the other.

"We've found a weapon," said Maistre, "a SIG that belonged to you and your gang a few years back. Does that ring a bell?"

"I've never had a gun, boss."

"Bullshitting already! Look, Jérôme, you're going to change your tune, because you and I haven't got any time to waste. This weapon, we're not trying to pin it on you, because we know you've got nothing to do with this business. Only it's killed somebody, and it used to belong to you. So, as we're decent people, and know that you're a real man, we've come along to talk to you respectfully."

Maistre walked over to the gangster.

"Respect, Jérôme! But if you mess me around, you'll be explaining yourself to the magistrates."

"O.K., boss! Respect. It's just I don't get why you've come to see me. Because the guns from back then were captured."

Maistre and de Palma glanced at one another for a second.

"I was even questioned about that SIG. It had my prints on it. You should look in your own house, boss!"

Maistre took a handkerchief out of his pocket and wiped his brow. He nodded to de Palma to indicate that he could now join in.

"They say that you're working off and on for Le Grand. Is that true?"

Lornec's expression changed at once. He was angry, and bristling with violence.

"I don't know who you're talking about."

"Are you taking us for idiots? Don't try and be smart. Does the 421 ring any bells?"

Lornec scuffed up the street dust with the tip of his shoe.

"You know where I mean? The nightclub, near Marignane, with the dice-shaped neon lights on the front."

"I go there sometimes."

"I know, and once you were seen with a certain Morini. You know who I mean."

"Don't know him," Lornec said, shrugging.

"The snag is, kid, that we've got photos."

De Palma walked into the middle of the road. It was deserted. He kicked a tin can hard, making it bounce against the wall.

"In your opinion, how many people know that you're talking to the pigs? How many, apart from your tribe?"

"I couldn't give a fuck, boss! Everyone knows I'm no grass."

"For now they do, Lornec. For now. But I'd advise you to watch out in the future. Because I'm going to put the word around."

Lornec clenched his teeth. His eyes looked as though they were going to pop out of their sockets. The veins in his arms stood out.

"What do you want from me? For me to tell you I'm with Le Grand? Everyone's with him these days, you prick. You know that as well as I do!"

"O.K., cool it! Just try and understand what we're after."

De Palma took out his notepad.

"The scene is the northern suburbs. The three boys who might have used that SIG are in the same gang. Their names are Lornec, Vandevalle and Santiago. They're travellers. Vandevalle was nailed in 1988 for armed robbery, he went down twice, including five years for pimping. He died in 1997 in the scrubland round Carpiagne – it was the start of the barbecue season. Santiago: done for armed robbery in 1990. He was the youngest. Three sentences: possession of a weapon, robbery and criminal conspiracy. Died in April 1998."

"A work accident?" Maistre asked.

"Exactly."

"Still nothing to say, Lornec?"

"No, not about that gun. I've told you everything."

"So what's Le Grand up to at the moment?"

"No idea, boss. Honest."

"Try and find out, my son," Maistre said. "We're not here to hassle you. Respect, O.K.? Respect. But Le Grand is playing the fool right now. Tell us what you know, or else the shit will hit the fan. If we're talking like this, it's because that SIG was used to shoot someone."

"Who, boss?"

"One of ours," said de Palma. "And that's really not good news."

"I don't shoot cops, boss."

When they were back in the car on the motorway that passed by the port, Maistre and de Palma remained silent. Lornec had put them in their place. If he was telling the truth then a SIG had vanished either from police headquarters or from the clerks' office after it had been seized. Apart from the enormity of the event, there was also the difficulty in following up this sort of lead.

"I'm on duty at 5 o'clock, Michel. I'll have to drop you off in town."

"Wherever you want, Le Gros."

"I'll deal with the SIG."

13.

Voices were rising from out in the darkness. Christian Rey could hear them intermittently. When he had completely woken up, the voices had melted into the reality that forced itself back once again.

How many days had he spent without eating or drinking?

His mouth was now no more than an open wound. His lips had split open from thirst. The stench of his guts filled his mouth, as if he'd swallowed barrels of putrid wine.

His tongue had shrunk. He was sure of it. It felt like a little piece of black horn, as hard as a knife handle. It clattered against his palate each time he moved it.

His eyes burned in their sockets, the final flames of life in his battered body; a timid blaze rising from the warm embers of a fireplace. He remembered how in his last dream he had called on death, but death had not come.

Death does not come just like that. He had been its delivery boy often enough, too often, to know that.

How many people had he killed? Gangland small fry, and big-time chisellers too. How many?

Faces appeared. Faces compressed by the forceps of memory, distorted as though pressed behind a window. He remembered the number twelve. No more, no less. He obeyed the law of the jungle. There was no fixed price, despite what was said in the press and by experts on the box. He killed to order, and his rate ranged from nothing to a hundred thousand.

The police had never found out about him. They just had their suspicions. Nothing more. All they knew about was the machines.

"A big hello from uncle" – that was what he used to say before pressing the trigger of an anonymous .45. "A big hello from uncle."

"SAY HELLO TO HIM FROM US!" the voices out of the void seemed to yell back.

He wanted to shout, release a little suffering from his guts, from the rubbish chute of his memory. But sounds no longer came: his throat was like a red-hot exhaust pipe.

Half dead, he listened to the shadows that were smothering him.

Someone or something was moving a few metres away. On the other side of his prison wall. A panting sound and banging. As though a heavy object was being dragged across the ground and a door or a cover being closed. It made a dull crack. He analysed the sound and found nothing in his memory that might fit it. The sound was not sharp, like two objects banging together.

Rey moved around as much as possible in order to make a noise: so someone might hear and bring help. He crouched on the ground like a limbless saurian and tried to wriggle over to the wall.

But he could not. And behind it, just metres away, the sounds continued. Something was moving more and more. He thought he could even hear a human voice.

There was a furious shifting and snuffling. Like the sound of an animal. He was sure of it now. It was long breaths coming from a huge maw, interspersed by the sound of feet running over what sounded like damp earth, possibly mud. A heavy, sucking sound.

One last time, he tried to cry out.

Then he flopped on the floor, beaten.

He thought again of his childhood. He said to himself that so long as he had a spark of consciousness left, he should remember what had been sweet in his young life. But the images rebounded off each other, visions from nowhere, faces he had never seen, situations he had never imagined. Everything jumbled together, in close-up, behind his half-closed eyes.

He realised that his mind was playing magic tricks on him before making its bow and allowing death to do its job.

It felt as though he were appearing before the god of mobsters, the one who counts the ill deeds and buggers you if you interfere.

148

The god of thugs, who had lost his place on the Capitol and was now doing overtime in the corridors of pain. The god of the lightless.

For days now, Rey had been wondering when exactly things had gone wrong for him. He supposed that it must have been after his mother's death.

He was seventeen. Prison had followed. Then the years of pimping, of slapping around his meagre herd and fucking them fast at night, after everyone else. The pimp always comes after everyone else.

He had dipped his dick in the come of the customers of the two fat whores who worked for him. That was when things had started to go wrong. Really go wrong.

The evening when Betty the brunette had told him about missing her periods, he had roughed her up more than usual. He remembered having got drunk and starting all over again. It wasn't right, he knew it, but it had not bothered him. He had dumped Betty in a disused well between Maussane and Eygalières and then gone back to his bar and stuffed himself with khemia and pastis.

The gendarmes had found the body, but that was all. Impossible to identify.

Death was in him now. That would not really bother him, but he wanted to know WHO and WHY.

On the other side of the wall, the din kept up. He heard a long clanking of iron and sheets of metal clashing together. It was a sound he knew, the kind that the door of the barn made on the farm where he had spent the only holidays of his youth. A big door mounted on a rail was being opened. He was sure of it. It brought back memories.

Images surged up from his agony.

And then a voice rose in the darkness. A high-pitched voice.

"Lagadigadeu, la tarasco, lagadigadeu . . ."

Then a second, deeper one:

"Laïssa passa la vieio masco . . . Laïssa passa que vaï dansa . . ."

The two voices joined together.

"La tarasco dou casteu, la tarasco dou casteu . . ."

Rey recognised that song from his distant childhood.

*

De Palma and Maistre made their way through the tourists who were congesting the rue Boulegon. When they reached place de l'Hôtel de Ville, it stank of melting sandals, redheads' armpits and pavement deposits. De Palma spotted Le Grand in his lair: the Café des Deux Mondes.

Standing a few metres from the entrance, he analysed the scene with precision: minimal risk. Marc Morini alias Le Grand was quietly sipping a beer, his back to the door, with his bodyguard facing any possible danger. Just like all gangland bosses. And this morning, no-one was expecting any danger. In Aix, the underworld feels at home.

De Palma approached. The bodyguard stood up.

"What's your problem?" he said, taking off his Ray-Bans.

De Palma produced his warrant card and stood in front of Le Grand. Maistre arrived behind him.

"Police, sir," said Maistre, his hand on his Beretta. "Keep your hands on the table and identify yourself."

"Vincent Lopez."

"L.O.P.E.Z.?"

"That's right."

Morini's lips were blue and taut. He took a gulp of beer and put the glass back down firmly on the table.

"Not in front of the customers, gentlemen," said Morini.

Maistre stared at him then told the three customers drinking at the bar to get lost.

"And who are you?"

"Marc Morini, the owner."

"O.K., so do like your pal. Hands on the table."

De Palma went round the table and searched the bodyguard.

"Just a second . . . lucky-dip time . . . and we win a Glock! This gentleman has taste. A brand-new 9 mm."

The Baron pushed Lopez down onto the table and slipped on the handcuffs.

"How are things, Morini?"

"I don't know who you are, sir . . . or why you're talking to me like that," the mobster said, his cheeks and double chin wobbling. "Do you have a warrant?"

"No-one mentioned any warrant," said Maistre, raising his hand. "Start by shutting the fuck up or I'll blow your balls off."

Morini lit a cigarette and exhaled the smoke like a bull about to charge.

The Baron checked that the toilets were empty and that there was no-one in the kitchen, before closing the door of the bar and drawing the curtains. He then went behind the counter and opened the drawers one by one. Just below the till he found a second gun: a loaded C.Z. 9 mm, with a bullet in the chamber.

"Well now, Jean-Louis, this is starting to look like criminal conspiracy here, with the arsenal and all. Do you think we'll find a little powder, or shall we wait a while longer?"

"Why, have you got some with you?"

De Palma went over to Morini and stared straight into his eyes.

"So you're the big boy round here! A simple bar owner in the centre of Aix. The same old story: a little café, to justify the earnings, no messing . . . Look, Jean-Louis, there's even a fruit machine!"

"Yes, but then there's everything behind it, and we're no fools."

"So, now, all together, we're going to the back of the bar. We've got things to talk about, lads. And you, the thug, we'll put you in the kitchen."

Marc Morini mumbled something incomprehensible as he sat down on the plastic upholstery on the bench at the far end of his bar.

"I'll be brief," said de Palma calmly. "Either you tell us a bit about your projects in the Camargue, or else we dip you seriously in the shit. I'm sure if we look hard enough we'll find some dope. We're here informally, but our friends at the commissariat will join us if we call them. And they'll find whatever we choose to show them."

Morini's head had sunk into his shoulders, like a boxer who knows that this round is not going his way.

"Does S.O.D.E.G.I.M. mean anything to you?"

Le Grand shook his head and exhaled through his nose.

"What, lost your memory?"

De Palma put two sachets of what could well have been heroin down on the table. Morini pulled back.

"What do you think you're doing?"

"It was a commissaire from Paris who taught me this trick. It goes back to the French Connection. In the report, these two bags will be what I found behind the bar, just next to the gun."

"Bastards . . ."

The Baron shoved a finger into the flesh of Morini's cheek.

"No swearing, Morini, or things could turn nasty."

Maistre heard a noise from the kitchen. He stood up and drew his Beretta.

"What's all this about S.O.D.E.G.I.M? It doesn't exist any more!"

"There we go. And what about Philippe Borland?"

Morini breathed in sharply then glared at the Baron, his tiny bright eyes full of fury.

"O.K., O.K . . . he was a manager. I wanted to invest a little money, but as I can't do it officially, I took him on."

"Fine. So nothing belongs to you, but everything is yours. Now tell me about that park in Provence, the Big South."

"I . . . dunno. What's that?"

"Don't fuck with me, Marco. The amusement park in Provence. How about a little cooperation?"

"It's completely on the level, boss. There's nothing behind it, I swear."

"Nothing except your dosh, which stinks at long distance."

Maistre came back holding a mobile.

"The little shit was trying to call his friends. So I gave him one. He's sleeping now."

Morini had clasped his hands in front of him. He was looking towards the door of the bar and rocking his head from side to side, as though carrying out a clever calculation between what he could say and what he should conceal.

"O.K., let's continue. It was on the level, nothing behind it. Right?"

"Exactly," Morini said, without taking his eyes off the door.

"The trouble is that there are people who get in the way. And I have the feeling that you decided to dissuade them from continuing. Have you been felling a few trees to get a clearer view by any chance?"

"I don't know what you mean."

"Does the name William Steinert ring any bells?"

"Yes, but I don't know him and he has nothing to do with all this."

"Have you ever met him?"

"No, never."

"I know that he was at the drinks party for the launch of the Big South."

"But I wasn't."

De Palma stepped back and examined Morini, who had his chin cradled in his hands, and his elbows on the table. The gangster had his predatory senses on red alert. He only answered when the question concerned him personally. As for the rest, he knew he was running no risk.

"For that business, I put up some cash, and that's all. I don't deal with anything, my name doesn't appear. A real ghost!"

"And you can say that honestly?"

"I'm telling the truth, that's all."

De Palma was beginning to have doubts. He sensed that Morini was stalling, and knew that he was capable of doing so for hours on end. But time was short.

"O.K., I'm not going to beat about the bush. Steinert's dead. Contrary to what was announced, an investigation is ongoing, and you're right in our sights."

"You've got nothing on me!"

"Oh yes we have. We dropped in on your pal, Jérôme Lornec, the gyppo."

Morini's lips stretched so far that they finally formed a smile on his flabby face.

"What's he got to do with all this?"

"It's a long story. When he was a little thug, he used to use a SIG. And then this SIG vanished for several years. Then it suddenly resurfaced and took a shot at me while I was checking out William Steinert's place. What do you say to that?"

"I don't follow you. The last time I saw Lornec was in prison, I think."

De Palma stood up and went behind the bar to pour himself a whisky. Maistre kept his eyes on Morini.

"Right. I'll tell you this one thing. I intend to find out who killed William Steinert, and I advise you to keep your filthy paws off my investigation. Otherwise it will be war. A war that you will lose."

"Now you listen to me, officer. I'm not at war with you. You can investigate Steinert all you want, but it wasn't me or one of my lads. It's quite true that I put a load of cash into that proposition for a theme park. I was born in Tarascon. It's my region and I love it. I want to give it something beautiful. I'm ready to pay whatever it takes."

Morini banged on the table then lowered his head.

"You're almost touching when you try hard!"

"You're just trying to scare me with all this hoop-la," Le Grand said, raising his stubby fingers in the air. "And to get me talking. But you've got it all wrong, lads. I've heard of Steinert because I live in Maussane, otherwise I couldn't give a fuck about him."

Maistre moved towards the gangster, who instinctively recoiled into his seat.

"Don't play the wise guy with us, Morini. Or else I stick shit on your arse and tonight you'll be sleeping in the can. Get me?"

Morini only stared back at him with the eyes of someone who had not been scared for years.

14.

Tarascon was waiting for the feast of Saint Martha. That year, the day of the patron saint of housewives fell on a Tuesday. Tuesday, July 29.

Out of the sun, between the panelled walls of the sacristy, Father Samuel Favier was putting the finishing touches to his sermon.

From time to time, street noises reached him and broke his concentration. He was looking for an ending, a real conclusion that would make the faithful think. But all he could find were commonplaces, the kind of liturgical clichés he'd been taught in the seminary.

On the cork noticeboard on the wall, next to the schedule of services, he had pinned up a simple drawing by a child in catechism classes. It was the picture of the week: Saint Martha as Terminator, overcoming a terrifying Pokemon. It was the version that he preferred of the miraculous Lazarus's young sister, who had arrived on the beaches of the Camargue two thousand years before with a band of apprentice saints, ready to get to grips with the prevailing paganism.

Martha, the patroness of housewives, but also of Tarascon.

Martha, inseparable from the monstrous Tarasque, which was half man and half reptile. The saint had delivered the people of Tarascon from this spawn of the devil, quite simply by speaking to it. Martha had sweet-talked the beast with a few kind words and the help of the Holy Ghost. Then she had tied her belt around the monster's neck and led it to the Rhône, where she made it promise never to terrorise the people again. The Tarasque had promptly vanished beneath the rock that now bears King René's Castle.

In his past life, Samuel Favier had been an emergency doctor, until he had met God on the battlefields of the former Yugoslavia.

155

Saint Martha was his first parish, and his sermon about the Tarasque the first real obstacle that the Almighty had placed in the young priest's path.

He was trying to find something edifying to say about this legend dressed up as a religious thriller. The ex-doctor in him wanted to be high-brow, and talk about man's reptilian brain, about the Tarasque that survives in all of us, ready to gobble up morality and common sense at the slightest disturbance of the ego. The Tarasque, that colourful version of the instinctive, raw, terrifying violence of the human race. That was what Favier wanted to highlight.

And yet his predecessor, old Father Bessodes, as he gave him the keys to his church, had warned him not to risk a schism: "Don't go too far with the Tarasque . . . they don't like that! You'll be taking a big risk. They're very sensitive about their tale of a monster, and can't stand it if you diverge from the official version. All that matters in this town is tradition. They'd be lost without their monster. If you tell them that the Tarasque is more a symbol than anything else, and that it never existed, you'll expose yourself to the fury of good society, the mayor and the bishop. Remember that they're all more or less cousins or friends, and they're the people that run the place."

During the service the previous Sunday, he had announced that he would be saying a grand mass on Tuesday evening at 8.00 p.m., so that all the townspeople could attend.

It was now Monday. He was rereading the opening passage of his text when he heard the church door creak. The big sacristy clock indicated 10.00 a.m. precisely. The *Tarascaires*, the Knights of the Tarasque, were early.

"Good morning, Father. I've come to fetch her."

"Really? I thought you'd come to confess, you wicked sinner."

Favier warmly shook the powerful hand of Marc Gouirand, the leader of the Knights.

"Tell me, Marc, how long have you been taking care of this creature?"

"The last festival made it twenty years."

He whistled with admiration. Marc Gouirand was a solid fellow, forty-something, muscular, with a jutting chin and the look of a cheeky brat who had strayed into the world of adults.

"So, why do you look after the Tarasque?"

"My wife says that she's my mistress . . . It's a tradition, Father. And without traditions, we're nothing."

"There's always Him up there," said Father Favier, pointing towards the top of the church.

"Yes, true. But . . . I've been seeing the Tarasque ever since I was a little boy," he replied, rubbing his chin. "When I was a child, all I dreamed of was being able to push her. And now here I am, right behind her."

"I've been told that it was you who repaired her."

"If you'd seen her, twenty years back when I took her over . . . she was in a real mess. Like a hippy, or a tramp. Good grief! No-one had given her the slightest lick of paint since the end of the First World War. Think of it . . . since 1918 . . . She was hideous, really hideous."

"Why, do you find her beautiful then?"

"She's magnificent! Come and see."

Marc Gouirand led Father Favier into the depths of the nave. The Tarasque was there, its bulging eyes wide open, both menacing and familiar, motionless in its special chapel. In the half-light, its huge Jurassic reptilian body could be made out, with its scales still filthy from the weeds of the Camargue and its red crest raised.

A gold and mauve ray of light lit up its face on the slant, making it look like a moustachioed villain. The Tarasque had the face of a turn-of-the-century wide boy or an Apache battered by fate.

"There she is, our famous beast," Gouirand murmured, instinctively standing back.

"Is it a male or a female in your opinion, Marc?"

Its jaw drooping, the monster stared derisively at the entrance to the crypt that contained the tomb of Saint Martha.

"A big question, Father. La Tarasque is a female name, but it's a monster. For me, she's female, but people see her as they want."

Favier went over to the legendary reptile and stroked its mane. He noticed that some chips of wood were missing from its face, especially on the right cheek and ear. A piece of moustache had also been broken off.

"Whatever happened to this poor monster?"

"We hit a car. Someone was double-parked just in front of the castle. It's hard to stop her sometimes."

The Knight raised the beast's heavy head and made the fearful white teeth in its jaws clack together. Their massive impact echoed through the vaults of the church.

Favier glanced at the crypt of Saint Martha, hoping that the din of monstrous teeth would not rouse the holy lady in her marble sarcophagus.

Gouirand kneeled down in front of the reptilian mouth.

"It's going to be a pain in the . . . to stick back the missing bits of wood. We'll have to make repairs . . ."

The priest went over and bent down to look at the extent of the damage.

"You'll have to find a wood carver. And a good one!"

"That's no problem. For the Tarasque, everyone pitches in."

Gouirand walked around it, examining the fabulous creature's scales which were highlighted with gold and grey, as well as its bright red spikes. He finished with its tail, which was tied in a knot and tipped with the blade of a lance.

"And maybe a lick of paint on her tail . . ."

"And how about a little blood on the teeth?"

"Why not? She loves blood. If she could eat a couple of towns-folk before Saint Martha's day, then she would."

"Yes, but don't forget Saint Martha herself!"

"Don't you worry, Father. We're not about to forget your lady friend."

With surprising ease, Gouirand pulled the Tarasque towards him, taking care that the tail did not damage the altar behind it. The jaws clacked again as he turned it towards the church's main door.

"How much does this contraption weigh?"

"Six hundred kilos, and she's five metres long."

"And you're just going to walk it through the streets of Tarascon like that?"

"I'm used to it. She listens to me."

Father Favier opened wide the double doors of the church and let out the Tarasque, led by its most loyal knight. A raw light invaded the transept, and the priest closed up again fast, raising a din that made the entire Gothic façade tremble.

Inside, quiet footfalls were echoing in the apse. Probably the first tourist of the day. Even though it was not yet visiting time.

Father Favier crossed the choir and went round the ambulatory to ask the visitor to come back in the afternoon. But he saw no-one. He searched the house of God from top to bottom, including the crypt of Saint Martha. No-one.

Yet he was sure that he had heard footsteps.

He went back to his sermon, with the unpleasant sensation of suffering from auditory hallucinations. And also with the certitude that he should not upset cranks like Gouirand. Especially since his parish was full of them.

A warm breeze was rising from the sea and blowing along the dirt track that led up to the sparse meadows of the Alpilles. Eugène Bérard's sheep were sheltering from the heat of the sun beneath a limestone overhang.

The shepherd kept his eyes fixed on the Baron. His luminous stare was analysing each gesture and each expression.

"Have you hurt your hands?"

"Can't hide anything from you!"

"You look as if you've been fighting the whole earth."

De Palma smiled, rubbed his hands together, then stuck them into his jeans pockets.

"Last time, you told me about the Downlands. Do you remember?"

"That's the land on the other side of the Maussane road. It's called the Chemin de Galibert. On the top, there are vines and some lavender. It belonged to poor old William."

"And this land is cursed?"

"Those are ancient beliefs . . . In the old days, people used to say that there was the statue of a Roman god there. I can't remember his name."

"Hercules, or Heracles."

Bérard glanced at the Baron, a flash of fire in his eyes, like a flame from a canon's mouth. His voice grew harsher.

"Who told you that?"

"I looked up a few archaeological records that mention it."

Bérard was now on his guard. He took a step backwards and leaned on his stick.

"I didn't know there was anything about that in the books."

"And you? Why don't you tell me a little bit of what you know about the Downlands."

"Oh, they're not worth much. They're full of stones as big as houses. There's nothing to be done with them."

"So why did they mean so much to William Steinert?"

"I can't answer that."

"I'm sorry, but you'll have to."

Bérard just whistled to his dog.

"You'll have to, M. Bérard. Steinert was murdered."

The shepherd stood up, like a bamboo rod that had stayed bent too long. De Palma had not been expecting this reaction. In the old man's face, he read an expression of great sadness.

"I think you ought to tell me the truth. There are powerful forces at work that are threatening everything and everyone around here."

"Oh, those forces won long ago, M. de Palma. All the land now belongs to outsiders."

Bérard turned back towards the valley and fell silent for a moment.

"Outsiders like the Steinerts?"

"William was different."

"Could you tell me a little about him?"

The shepherd bent down and plucked a blade of grass which he split between his nails and stuck in his mouth.

"Do you have time?"

"I'm at your disposal."

"I'll have to take the animals back. Come with me to the farm. It's not far. Then we'll talk."

Eugène Bérard lived in the farmhouse of Les Fontaines: two buildings, one for him, the other for the sheep, formed an L in front of a large barn, in which slept a 1960s Massey-Ferguson, a harrow and a haymaker, all of them covered in rust.

His flock pushed its way through the entrance to the fold. Lambs that had lost their mothers were bleating. The shepherd went up into the barn to fetch some hay for the mangers, then he gave the lambs their ration of barley.

"Goodness, they're hungry! With this heat, there's nothing left to eat in the pastures."

"You take good care of them."

"I certainly do!"

Despite his great age, he still moved among his jostling charges without losing his balance.

"William often used to come here. Sometimes he gave me a hand. But he didn't want anyone to know that. It reminded him of his childhood, when he helped with the harvesting or haymaking."

A last ray of dusty sunshine came in through the double doors. The air was charged with the animals' vitality and the grinding of their jaws as they quickly reduced their hay to a fragrance of mint and thyme.

"Come on, we've earned a drink."

The farmhouse living room was plunged in total darkness. Bérard opened the shutters to let in the evening light. He placed a jug of water, two glasses and a bottle of pastis on the table. Then he disappeared.

The room was partly taken up by a huge table covered with oilcloth. At the far end, there was a large freestone fireplace and a modest grandmother clock. The only other piece of furniture was a tall, dark, walnut cupboard.

Bérard returned with a small package under his arm.

"I knew William when he was very young. His father came here, before the war."

He poured two pastis and raised his glass.

"Your health, sir."

The old man rummaged through his papers, careful not to let de Palma see anything.

"William's father carried out digs in the region. He was looking for sarcophagi and old stones. One day, I bumped into him not far from here, just as I did with you, and the two of us got on. Look, here's a photo of him."

Steinert senior was standing beside Bérard, his hand on his shoulder. Both of them were smiling at the photographer.

"That was the day when we found the statue of Hercules. I was the only one who knew where it was."

The old man sat down in front of the Baron.

"William's father was a good man. His name was Karl. He'd studied archaeology back in Germany."

"Archaeology?"

"He was interested in the ancient Greeks and Romans who came to this region. And as the people round here knew that I was interested too, they sent him to see me. That's how we got to know each other."

The old man pushed his cap back, freeing a lock of silver hair which stuck onto his damp forehead. He took a swig of pastis.

"And then the war broke out. Round here, we didn't see much of the Germans. Just a few patrols. After all, nothing much happens in the countryside! Then, in 1942, Karl came back with a whole gang of Boches. They were students from Munich University. They started digging again . . . this was the time of the Vichy government. They worked with some students from France."

He let his big hand drop onto the tablecloth. The mechanism of the clock started up, and seven chimes filled the room with sound.

"And did they find anything?"

"Nothing much . . . but they all stayed at La Balme, except for William's father, who refused to live in the farmhouse. So, you see, he lodged at the central hotel in Maussane, while the youngsters slept in the barn! But all went well. I mean, this wasn't a crowd of Nazis. I can still picture them all in the farmyard. They were nice and helpful. But then, in 1942, the Wehrmacht turned up, and everything changed. Some of the students left, while others put on army uniforms."

Bérard showed a photograph from the war years. To judge from the various people's dress, Steinert was surrounded by local worthies.

162

"That's the old mayor of Maussane, and this is the father of the present mayor of Eygalières."

De Palma waited for the old shepherd to resume the conversation of his own accord. Bérard stood up, walked over to pat his dog's head, then took a packet of tobacco down from the mantelpiece.

"At the end of the war, we were visited by bogus members of the Resistance from Marseille, Arles, Tarascon and round here. They were real thugs. Especially the ones from these parts . . ."

Bérard paused. He clenched his teeth and seemed to be short of breath.

"I must tell you that I was in the Resistance and Steinert knew it. I was in the Vincent network. It was a small organisation that we set up with some local lads. Steinert even helped me out a couple of times. But try and explain that to a load of lawless ruffians."

"What happened?"

"They shaved the head of Mme Maurel, the owner of the farmhouse, and they shot one of her brothers. If you go into the farmyard, you can still see the bullet marks in the barn wall, to the right of the door."

Bérard thumped down his empty glass and stared into space. The clock chimed the half-hour. He removed a deckle-edged photo from the pile. It showed a young woman of about twenty, with a beautiful face lit up by rather a fixed smile and tender eyes.

"This is Simone Maurel . . . I could do nothing to help them. Not a thing. Poor old Emile. His body had been torn apart by the time I got there."

"What about Mme Maurel?"

"She died shortly afterwards. Of shame . . . How can you live with that?"

The shepherd sat back down. His figure had shrunk once more. Through the window, he watched the dust in the yard rise up towards the sun.

"You'll have another one, won't you?" he asked, pouring out a fresh glass without waiting for a reply.

"What about the other brother?"

"He died too. But much later . . . A tractor accident. He'd got a job on the Janson farm."

The shepherd finished his sentence with a gesture that de Palma did not understand. Evoking the past had evidently upset him. He was an emotional man concealing a long-standing anger.

Outside, the two tall olive trees in the yard were changing colour in the evening light. The dog went out and growled.

"In 1946, a man came to see me. I never learned his name. He simply told me that Steinert had sent him and that he was going to buy La Balme. Then he asked me if I'd agree to look after the land. And I did so for several years. I don't have much in the way of land myself! After my wife died, in the 1980s, they bought the Downlands. William arranged the purchase. His poor father was already dead."

"And you knew there was this real estate scheme?"

Bérard's eyes filled with anger.

"If they ever do that . . ."

"So long as the Downlands aren't for sale, they won't be able to do anything!"

"Don't you believe it! I own part of it, and I'm very old. I'd left everything to William. But now he's dead and they could turn us out if they want. They make the laws, and adapt them as they want. And now William's gone. He knew what he was doing, plus he had money and lawyers. No-one argued with him! But poor people like us . . . we count for nothing!"

"And is the mayor of Eygalières in on this?"

"Of course he is! All the big cheeses are in the know. Anyway, I'd rather not say any more. There's no-one left to save our little corner of Provence."

"There's still William's wife! She's very rich too, and the Downlands are hers now."

"I don't know if she'll stay. I don't think so, without her husband . . ."

Bérard had spoken as though he was expecting an answer.

"His wife intends to stay."

"I don't know if William told her."

"Told her what?"

"William was Simone Maurel's son. He was born in 1942. It was poor Simone's only sin: having the child of a man she had loved during the war."

De Palma was lost for words. The light had changed. In the cooler air, the birds were starting to sing, while the sheep had fallen silent. There was a smell of sweat, rancid wool and strong milk.

"She died and left her son behind . . . When she was shamed like that, she sent him to his father, in Germany . . ."

Bérard shivered. These memories were exciting his heart. For a moment, his features changed; his face emptied of the remnant of life that had been driving him on just a few minutes before.

"What I've just told you, no-one else knows. William found out when he was much older. I told him. When his mother died, he was only three. He didn't remember her."

Bérard blew his nose loudly.

"William was like a son to me."

On the road that led down towards Fontvieille, de Palma tried to put his ideas in order. The day before, he had learned nothing from Morini, except for the confirmation of what he already knew: the mob in Aix was laundering money in business deals such as this amusement park. There was nothing surprising about that. The only detail that provided any progress was Morini's origins: he came from Tarascon. One day, that could turn out to be relevant.

On the other hand, this meeting with Bérard had sent his mind into a panic. He had been expecting anything but that, and suddenly whole sections of the mystery had fallen. He now understood why La Balme farmhouse had meant so much to Steinert and why he had changed nothing in most of its rooms.

He stopped beside the vines that grew along the Downlands. To the right, between the white crests of the rocks that rose up as far as the fortress of Les Baux, the sky was still red from the sun. In the valley, a silvery light flattened out the contours.

The Baron went in among the pines, took a few steps, then stopped. There was a smell of warmth and roots. As far as the eye could see, there were the twisted trunks of oaks and stumps rotting on a bed of needles. As the night fell, the pines and mastic trees stood like threatening sentinels.

The Baron retraced his steps. In the distance, he could hear cars driving up to Les Baux, and a solitary cuckoo among the creaking branches.

It must be warm on the beach.
The sand is golden with pink and violet glints.
The image is slightly hazy,
Stippled by time.
Isabelle is in her swimsuit.
She's fifteen and a half.
She's walking across the sand like a clown.
Close-up. A smile at the camera.
She's just been for a swim. Her swimsuit is taut.
Her breasts are hard.
She has sand on her calves and the tops of her thighs.
Her grandmother is watching her and waving at the lens.
Then the letters and numbers stand out on the white background.
Maistre turns off the projector.
Marceau stands up.
De Palma doesn't move.
He's turned round his chair and leaned his forearms on the back rest.
He yawns.
"What's the time, Jean-Claude?"
"Three o'clock. I'm knackered."
"Me too," Maistre adds.
"You coming, Michel? Let's go and get a bite to eat at the Pied de Cochon."
The Baron grimaces.
"You want to eat after what we've just seen?"
"Yes, Michel, I still want to eat. Because we have to keep our strength up if we want to find that fucker."

That night, de Palma leafed through the pages of his notebooks, looking for a truth that was receding a little more each day. Isabelle Mercier had been his only failure. He had found answers to all the other investigations, even if the courts had not always delivered the verdicts he was hoping for. There were policing certainties and then there were judicial truths.

He had sent to prison a countless number of people who had committed bloody crimes. Most had received maximum sentences: a life behind bars, as well as few executions when he was a young officer.

Each time, the truth had emerged, and that was what really mattered for him.

Except for Isabelle Mercier.

He remembered the feeling of powerlessness that had gripped him and which he had shared with Maistre and Marceau. He felt the same way now. He did not understand why Steinert had died. The little voice that whispered to him that it was for a few hectares of land did not satisfy him. Morini did not kill people without knowing the whys and wherefores of his action. That much he was sure of.

On the day of the billionaire's funeral, he had glimpsed a truth: Steinert had died accidentally. Yet he knew that the context of this accident had not been natural. Around the edges of that accident he could vaguely discern a meshing of events that went beyond the harshnesses of life and had made death inevitable.

15.

Tuesday, July 29. 10 a.m.

Marceau was the first on the scene. He was alone, having intercepted an urgent message on the Homicide frequency. The call had mentioned the cleaning and maintenance depot of the town of Tarascon. The operator had then specified: "In the municipal garage".

A patrol was on its way.

The first thing Marceau saw was the Tarasque, then Marc Gouirand and, sitting beside him, Father Favier, who had raised the alarm. The monster had been placed amidst a stack of equipment, in the very place where Gouirand had left it the day before to treat it to a wash and brush-up. In front of its maw lay a horribly mutilated body: a torso, a head and an arm caught in its wooden teeth.

Like a barbaric offering to the hideous creature.

"Have you touched anything?"

Father Favier advanced towards him.

"No, nothing, sir. I was a doctor before I became a priest. I know the police's methods."

"What about you, sir?"

Gouirand did not respond. He was sitting on a low wall, his head in his hands.

Favier took Marceau by the arm.

"I think it would be better to wait. He's still in shock."

A patrol arrived and started to trample over the scene of the crime, before coming to a halt at the sight of the corpse. Marceau shooed them away at once. He did not approach the body straight away, but stood for some time in silent observation. Then he took out his mobile, asked for the forensic unit in Marseille, hung up and turned towards Favier.

"O.K., Father. Can you tell me exactly what happened, between the moment when you discovered this horror and now?"

Favier took a deep breath.

"I was about to go through my sermon for this evening's mess one last time, when I got a phone call: it was Marc Gouirand, to tell me . . ."

"What did he say precisely?"

"Not much."

"Try to remember."

"He was having trouble speaking. All I understood was Tarasque and municipal garage. That's all."

"But you realised that something was wrong?"

"I used to be an emergency doctor. I'm very familiar with accidents and tragedies."

"And then?"

"Then, I came here. Marc was sitting just as you see him now. He hasn't moved since. I saw the corpse and called the police. Three minutes later, you got here."

Marceau looked at his watch. It was now 10.20 a.m. Favier's version of events fitted perfectly. He looked at Gouirand, who still had not moved. In a few minutes' time he would question him.

Meanwhile, he went back to his car and radioed to ask where the Marseille forensics team was.

"On their way," yelled the voice on the radio.

At 10.45, Larousse arrived, accompanied by the deputy public prosecutor: a pretty and slender brunette with square glasses and a little upturned nose decked with freckles. Marceau had never seen her before.

Larousse introduced them.

"What do you think, Marceau?"

He scratched his head.

"A real act of barbarism. The work of a lunatic. I haven't seen anything this vile for ages. This is Father Favier, who alerted us."

The young deputy prosecutor tried to move closer to the body, but Larousse held her back by the arm.

169

"We'd best stay here in case we disturb something. Let's wait for the technicians. They should be here soon."

Marceau glanced at Gouirand. He noticed that he had now raised his head and was staring into space. The detective decided that it was time to ask a few questions. He went and sat down beside him.

"How do you feel?"

Marceau held out his hand, but Gouirand took no notice.

"That's Christian in front of the Tarasque."

"Christian who?"

"Rey. A former knight."

Marceau offered him a cigarette, but he refused with a shake of his head.

"And did you know this Rey well?"

"He's a childhood friend."

Marceau drew a little nearer to Gouirand.

"And you said he was a knight?"

"A Knight of the Tarasque! One of those who push her and attend to her."

Gouirand raised his eyes and looked at the corpse which was just a few metres away. A smell of panic and death hung over the municipal garage.

"What happened when you got here earlier?"

"I discovered him, just as you see him now. I didn't touch anything. Can you imagine?"

Gouirand buried his head back in his hands. Marceau saw that he was not going to get anything more out of him. He stood up, gave him a friendly pat on the shoulder, and went back to Commissaire Larousse.

"You know who that is in front of the Tarasque?"

"No."

"Rey."

"Christian Rey?"

"That's right."

"Can you explain?" the deputy prosecutor butted in, a hint of authority in her voice.

"An old acquaintance of ours," Larousse replied. "Christian Rey:

170

pimping and illegal gambling machines. We also long suspected him of being the local mob's executioner. That's who."

"Do you think this could be a settling of scores?"

"Why not? That would be the classic scenario."

"I don't think so," Marceau replied.

"Really?"

"Yes, really."

"Well, we'll see," Larousse concluded coldly.

The team arrived from Marseille. Marceau gave them a very brief run-down, then he put on some gloves and overshoes before following the technicians towards Rey's body.

After each step, the technician in charge placed a yellow marker on the ground with a big black number written on it. Behind him, his colleague took a photo of each one.

A couple of minutes later, they were two steps away from the corpse and bent down to catch their breath.

A chest. Arms without hands. And a head, which was weirdly intact. The body had been severed across the torso.

Gaping wounds. Bones sticking out. Marceau noticed a vertebra and a rib, cut clean through by what he supposed must be a machine.

The face gave out a ghastly impression. The cheeks were phenomenally hollow, as though there was nothing left but leather over the jaws. The teeth stuck out, while the eyes seemed to be still biting into what remained of the visible world.

Marceau had rarely experienced such a sensation of animal terror. It felt like being transported years back, to Paris, when he was a young inspector and doing his apprenticeship in horror.

Rey's skin was still pink. There was no trace of decay, while the blood had already coagulated on the surface of the wounds.

The police officer examined the skull, but saw no wound. There was no round hole, the sign of a bullet. No ecchymoses or haematomas either.

Marceau took a step back.

"I'll leave you to it," he said to one of the team. "We'll see during the autopsy."

He went back, carefully placing his feet in the traces of the outward journey.

"So?" Larousse asked.

"So, you'd have to be a genius to say what exactly Rey died of. Whatever it was, it wasn't a good old 11.43."

"You're thinking of something in particular?" the deputy prosecutor said.

"Yes. A machine. Only a machine could amputate a body like that. Something like a huge pair of shears."

"And that's not going to happen in the context of a gangland killing?"

"That's not what makes me wonder. Because they don't always gun each other down."

"So what's the problem?"

"The Tarasque."

"The what?"

"The Tarasque."

"Oh right, that nasty great thing over there."

"Michel? Jean-Claude here. I've got a stiff on my hands. A Christian Rey. Does that ring any bells?"

"Jesus, Christian Rey. There's definitely a time and a place for everything. And some people will be saying that it was high time."

"Yeah, but there's a catch."

"What's that?"

"He was found practically in the mouth of the Tarasque. This morning."

The Baron let a silence pass by.

"And what are you thinking?"

"I'm thinking it's more than just a gangland killing. What about you?"

"I don't know. It's all news to me. Have you got anyone who's talking?"

"The one who discovered the body. He told me that Rey was a Knight of the Tarasque."

"A what?"

"One of the people who push the thing when they take it out for the carnival."

"The Tarasque, you say!"

For a few seconds, the Baron hesitated. Ideas were spinning through his mind.

"Is the prosecutor there?"

"His deputy. A skirt. She's new and she looks to me as thick as they come."

"And where are you at with Steinert?"

"The case has been closed. I've just heard the news. Officially, there's no more Steinert case."

"But I still think he was killed."

"The only thing that's certain about it is that the prosecutor's closed the case."

"O.K., we need an urgent talk, Jean-Claude."

"Why urgent?"

"See you later, my lad. I'll be there this afternoon."

Marceau's office stank of stale Gitanes and sweat. He was sitting in front of his computer, with his feet on the table. De Palma was standing in front of him, staring intently, his face tense.

"And you're telling me that you went to see Morini, just like that, with Maistre?"

The Baron did not respond.

"And then you tell me that it won't be the last time. That you've been shot at and you've got some names!"

"Affirmative," de Palma said, his voice slightly muted.

Marceau suddenly stood up.

"Affirmative, my arse! I reckon that you're operating more and more like a cowboy and that you're putting your fellow officers in danger. You have an influence on Maistre, don't abuse it! He's a father. I thought I'd just remind you of that, in case you'd forgotten."

De Palma relaxed.

"I hope you still have a scrap of conscience left, to show you the possible consequences of your foul-ups."

"I needed to know. That's all there is to it."

"What did you expect Morini to tell you? In the police we don't always know everything. That's the way it is."

"And you can live with that?"

"For ages now, I've learned to live with small truths and big lies. And with more and more unknowns in this big equation of shit."

De Palma folded his arms over his chest. He glanced at the missing persons notices stuck up on the walls. Steinert's was still there.

"Does Morini come from Tarascon?" he asked, opening his pad.

"He was born in rue des Archives, and he's still got plenty of friends in the neighbourhood. What's more, he does a lot of business round here. I'd advise you to watch your back in these parts. Tarascon is a bit like his manor."

"Born in 1943 in Tarascon, Bouches-du-Rhône," de Palma said laconically. "Arrested for armed robbery in 1963, then for procuring and so on and so forth. The irresistible rise of an arsehole. A big lie, as you put it, on legs."

"What do you expect me to do about it? They say that he lunches with the mayor and mixes with freemasons as casually as you go to the barber's . . . People say a lot of things about Morini."

"Do you know where he lives?"

"He's got a huge villa in Maussane, just in front of the village. And land all around it. Enough to spot an enemy coming."

"That must make a change from his lousy little bar in Aix. Because he can't spot an enemy coming there. Can you show me on the map where the fucker lives?"

"I've got it on my machine."

Marceau clicked his computer mouse to open a file.

"Here, that's where it is. On the road to Eygalières. Just by this big forest to the right on the way up."

De Palma suddenly realised that he meant the Downlands. In other words, Steinert and Morini had been neighbours of a sort.

Marceau sat down again.

"They say that he runs all the one-arm bandits from Nîmes to Toulon, including all the small towns to the north as far as Valence, and maybe even Lyon. Plus the whores, and the nightclubs. He's not much into drugs, as far as I know. Morini's thing is gambling. Christian

Rey was one of his men, by the way. He used to be the local debt collector."

Marceau lit a Gitane and watched its blue smoke rise towards the ceiling.

"Him and another guy, an ex-cop called Bernard Dominguez."

"I know him," said de Palma. "He was a good officer until he started screwing whores all day long."

"I'd just love to nail him . . . Anyway, apart from that, there isn't much to say about Morini. In the end, he's a classic godfather. He's got a hell of a reputation, but in fact he's just like the rest of them."

He stubbed out his half-smoked cigarette.

"Which is bad enough already!"

Marceau suddenly looked tired. He seemed sad and empty. He closed the windows on his computer screen and lit another Gitane.

"I haven't forgotten Isabelle either. Sometimes I realise that I haven't thought about her for the past two or three days and I feel guilty. Jesus, do I feel guilty."

That day, there was a space between the two men that nothing could fill, not even their memories.

"It was you who gave Chandeler my number."

Marceau simply raised a hand and lowered his eyes, while trying to look indifferent.

"I'm not holding it against you, Jean-Claude."

A long silence.

"And Maistre, what does he say?"

"You know Jean-Louis. It all goes on inside. He's not much of a talker."

There was quite a crowd on place de l'Hôtel de Ville in Aix. It was market day. Marc Morini was sitting on the terrace of his bar, with his bodyguard in front of him. The man took out his 200 mm and took two photographs.

Just like last time, the man noticed that the nearest stall to Morini's bar was an Italian cheese seller. He went over and ordered five hundred grams of parmesan and a chunk of mozzarella. From there, he had a three-quarters view of Morini. He took a third photograph.

The clock chimed eleven in the town hall belfry.

The last time he'd come, he had seen some policemen he did not know go into the bar. They had stayed for a good fifteen minutes and then had come out with stern faces. Some time later, a bunch of shady characters turned up.

So Morini wasn't easy to get at.

This seemed to be the same situation. Morini was sitting in the same position.

He picked up his portions of parmesan and mozzarella and went back into the centre of the market. One more anonymous face.

He bought some candied almonds and was opening the box when he saw Morini's bodyguard stand up and go inside the bar.

Le Grand was alone. Still with his back to the street. The man did not wait a moment longer. He felt buoyed up by all the wonders that the Beast had revealed to him. He got out his Colt .45 and made straight for his prey, his gun pressed against his right thigh.

Morini did not have time to say or do anything at all. His predator's instinct deserted him the moment the Beast's servant stuck the barrel of the .45 into his fat neck.

"On your feet, shit-face. And quick."

Morini did so in silence. Lucky for him, or the man would have had to finish him off there and then.

"Hands behind your back."

"But you can't do this. Who are you?"

"I'm the police," the man said, flashing a tricolour card.

They walked some thirty metres along the square then ducked into an old 406 estate.

When Morini saw a parking ticket was stuck behind the left-hand windscreen wiper, he knew instinctively that there would be no official questioning or police custody at the end of this journey.

This was the end of the line for his life as a predator. He had been expecting it for a long time, but not like this.

Marceau's clearest memory of Christian Rey went back to his time with the *Brigade de Grand Banditisme* in Marseille. Rey had been questioned about a gangland killing. He was suspected of having offed the rebellious owner of Le Nain Jaune, a bar in central Avignon. Judge Bonnardi wanted the gangster questioned, and the gangster had been questioned. Nothing had come of it.

Today, Rey had been half eaten by some internal machine and was lying on the chrome-plated dissection table of the forensic surgeon at La Timone hospital.

With Dr Mattei in charge. The doctor of the dead.

"There's not much left of our friend."

"What do you make of this wound?" Marceau asked.

"Hard to say."

"Could it be from a machine, such as a grinder or something of that sort?"

"Maybe yes, maybe no . . . it looks to me more like a bite."

"Hang on, Mattei. I might have told you that it was found in front of the Tarasque, but there's no need to start telling stories."

"I mean it, Jean-Claude . . . I really do."

Mattei stood back from the table, both arms raised, a scalpel in his left hand.

"I saw this kind of bite wound when I was working in Mauritius, just after I'd qualified. It was a fisherman who'd been attacked by a shark, in the lagoon. He'd been half eaten. Just like this."

Marceau ran his hand over the nape of his neck to wipe away the sweat that was dripping down his back.

"Leave it out, Mattei. There aren't any sharks in Tarascon. What else have you found?"

"Lots of interesting things: algae, traces of earth under the finger-nails, and so on . . ."

"You said algae?"

"Yes, and silt. But from fresh water, I'd say. There are no traces of salt or anything that might suggest sea water."

"So what are your conclusions?"

"That our customer spent some time underwater. Stagnant water probably. A bit like the one the other day."

"William Steinert?"

"Spot on. Except that Steinert drowned."

"You're sure about that?"

"Of course I am! There can't be any doubt about it. Steinert died of drowning just as surely as this one died of being eaten by something. Got it?"

"Loud and clear, boss."

Marceau looked at Rey's body. He tried to recall the mobster he had encountered when he was in custody: his face had shrunk, it no longer looked the same, Marceau was sure of it. In his memories, Rey had been fairly chubby, though without a belly, tall, and built like a prop forward. The half man that they had in front of them must have suffered horribly, suffered a gangster's Passion, followed a scumbag's stations of the cross.

"He was tortured before being finished off," he said, as though throwing a card down on the table.

"What do you mean by that?"

"Tortured. No water or anything else for days. Look at his cheeks." Mattei turned towards Marceau.

"You'll end up getting my job one of these days, Jean-Claude!"

"Not yet, doctor death. But I'm working on it."

Mattei pointed out traces of burns on Rey's wrists. One or two old scars. A tattoo on his shoulder.

"Nice tattoo," he said.

Marceau leaned over to see.

"What is it?"

"An impossible monster: a Tarasque. That fits with what Gouirand told me."

With a twirl of his scalpel, Mattei drew a circle around Rey's skull and asked his assistant for the saw.

"I don't think I'll find out much more today. We'll have to wait for the D.N.A. results and chemical tests."

"How long?"

"For the chemistry, tomorrow at the latest. It's being done in Marseille. But I'm sending the D.N.A. to Nantes, so it could take some time."

"Why didn't you go with Bordeaux?"

"We don't work with them any more. Too many foul-ups."

"So let's wait for the labs. They're the real police these days."

The skin of Marceau's face was so taut that his skull protruded clearly. He went over to the corpse while Mattei was lifting its scalp. As he pondered, he clenched his teeth, and his jaw muscles bulged when he did so. A cold gleam glazed his eyes.

16.

It had been raining since the middle of the night. The water had gathered black trails of dust on streets and pavements overheated by the sun.

The day before, de Palma had had the stitches removed from his shoulder wound. Apart from a slight tugging on his skin, he no longer felt a thing.

As soon as he emerged from the automatic gate of Résidence Paul Verlaine, he felt the touch of eyes from across the street.

He could not tell where the danger lurked, but he could sense it. For the coming night, he had decided to sleep at Maistre's place. After that, he would see.

If he was sure of one thing, it was that Morini would not let up. He had gone too far: his visit to Lornec and then the threats he had made in Aix were too much to swallow. But it was a long step from there to taking out a contract, even if Morini had built his empire on the basis of incredible violence. Even if he had wiped out rival gangs like a butcher. He was a psycho who enjoyed just two things: getting himself invited to the orgies of the great and good, and offing someone. All the same, he never did so without a good reason.

As he turned into rue Laugier, he looked in his rear-view mirror and saw a Scenic following him. He made out the driver's face, and he had seen enough gangsters in his life to realise that the man on his tail was no part-timer.

He accelerated suddenly, putting a good fifty metres between them, then found himself face to face with the number 18 bus that was coming up avenue de la Capelette. Behind him, the Scenic's driver picked up his mobile.

De Palma turned off the avenue and drove the wrong way up rue Saint-Jean. The car was no longer there in his mirror. He stopped, checked the clip in his Bodyguard, picked up his .45, racked the slide and laid in on the passenger seat.

Was he succumbing to hallucinations again?

He was still wondering about that when, thirty metres away, he saw a motorcycle heading straight for him with two men in the saddle.

De Palma floored the pedal and drove straight at them. They swerved to avoid him.

In front of Saint John's church, he just missed a couple of kids who were kicking a football.

He wrenched the wheel to the left, like someone on a stunt-driving course, then drove along the railway track, the Alfa hugging the tarmac.

Left again, in a screech of tyres.

On the pavements of the old industrial estate there were holes, burned-out mattresses, wrecked fridges, a blind T.V.

The old pith helmet factories, scheduled for demolition for years, were still standing. A glance in the mirror: no-one.

The Baron parked his Giulietta in front of the watchman's hut, by a time clock now swollen with rust.

At that moment the motorbike braked. De Palma threw himself out of his car, rolled over and stood up, legs bent, aiming his Colt at the target, his left palm bracing the butt.

The gun jumped in his hands, like a toy with a mind of its own.

The first two bullets made little volcanoes of dust in the walls of the electric plant.

The driver tipped his bike over and crouched behind it. The other ran in a circle to outflank de Palma.

A third shot. A direct hit. Under the impact of the 11.43, the bike shuddered.

One hit. Two. The shells hit metal. CLANG. CLANG.

And then a great BOOM.

Heat everywhere. Hydrocarbons and benzene combined.

The black leather-clad body rose into the sky and bounced off the grey stones of the wall. Then it fell back, one leg over its head, disjointed by the explosion.

The Baron bent double and scurried behind the watchman's hut.

A pile of rubble hid him from the old works canteen. It smelled of tramp shit and dog piss. The fetid stench started to crawl over his skin and invade each pore.

A T.V. set wobbled under a burst of fire. The Baron felt the first kiss of death. Right in the shoulder. In the same place as last time, but deeper. He fell to the ground and saw the blood oozing between his fingers. Drops of life on his finger nails.

One bullet. Two. Three. And click.

Shit, the spare clip was in the car.

He pulled out his Bodyguard.

A .38 special. The famous police issue.

He moved forward, his pistol in his left hand. Nothing.

He waited in the silence.

How much time had gone by? Hours. An eternity. Just a few seconds. De Palma knew how time dilated.

He cocked an ear. Someone was running down the slope away from the factory, fleeing towards the ruins of the sulphur plant.

De Palma went back to the driver. With the tip of his gun, he lifted up the helmet's visor. The right eye was puffy. Vincent Lopez. Final contract.

Suddenly, he heard sirens toiling through the traffic down below, in La Capelette.

He took a few steps and sat down on the pavement. There was a smell of melted leather and petrol fumes.

When his colleagues zoomed in, de Palma stood up on his long legs, produced his police card and put his hands up.

Anne Moracchini came into the hospital room with Maistre just behind her.

"How's it going, Michel?"

She planted a kiss on his forehead. She was wearing the same musky perfume as on their night at the opera.

"It hurts, but the quack says it's nothing and I can go home tomorrow if I want."

"In any case, you shouldn't stay here, as long as this hasn't been sorted. I'm afraid the hacks have not only mentioned your name, but also the hospital where you're being treated."

"Kind of them. I hope they've also published the room number."

"You're staying at my place," Moracchini said.

"Don't take advantage . . ."

She took a chair and drew it up next to him. Delicately, she placed her hand on his.

"As soon as we found out, we went on a little trip to Aix," she said softly. "Maistre, Romero and I."

"He was there?"

"No," Maistre murmured.

"And?"

Moracchini lowered her eyes.

"His thug told us that he hasn't been seen since yesterday."

"The poor lad must be worried!"

"And so he should be," Maistre said. "Just imagine, you're sitting talking to someone, you get up for a slash, you hang around a bit because you're taking a dump as well, and when you come out again, no Morini!"

"You're kidding me!"

"You heard correctly," Moracchini said. "The heavy's name is Serge Mondolini, remember him? He's one of our regulars."

The Baron frowned.

"So, he goes to the crapper, and when he comes back Morini has vanished in a puff of smoke. He's making it up."

"I don't think so. Really I don't. He even told us that he feared the worst and would give us all the help we needed."

"I'll go and see him, in a few days' time."

"That's right, go and put your oar in," Maistre said, glancing out of the window. "Tell us where you'd like to be buried."

"Next to my father."

Moracchini stood up.

"Michel, you're going to have to choose between your friends and your bullshit. When you get out of here, you're coming to my place. And I don't want to see you hanging around La Capelette. As for Morini, we'll deal with him."

"Who knew that I lived at 102, boulevard Mireille Lauze?"

"They know lots of things."

"No, there are very few people who know that. Very, very few. Except for my close friends."

"They simply tailed you, you dummy."

"Except that, since going to see Morini, I've been really careful. I go home via traverse de la Barnière by jumping over the wall. After that, no-one can see me. So what do you think?"

"I . . . I don't know."

"Well, I do! Some fucker has been out for my blood ever since I took an interest in this case."

De Palma stopped for breath. An arrow of pain pierced his shoulder.

"This is serious, Anne. Very serious. It goes deeper than just the no-good local mob."

"Obviously what you're saying fits in with the first attempt too."

"No it doesn't."

"Why not?"

"When you use a SIG, you don't miss."

"What do you . . ." Maistre stammered.

"The first time was to scare me. This time it was to kill me."

"That's all very well, Michel, but you haven't even asked who's in charge of your case."

"And so?"

"I am," Moracchini said, with a glint of defiance in her eyes.

He looked at Maistre, who seemed lost in very distant memories.

"And our initial investigations have turned up a bullet from a SIG."

"Where did you find it?"

"On that pile of rubble, in a big lump of plaster. It had been fired in a south–north direction. In other words, it came from the one who got behind you. Not the driver, but the passenger!"

"That's the news of the day."

He took the remote control in his good hand and raised his bed to the sitting position. The doctor on duty came in.

"How are you feeling?"

"Fine, it just tugs a bit."

"That's normal, it's the stitches."

The doctor raised the dressing and adjusted his glasses.

"Is there anyone at home who can change dressings?"

"Yes," Moracchini said. "I've had experience."

"O.K., so you can go home if you want. I'll take out the stitches next week."

Moracchini's living room led out to a cool garden with two huge oaks at the bottom, on the bank of an old irrigation canal. She had planted some rambling roses and wisteria, as well as strewing potted plants all around it.

De Palma felt good. He watched his colleague and realised that it was the first time that he had seen her at home and entered her personal space.

She sat down next to him, with some lint and gel. As she changed the dressing, he felt her breath on the nape of his neck.

"He shot you just where he hit you the first time. He's a maniac."

She put on the lint and two strips of plaster, then rolled down his sleeve.

"Do you want a drink?"

"Yes, something strong, I've earned it."

She mixed a jug of Morito, with crushed ice and fresh mint. They drank in silence, savouring the chilled liquid.

She had bunched her hair up over her neck, which highlighted her features and made her look like a young girl. De Palma said so, and she smiled with affection.

She told him about her father, who often paid her compliments. He was a man of few words and unfinished sentences. She had spent much of her teenage life trying to make sense of this man, whom she adored more than anything, and what he meant by the words he left hanging. He was a lawyer, born in Algeria, who reserved his eloquence for the courts.

So she came to realise that she was a woman destined for silence and contemplation.

"It's strange that you're now telling me about your father!"

She slapped him on his good shoulder.

"It's because you impress me, M. de Palma! So I have to defend myself as best I can."

"I impress you, do I?"

"Yes, and sometimes you should realise that."

She stood up and winked at him.

"Come on, let's go back inside. We'll be more comfortable."

She lay back on the sofa, propped up on her elbows.

"Now, you can tell me something about yourself."

"There's nothing to tell."

"What were you like as a little boy?"

De Palma rarely thought about his childhood and what he had been through with his brother. It plunged him into unending sadness. His brother had died of leukaemia, and he had nursed a sense of guilt that still had not left him: guilty of failure to help, a terrible feeling, and one that haunted him. He had never spoken about it to anyone.

"There's one memory I have of those days, it was when we used to come out of the conservatoire on place Carli after our music lessons. Our heads were full of demi-semiquavers. I don't know why, but in my memories, the sun is always setting . . . Anyway, we'd walk down to the opera house with our friends. It was magic. We went by the Gare de l'Est and bought slices of pizza from the Italian place that used to be on the corner of the Canebière. Then we'd eat them as we went through the red-light district, staring at the whores in thigh boots who would wink at us."

"Why did you go to the opera?"

"I was an extra."

"You used to sing?!"

"Extras don't sing, Anne. They're just part of the crowd, priests, guards or pages, or whatever. They play no part, but without them the show lacks sparkle. They're magnificently pointless. Can you imagine *Aïda* without the soldiers? I was a high priest with a ropy wig and foundation all over my face, standing right next to Radames. On another occasion, we executed Mario in *Tosca* . . ."

186

He fell silent. In the half-light, he was looking for an attitude of pride, something to hide behind while his feelings had time to subside.

He regaled her with tales from the stage: the terrible flops, when screwed-up programmes and loose change would rain down on the boards like drops of humiliation, and the splendid successes that made the lines of velvet seats explode.

He had spent more than eleven years on the boards of the municipal theatre; eleven years of electric warmth in the dark, secretive wings; in the white lights of the Svobodas; the warm shadings of liquid blue and ochre in the distance, stage left or right, or else on the proscenium, the only place where the gleaming, serious, anonymous faces of the audience can be seen.

Eleven years of interpreting the anxieties of opera stars during the long minutes of waiting before going on stage, the suffering that sends voices wafting above the violins and carries them right to the end, up there in the heights of the big theatre.

Moracchini suddenly realised just how much a man like this must suffer in the Marseille police force. With a gesture as soft as a sigh, she stroked his shoulder. The Baron shrank into himself.

"The world is divided in two: those who love Callas and those who love Tebaldi."

"What about you?"

"Tebaldi in *Aïda* and Callas in *Norma*."

"Trying to have it both ways are you?"

He stretched and poured himself a glass of water. She moved closer.

"When I was a kid, there were Stones fans and Beatles fans. Two different schools."

"I remember that. And so?"

"All of them were often complete idiots. Some were even top of the class, the sort who understand nothing and feel nothing unless you can stick a label on it. But luckily enough, there are also people who love music."

She drew him towards her, kissed him maternally on the lips and forehead and smiled into his eyes. He buried his face in her hair, and moved down the suntanned length of her neck.

With a heave, she turned onto her back, and a violent stab of pain in his shoulder made him cry out.

Slowly, he undid her fine silk top, freeing her heavy breasts, which he took into his hands and covered with kisses. Then, he lost himself in the hollow of her stomach and breathed in her pepper-scented closeness.

17.

De Palma gave his temples a long massage. For the past two days he had been convalescing at Jean-Louis Maistre's place, on the heights of L'Estaque. He had left Moracchini's house to avoid settling into a relationship that still scared him.

He stood up straight and breathed in deeply. The breeze was blowing the sea air up to the houses on the side of the hill.

The sky was azure as far as the eye could see. The city in the distance was white, the colour of precious shells. The seawall cut its way through the waves, looking like a huge exclamation mark at the end of a long sentence of tiny patches of land, with burning roofs and hills.

"How's life, Baron?" Maistre asked. "You haven't been too bored all day long?"

"I slept a lot. The boss wants to see me, tomorrow."

"Oh," Maistre said, pouring two pastis.

"I couldn't give a toss what they say. Anyway, they can't touch me."

"Especially when your 11.43 shells are lying in a drawer in my office."

The Baron turned towards his friend.

"Anne really loves you, I'm telling you. Between you and me, she's washed you whiter than white. If you feel you're looking like a fridge door or an aspirin, then it's down to her."

De Palma sat down on the low stone wall that Maistre had built last winter to keep in place the little earth his garden possessed.

"She even put a few shells from your piece on the scene of the crime. Not bad, don't you think?"

"I . . ."

"As far as I'm concerned, I could beat you senseless . . . What the fuck are you still doing with your 11.43? Throwing it away might have been a good idea after what happened."

When he got angry, Maistre's proletarian Parisian accent came back. He had never really lost it.

"If you're just going to get in my face, Jean-Louis, then I'm off!"

"Alright, don't get into a sulk. Anne will be here soon."

"I'm going to need another piece."

Maistre disappeared for a moment into the shade of the house, and emerged with a black box which he handed to de Palma.

"This is clean?"

"Of course it is, you idiot. It's mine, I bought it with my police pay."

"So what am I supposed to do with it?"

"It's a last resort, Michel. It's never been used, but it's been around. A Corsican sold it to me. What's more, I had the barrel and hammer changed. Not bad, eh?"

It was a snub-nosed Colt Cobra. A marvellous gun. As black as death and as slim as a dream. De Palma weighed it in his hand. He liked its bulk and its varnished wood grip. Both sober and classic.

He clicked open the cylinder and slipped in six .38 shells.

When Moracchini arrived on the patio, she glared at the Cobra while placing a soft kiss on the Baron's neck.

Just then, his mobile rang.

"M. de Palma, Ingrid Steinert here."

"Hello," he answered, moving to one side.

"I'm very worried. I read in the papers that you've been shot. And that you killed someone . . ."

"You shouldn't believe everything you read in the papers, you know."

He noticed that Moracchini was watching him and seemed to be trying to lip-read what he was saying.

"I don't know . . . I mean . . . were you wounded?"

"Nothing serious."

"When will we meet again?"

"I'll call you tomorrow. Right now, I need some rest."

"O.K., speak to you tomorrow then. Take care."

As he hung up, he felt Moracchini's gaze on his back. He turned round. She was standing just behind him.

"Was that Ingrid Steinert?"

"Yes, I must admit that I'd rather forgotten . . ."

"What did she want?"

"She'd seen in the papers that I'd killed someone and been wounded. That's all."

"We're going to have to sort a few things out with her."

"As you say . . ."

Morini lost his balance. He fell flat on his face and it took him some time to get to his feet again.

Since being locked up in total darkness, this was the second time he had fallen. First his head spun, as though he no longer knew which way was up and which down, then his huge body collapsed.

The last memory that he had of light was a flat expanse half covered in water and a white-walled hut in the background. What struck him was that his kidnapper had blindfolded him, and had only restored his sight when they arrived in this marsh.

And then pitch darkness. Not the slightest gleam of light came in from outside. He had now lost any sense of day and night. Hunger gnawed at his stomach. He was terribly thirsty.

He felt his way around the walls of his prison and located the door. He hammered on it. Several times. Just as he had done when the judge had put him in solitary in D block of Les Baumettes prison.

"Open up!"

The only answer was the enormous silence.

"Open up!" he screamed, before he broke down sobbing.

In the car, he had tried to negotiate with his abductor. He was sure he'd seen him before somewhere. Tall, with greying hair around his temples. Well into his forties. With an odd accent. This accent did not match the man's appearance. Morini had initially supposed that he was a police officer, then he wondered if he might be a mobster from a rival gang. This thought process had lasted for about a minute.

He had tried to sweet-talk him, then he had got irritated and turned to threats. Until the man gave him a thunderous slap and gagged him.

Jesus! He'd been caught like a baby. That thought tormented him even more than the thirst. He had mistaken a gangster for a cop. Even worse: he had failed to distinguish between a gangster and a raving lunatic.

His instinct had deserted him.

He told himself that he no longer deserved to live.

18.

Above La Balme farmhouse, the last glimmers of day were covering the limestone crests of the Alpilles with red lace.

Maistre's 205, covered with dust and with wrecked shock absorbers, bounded over the last rock in its path. But it was better than the Alfa Romeo, which everyone now seemed to recognise.

That morning, de Palma had gone to see Brissonne. His grass had not been very reassuring. Morini had lost it after their visit and had almost killed Lopez with his bare hands. The underworld was buzzing with their meeting. But the contract had been put out by Lopez, not Morini.

Brissonne also had a warning for de Palma: Morini had well and truly vanished, and people were wondering who was behind his disappearance. The big guns were going to start doing the talking in a few days' time if he did not resurface. A mob war was going to break out. It was inevitable.

"You should make yourself scarce, Paulo. Take a few days off!"

"I'm going on a trip to Italy. I've got a few friends there."

The mobster frowned at the Baron.

"Watch out for yourself, Michel. There's a storm brewing, and you know what that means."

Madame Steinert was alone, wearing a black blouse and a thin floral skirt that clung to her slim figure. She was walking slowly beside the pool, with bare feet.

De Palma got out of the 205. Instinctively, he checked that the Cobra was there on his hip, then glanced all around before going towards her.

She waved and came to meet him.

When they were close, she extended her cheek to him. For the first time.

"It's good to see you, Michel. Those journalists are idiots. The way they put it, it sounded as though you were at death's door. It's *furchtbar* . . . awful."

"It was just a flesh wound."

"I hope so."

Her voice was deeper than usual and she did not look straight at him. Instead, she gazed at the turquoise surface of the pool.

"I asked to see you because I think I've got something new to tell you."

"Really?"

"Yes, but first, let's have a little drink. What do you say, Michel?"

He felt awkward and simply nodded.

On the patio, she rang a small bell and a young woman emerged from the kitchen. She said something in German to her, and de Palma realised that this was the first time that he had heard her speak the language. He found it rather pleasant.

"I'd like you to try the white Muscat that we make here. It was William's idea. He had preserved an old vine behind the pool house over there. I must say that it's really good. It's my favourite."

The Baron's throat was dry. He drank back half of his glass at once. The sweet wine filled his mouth with a bouquet of honey. She winked at him.

"You're my guest this evening. Do you know the Val d'Enfer?"

"No."

"It's a mysterious place below Les Baux. Taven the witch is supposed to have spent time there."

"My father used to tell me stories about witches."

"Was it him who introduced you to Cathy and Heathcliff?"

The Baron put down his glass, and clumsily knocked an olive onto the ground.

"Yes, it was him. How . . ."

"I'm good at guessing things. William was always impressed by my gift."

"You also have a good memory."

194

"Yes, sometimes. When people interest me."

She raised the Muscat to her lips.

"I wanted to invite you to have dinner with me in a restaurant near Val d'Enfer. What do you say?"

"I don't know if I should accept!"

"Unless you'd prefer to eat here. Our cook, Robert, has made a pistou soup which is like nothing you've ever tasted before. So what will it be: gastronomy or simplicity?"

"Simplicity," he said.

"I'm touched by your tastes."

She stood up and went into the living room. He watched her supple sway and thought that fate had played a hell of a trick on him between the shanty town of La Capelette and the farmhouse of La Balme.

He filled his lungs with air full of the fragrance of olive trees and ripe grapes. The image of his mother placing the tub in the kitchen to give him his evening bath crossed his mind. He could picture himself again in that soapy water with his grazed knees and black hands after playing knucklebones in the primary school playground on rue Laugier. The tub and coal stove had four rooms to heat.

He stood up and walked over to the pool. A cricket was picking out a melody somewhere in the clump of lavender.

A delicate hand was placed on his forearm.

"I'd like to show you something, if you wouldn't mind."

"No, not at all."

She had changed and was now wearing a very simple pale pink dress that revealed her shoulders and stopped above her knees.

They went into the building through the main entrance. De Palma recognised the reception room where she had welcomed him the first time he had visited the farm. Then he followed her to the first floor up a broad white-stone staircase of a quite surprising sobriety. No decorations, no frills. The whitewash smelled old.

Here, too, William Steinert had not wanted to change a thing. No doubt to preserve the memory of the mother he had never known.

"I want to show you a few documents that I found this week while I was sorting through William's things."

She opened the door of a large room which had been furnished as a lounge or reception room, with a billiard table in the middle, settees upholstered in Marseille piqué, and knick-knacks all around: a chess set on an occasional table, an old pinball machine and a 1950s Wurlitzer jukebox. There were oil paintings everywhere.

She noticed that he had paused for a moment.

"Do you like the style?"

"It's one hell of a mixture!"

"They're all collector's pieces. William used to call it his museum. Everything you see here was picked up in markets across the world. They're real rarities. I wanted you to see them so that you could understand what sort of man he was."

In a glass case, he noticed some wax cylinders, a letter signed by Blaise Cendrars and some Egyptian and Greek antiquities. There was also a statue measuring about a metre high.

"It's a marble kouros."

It was smiling into eternity, its lips raised at the corners of a stone mouth.

"It's from the end of the archaic period. It's magnificent. There are many museums that envy us."

"The line is simple, but perfect. It looks like the Rampin Horseman."

"Are you a connoisseur, Michel?"

"An old memory from history at university. I loved Greek art."

"Oh, I see . . ."

She drew nearer to him, as though seeking greater closeness.

"Would you like another glass of Muscat?"

"Yes please," he replied, without taking his eyes off the kouros.

"Come and sit down. Laura will bring us the necessary."

She sat down in an armchair and crossed her legs. Slightly embarrassed by her stare, which never left him, the Baron sat down opposite her.

"Why did you join the police, Michel?"

"It's funny. Every time I trot out the little culture I possess, I'm asked the same question."

"That's fair enough, isn't?"

"Yes, perhaps . . ."

"But you still haven't answered."

"Because I come from a poor neighbourhood in Marseille, and I didn't have much choice."

"I think we always have a choice."

"Maybe. But you may have to be more courageous than I am."

"It isn't a question of courage. But why did you stay?"

It was an ordinary question, but it took him unawares.

"Perhaps because of a girl who looked strangely like you."

"Could you explain?"

"I can't."

"She's dead, isn't she?"

Laura arrived carrying a tray with two glasses of Muscat. De Palma took one, and took his chance to stand up.

"She's dead and you never found her killer. Am I right?"

"I . . . I'd rather not talk about it. If you don't mind."

"I quite understand. Come on, I'll show you something."

At the far end of the room, there was an art deco-style table with curved legs, on which Ingrid had placed a whole pile of papers and photographs.

The photographs were shots of the Camargue. De Palma saw lagoons that disappeared over the horizon in the light of dawn or dusk. There were also some shots of birds: raptors, herons, and other species he did not know.

He paused over some photographs of large white birds.

"They're white spoonbills. The last pictures he took, as far as I know. Laura went to fetch them from Tarascon today."

"They're magnificent."

"Yes they are, aren't they?"

"Did the photographer say which day your husband dropped the film off?"

"The day he disappeared. June 24. I thought that might tell you things."

"And you're quite right. So we're now sure that he vanished on the 24th. What are these documents?"

"They're notes he left in his car. The police didn't take them away."

De Palma read:

1 – *La Capelière. At the far end of the large meadow? Turn left then right towards the dead tree in the water. Ten metres to the left. In the coppice.*
2 – *From the guardian's hut, towards the marsh.*

"They look like directions, don't they, Michel?"

"One of them gives the exact place where he was found."

"I hadn't noticed that."

On another piece of paper, which was folded in four, Steinert had written:

Rush hut number 2, well hidden after the reed bed. A good place for sunrise. Mention it to Christophe.

"Did your husband often make notes like this?"

"All the time. His memory wasn't very good, he was always forgetting things, so he kept notes."

"Do you know this Christophe?"

"It's Texeira, the director of the reserve. We've met once or twice."

She put the photographs back into their envelope.

"There, that's all I wanted to show you. The rest is just snippets of his existence, nothing of any great interest."

"In a life, everything is of interest."

She stared at him with a little girl's eyes.

"Come on, Michel. Let's have some of that famous pistou soup. We'll talk about something cheerful. William wouldn't have liked us to be sad."

19.

Maistre's investigations into the career of the SIG had so far not been conclusive, except in discovering that the proper series number had not been recorded on the list of exhibits from the grocery hold-up. That was why he'd had trouble locating it. The number recorded by the police differed from that used in court. In the paperwork of criminal justice and the police, the weapon no longer existed. Maistre had never seen such a disappearing act.

This was also why he had decided to take his time, and avoid arousing colleagues' suspicions. Because one of them was involved in this story, and sooner or later he knew that he would find him.

Late in the afternoon, the Baron was driving through the sweltering heat of the Vaccarès reserve. Texeira had called him: the voices had returned.

Along the banks of the lagoon, there was an overwhelming smell of dead algae and dried-up slime. Every available space along the road was occupied by a mobile home or caravan. Some holiday-makers were Dutch, others were German, with red thighs and faces consumed by the sun.

He turned onto the road to La Capelière before parking the 205 between two tourist coaches.

The reed bed was rustling in the furnace. The tips of the reddened canes swayed almost imperceptibly, moved by an invisible breeze.

Texeira was standing in the middle of a group. He was handing out brochures and visitors' guides to the reserve. When he looked up, he saw de Palma waving at him.

"I'm coming, I'm coming . . ."

De Palma signalled him to take his time, before retreating from the sun into the ecology museum. Texeira joined him a few minutes later.

"Good afternoon, M. de Palma. I'm up to my neck right now. But come to my office in five minutes' time and we can talk."

The Baron decided to explore the museum a little. He had a good look at an exhibit showing the composition of the flora in the marshes. He had had no idea that there were so many different species of plants, and especially algae.

When he had finished, he bought a plan of the reserve, a brochure about the birds of the Camargue and an ordnance survey map of the area.

Texeira was in his office looking through his binoculars when the Baron appeared in the doorway.

"We've now got all the time we need. I suppose you're here about the voices."

"That's right."

The biologist stowed away the Petri dishes that were scattered over the draining board. Then he placed both his hands on his binoculars.

"I heard voices. It was past one o'clock. They were coming from the far side of the marsh, from around the old hut. There were voices and footsteps."

"And what were they saying, these voices?"

"It's very hard to say!"

"Why?"

"Because I think it was in Provençal, or something like that."

"Provençal?"

"Yes, they said: *La Tarasco, la Tarasco . . . Lou Castéou.* The Tarasque, in other words. That much I understood. And it does sound like Provençal, don't you think? The rest, I can't tell you. I just can't remember."

"One voice or several?"

"I think there were two, because one was high and the other lower."

"Did Steinert mention these voices to you?"

"No, why?"

"Just asking."

Texeira sat down on a swivel-chair. He folded his arms and raised his shoulders.

"I did say I'd keep you informed. But I don't see what can be important about all this. There are just some idiots who come here to kick up a din at night. There are so many loonies around these days."

"Another thing: why didn't you tell me right away that you knew Steinert well?"

"I was cross with myself afterwards. I was being selfish. I didn't want any trouble, that's all. Anyway, what I know about him is quite irrelevant."

The Baron gestured broadly to tell him to stop making excuses.

"Tell me about him instead. What was he like?"

Texeira took off his glasses and started to clean the lenses with the lapels of his white coat.

"He was a very impressive character, even if you didn't quite know who he was. When he turned up here in the evening, before bivouacking in the marshes, he used to speak about all sorts of things and – how can I put it? – he was radiant. He had a presence, with quite exceptional magnetism. A great, very great man . . ."

"You seem to have respected him."

"We had the same opinions about ecology, the protection of animals . . ."

"Meaning?"

"He thought, like me, that we can't ignore the human factor, that ecology is a whole, and that protecting nature also means protecting a region's cultural and human heritage. I know that he fought hard for that, especially when it came to archaeology. He was always up in arms against this or that mayor of some town in the backwoods of Provence. If wanted to, he had the means to make their lives difficult, but he always preferred to negotiate. He was a good listener. When I spoke to him, he attended to what I said as though he was a student. It was rather impressive when you bear in mind that he was a real capitaine of industry in his country."

"Do you know his wife?"

"No. In fact, he never mentioned her."

"But she says that she's met you!"

"Honestly, I don't remember that."

"You mentioned his campaigns. Could you tell me anything more about that, or give me some examples?"

"That will be hard, he was quite discreet about his concrete actions. But I do know that he forced the gendarmes to investigate the world of seasonal workers. There are loads of illegal immigrants around here. It's a real form of slavery."

De Palma leaned against the bookcase, and a dark gleam lit up his face.

"Did he come here alone?"

"Yes, always alone. He would park his huge 4×4 beside my car then come up to see me. But he never came here when there was a crowd."

"Did you ever wonder why?"

"I asked him and he told me that he didn't like the company of tourists. They were what he hated the most."

De Palma went over to the window and looked out at the marshes.

"M. Texeira, do you still have my phone number?"

"Yes, of course. It's in my diary."

"If you ever hear these voices again, call me at once."

"O.K. As you want. Is it that important?"

"I don't know. But I do think that it's far more important than you imagine."

The Baron wiped his forehead with his handkerchief.

"Are you here every night at that time?"

"Yes, usually."

"And are you asleep then?"

"I never go to bed before about half-past one or two."

"Now, could you show the place where these voices were coming from?"

"Follow me."

On the path that ran beside the reed bed, the earth was as hard as old cement, and covered in cracks despite the recent rain. Texeira strode ahead rapidly. From time to time, he glanced towards the creek.

"The level is going down," he said, pointing at the water which was frothing like detergent.

They entered a clump of ash trees. Texeira turned left, went up some wooden steps that were hidden among the trees and vanished into a hide. Panting, de Palma did likewise.

"Here we are. The voices came from the far side of the marsh. Over there, in that large reed bed."

"What exactly did you hear?"

"As I told you, two voices, some words in Provençal, and some noises."

"What sort of noises?"

"Splashing, the sound of feet in water . . ."

"And then?"

"That's all. They sang, then everything stopped."

"They sang?"

Texeira looked annoyed by the officer's avalanche of questions.

"Yes, so what?" he said with a sigh.

"Look, M. Texeira, you hear voices in a place where no-one can go, then you tell me that people were singing, and after that, that there were sounds of splashing . . . and all this subsequent to someone being found dead on your reserve in extremely suspicious circumstances. You also forget to tell me that you knew this person. Do you see now why I'm asking questions?"

"I'm sorry, M. de Palma, really I am, but I thought these kinds of detail wouldn't really interest you, and then I didn't want to have to deal with you."

"How can someone get over there?"

"Actually, I've never been there and don't see how anyone could without getting soaked."

"In a boat, perhaps?"

"We'll take the reserve's punt."

The marsh was a good hundred metres wide by two hundred long. It lay amid practically virgin territory, which seemed to be returning to life as the sun set.

At the far side of the pool, an egret took flight, slapping the surface of the water with the tips of its wings.

Texeira stood up in the flat-bottomed punt and pushed with a long pole, which sank deep into the silt, making wide brown stains in the greenish water.

In under five minutes, they arrived at the edge of the reed bed. De Palma made to stand up, but Texeira stopped him short.

"Watch out, there's quicksand around here. Let's look for a patch of solid earth then move slowly. If you see any birds on the ground, try not to frighten them. They've taken up their quarters for the night."

They crept around the reed bed in a northerly direction. Texeira tested the ground on the bank, metre by metre. It was only after a hundred metres that the punt touched bottom.

Texeira prodded a few more times, then nodded: they were now on a sand bank that emerged from the water in the middle of the reed bed.

When they leaped over board, de Palma laid his hand on Texeira's shoulder.

"Thanks for all this. Now we'll have to keep our eyes peeled. The slightest thing you find unusual, please show me."

"No problem."

"I'll follow in your footsteps. Take your time, because you'll probably notice things that I wouldn't. I'm counting on you."

Texeira advanced slowly. Soon they were standing in about ten centimetres of water. All around, the Baron observed hordes of creatures that were unknown to him. All around him, the marsh was crawling with life.

Suddenly, Texeira stopped.

"There are some footprints here."

De Palma walked over and saw on a strip of earth that rose above the water the trace of a footprint: a man's, with size eight or nine shoes. There was just one, because the person who left it must have walked through the water, just as they were doing now. A footprint made by a sole with crampons, and which was easily recognisable to a knowledgeable eye – Vibram soles.

"This is a real surprise," Texeira said. "You can't come here unless you really know the place well."

De Palma regretted not having brought a camera with him. He removed a piece of paper from his pocket and stuck it on a reed stalk. Then he produced his notepad and made a rough sketch showing the direction of the foot: just about due north, according to Texeira's indications.

"Let's go on."

"We can't be that far from the hut."

They walked on a few metres further. The reeds grew less dense and opened out onto a second marsh, smaller than the first. In the distance, a reed hut with rather dingy white walls stood on a mound of earth between two poplars.

"How many huts are there like this one?"

"Just two."

"And have you ever been inside this one?"

"No, I must admit I haven't. It's silly, but that's the way it is. One of my students went in last year. And he told me that there wasn't much there. It's just another hut. Also, it's not in a very good position for observation. Ever since they've dammed the stream you saw earlier, the water has risen here and you can't get to it by foot."

"O.K.," de Palma said. "Let's try it anyway."

"In that case, we'll go back to the punt and carry it to here."

Half an hour later, de Palma and Texeira set foot on the mound and went over to the hut. They walked all around it before going inside.

It was an oval room. In the middle stood an old table gnawed by wood lice. There were three chairs with broken straw seats, an ancient haversack and some glasses full of dust.

De Palma scrutinised every nook and cranny. The only thing of interest that he found were traces of a recent presence. Very recent, judging by the marks that could be seen, especially in the dust on the table.

The earth floor had been swept, and then the traces of the broom removed. When he bent down, he saw that it had been cleaned recently.

No more than three or four days ago, he thought.

Texeira called him from outside.

"Look."

On the bank, the earth had been turned over and the sand below the water ploughed up by someone or something.

"It's as if a large animal has been blundering around."

"Which would explain the sounds of splashing," Texeira said, pointing at the marks.

"And you heard that noise the second time?"

"No, probably because I was further away. Or maybe because I didn't pay attention."

The traces on the bank were also recent. They went down into the water and vanished into the silt. And yet some hollow, wedge-shaped marks could still be seen. The water of the marsh had dug deeper around the marks.

De Palma noticed that on the bank everything that might have been recognisable had been wiped away. That much was clear.

A heron landed on a dead tree which was rocking on the grey waters. At that moment, the natural world quivered. On the tips of the reeds, a pink light glittered briefly. The sun was setting, in the distance, on the far bank of the Vaccarès.

"No, Michel, I can't answer that! I don't know if William was a freemason or not. He was very discreet about his private life. And don't imagine that I was part of his private life."

Mme Steinert was agitated. Her hair was still damp. She had tied it up over her neck, and secured it with an ebony chopstick.

After leaving the Vaccarès, de Palma had gone to see her at La Balme. He had warned Maistre that he would be back late that night. Maistre had grumbled, Moracchini had thrown a fit of jealousy, and the Baron had done as he pleased.

"I'm sorry to disturb you for so little reason. I'll go."

"You're not disturbing me, Michel. I want you to stay to dinner."

"I'm afraid of upsetting you with all my questions."

"Not at all. Don't forget that I was the one who put you in this position."

De Palma squirmed in his chair.

"Have you heard from Chandeler?"

"No, not since I decided to dispense with his services."

"And may I ask why you decided to fire him?"

"Quite simply because he was too greedy. Too voracious. In fact, he only handled a tiny part of the family's business."

From her frown, de Palma guessed that Chandeler had probably tried his luck with her and had been turned down.

"Can you tell me more about the Downlands?"

"We could go for a stroll there."

"But it's nighttime!"

"Then we'll go tomorrow."

"Tomorrow?"

"That is, if you agree to sleep over at the farmhouse. There's plenty of room to spare, you know."

All the Baron did in answer was to gaze up at the white drystone walls pierced by little windows. The house had three floors. On the top one, a few of the windows glowed in the darkness. They must be the servants' quarters.

"Did you ever wonder why your husband was so determined to keep this place as it is?"

"I'm sorry?"

"Why he didn't want to change anything, or hardly anything?"

The question had caught her unawares. She seemed almost upset, as though he had just made her realise that she had never really worried about her husband's strange behaviour.

"I don't know. I think that he was very concerned about authenticity."

"There was more to it than that."

Her turquoise eyes peered at him cautiously. Then, slowly, she picked up a cigarette, placed it in her lips and flicked open her lighter.

"It's because William was the son of the house's former owner, Mme Maurel."

Ingrid put her lighter down slowly, and looked at him hard. Clearly, she had not known the truth. She looked away. He saw that her eyes were shining.

"I didn't want to shock you, but I think I owe you the truth."

She undid her hair and let it tumble down, still damp, onto her golden shoulders. Then she folded her hands over her chest with a gesture of self-protection and squeezed hard.

"I'm not blaming you. That was the real problem with William. He hid so much from me. I think you can now understand . . . life with him wasn't easy."

She stood up and paced towards the swimming pool. Her dark shadow undulated over the blue surface.

"It was Bérard who told you that, I suppose?"

"Yes."

"He knows a lot of things about my husband."

"Yes, it would seem so. I think you should go and see him."

Suddenly, she looked fragile. She trembled. A wrinkle appeared on her forehead. She stubbed out her cigarette.

"I . . . stay here tonight, Michel. This . . . this isn't an invitation, it's a demand. Do me this service . . ."

"I don't want you to consider it as a service."

"In my world . . . I mean, in my . . . Um . . . I feel really clumsy this evening."

She put her hand back onto her cigarette case and took out another, which she lit and dragged on deeply. De Palma realised that he did not like seeing her smoke. It made her seem too familiar. He looked away.

"One day, I was summoned to what we call the scene of the crime. It was years ago. When I'd just joined the force. I was in Paris. And I can remember it like it was yesterday.

"Her name was Isabelle Mercier. She was sixteen. Blonde . . . a beautiful girl. Or rather, I didn't know that till later, if you see what I mean. When I saw the photos and films that her father agreed to show us.

"I've searched for a long time. A very long time. Without ever letting up. I have entire books full of notes and statements. Ever since, I've been out to get the person who made her suffer what she went through . . . And I might die like this! But I'll never stop searching. I'll construct a thousand different scenarios. I may never find the right one, but that's just too bad. You know, it's rather like an endless quest."

She drew heavily on her cigarette then stubbed it out in the ashtray.

"She looked like you, Ingrid. The resemblance is terrible. Terrible."

"Stop it, Michel, you're scaring me."

She crossed the living room then stopped in a doorway that presumably led to what she called her "private domain".

"Goodnight, Michel. You'll find your room on the first floor, opposite the lounge you're already familiar with. I'll see you tomorrow."

She let her arm drop down beside her, then vanished into her own quarters.

Morini tried to lift himself up on his arms, but failed. His muscles had melted away. His legs were barely responding any longer.

He remembered the voices that he had heard the day before, or just now. This morning or last night. It made no difference.

The voices had been so distant it was as if they were being filtered through thick layers of cotton. He remembered yelling out, but he wondered if his voice had not remained stuck to his lips, or in the depths of his burning throat.

After that, he had drunk his urine and his thirst had eased off for a while. But only for a while. Before long, an acidic slime had built up in his mouth and on the edge of his tongue.

But he could clearly remember the voices. One had said: "Everything's been cleaned up here", or something like that. And the other one: "There are still some traces in the water." They were two men who did not know each other very well, to judge by the way they spoke.

Of that he was sure.

He fell asleep, exhausted by this effort of recall. An enormous racket woke him up. A sound of splashing in the water, just on the other side of his prison wall.

And then a song surged up into the darkness. As high-pitched as a child's voice.

"*Lagadigadeu, la tarasco, lagadigadeu . . .*"

And then a second, far deeper voice. Like the cry of a farmer calling in his herd.

"*Laïssa passa la vieio masco . . . Laïssa passa que vaï dansa . . .*"
The two voices then blended into a strange duet:
"*La tarasco dou casteu, la tarasco dou casteu . . .*"
This chant brought back fond memories. It was the song that the Knights of the Tarasque sang when pushing their papier-mâché monster through the streets of Tarascon, before charging the terrified crowd.

And him, Morini, in the pure white uniform of the Knights, with a musketeer's hat. He had been a little boy the first time he had seen the Tarasque, raised on tiptoe, his chin resting on the windowsill.

He swore that if he ever got out of this alive, then the amusement park would be named after the Tarasque. He was Le Grand. The person everyone listened to. Whom everyone obeyed.

He would have liked to remain a Knight of the Tarasque . . . if prison hadn't interfered with his fate. Since he had left the monster, there had been a void in his life. That was why he had put so much effort into the Big South.

The park must carry the stamp of the monster. Or at least its image. With entertainments wholly devoted to it. His father would have liked that idea. Not his mother, but he did not care about that.

The ceiling of the prison opened suddenly. Earth fell down onto his face.

A fierce light struck his eyes like a slap. A superhuman force seized him and dragged him up into the dark sky.

De Palma woke early. The farmhouse was deserted. He went out onto the patio and savoured the fading freshness of the morning. The farm workers had gathered around a huge tractor in the garage and were discussing the coming day's work.

An intense light surged up between the breasts of the Alpilles. In under an hour, La Balme would be inside the furnace.

He looked at his watch and found that it had stopped during the night; it still said 11.30, the time he had gone to bed.

He took out his mobile, switched it on and found that he had nine messages. The recorded voice told him that the first message had been left at eighteen minutes past midnight.

"M. de Palma, Christophe Texeira. I'm sorry to bother you so late, but the voices are back again. Call me back as soon as you get this message."

He cursed himself for having turned off his telephone while in Ingrid's company.

He listened to the others. They were all from Texeira, who had tried to contact him all night at various times; the last message had been at 2.19 a.m.

He telephoned him back at once.

"I heard them around midnight."

"Midnight?"

"Yes, that's right. The same routine in Provençal again. But this time I had a great idea: I recorded them."

"How's the result?"

"Come and listen!"

De Palma did not wait to say goodbye to Mme Steinert. He got into the 205 and made straight for La Capelière.

There was thunder in the air. Clouds were drifting up from the sea and gathering over the vast meadows of La Crau and the swamps of the Camargue.

When he turned into chemin de la Capelière, heavy drops exploded onto the Peugeot's dusty bonnet.

Texeira was waiting in the little museum's doorway. De Palma ran over to him.

"Good to see you, M. de Palma!"

"Good to see you too!"

"Let's not waste any time, come inside."

Texeira placed a small tape recorder on his desk, of the kind the Baron had often seen in old-fashioned listening devices.

"It's a Nagra," Texeira said with a hint of pride in his voice. "And here's the magic microphone."

He showed him a long mike, rather like the ones used by the police during stake-outs. It had SENNHEISER printed on its body in chrome letters.

"It's old, but when used with this parabola the results are quite extraordinary. We use it to record birdsong."

"Great," said de Palma, who was losing his patience.

"An ancient piece of kit, but effective! And here's what I recorded."

He pressed 'play'.

The first sounds were of footfalls and breathing. Like someone in a big hurry.

"That's me, running to get as near to the voices as possible."

Then, suddenly, the footsteps stopped . . . Texeira's panting could still be heard, then nothing. The biologist had presumably turned the mike in the opposite direction.

"Here we go."

At first, there was the sound of a heavy tread through fairly deep water. Someone or something was going through the marsh at a distance that de Palma couldn't estimate. Then the sound stopped, just a faint splashing before the first voice started up. It was so sharp and strange that de Palma recoiled from the machine:

"*Lagadigadeu, la tarasco, lagadigadeu . . .*"

There was a loud noise of water, as though something was stirring in the depths of the swamp, followed by a second far deeper voice:

"*Laïssa passa la vieio masco . . . Laïssa passa que vaï dansa . . .*"

The two voices joined together like a terrifying choir in the middle of the night and the marshes.

"*La tarasco dou casteu, la tarasco dou casteu . . .*"

There were other sounds that de Palma could not really identify. It sounded like footsteps in mud, but he wasn't sure.

The two voices rose again in the night.

"*La tarasco dou casteu, la tarasco dou casteu . . .*"

De Palma noticed that the two men had apparently moved; their voices had grown muffled. They had moved away from the mike, either going into the undergrowth or behind a wall.

"They went into the hut," he exclaimed.

"You think so?"

"It's a possibility."

"Hang on, the worst is yet to come."

Texeira turned up the volume.

"This microphone can often pick up things that are inaudible to the human ear."

There was a strangled cry. It was barely discernible, but de Palma knew it at once: the last screams of a man being put to death.

Texeira stopped the tape. His hand was trembling.

"That's all. There's nothing after that."

"Can you play the last minute again?"

The Baron listened with his eyes closed. He mentally reconstructed the scene, as captured by the mike in the darkness of the swamp.

"Christophe, have you been back to the hut?"

"No, I remembered what you told me."

"I think that you've just saved your life."

"Really?"

"One hundred per cent sure."

Texeira looked him up and down.

"I suggest we take a look at the hut. Do you have time?"

"Not really. But I must admit that I'm dying with curiosity."

For over an hour, the sea breeze had been driving the stink of the cellulose factory on the Rhône back up towards Tarascon.

Despite the few drops of storm rain, it was still hot. The heat seemed trapped in a bag that nothing could penetrate.

When he saw the crowd that had gathered, Marceau quickly wiped the sweat from his forehead. He had some trouble making his way through the onlookers before finally reaching the heavy doors of Saint Martha's church.

The officer who opened them for him was looking suitably grim. Once inside, an old veteran whom Marceau had known from the territorial brigade pointed to where the action had happened.

At the far end of the apse, the forensic team had stretched a yellow tape across and placed a few markers. The gate leading to the crypt was open. Marceau noticed blue glimmers rising from the underground depths of the church: the technicians were using a CrimeScope to scan the scene on wavelengths invisible to the naked eye.

Marceau kept his distance, allowing the forensics team to finish its painstaking work.

"Oh, you're here!" Larousse said, looking as rough as he always did when something important had happened. "We've managed to limit the damage in the press."

"What have you told them?"

"That a visitor had discovered the lifeless body of a tourist, and for the moment the police are pursuing their investigations."

"Why, isn't that true?"

"You mean you don't know?"

"I was on leave yesterday."

Larousse took Marceau by the arm and drew him to one side.

"It's the same scenario as last time."

"Christian Rey?"

Larousse nodded.

"The body was discovered by a visitor, just after opening time. A Danish tourist called Thomas Nielsen. But this time we've got a really big fish on our hands. Morini. How does that grab you?"

"Morini!"

"Indeed. After Rey, his lieutenant, we now have the boss himself. Who's going to be next?"

"So you think we've got a serial killer on our hands?"

"What would you call it?"

Marceau glanced round at the crypt. Larousse turned towards him.

"Where are you at with Rey?"

"We've got the D.N.A. results."

"And?"

"Unknown D.N.A. on the wounds."

"And so?"

"So we have some totally unknown D.N.A."

"What do you mean by that?" Larousse snapped.

"I mean that it is traces of saliva that were found."

Larousse stared up towards the ceiling of the church. He took a deep breath.

"And you have made all the necessary comparisons with other D.N.A. . . . I don't know, say . . ."

"Saliva on a wound generally indicates a bite."

"Do you realise the size of the wound, Marceau?"

Jean-Claude raised his hands before letting them drop again.

"I called Nantes last night. They do very good work, but this time they have no idea. No idea at all."

"What about the genetic records?"

"Nothing doing either. D.N.A. unknown."

A member of the forensic team appeared in the entry to the crypt. He took off his gloves and mask and threw them into a yellow box. After that, he beckoned to Larousse and Marceau.

"Hi, Jean-Claude, how are things?"

"I'm getting by. How about you?"

"It's not a pretty sight down there. Jesus, I've never seen anything like it!"

"Can we go down?"

"Right away. We've just finished."

Larousse and Marceau put on their gloves and overshoes then walked through the Gothic door.

As they went down the steps, Marceau felt the stench grip his throat. He stopped and put on the gasmask that the technician held out to him.

"What a fucking stink."

Larousse was behind Marceau and squinting over his mask, which gave him a pig's snout.

A little lower down, the photographer was taking several pictures of a bloodstain on the railings of the tomb of the chevalier Jean de Cossa.

When they got to the crypt, Marceau stopped dead.

Morini's body was placed in front of the sarcophagus that contained the remains of Saint Martha. His head lay with its left cheek pressed against the flagstones, looking towards the monument with bulging eyes. The bottom of his torso and his legs were missing. Marceau's gaze was liquid and brimming with anger.

"Have you got anything to tell me?" he asked the technician.

"Sure, where would you like me to begin?"

"Tell me about the wound. I'll read the report for the rest of it."

"It's the first time I've ever seen a wound like that," the technician replied, shaking his head. "Just look."

They bent over the body.

"You get the impression that the flesh has been torn away. The inner organs have gone. It's a completely empty torso."

Marceau pointed at a whitish gleam on the blood.

"And what's that?"

"It looks like either saliva or sperm, I can't tell yet. But I'd say it was saliva."

Larousse was standing to one side and looking away from the body. Marceau stood up slowly and stared at Saint Martha laid out on her deathbed: her fine, delicate figure draped in marble. Her face was spattered with blood and her body crisscrossed with brown marks, as though the madman who had desecrated the shrine had tried to scratch the stone.

"The death certainly occurred last night. I think the body was left here early this morning. Probably between eight and nine o'clock."

"Are you sure?"

"Almost. Some of the bloodstains aren't quite dry yet."

"Not coagulated?"

"Yes, coagulated, but not completely dry."

"Which means that the body was brought here just after the murder. At most thirty or forty minutes later. Otherwise, the blood would already have coagulated and there wouldn't be all these stains."

"I completely agree."

"Also, he transported it in a bag or something like that. There are no traces anywhere else."

"Good point," said Larousse. "So what's your conclusion?"

"I don't have one," Marceau said, gravely. "Nothing at all. Morini must have been slaughtered not far from here, then his body was brought here and staged like this. Where's the priest?"

"He's in the sacristy. Delmastro is questioning him."

"I want to see him at once."

Above the saint's head, the inscription *Sollicita non turbatur* had been crossed out with several streaks of blood.

"*Sollicita non turbatur*?" Marceau read. "Does anyone know what that means?"

"I lost my Latin years ago," Larousse replied.

"But it seems to have meant something to him. Look at how he crossed out the words."

"Whatever happens, not a word to the press for now," said Larousse. "I don't want to see a single hack in the vicinity."

The Commissaire turned on his heels and went back upstairs. Marceau stepped back and observed the entire scene. This was a vision like none he had ever witnessed before. Morini had been left like a sacrifice at the feet of a saint who was particularly loved in Tarascon. This staging must contain the answer to this slaughter.

Back on the surface, Marceau tore off his mask and gloves.

"I've just had a call from the prosecutor," Larousse told him. "This case is being given to the *Police Judiciaire*. There's nothing more for us to do here."

"I was expecting that." Marceau cursed as he threw away the gloves.

"They'll be here any moment now."

"Who's on it?"

"Moracchini. Plus someone I don't know called Romero."

"I know Moracchini, but not the other."

"Sorry, Marceau, but this is too big for us. This is the second gangster we've found half eaten. We don't have the resources for this kind of thing. The prosecutor's right. It's a case for the P.J. At least that way we're in the clear."

De Palma took an initial photograph of the sandbank, then a second of the thin band of earth that wove through the reed bed.

Texeira had lent him the digital camera that belonged to the reserve. The Baron checked the image, then walked on.

"Same principle as last time, Christophe. The slightest detail could be important. Even the smallest."

Texeira stared at the ground and frowned. A quarter of an hour later, they were standing in front of the footprint they had discovered the day before. No-one had touched the marker de Palma had left there.

He took three more photographs, then he placed the measuring rod that Texeira handed him next to the print and took another snapshot.

After a further fifteen minutes, they reached the stretch of water that lay between them and the reed hut.

There was not the slightest breath of air. The only sounds being made by the rotting life of the swamp came from bubbles rising from the depths of the silt and bursting on the surface.

The Baron signalled to Texeira to crouch down.

"Look closely," he said. "Has anything changed?"

Texeira gazed towards the hut. He took his time before answering.

"The door," he said.

"Exactly."

"Last time, it was closed. I shut it, in fact."

Half an hour later, they set foot on the mound of earth that the hut stood on. The Baron took out his Cobra and motioned to Texeira to hang back.

He walked on gingerly, almost in slow motion, as tense as a big cat.

The ground around the hut had been meticulously cleaned. On the bank, he found the same traces as during their first visit. He decided not to linger over such details and instead go straight inside.

Gently, he pushed the door open with his foot, pointing his gun into the gloom of the hut. The door creaked loudly. Texeira followed him inside.

On the table, he noticed some finger marks. He looked closer and saw that the person who had left them had taken the precaution of wearing gloves. The dirt floor had been swept.

"I don't understand," Texeira said.

"Well I'm starting to get an idea."

"Lucky you!"

"On the tape, you can clearly hear that the voices fade away, or they're muffled."

"That's right, just before the scream."

"So let's picture the scenario: two men come in here with a third person. They are on the bank when they're singing, then they come inside."

218

The Baron gestured to illustrate his version.

"Why two men?"

"It's very clear on the recording, when the scream is heard. So there are three voices."

"That's true, you don't hear the third one before."

"No, you don't hear . . ." the Baron repeated thoughtfully.

"What you say is perfectly obvious when you think about it."

"Before . . . Jesus, the third person was already here!"

"Are you sure?"

"It seems the most likely scenario."

The Baron retreated to the door, took several paces outside, then came in again.

"They come in singing, then, at that moment, they strike down the person who's in here."

"Strike down?"

"And maybe killed him. Look, they've cleaned everything up."

He gazed around the floor. Then he bent down to peer beneath the table. The ground was marked with what looked like wide sweeps of a broom. He retreated again to the room as a whole, then moved closer again to peer at the traces from different angles. He took the measuring rod and scratched the floor in several places.

"It's really odd," he said. "Really it is."

Texeira observed him tensely. He didn't miss one of the policeman's gestures.

"Weird . . ."

All at once, the Baron drew some long lines in the dirt. He did it several times in all directions, and lifted some earth. He kept going until the tip of the rod hit an obstacle. Then he kneeled down and rubbed at the place the rod had hit. In less than thirty seconds, he had uncovered a trapdoor.

He stood up abruptly and pushed the table aside.

"Help me lift this thing up. Or rather, lift it up in front of me, while I keep my gun trained on what's inside. You never know."

Texeira raised the panel of wood. A fetid smell invaded the room. De Palma recognised the stench of decomposing human excrement.

Texeira produced a torch from his pocket and handed it to the Baron.

The trapdoor led to a long tunnel about a metre wide. In the torch beam, de Palma could see the entrance to an underground room at the end of the tunnel; a sort of cellar dug out of the raw earth.

"Can you see anything?"

"Nothing that exciting. We'll have to go down and see. But we won't be doing that for the moment."

He retreated, and took two snapshots. Then he photographed the interior of the passage, while Texeira held open the trap.

"We're going to leave everything as we found it, so that no-one will guess that we've been here."

Ten minutes later, they crossed back over the stretch of sleeping water. De Palma stared at the reed hut, which danced before his eyes each time Texeira pushed with his pole.

In the humid light, a buzzard emerged from a clump of stunted ash trees and poplars; it beat its wings heavily then glided above the surface of the reed bed before vanishing behind the curtain of rushes.

The bells of Saint Martha's church were ringing the angelus when Anne Moracchini and Daniel Romero parked their unmarked Xsara in front of the building.

They presented their tricolour cards to the guard on the door, who was looking increasingly confused.

"Commissaire Larousse?"

"He's just left."

"Commandant Marceau?"

"They left together in fact."

"Perfect," Moracchini said. "The P.J. always gets a warm welcome. How nice."

She went inside the church and headed straight for the entrance to the crypt.

The forensic team had put away their equipment, and the clean-up teams were ready to start.

"Where's the body?"

"It's been taken away, just five minutes ago."

"I see," Moracchini said. "They haven't heard the last of this."

She went down the crypt steps, followed by Romero. It was Romero's first real investigation with the brigade, and the squabbles had already begun.

When Moracchini saw the bloodstains on the statue of Saint Martha, she paused for breath, went over slowly and tried to picture the placing of Morini's body.

As the technicians had removed their powerful lamps, the saint's burial place had returned to its sepulchral gloom. The smell of the corpse had practically vanished.

A brigadier from the Tarascon commissariat arrived in the crypt.

"Who took the body away?"

"The emergency services. They took it to Marseille for the autopsy."

"I mean, who gave the order to move it?"

"It was Marceau, he . . ."

"O.K., O.K. . . . What time was that?"

The brigadier walked over to the light to look at his watch.

"Just half an hour ago."

The two officers looked at each other in silence.

"Pick up all the details you can, Daniel. I'm going to try and get hold of Michel. I'd like him to have a look."

"O.K., Anne. Do you want me to take some photos?"

"In this light?"

"I've got flash."

"Try it, and if not you ask them to put the juice back on."

The team of cleaners appeared in the doorway, two black figures in the blue gleam.

"Don't touch anything," Moracchini said, pointing at them. "Go back upstairs at once."

"Commandant Marceau . . ."

"I don't give a shit about your Commandant Whatsisname. We're from the P.J. and I've been mandated by the prosecutor of Tarascon, clear? And I'm ordering you to go back upstairs."

The two officers did not wait to be told twice.

"Do you want me to call Marceau, Madame?" the brigadier asked.

"I'll have him sent for . . . if he wants to play games like this, then I'll get him summonsed by the magistrate as soon as possible. He's going to see who's in command here!"

Moracchini found a quiet spot in the car park in front of Saint Martha's church, just a few metres away from King René's Castle, and dialled de Palma's mobile. In vain. She tried his home and got the answering machine but did not leave a message.

Furiously, she stuffed her mobile into the back pocket of her jeans and went back inside Saint Martha's.

Father Favier was pacing around the sacristy, utterly bewildered. From time to time, he stopped, opened drawers that contained various sacred objects, then closed them again with a nervous twitch.

"Try and calm down, Father," Romero said. "We need you to tell us everything you know."

"Sorry, but I don't know anything at all. Nothing! During my ten years on emergency wards, I never saw such viciousness. It's unspeakable."

"I know," Moracchini said, glancing over at Romero. "We're just trying to put your movements together. After that we'll leave you be, alright?"

The priest came to a halt.

"Alright."

"What time did you discover the body?"

"I didn't. It was a visitor."

"Never mind! We'll get his statement later."

"It must have been about nine o'clock. But I'm not sure."

"What time did you call the police?"

"Straight away."

Romero noted down all these answers carefully, as well as any details that seemed important to him, such as Favier's attitude on being asked each question.

"Did you hear a noise or anything earlier?"

"No, not that morning."

"But yes, you did before?"

"Two days ago. I had the impression that someone had slipped into the church. But there was nobody there."

"You mean that you heard sounds suggesting an alien presence, or something unusual, is that it?"

Father Favier nodded then started pacing up and down once more.

"We'll leave you in peace, then talk to you again later, O.K.?"

Favier muttered something that neither of the officers could hear.

The judge immediately sent a warrant to the offices of the *Brigade Criminelle* in Marseille, giving permission to search Morini's residence. Moracchini and Romero arrived just after the gendarmes, who had surrounded the gangster's house.

"I'm Commandant Bonin, of the Tarascon company," said the gendarme, shaking the capitaine's hand. "We were expecting you."

Morini's wife had just been informed of her husband's death. She was hysterical. Moracchini made her sit down in the living room. Without waiting for reinforcements from Marseille or the local boys from Tarascon, she started the search.

"It's 14.00 hours, Daniel. Note down: Began search in the presence of Mme Morini."

The two floors of Morini's home must have measured a good three hundred square metres.

On the ground floor, there was a huge entrance hall, decorated soberly, with white walls, a few paintings by minor Provençal artists, two classical sculptures and green plants everywhere. To the right, it led into a vast living room with pale green walls, several leather sofas of different styles, padded armchairs and heavy curtains with huge pastel flowers.

On the walls, the crime boss had hung a series of photographs of old Tarascon featuring the centre and the castle before the reconstruction work had been done on the river and the town. Above one of the sofas hung a poster for the Tarascon carnival, dated 1932. Beside that, a sepia photograph depicted the Tarasque surrounded by its Knights. A Regency glass case contained a set of miniature bronze or ceramic Tarasques, as well as a collection of various monsters made of terracotta or copper.

223

At the back of the room, there was a bar of real zinc, which the gangster must have picked up somewhere shady. An antique one-armed bandit stood beside it.

The bay window looked out on a twenty-metre pool and a neoclassic-style pool-house. Further on, there was a forest of pines and oaks: the part of the Downlands that belonged to Morini.

On the first floor, seven bedrooms were laid out as suites complete with jacuzzi and desk each in a different style.

"We'll start with the bedrooms, Daniel. Let's get going."

Only two of them were used regularly: one contained Morini's personal belongings, the other his wife's.

"So the two of them didn't sleep together!" Romero said.

"You know, mobsters aren't people like the rest of us!"

The two officers went through everything in the wife's room. They found nothing except a collection of lingerie that made Romero blush.

Then they searched Morini's study, where they came across a few telephone numbers jotted down on Post-its. Moracchini placed them in a plastic envelope. The four mobile phones that lay on the bedside tables were also seized, as well as Mme Morini's address book.

Moracchini went back downstairs to the entrance hall. She gave instructions to the reinforcements that had just arrived, then went to see Morini's widow. The young woman was sitting on a thick leather sofa, her eyeliner running down her cheeks. She smelled distinctly of gin.

"Can we speak to you Mme Morini? Are you feeling any better?"

She must have been a good twenty years younger than her husband. Her black hair was tied up over her fragile neck by a knotted velvet ribbon. She wore a white dressing-gown, over her suntanned skin, and beneath it a bikini with bright red and yellow flowers.

"You can ask me whatever you like. I know nothing. He never told me anything . . ."

She spoke with a slight Marseille accent.

"What's your name?"

"Stéphanie. And that's practically all I can remember about myself!"

She looked up at Moracchini and stared into her eyes. She was quivering with rage.

"Anyway, I suppose it had to happen sooner or later."

Moracchini sat down next to her.

"Had he received any threats?"

"He seemed more nervy than usual, but you never really knew with him. It depended on what business he was doing."

"When did you see him last?"

"About a week ago. I can hardly remember, in fact! It's a bit like living in a parallel world. He said he was going to Aix and would be home in the evening. He never came back."

Moracchini guessed that Stéphanie must have been taking large quantities of some sort of dope to put up with a pig like Morini.

"Did he phone you to tell you he wouldn't be home?"

The young woman pouted cynically.

"Are you joking or what? When he didn't come home, he never said anything. But, this time, he said he'd be home."

"I mean, since his disappearance, have you received any calls from him, or anyone else?"

"No, Madame, nothing. But I do remember, on the day before he disappeared, he wasn't in his normal state of mind. He stayed for ages in his bedroom whispering into his telephone."

"And that wasn't usual, if I understand you correctly?"

"Exactly. But, you know, when you live with someone like that, you soon learn to be like the three little monkeys: you hear no evil, speak no evil, see no evil . . ."

Moracchini could not stop herself from looking scornful.

"O.K. You stay here. I'll be back to question you again later. In the meantime, get dressed."

She then went out into the garden and made a long telephone call to de Palma.

It was just after midday when the Baron turned into the driveway of La Balme farmhouse. The heat was stifling and he had problems keeping his grip on the steering wheel of the 205.

For the first time in a while, he noticed one of the young woman's bodyguards, who vanished behind one of the buildings when he approached. Mme Steinert must have seen him coming, because she was waiting for him on the patio, with a stern expression on her face.

"We missed you this morning for breakfast."

"I'm sorry I had to leave you like that. But I had to make a trip to the Camargue."

"Oh really?" she said, crossing her legs.

"Yes, one or two routine checks, as they say."

"And ideas like that suddenly grab you! I know, I'll go and check some details in the Camargue . . ."

As she spoke, she snapped her fingers in the air. Her voice had grown metallic.

"You've arrived at the right time, Michel. I've sent my chauffeur Georg to go and fetch M. Bérard for a lunchtime drink. And here he comes."

The Mercedes 4×4 steered a wide circle in the courtyard. The Baron recognised Georg. He was the bodyguard he'd spotted the first time he had seen her in Marseille. He was wearing sunglasses.

Bérard would not let the bodyguard help him out of the car. Bent double, he then came to shake Ingrid's hand. When he saw the Baron, who was standing to one side, he whistled softly.

"So the policeman is here too!"

"A policeman, but above all a friend," Ingrid said, still clutching his hand. "Come on, we're going to have something to drink."

"Oh, I can't stay long. Especially in this weather. You know, my charges are waiting for me. *Quand plòu en Avoust, tout òli e tout moust.*"

"What does that mean?" Ingrid asked with a smile.

"When it rains in August, all is oil and grape must."

"That's good news, isn't it?"

He stared at her, then twitched his head with a twist of his lips.

"Don't you think so?" she asked.

"It's the beginning of August. And there was thunder this morning. Good God! *Quand trono lou matin marco d'auro.* You don't understand!"

226

She raised her hands then let them drop to her sides.

"When there's thunder like this morning, it's often a sign of wind. Sweet Jesus, I'm afraid it'll start blowing, and what with all those fires around here . . ."

"*Fängt der August mit Donnern an, er's bis zum End' nicht lassen kann*: if it thunders at the beginning of August, it will continue to the end of the month," she replied.

Bérard lowered his eyes and stared at his feet for a moment. Then he adjusted his beret, uncovering a lock of silver hair.

"Goodness, William understood patois."

"It's true, he had learned Provençal."

"He spoke it better than I do," said Bérard with a whistle. "He had really studied our language."

"Come on, M. Bérard. Let's have a drink in the shade. You'll feel better."

"Oh, don't worry. The sun doesn't bother me."

Bérard was feeling embarrassed. He was glancing around darkly. De Palma was impressed by the vigorous aura given off by this man who was almost a hundred years old.

"So you asked me to come to tell you about the former owners?"

He looked at the Baron.

"I thought it preferable for Mme Steinert to know what you told me when we last met. But it wasn't me who asked you to come today."

Bérard gave Ingrid a long stare.

"It's all ancient history. Especially now the poor soul's dead."

"Did you know his father?" she asked.

"Oh yes. In the prewar days, before everything fell to pieces. He used to come here in search of antiquities and, as I knew a lot about such things, he used to ask me questions. Sometimes, we went for a walk together and I showed him places."

"Such as the Downlands," de Palma said.

"Yes indeed. We went there . . . I remember as if it were yesterday. He was walking behind me, on a day like today. Really muggy! We started on the Fontvieille road then went as far as the big oak up there. That's where I showed him the old stones, as we call them."

"That's where the statue of Hercules was?"

Bérard looked up at the Baron.

"He called him Heracles. That's the Greek name. Because in fact the stones came from Greece. The Romans only arrived later. I read that in books."

Bérard wetted his dry lips with his pastis. Then he took an olive.

"Ah, Carpentras black. They're excellent!"

"We're going to plant some more."

"Wait for the spring then put them in that large plot you have by the road up there. It's neither too damp nor too dry."

Bérard took a good swig of pastis, then looked with interest at Ingrid.

"If you mean to plant, does that mean you're going to stay?"

"Why, were you afraid that I'd leave?"

"Yes, after William's death, I was really afraid of that."

"No, we're staying."

"Well, in that case . . ." Bérard said, flapping his hand.

De Palma waited for a moment.

"What do you mean by that, M. Bérard?"

"Some people aren't going to be best pleased."

Mme Steinert was about to say something, but the Baron motioned to her to stay out of this.

"Who do you mean?"

"The ones who want to open the park. They came to see me the other day. I told them that I wouldn't sell them an inch of land. That they'd have to wait till I was gone. And that anyway, I'd left everything to William."

"Can you describe these men to me?"

"They looked very respectable. One of them told me his name. It sounded German or something. Not like a name from these parts."

Ingrid started.

"Not M. Chandeler, by any chance?"

"What was that?"

"Chan – de – ler."

"It could well have been that."

"What did he look like?"

"Tall, very tall. With nicely combed hair. Forever smiling, like a salesman. Like, like . . . the people who work in banks. Know what I mean? They're always trying to sell you something. But don't worry, they left me a calling card. I'll show it to you. But I reckon it was the same name as the one you just mentioned."

"And the other?"

"The other man was fat. He was a tall man too, but fat. And he looked like a real crook."

"Did he give you his name?"

"No, no. He didn't say much. And outside there was another one waiting in the car."

De Palma's head was racing. There was nothing surprising about Chandeler being there. He was simply a lawyer who was trying his luck. But who was he working for? And who was the fat man who came with him?

"Tell me, M. Bérard. Do you remember what day this was?"

"Goodness, no. I sometimes lose track of time a bit. I might tell you something wrong."

"But it wasn't yesterday?"

"Definitely not," he replied, raising his hands. "It was a few days after poor William's death."

"It doesn't matter."

The shepherd took another swig of pastis, then stood up.

"I must go back, my flock is waiting."

Ingrid took both his hands. She looked at him affectionately.

"Can I come to see you one of these days?"

"Oh, my house is a poor place, you know! Only William used to come by, he didn't mind. My wife's dead and gone these twenty years now. So things aren't kept as they should be."

"It doesn't matter . . . Or else I'll come to see you while you're watching your sheep."

"Alright. I'll be by the rocks a little later, when it's not so hot."

The Baron's mobile rang.

"Where are you, Michel?"

"In Provence, Anne."

"Still with Ingrid?"

"There's no hiding anything from you."

"Go straight away to the forensic unit in La Timone."

"Why?"

"They've taken Morini there. But we're on the case."

"I'm on my way."

"But don't go inside, Michel! Remember, officially you're not involved in this investigation."

"O.K. I'll join you in a couple of hours' time."

He arranged to meet her in a café on boulevard Baille, just by the hospital.

Bérard sat back down on a wicker chair. De Palma noticed that Ingrid's eyes were wet with emotion.

"See, what did I tell you? The wind's rising. That's not good."

A greenish light fell from the neon lamps in the dissection room. Moracchini and Romero, dressed in green overalls and with masks on their faces, were standing behind Doctor Mattei and his assistant.

Mattei looked at Moracchini and pointed his scissor's at Morini's injuries.

"There's saliva on the wounds. The same saliva as last time, at least I think so."

The doctor of the dead indicated a dangling strip of flesh.

"Look, his dermis, epidermis and muscles have been completely ripped apart! As if something had bitten him, then pulled to remove the piece."

Moracchini looked at Romero. Above her white mask, her eyes looked anxious.

"Any ideas, Doctor?"

"None."

"I think that the D.N.A. will help us out once again. And I'm ready to bet we'll find the same as last time."

"So?"

"He's been fed to something. That's how he died. What do you think, Mattei?"

"I can't think of anything at this level. I can't imagine jaws that powerful. Unless there were several animals at the same time."

230

Mattei bent down once more to examine Morini's wounds, almost touching them with his nose. He frowned and held his breath.

"The spinal column has been bitten in two by jaws. It's not possible otherwise. It's just like a dog bite, but ten times bigger. And it reminds me of men I saw in the tropics, who'd been attacked by sharks . . ."

Mattei had slit open the thorax and neck up to the chin. He had levered the thoracic cage open before removing the lungs and heart.

"There was adrenalin in the heart and water in the lungs. I also found some algae on the body."

"So it's just the same scenario as with Christian Rey. Exactly the same . . . The guy is dropped in water, then he gets eaten."

"And it's fresh water, too. So no sharks . . . A crocodile maybe . . ."

"Why not a Komodo Dragon? What a headache! I just don't get it."

She looked at Romero and noticed that his eyes had glazed over. She had not known her new colleague very long, but she had worked out that this was the sign of intense mental activity.

"The Tarasque," de Palma murmured.

Moracchini's eyes were red with fatigue and disgust. She had picked up the Baron and was driving down the motorway towards Château-Gombert.

"What are you muttering about?"

"The Tarasque. That's all."

"You wouldn't be starting to lose it, by any chance?"

"No, no . . ."

"But the Tarasque doesn't exist!"

"Perhaps not. But someone is crazy enough to play the monster for us."

The overhead metro overtook them. She noticed a group of youths horsing around in the last carriage.

"Someone is staging a scenario? Now that's more like it!"

"The bite, the algae . . . it all fits together. There's someone somewhere who wants to resurrect the Tarasque."

"That's one possibility. But what might also have happened is that

Morini and Rey were quite simply snuffed by their little chums in gangland. There wouldn't be anything very surprising about that either."

"Not the right modus operandi."

"How can you be sure, Michel? They're getting crazier and crazier, you know that as well as I do."

The Baron waved away her suggestion and pursed his lips. His face was almost ashen and a headache was starting to grow at the base of his forehead.

"Romero's gone back to Tarascon to pick up Marceau's report. The bastard, he couldn't bear us being given the case. He'd had our friend removed before we got there."

"It doesn't really matter, Anne."

"What are you talking about? We've got nothing and he's maybe hiding things to keep us slaving away like idiots."

She drove under the metro line and accelerated suddenly, as though she was fleeing something. Her hands were clenched on the steering wheel and the headlamps of the cars on the other side of the road glittered in her damp eyes.

The next evening, at 7 p.m., the Baron leaped over the surrounding wall of the Résidence Paul Verlaine, drew his Cobra and made a panoramic scan.

He let a neighbour from the third floor go by, holding his son by the hand. Then, when no-one else was in sight, he went along the path leading to his building, careful to stay close to the pines and the shrubs that bordered it. The Cobra was tight against his thigh. In case of sudden danger.

It was the first time he had been home for three days. It smelled musty and full of bad memories.

The answering machine flashed up ten messages. Two of them were people hanging up, while the other eight were from his mother, whom he had not called for a week.

Without wasting any time, he went into the bedroom, grabbed a travelling bag and threw in two pairs of jeans, a pair of trainers, a few T-shirts and a drawer-full of boxer shorts and socks. In the wardrobe, he noticed the box in which he kept a hoard of souvenirs. He looked inside and found a notebook that contained a photograph of Isabelle Mercier. He examined it for a moment, before noticing something that had hitherto escaped him, despite the scores of times he had stared at it: she had a beauty spot shaped like the ace of spades just between her ear and the angle of her jaw.

He had spotted this detail only today. And he knew why. Because he had also seen it somewhere else. On Ingrid Steinert's cheek.

He lay down on the bed and sank into the dark waters of his memories. As ever, all he could see was a face that no longer existed, and a body already stiffened by death. A single eye that still stared at him over all those years and sleepless nights.

For a long time, he stayed in the shadows of his bedroom, watching the daylight gradually fade away between the slats of the shutters. Isabelle had been the first victim, but how many more corpses had he seen since then in his life as a detective?

At least three hundred. Maybe more.

The number made his head spin.

At the beginning, he had thought that he should hang on to all of them and hold them in his memory. It was his debt to the dead, because the dead know that they exist so long as someone pictures them. And if they are forgotten, it is all over.

As a little boy, he would sometimes walk in the alleys of Saint Peter's cemetery. He liked to read the names of the deceased on the slabs of granite and to invent their life stories, little novels in a nutshell telling of their vanished destinies, instant dramas in which love and wonders played leading roles.

Starring roles.

He jumped up, closed his bag and headed for the door.

Outside, the night had stretched its canvas. He waited for there to be nobody near his building, for the stairwell and hall to be plunged in darkness, then he walked out into the gloom of Marseille.

Thirty minutes later, he was bounding up the stone staircase that led through the prickly pears to Maistre's patio.

He served himself a kir then sat down on the low wall that overlooked the little houses of L'Etraque. In the distance, the sea was like a vast black slick running from the harbour wall as far as Maïre and then to the flickering star of the Planier lighthouse.

Maitre was browsing through a boat supplies catalogue. The murmur of the city could be heard from afar.

"Do you think we'll ever find our fishing boat, Michel?"

The Baron answered with a grunt.

20.

Controller General Lamastre had been regional head of the P.J. in Marseille for five years. He was rather a stylish man, he was in the town hall's good books, and didn't like disciplinary scandals.

That morning, Lamastre was getting impatient. He picked up the F.B.I. special agent badge which he always kept on his desk; it was a souvenir from his stay in Quantico years before, when he had decided to try to adapt the American super-cops' profiling techniques to French procedures. The badge had been given to him by James Lehane Jr, one of the best manhunters in the U.S.A.

"Take a seat, Michel. I don't like having to talk to you like this, but I have no choice. How are things?"

"Fine, sir. I've completely recovered. And I'm longing to get back to work."

"You knew Lehane too, didn't you?"

"Yes. He was a great guy. I've read both of his books and must admit that I've used his ideas a lot."

"Indeed," Lamastre said, putting down the badge. "Quite a detective. Let's drink to his health before I give you a scolding."

Lamastre came from Normandy. His blue deep-set eyes, perpetual three-day beard and a complexion fired by alcohol did not undermine his natural elegance. He produced a bottle of Jim Beam and two glasses from his desk drawer.

"The news isn't good," he said as he poured out the bourbon. "Certain people around here want your balls on a plate, Michel."

"I know."

"In this country, cops like you are becoming a rare commodity . . .

and certain people like that fact. To be quite honest, I'm seeing what can be done to avoid your being charged."

"They've got nothing against me, I've done nothing wrong."

"The problem is that you were seen having a rather physical conversation with that bastard Morini, just a few days before he passed on. Do you follow?"

"Of course I do, but . . ."

"Don't try to explain yourself, Michel. I know full well that it wasn't you who cut him in half and I've already rejected any such insinuations. Don't forget, however, that they exist. But the snag is that we have a statement from a customer of Morini's bar. He saw you and he's willing to sign, with his elbows if need be."

"I don't follow you . . ."

"Leave it out, Michel. I'm not out to get you."

Lamastre handed him the official report.

"They want your arse, and they'll get it if you carry on like this. Our friend here apparently saw everything. Just read the statement! It's highly detailed."

"O.K., so I talked with Morini and I handcuffed his bodyguard."

"And both of them died within the next few days . . ."

The Baron sat back in his chair. Lamastre picked up his badge again.

"I need to know why, Michel."

"It's a bit complicated. I don't know where to begin."

"I've got all the time in the world, and there's plenty of bourbon left. This is a friend asking, Michel!"

Caught in the trap, the Baron stayed silent for a while. He was going to have to talk, but first he wanted to find out exactly how much his boss knew. When he reached out his hand to take the report, Lamastre gripped it.

"Don't play silly buggers now. The report is mostly about Lopez. The man you blew to pieces not far from where you live. It's all rather messy, isn't it? As for the rest, I honestly couldn't give a damn!"

He raised his hand.

"Who cares if you put the shits up that fucker Morini? But for

236

two magistrates who specialise in organised crime to try to pin the death of good old Lopez on you – that I can't abide. So I need your version of the truth. And it had better be truer than that of our learned friends. Message received?"

"Loud and clear."

De Palma knew that Lamastre was extremely rigorous, absolutely honest and quite ready to stick his neck out for his men. So he had to play it straight while also hiding both his strengths and his weaknesses. Otherwise, the trap might close on him for good.

"This customer's statement is a tissue of lies," he said.

"That's not what I want to hear, Michel."

"Between you and me, boss, this is pure perjury. But, O.K., I'll tell you everything."

He started at the beginning: the meeting with Mme Steinert, the shot in the dark . . . He also mentioned the grass who had put him on the track of Morini.

Lamastre listened, still clutching his badge.

"You're in it up to your neck," he said. "You know what being charged means for a police officer?"

"I know, Chief."

The Controller General threw his badge down on a file marked "De Palma".

"As far as I'm concerned – I mean the Marseille P.J. – I'm going to give you a clean slate. When do you start work again?"

"Next Monday."

"O.K., let's say that de Palma's great return is going to be postponed slightly. Get yourself another month or so of sick leave. Time enough to let things run their course. We'll see how things stand when autumn comes. And I'm going to visit your friend the prefect later today."

"Say hello from me."

"It's lucky for you that you've been friends these twenty years."

"We go back to our days on the *Brigade Criminelle*."

"I know, I know, the pests in Paris. There's more to life than Maigret, you know."

"He was a young Commissaire at the time."

"Stop, you're bringing tears to my eyes."

Lamastre poured out two more shots of Jim Beam.

"So, Steinert you say?"

"Yes, boss."

"That case stinks, don't you think?"

"It isn't a case. I mean, everything possible has been done to turn it cold."

"Yes, I heard they'd decided he drowned."

"It was a murder. As sure as two and two make four. And someone big was behind it: property deals and so forth!"

"I'm ready to believe you, but it won't wash. People are judged on the facts, not on intellectual constructions."

Lamastre knocked his glass back in one and grimaced as he felt the burn go down.

"There are hundreds of poor bastards who get murdered and are put down as suicides. Do you know why?"

The Baron shrugged and picked up the F.B.I. badge.

"Because there's a two-gear justice – everyone knows that. And a two-gear police system. A D.N.A. test costs between 300 and 800 euros, do you follow me, de Palma?"

"Of course . . ."

"I know, I'm stating the blindingly obvious . . ."

He poured himself another shot.

"And I advise you to lay off the Steinert case during the month on sick leave you're going to take."

When he emerged into the courtyard of police headquarters, de Palma tried in vain to contact Marceau on his mobile. So instead he telephoned the commissariat, only to be told that his old colleague had gone on holiday abroad two days before.

The Baron was about to pull away in Maistre's 205, when Romero's head appeared at the window.

"Good day, boss. How are things?"

"I've just seen Lamastre. He'd rather I stayed ill for a while."

"No surprise there. You're much talked of right now, and not all of it good!"

"That's nothing new." ·

"Things are drifting up to the surface."

"Who cares?"

Romero stuck his head into the car.

"I went to see Maistre yesterday. As we got nothing out of Lornec, we took a little trip to the Belle de Mai to see what we could find out about those old hold-ups."

"Anything new?"

"Not much. But there's one thing of interest. At the time, it was Marceau who was in charge of the investigation. You should give him a call."

"That's right. He was on the B.R.B.* at the time. I should have thought of that. The snag is that he's on leave right now. The bugger's abroad and no-one knows where. We'll have to wait for the end of August."

"Shit, that's a shame."

"That's one way of putting it. Anyway, nothing is panning out at the moment."

"Anne's here. Do you want to speak to her?"

"No, my lad. I feel as though I stink of something dead right now."

"Come on, Michel, forget it!"

"You don't know them. They're as jealous as divas."

"Whatever. Let's try and get together as soon as possible. O.K.?"

"No problem. See you around."

The Canadair banked over the summits of the Alpilles before swooping towards the Downlands, barely thirty metres above the ground.

With tears in his eyes, Bérard watched it fly in line with the lavender fields, which were half hidden by the black smoke. Madame Steinert had taken the old shepherd by the arm because he could not keep still.

Once past the Route de Maussane, the Canadair dropped its tons of water over the burning torches of resin and oak, before vanishing into the blue sky smeared with black.

* *Brigade de Répression du Banditisme.*

"M. Bérard, you can't stay here. The firemen are telling us to leave."

The old man did not move. He murmured something inaudible, like an incantation, as he watched the inferno advance on a turret of limestone.

A quartermaster of the Marseille fire brigade shouted above the tumult and the cracking of tree trunks torn apart by the flames.

"You can't stay here," he called, unrolling a hosepipe. Move away! This is no place for you."

Madame Steinert guided the shepherd to the other side of the road. The wind drove the smoke towards them. In a swirl of fury, everything grew dark and sparks danced in the scorched air. She took him by the shoulder and led him towards her car. It was at that moment that she saw de Palma emerge from behind a fire engine.

"You've got to go," he said. "Get into the car, M. Bérard, you'll make yourself ill. The air is toxic."

The Baron motioned to Ingrid to take the driver's side, then he sat Bérard down in the passenger seat. The old boy was like a puppet. He no longer reacted to what was going on around him.

The Baron sat in the rear of the Mercedes 4×4, and they drove off towards Eygalières. The firemen had set up their command post in front of Morini's house and were fighting the blaze just a hundred metres away from the façade.

"Let's take M. Bérard home."

She nodded and overtook a Maussane firemen's ambulance.

"Where is your flock, M. Bérard?"

The old man did not reply. De Palma saw that he was crying, his eyes wide with terror.

When they arrived in the courtyard of Les Fontaines, Matelot the sheepdog didn't move. De Palma realised that something terrible had happened before or during the fire. He motioned to Ingrid to stay in the car.

"Drive off as soon as I'm out."

Ingrid had her hands clamped on the wheel. Bérard was staring ahead, as though what was happening no longer touched him.

The Baron threw himself out of the car and ran over to the dog's kennel, his Bodyguard drawn. Ingrid pulled away at once.

Matelot had been shot in the head. His skull had exploded, scattering brain matter all over the kennel.

De Palma went into the barn and listened. He heard the Mercedes leave the farmhouse turning and head towards Eygalières. Then there was silence.

Les Fontaines was in a state of stunned suspense. Flies were buzzing around in the heavy air. The sheep were gone. The gate of their pen was wide open. On the ground, the straw had been disturbed and scattered over the yard. It made a long yellow track that led towards the fields. The herd had been stampeded. Behind a manger, a lamb was breathing feebly, its back broken when the herd had trampled over it in panic.

He pushed open the front door of the house and pointed his gun inside. He smelled the old man's odour, newly mingled with the smell of wood ash that clung to the ancient furnishings. The overwhelming stillness had something disturbing about it. The only sign of life was the ticking of the clock.

He walked slowly inside, still on his guard.

The pantry door was open and a tin of biscuits had been spilt over the floor. Beside it lay some papers which looked like bills and a few carefully folded ten-euro notes.

The Baron glanced into the cupboard. It contained three shelves. The top one contained a line of bottles of liqueur and empty jars. Beneath it, a pile of dishcloths had been ransacked, leaving an empty space beside it; presumably where the tin had been. On the bottom shelf there were some cans and bars of chocolate, which had also been turned over.

He went all around the room then headed for the only door, which was in the far wall. It was closed. He turned the handle but could not open it. It was either locked or jammed. He tried again, and gave it an angry kick, but it wouldn't budge. He realised that it must be locked from the inside.

A meow broke the silence. A cat appeared in the front doorway, no doubt the only surviving witness of the terrible scene that had played out in the farm.

The big clock chimed six p.m. Outside, the air smelled scorched. The wind had risen and was blowing the smell of the fire towards Les Fontaines.

The Baron was about to leave when he heard the sound of a body hitting the ground. He just had time to duck when two gunshots rang out. A window shattered. Then there was a sound of rapid steps. A man was running towards the far side of the buildings. The Baron stood up and took aim.

It seemed to happen in slow motion. He fired once and saw the .38 bullet hit the ground. When the man turned round, he corrected his aim and pressed the trigger. The shot hit the man in the left leg; he made to fire back but the Baron put a second round into the same place.

The man fired once, and then again. The Baron just had time to duck before another window blew apart. When he stood back up, the man had vanished. De Palma ran out after him.

He stopped dead when he heard a powerful motorbike roar away on the dirt path.

The farm was still vibrating from the shots and there was a reek of burned powder. Most of the sheep had taken shelter in the field just behind the barn, a few more were lingering in the garden.

De Palma went back to the dining room. The lock on the door that led to the bedrooms was an old model, easy to open. In the farm's stock of tools he found a length of thick wire and fixed up a makeshift key. Thirty seconds later, the lock gave way.

The walls of the shepherd's bedroom were covered in a faded yellow wallpaper dotted with pale blue and pink flowers. To the right of the window, a huge wardrobe occupied all of the space; to the left was a single chair, with a black suit jacket draped over its back. The brown walnut bed was covered with a thick eiderdown and a hand-knitted bedcover.

He opened the wardrobe. On the upper shelf, there were some piles of ironed shirts and below that some carefully folded black corduroy trousers. An old hunting rifle lay in front of the pair of trousers. He opened the breach. It was loaded with two Tunet double zero cartridges.

The rest of the room told him nothing. There was a Christ made of yellow metal mounted on ebony on one of the walls, and a dried olive branch nailed up above the bedstead.

At the far end, a door led to another connecting room. When he opened it, it felt as though something invisible had been released, as if an impalpable form passed by him and fled outside.

There were a few dusty sticks of furniture and some old photographs hung on the walls: sepia portraits of past generations; a group of people in a glass-fronted frame; a papier-mâché Tarasque with a man in a costume like a musketeer's, with knee breeches, buckled shoes, frilly shirt and broad hat. It was Bérard, posing beside the monster as a Knight of the Tarasque. Other knights were standing behind him.

To the left of the beast stood several officials, no doubt from the Tarascon town hall, and two taller men in Nazi uniforms.

The Baron remembered what Bérard had told him about the Resistance and the protection old Steinert had given him. He took the photograph down and turned it over. Behind it, Bérard had written in a fine hand: Festival of the Tarasque, 1942.

He hung it back up, then looked around the room. He saw at once that it had been ransacked. The chest of drawers had been searched. There were two dog-eared breviaries, a copy of the Provençal edition of Frédéric Mistral's *Mireio*, a *Trésor du Félibrige* and a few books by Roumanille and Daudet. As he closed one of the drawers, his foot struck some object. He bent down and picked up an ancient tome from the floor: Agrippa's *La philosophie occulte ou la magie*. The preface stated that this edition dated from 1911, but that the text had been written in 1540. It was a work for an initiate.

He sat on the bed and thought for a moment. Someone had come to search the place and had been disturbed. What had he been looking for? A book about magic?

De Palma reconstructed the scenario: on seeing him arrive, the man had locked the door leading to the bedrooms and had escaped through the rear window, which was not very high. So he probably had not had enough time to find what he had come for.

De Palma searched both rooms meticulously, but found nothing unusual apart from that book about magic. He thought of the tomes he had seen in Steinert's office and tried to make connections, but he had to give up: he did not know enough about the occult arts to take this line of inquiry further.

He took down the framed photograph again and studied it closely: 1942, the festival of the Tarasque, with the Nazis in attendance . . . But it was just a picture like thousands of others.

All the same, Bérard had gone out of his way to tell him about that period. It had been the childhood of Steinert, the Boche's son, as they called him after the war. William's father had saved him from that shame, but his mother, Simone Maurel, had had her head shaved and her brother had been shot in the yard of the La Balme farmhouse.

He replaced the photograph and stepped back. The men and women posing beside the Tarasque were staring at the camera, their smiles fixed for posterity, not realising that they were covering themselves with shame by consorting with the enemy.

They all seemed to belong to a single family, gathered around a ridiculous monster. One of them had placed his hand on a Nazi officer's shoulder. Bérard was puffing out his chest.

De Palma was sure that it was all there, in that photograph, but he was incapable of decoding it. Only Bérard could do that. The south wind pushed the black smoke of the blaze towards Les Fontaines.

The sheep had returned to the yard and were bleating for their missing master. De Palma let them into the pen and tipped some bundles of hay into the mangers. As he closed the doors again, he realised that he was going to have to return to the scene of the fire on foot.

On the road from Maussane to Fontvieille, several fire engines were parked end-to-end on the kerb. Groups of firemen were talking, their faces running with sweat, their white hoods lowered round their necks.

When de Palma arrived, he saw that a gendarme officer was conferring with the commandant of the brigade.

"Good evening, Capitaine. I'm Michel de Palma from the Marseille P.J. Can I ask you a couple of questions?"

"Have you got your papers?"

He produced his tricolour card and brandished it under the gendarme's nose.

"So how can I help you?"

"I just wanted to know whether you consider this to be arson or not."

"It was arson," the head fireman replied. "No doubt about it."

The gendarme glared.

"Look," he said. "I want to know what you're doing here."

"I'm investigating. On my personal initiative."

"Initiative my arse."

"Listen, Monsieur, I have every reason to believe that this fire is connected with a case that we are investigating. Now, you can always refuse to talk, but I'll mention that fact in my official report. What do you say to that, Capitaine?"

"Piss off," the gendarme replied, and turned on his heels.

"He's had a hard day," the fireman said. "He's got his knickers in a twist."

The capitaine slammed the door of his 406.

"As I just told you, this was definitely arson. A classic technique: an insecticide spiral, a wick on the end, and petrol in a container. You light it then walk away. The spiral burns down, and the fire starts several hours later."

"I thought so," de Palma said. "If you find out anything else, could you give me a ring?"

"No problem," the fireman answered, taking the card that the Baron handed him.

Ingrid had put her arm through Bérard's and was walking him up and down the patio of La Balme, like a nurse.

"How is he?" the Baron asked.

"I've been expecting you for some time . . . I think he should be taken to hospital," she whispered. "He seems to have lost his reason."

Bérard's face was still just as listless. He looked as though he was staring into an unknown world, and had lost the spark that kept him so bright.

"Can you hear me, M. Bérard?"

The shepherd did not answer.

"I'm the police officer from the other day. Do you remember me?"

"I'm sure that he's in a state of shock, and should be hospitalised. I called the mayor of Eygalières. He told me that Bérard has no family, and that no-one there will have the time to deal with him until tomorrow."

"And you think it can't wait till then?"

"Not only think. I'm sure it can't! And you can't expect him to go home by himself in that condition."

An ambulance from Tarascon came to fetch Bérard at 8 p.m. Ingrid and the Baron decided to go with him.

At 10.32 p.m., the old shepherd died. The doctors at the hospital failed to make any real diagnosis. They just mentioned his great age and the psychological shock.

That evening, Ingrid took de Palma's hand and squeezed it tight. She put up her hair, which had tumbled down over her shoulders. Her profile stood out against the crude light of the neon lamps. Between her cheek and the lobe of her ear, there was a beauty spot shaped like an ace of spades.

At two in the morning, de Palma dropped Ingrid off at La Balme. He told her about the photograph he had seen on the shepherd's bedroom wall and realised how hard it would be to use it now that Bérard was dead.

He left the farmhouse, drove up towards Eygalières and parked Maistre's 205 by the entrance to an olive grove, where the road to Maussane met the sunken track that led to Les Fontaines. No-one could see the car from the main road.

He took a torch from the glove compartment, closed the car door quietly and headed off down the path, keeping the beam of light fixed on the ground.

To the right, the dark ranks of vines looked like ridges of coal in the shadows. There was a fragrance of ripe grapes and warm pine resin. Each footstep crunched in the sharp little stones along the

246

track. Suddenly, the Baron dived in among the trees and advanced into the darkness.

Les Fontaines farmhouse was about forty metres away, out in the open. He switched off the torch and felt his way forward in the moonlight. Five minutes later, he was crossing the yard.

The flock was calm. He slipped into the doorway, used his wire in the lock and went straight up to the bedrooms. Everything was eerily silent. He found the photograph, took it down and played his torch over the faces of the people around the Tarasque.

It was at that moment that he sensed he was not alone.

The photograph comes to life.
  The crowd surges with clamour.
  "La tarasco, la tarasco . . ."
  The crowd opens like a wound.
  Before the papier-mâché monster that is rushing towards it.
  "La tarasco, la tarasco . . ."
  Bérard is holding on to the monster's tail.
  He steers it with precise gestures.
  "La tarasco, la tarasco . . ."
  Bérard calls out: "Laïssa la passa . . . Laïssa la passa . . ."
  The knights join in: "La tarasco dou casteu . . . Lagadigadeu . . ."
  The children run away screaming.
  The monstrous mouth clacks its teeth.
  One of its knights finds a girl in the crowd.
  She is beautiful and dark, like a gypsy virgin.
  The beast's servant captures her.
  Two other knights force her up onto the animal's neck, chanting:
"Lagadigadeu . . ."
  The virgin roars and wriggles her bare legs.
  "La tarasco, la tarasco . . ."
  Bérard grips the beast's tail so as to make a seasaw movement.
  The entire crowd sings: "La tarasco, la tarasco . . ."
  The neck rises.
  The virgin bounces upwards.
  "La tarasco, la tarasco . . ."

She straddles the Tarasque.
Her thighs are half naked.
She grabs at the hideous monster's mane.
"La tarasco, la tarasco . . ."
People are laughing and giggling.
People are sparkling, their eyes lit up with pastis.
Glasses clink.
On the terrace of the Café du Centre, people are chatting in German.
In German and in Provençal.

De Palma spun round and pointed his torch at the window. A livid face stared at him from outside, its features carved out by the beam of light.

He drew his Bodyguard. The face vanished at once, and he heard the thud of a body landing on the ground. He ran to the window, opened it and played his torch over the farmyard. It was empty. In the pen, the sheep were jostling each other, barging against their mangers.

21.

The temperature had dropped. The muggy heat of the past few days was over. Breezes were blowing between the clumps of rushes, making wrinkles on the smooth waters.

Moracchini and the two forensic technicians jumped off the punt that Texeira had lent them. Just behind them, de Palma and Romero were sitting in an inflatable dinghy, making a first reconnaissance tour around the reed hut. At each push, Romero's pole splashed loudly in the water.

Richard, a forensics veteran, entered the hut first. He stayed there for half an hour before emerging carrying an armful of bags which he placed in a plastic crate.

"We'll put the seals on later, when we get back to the office," Romero said. "I'll just note down what they are."

"There's quite a lot of stuff," said Richard. "It looks rich."

"That's good news," Moracchini said, looking at the packets.

Richard had listed the contents of each sample and the number of the marker.

"I'm just going to take a couple more shots, then we'll go down into the hole."

"As you like."

De Palma and Romero examined the bank that ran around the hut. They didn't see much, apart from bird tracks in the sodden earth. They were all over the place.

But no traces of human feet.

They went back to the place where de Palma and Texeira had noticed, some days earlier, that the bottom of the marsh had been disturbed.

The water level had risen slightly and there was nothing usable. But the Baron still wanted to explore in the northerly direction given by the footprint he had found. He advanced through the reeds, but the vegetation grew so dense that he had to concede defeat: it was impossible to go this way.

"Let's see if Richard's finished with the hut. I want to be there when they go down into the hole."

Richard was finishing taking photographs. His colleague, Patrick, hadn't found much around the hut except for a few feathers.

"Michel's right. Someone has cleaned up. And I must say the guy has talent. You'd think they belonged to our team."

"Don't tempt fate."

"No really, it's as if they'd had police training."

Richard came out of the hut and put his camera down on its case. He wiped his forehead and took off his gloves.

"We'll wait for Michel, then down we go."

The smooth slope that led down to the underground room was about two metres long. The room itself measured two by three metres – high enough to stand up. It had been dug out of the earth, which was quite hard here, and then the floor had been crudely concreted over. The walls had simply been smoothed down, like cob.

It all formed a proper room, which, in its shape and conception, recalled the underground hides of the Viet Cong.

"It stinks down here," Moracchini said.

"Yeah," said Richard. "Shit and piss. Human, and not that old. It's like being in a lair. I'll put the CrimeScope over it, but at first sight there isn't much to find."

Moracchini pulled herself up out of the tunnel and sat down next to the Baron. She produced a packet of cigarettes and offered him one. He waved his left hand to say no.

"You've really stopped smoking, Michel?"

"It's bad for migraines. So I'm trying to stay stopped."

"What do you think about all this?"

"I don't understand a thing. We're finding a new piece of jigsaw every day. On the one hand, there's a lunatic wiping out mobsters one after the other. Then there are voices, here, in the arsehole of the world. Voices talking about the Tarasque in Provençal. Plus a billionaire who drowns in the same patch. Add to that the bastard who's trying to shoot me, then you have the entire picture. It you can find the least bit of logic in all this, then let me know."

"Maybe not everything's connected. O.K., they intersect, but they're not necessarily linked. It's happened before."

"I'd put it differently: there is a connection, but no logic. That's what makes it all so hard."

"And what's the connection?"

"The Tarasque."

She looked up at the ceiling.

"You really believe in all that?"

"I don't believe, I'm making an observation. Steinert was interested in the Tarasque, Christian Rey was a Knight of the Tarasque, so was Morini, who was even born in Tarascon. Plus he was a neighbour of Steinert and had an interest in the famous Downlands. I also found out that he knew Rey, who worked for him collecting his slot machines takings. Is that a link, or isn't it? Then there's the fact that the corpses are found in places or next to places that have something to do with the Tarasque."

"O.K., so this isn't all coincidence. Steinert was into the Tarasque. O.K. Everyone in Tarascon is into the Tarasque. Voices have been heard here. O.K. Steinert died nearby. Right. But what tells you that there's a link between the two bodies?"

"The adrenalin."

"What?"

"Adrenalin. This blasted adrenalin. It's in every body. Loads of it. Mattei is adamant. The people who died around here had the fright of their lives before they died. That's the only true, definite link. And it's a good scientific one. The rest is still hazy, I quite agree, and I must admit that it's been messing with my head for days now."

In the series of hold-ups involving Lornec and his gang, Marceau had signed most of the statements and almost all of the reports. Just a few of them bore the signature of Alexandre Vander, a capitaine in the B.R.B.

Maistre leafed through scores of pages trying to get to the essentials. There were statements by Lornec, Vandevalle and Santiago. The last two had been killed. Only Lornec was still of this world.

The reports were uninformative. Everyone had denied everything and had provided bogus alibis: Lornec was supposed to have been at his sister's place, Santiago had gone to see a friend in Nîmes, while Vandevalle claimed that he had been watching the semi-final of the European Cup.

According to the list of exhibits, some weapons had been seized at Lornec's house. But a SIG automatic pistol was not among them. Maistre flicked through Marceau's conclusions, closed the file with a sigh and returned it to the secretary of the records department.

On his way back to his office, he dropped in on the B.R.B. Vander was there, typing up some phone-tapped conversations made during an investigation into stolen cars.

"How are you, Vander?"

"Fine, except that I'm spending all my time tapping phones. Jesus, that's no job for a real policeman!"

"I need your help, Alex."

"Are you inviting me to join the *Sécurité publique*?"

"No, I want you to think back to the case of Lornec, Santiago and Vandevalle. They did hold-ups during the Nineties."

Vander rolled his chair backwards and placed his huge hands on his thighs.

"That was the crew in the north. And they go back quite a way. We never got any real results. Two of them have been iced since then. But as far as I know, Lornec is still alive."

"Did you work with Marceau at the time?"

"Jean-Claude? Yes, we collared them together, but the case fell through."

"Were there some guns?"

"Yes."

"Do you remember the models?"

"Hang on, I'll have to get back in the mood . . . There were some hunting rifles, maybe a couple of revolvers. I can't remember. That's quite a poser you've asked me."

"Try and remember! An unusual weapon."

"Just a second. Wasn't it then that we found something a bit odd . . ."

Vander gripped his chin and closed his eyes.

"A SIG. Yes, I think there was a SIG. You don't often find a piece like that."

"Even nowadays?"

"No, absolutely not . . . it's the only time I've seen robbers using a SIG. They generally prefer big pieces, like an 11.43, and not fine artillery like that."

"And you don't know what became of it?"

"It was taken as an official exhibit, of course! What do you imagine? Get out the file and you'll find it. But if you're looking for the actual piece, I'm not so sure. It may be downstairs in records or still at court."

Vander glanced at his computer screen, clicking twice on "Save".

"You've got one hell of a memory, Alex."

"Haven't I just! You know, sometimes I can recall the phone numbers of people we were tapping three years back. Just imagine that!"

"You've always impressed me."

Maistre slapped him on his bulky shoulder. Vander pretended to wince.

"Tell me, why are you interested in all that ancient history?"

"I just wanted to check something out in a case. We've got a gun that's talking, and it's the same one."

"That's odd. Because at the time, it had never been used. It was brand-new."

"Are you sure?"

"Definite. No doubt about it. You remember the guns that mobsters use. They're like miracles at Lourdes! Just ask Marceau, and you'll see!"

"Thank you, my man."

*

Maistre waited to be in his car and stuck in a jam on the north-bound motorway before telephoning the Baron.

"This business about the SIG is starting to look funny. Vander tells me that he saw the gun and that it was officially recorded, but there's nothing in the file. What's more he says that the weapon had never been used."

"It's more than just strange. Have you checked out the chronology?"

"What do you mean?"

"The date when the exhibits were sealed, and the date when they picked up the bullet."

"I don't have the date on me. I meant to get it."

"The exhibits have the wrong number, but the date must be the same as for the statements!"

"Sorry, Michel. I don't think as fast as you do."

"Check the day they found the casing in the old grocer's shop against the day when Marceau and Vander pulled in the three little sods. If it's before, then there's no problem. If it's afterwards, then you'll have hit the jackpot. And you know what I'm hoping . . ."

"I'll call you back in five minutes."

Maistre pushed his knees up to steady his steering wheel and opened the file. It took him just five minutes to work out that there was a period of no less than two years between the two dates. This revelation gave him the heaves.

"Bingo Michel! The bullet was discovered later . . ."

"What's your conclusion?"

"That the weapon disappeared from our nice safe haven. And that some people are so cocksure that they leave things as gross as this behind them."

"And after all that, it wound up in the hands of the man who tried to kill me."

"Three times."

"Exactly. Well done. But we need to know more than that. Have you mentioned this to anyone?"

"Yes, Vander."

"There's no risk with him. But don't tell anybody else. Otherwise, we could really end up in hot water."

"O.K."

"And then, we mustn't look for links when there aren't any, if you see what I mean."

"Right."

"It's Lornec who provides the link. Lornec, then Morini. Lornec was working for him right up till his death."

"How do you know that?"

"I'm psychic."

"Leave it out, Michel."

"All the same, Lornec has nothing to do with this. He was just unlucky enough to be in the right place at the right time. But I'm sure he's not behind it all. A piece arrives at headquarters or the court, then it leaves. That's the real problem. And there are only two people who could have done it."

"Stop it, Michel. You're giving me the shivers."

"Either a magistrate or an investigator."

"Marceau!"

"Obviously. The judge had no interest. Too dangerous for him, and anyway they know the ground. In those days, the magistrate was probably Alonso; she was certainly not the kind to give a gun back to a mobster with a letter of apology."

"Why Marceau?"

"I have no idea. To be honest, I'm at a loss. This comes as a bomb shell to me."

"But, Michel, just imagine, we've known him for ever! Really, I can't believe it."

"I realise that. But if I remember right, four or five years ago there was a big shortage of guns on the market. That might explain it. Marceau has always had money problems. The Inspector General's office has already bawled him out on a couple of other occasions for similar reasons."

"I hope we're wrong about this!"

"I'd like us to be, Le Gros. I really would."

The Baron took a long look at the map. He wanted to avoid the area of the fire so that no-one would spot him. To approach from the north, on the Fontvieille–Maussane axis, was impossible. The same applied to the direction from Eygalières. He would have to go from the south, even if that meant cutting through private property.

The map showed several paths through the forest. The hardest part would be avoiding any fire patrols or the local police. He would leave the car as far away as possible from the place he was aiming for.

In Marseille, he had rented a 4×4 Nissan Patrol. It had cost him a fortune and he wouldn't get it back.

He folded up the map and drove as far as Raphële, where he took the road that led straight to the Alpilles. A quarter of an hour later, he was going down a track that led away from the main road into the wilds.

He drove for some time between two rows of barbed wire, then the road climbed through the first wood of pines and stunted oaks. The 4×4 gobbled up the steep slope and started to pitch like a boat. Then the road began to snake along increasingly rugged hillsides.

In the distance, the plain of La Crau melded into the sky, the sea, and the marshlands of the Camargue. It was a huge, flat expanse, hazy in the evaporating dew.

When he passed the final bend, which formed a pass, the first charred trees appeared. The landscape changed suddenly. Nature had been blowtorched; dark stumps stuck up from the earth like charcoal claws. The limestone formed a few white patches that stood out from a blanket of soot.

From afar, the Baron glimpsed the white turret that he wanted to see. From here, it looked like a big limestone cube jutting up from the ground, with four pine trees at its feet, twisted by the agony of fire.

He parked the Nissan Patrol in the shelter of two rocks, then set off on foot, moving at a trot. He knew that there would soon be helicopter patrols in the sky, checking that the fire had not been rekindled.

Fifteen minutes later, he arrived at the base of the rock in a sweat and started his explorations.

Bérard had mentioned old stones, and he could more or less recall the topographical charts he had seen in Steinert's study.

Above all, he had the few translations that Ingrid had made for him. All of the notes he had read spoke of this "white tower", a clear landmark in the valley, and of the village that was supposed to have existed at its feet during the first century B.C. According to Ingrid, this was where the large sarcophagus which now stood in the farmyard of La Balme had originally come from.

De Palma knew that he was going to have to act quickly to determine if the land ravaged by the blaze still contained any Greco-Roman ruins which might have blocked, or at least delayed, certain real estate projects.

He soon found what the shepherd had called the old stones. The fire had in fact revealed what had previously been hidden by the forest's undergrowth: perfectly carved blocks of varied dimensions, half buried in the earth.

They formed something like a limestone wall that led away towards La Crau before disappearing into the ground.

Old Karl Steinert had been right. There had been dwellings here. The text translated by Ingrid read:

. . . *According to Canon Malvan (the digs date from the nineteenth century), in the place called "La Tour Blanche" there are houses and a line of large stones which could well have been a boundary wall, but this has not been proved.*

The houses are not organised according to an orthogonal plan, but instead scattered around in complex plots, all quite different from each other. Presumably the initial construction was relatively recent, dating back to 30 or 40 B.C., and it was a house arranged around a courtyard with a portico . . .

Towards the south, there was perhaps a large garden or a vast area set aside for games and displays. But its current state does not allow us to say more, because the rather dense vegetation precludes the possibility of taking samples . . .

The text then described several ceramics which had been found in the vicinity, some of which went back to the second century B.C.

. . . On a limestone block there is a carving of a quite unusual monster: half man and half crocodile, it looks strangely like the Tarasque of Tarascon . . . This stone is situated at map reference 26 N / 84 E . . .

. . . This discovery, or rather rediscovery, was made by Monsieur Bérard, a farmer living in Eygalières, who owns the land. Monsieur Bérard has told me on a number of occasions that this land used not to be wooded, at least not as it is today.

Furthermore, I have Monsieur Bérard's agreement to make this land available if ever a dig were to be carried out.

Steinert, 23 October 1938.

Brambles and shrubs covered the edges of the ancient walls. It was impossible to get near them without pruning them back. The Baron took several photographs. Most of the stones were swamped by tree roots and scorched bushes. He walked once more around the rock, but saw nothing else of interest. It was only when he gained a little height that he saw the lines in the ground: squares, rectangles, and a few curves.

He took another set of photographs and decided to return home.

As he got back into the Nissan, he suddenly realised why the wood had been burned down, and above all who had done it.

At that very moment, the whirr of a helicopter arose above the Alpilles and spread out across the plain of La Crau.

22.

Marceau came out of his house, at 10 rue des Halles, at 11.45. It was his fifth day on leave, and he still had a few details to sort out before going abroad. This year it was Mexico.

He bought his newspaper from the kiosk over the road then went to the Café du Globe, where he ordered a coffee, just as he had done every day since being posted to the commissariat in Tarascon.

Motionless, the man observed him, the 200 mm in his right hand. If all went according to plan, Marceau should emerge again in less than fifteen minutes, time enough to drink his coffee and perhaps order another, as he had done the day before yesterday. There'd be time to take one or two snapshots.

But, today, Marceau was not working. The man had known this since last night.

"The commandant is on leave. You can contact him at the end of the month," a young female voice had said on the telephone.

He approached the stationer's opposite the bar, and pretended to be choosing a postcard in case the cop decided to change direction and move faster, as he sometimes did for no apparent reason.

Marceau emerged after just one coffee. He took a single snapshot, face on. Then the cop turned left at once and, instead of going home, walked up rue de l'Hôtel de Ville towards the theatre.

The man followed him. He was certain that his prey could not escape him.

On arriving at the theatre, Marceau looked around in all directions. He did not see the man who had just had time to slip into a doorway. Marceau stood still for a while before producing a bunch of keys and going inside the building which contained William Steinert's office.

This was unexpected. But never mind, the man knew how to improvise. He gave himself a few minutes' thought, and finally made up his mind to wait. Marceau was a daunting target.

It took a good half an hour before the door opened once more and Marceau reappeared. They both walked off.

The man told himself that today was not the day. Definitely not. The day seemed to be full of surprises. Unless luck smiled at him.

And that is what happened.

Instead of going home, Marceau stopped to make some photocopies. Then he returned to put back the documents he had taken from Steinert's office. Another thirty minutes went by. Marceau came out and threw into the gutter what looked to the man to be a pair of gloves. It did not matter.

After that, for some unexpected reason, Marceau decided to take the ring road. When he had almost reached the place where the man's car was parked, its owner came up next to him.

Everything speeded up. The man pulled his automatic on Marceau and forced him to put his hands behind his back. Then he put the cuffs on and removed the gun from his target's belt.

Thirty minutes later, he was driving through the byways of the Camargue.

Moracchini was savouring the fruits of her work. In less than forty-eight hours, she had managed to obtain the D.N.A. results, using charm and the promise of more.

And the tests were talking: the traces of saliva found in the wounds of Christian Rey and Morini came from the same source.

The fragments of D.N.A. found in the reed hut matched Rey and Morini. In this case, it was the genetic records department that had made the match, as both of the mobsters already featured there among the police's bar codes and alleles.

The conclusion was that both of the gangsters had spent time in that hole. She could almost reconstruct their last days: no water, no food and total darkness. The forensic report was definite.

Furthermore, Mattei was equally definite: both bodies had been bitten by a pair of outsize jaws, such as those of a crocodile. He recommended comparing them with any animals that the two men might have come into contact with. This seemed surprising, but it was his department's expert opinion.

Moracchini and Romero had then gone to grill Lornec about his possible connections with Marceau. The gangster had told them nothing, but had seemed put out. Moracchini was never wrong about that. Nor was her team-mate.

Gouirand, the head of the Knights of the Tarasque, had been questioned twice. But both sessions had been disappointing. Moracchini had been expecting a lot, especially when she had discovered Gouirand's CV in police records: he had been caught twice red-handed during hold-ups with his pal Rey. The two men had been friends. But the trail stopped there. Still, she remained optimistic.

"We've made pretty good progress, haven't we?"

Through the bay window of the department's photocopying room, de Palma stared at the dome of La Major which was glowing in the sunlight.

"Yes, great! Now I think we should go through the names of the characters involved in property deals with S.O.D.E.G.I.M. around Maussane, Eygalières . . . even as far as the Camargue. I mean projects such as entertainment parks, leisure centres and so on."

"Is that all?"

Moracchini had put her hair up and pinned it with a ballpoint pen. She was wearing a light dress and strappy sandals.

"Yes my dear, we're going to have to get down to it!"

"We've got time."

"In the force, we never really have time."

"I know, but when it comes to the Steinert affair, no letter rogatory has been issued to allow us to take evidence. In fact, we're working on the fringes of legality. I could claim it to be a personal initiative, but I don't hold out much hope there."

"It's tricky. We're dealing with village secrets here, things that go on behind our backs that are unbeknown to us. It would be logical enough for Morini to take out Steinert so as to get hold of his land.

But then there's Bérard. Was it necessary to kill him, too? Why didn't Morini's henchmen go and see the old man and talk him into selling? It's all pretty weird, isn't it? And why not do the same with Steinert? I can only wonder if we'll ever find out."

Moracchini untied her hair and shook it back.

"So you think these are family secrets?"

"Not only that! Do you have Gouirand's phone number?"

"Yes."

"Call him and ask if he knew Morini."

Moracchini picked up her mobile and telephoned Gouirand. She spent less than a minute on the telephone, but, from the expression on her face, he guessed that he had been spot on: Morini had been a Knight of the Tarasque in the 1980s, at the same time as Rey.

Marc Gouirand was standing in front of the town hall, cleaning the windscreen of the mayor's Safrane. He was wearing dark glasses, cotton trousers and a flowery shirt that opened to reveal his chest. Moracchini had been watching him for some time, sitting over a coffee in the Bar du Centre.

When he put down the chamois, she got to her feet and went over to him.

"Monsieur Gouirand, do you recognise me? I'm Anne Moracchini, from the Marseille P.J."

The head of the Tarascaires straightened and looked her up and down.

"I wanted to ask you a few questions about the death of Christian Rey."

"Now?"

"If it's possible."

Gouirand glanced at his watch.

"The mayor's still in a meeting. It should take about another three quarters of an hour. Is that enough?"

"It's up to you to make yourself available to the police, sir, and not the other way round. Are we clear?"

Gouirand's smile vanished and he lowered his gaze.

"Perhaps you'd rather come to the station in Marseille with me?"

"No, no, it's alright!"

"Fine, so tell me, when exactly did you first meet Rey?"

"That's easy: in primary school. We'd known each other as long as I can remember."

She pretended to note this down.

"And what about Morini?"

"The same goes for him. We were all the same age."

"You know he's dead?"

Gouirand simply nodded before giving the windscreen of the Safrane another wipe with the sponge.

"And they both used to be Knights of the Tarasque, like you?"

"Yes, we all started together."

"Then what happened?"

"I don't really know. After that, we all went our separate ways. They became crooks, and I got a job at the town hall."

She stared up at the building: it was very old, made of dressed stone that dated back to the Middle Ages, and covered with mullions, diamond-shaped stained-glass windows and extravagant sculptures.

"And have you been working here long?"

"Since 1987."

"Can I ask you what you do exactly?"

"I'm the mayor's chauffeur."

"I know that, but I've also heard that you organise the distribution of election posters and can use your fists a bit."

Gouirand shrugged. She glanced at the back seat of the Safrane and saw the handle of a blackjack sticking out of the pocket of an evening jacket.

"What's the blackjack for, opening bottles?"

"It's just in case the mayor gets into danger."

"So you're also his bodyguard?"

"Not really, but you never know."

"I think you'll be called in for questioning in a few days' time. So stay in Tarascon, O.K.?"

"Very well, Madame."

"De Palma, I'm a police officer."

263

The blonde at the door of Chandeler & Associés blinked, and her lips formed a pout.

"Do you have an appointment?" she said at last, observing the visitor over her glasses.

"Is Maître Chandeler seeing a client?"

"No, I mean yes . . ."

De Palma opened the door, the secretary followed him in.

"Sir, this gentleman . . ."

"That's alright, that's alright . . . you can leave us. I know M. de Palma."

She had barely closed the double doors when she heard a slap and a cry resound behind her.

Chandeler was on his knees, his spectacles in his hands. He paused for a moment, sniffed back the blood that was pouring from his nose, and got to his feet. The Baron stepped back and gave him a kick in the guts that bent him in two.

Chandeler rolled over before standing up again. He was about to call out when he noticed with terror that the Baron was holding a gun on him. A handsome Cobra with a cold, gleaming barrel, just two metres away from him.

"Sit down, you piece of shit."

Chandeler raised his hands in a gesture of appeasement and walked over to his chair.

"No, not there, here," de Palma barked, pointing at the seat intended for clients.

"Think about what you're doing, Commandant. You've already committed an action that will have serious consequences for you. Don't make matters worse."

The Baron went over to Chandeler and scrutinised his adversary's every tic. When he came in reach of the lawyer he let fly a punch that knocked his glasses back off.

"You're going to pay for that."

"You know that the old shepherd's dead?"

"I don't know what you're . . ."

Another slap shot out.

"Listen to me. We've got everything we need on you. We've even got a photo of you in Bérard's place with your pal Morini."

264

Chandeler doubled over.

"So either you start singing or I'll put the word out that I roughed you up a bit and you gave up all the others. To look at you now, I reckon that they'll all believe me."

"I'm only a cog in the machine."

"And a Knight too, as I see."

"Just a cog. There are big interests at stake, very big . . ."

"A Knight who is also an intellectual!"

"They're . . . it's a financial group . . . with . . ."

The Baron came over to him. He hunched up even more.

"A group of people with . . ."

"With Morini among them."

"Yes, that's right."

"You know that you're starting to get on my tits, telling me things I know already!"

The telephone rang.

"Answer and tell your secretary to go home. Anyway, it's time."

Chandeler did so, while drying the blood that was dripping from the corner of his mouth.

"O.K., let's try again. Morini isn't a scoop. I hope you've got something better . . ."

The Baron decided to play a card he wasn't sure of. He made a gesture, a simple gesture: he ran his index finger over his belly as though he was cutting through his torso with an imaginary weapon.

Chandeler opened his eyes wide and started to tremble all over.

"The problem is they don't want to sell, and in the region it's the only place where such a project can be carried out."

"What's all this nonsense? You can build a park wherever you want."

"Check out who owns all the land around the site, and you'll understand."

"Names, Chandeler, I want names . . . You know them, they're your clients."

"If I tell you, I'm a dead man."

The Baron grinned.

"And also if you don't," he half murmured.

"Why not do a deal . . ."

"A man has just died. He has to be avenged."

"O.K., there are some people from around here, then some Italians and Americans . . ."

"I want a list."

Chandeler went over to his desk, opened a file and handed a sheet of paper to de Palma.

"It's all there," he said, looking away.

"You see, where there's a will . . ."

He looked at the list of names. Morini's was not on it, but he recognised one or two cronies amenable to laundering his money.

"I just hope that the beast doesn't eat you, too!"

"I too have received the mark."

The Baron nodded as though he knew what he was talking about.

"Show me," he said.

Chandeler stared at the Baron with his eyebrows raised. He slowly opened a desk drawer and removed a plain white feather. It was just like the one de Palma had seen in Steinert's office.

"Who else received this mark?"

"We all have."

"All the rich bastards on your list?"

"Yes, that's right."

"Pray to the god of swine like you that the police you despise get him before he gets you."

The Baron backed away to the door, opened it and left.

Maistre was standing bolt upright facing the sea. It looked as though he were savouring infinity. After a while, he came alive again and poured red wine into a plastic cup.

"I've got the truth at last . . . or at least, part of it."

Maistre did not turn round. He kept his eyes fixed on the horizon which was still red with the fury of the sun. The siren of a roll-on roll-off boomed in the terminal of Mourepiane.

"If I'm not mistaken, the whole business was actually quite banal."

"That's often the way it goes, Baron. You think you're up against exceptional villains who are pulling off incredible capers, and

266

generally you end up with a couple of pricks not worth getting up in the morning for."

Maistre looked at his watch. Moracchini appeared at the end of the patio. She was wearing a linen dress that revealed her shoulders and slender ankles. She took off her sandals and walked barefoot across the limestone tiles.

"Delpiano already knows that you've given Chandeler a pull."

"Why, are they in the same chapel, I mean lodge?"

"He's just told me about it on the phone. He wants your hide, Michel. I have no idea why he's got it in for you so much, but it scares me."

She sat down just beside him. De Palma sensed his body turn electric from the stealthy contact with her dress. He quickly stood up, removing the sheet of paper Chandeler had given him from the rear pocket of his jeans. Moracchini took it and read it carefully.

"There are some people I know in here!"

"Yes, and some others you don't. It doesn't matter! But they all have a point in common."

"What's that?"

"Someone has sent them a feather like this."

"And what does it mean?"

"Not much for the moment, except that when I mentioned bodies that had been sliced in half to Chandeler, he practically shat himself."

Maistre picked up the paper and stared at the list.

"Jesus, there are two or three here that the financial brigade would like to nab: Grimaud, Landrace, Rossi . . . fuck me!"

"They're the ones who wanted to buy up Steinert's land, the patch they didn't want to sell, the famous Downlands. It belonged to his father, and Bérard presumably sold it to him before the war."

"You mean the woods that burned down yesterday?"

"That's right. But they weren't involved in the arson."

"Who was it then?"

"Bérard himself. He wanted everyone to know that there are Greco-Roman ruins in the forest so that no-one could build anything there."

Moracchini was rubbing her forearms as if she was cold.

"And you think that's why they killed Steinert?"

"It might look that way, but I don't think so. The problem is that I'm not sure we'll ever get to the bottom of this business. Unless we get a stroke of good luck at last."

Maistre lit a cigarette and drew on it nervously.

"There's something I don't understand," he said. "These people have got enough dosh to build their damned park where they want."

"You're right, Jean-Louis. But I think there are one or two things we're still missing. Around here, it was just about the only viable site. There are lots of tourists, and everyone had something to gain. The people selling the land could name their price. A plot where you can get planning permission in this Bermuda Triangle is worth a fortune: as much as 4,000 euros per square metre! Did you realise that?"

"Maybe so, but there's still the coast and everything. I mean, it's the back of beyond out there."

"I reckon that there's subsidy on offer, but above all it was a group of guys who'd known each other since childhood. A sort of clan. Morini and Rey were old pals!"

"Yes, but one was the godfather and the other the stooge!"

"You're right, Le Gros. We've now got to uncover their connections with the others."

Maistre stood up and got out two bottles of wine. He put three glasses on the table and uncorked the first bottle. The roll-on roll-off which was sailing out of Mourepiane gave another blast of its siren.

"Some guys who are rolling in it get rid of a troublesome billionaire. That works. Especially when you see the names on the list. But still you say that it's something else!"

"Yes, something else."

23.

Moracchini nearly spun off the road to avoid hitting a tourist. The Xsara swerved to the left and collided with the pavement. Romero laid his hands on the dashboard.

"Jesus, Anne, watch out. I've got kids, you know."

"Put the lamp and siren on the roof. We'll be more visible."

In front of the castle of Tarascon, she took the wrong turning, going towards the church instead of the ring road. She reversed back, then shot off the wrong way along the outside lane.

Just after the castle, a traffic cop appeared in the middle of the road and pointed left, towards the car park by the banks of the Rhône.

She parked the Xsara just in front of the security cordon.

"Ah, there you are, Moracchini. Jesus, what a mess. And you knew him, I think?"

Larousse's face was creased, his eyes almost hanging from their sockets.

"I'm sorry, I don't know the identity of the . . ."

"It's Marceau."

"What?"

"He's down there, on the rocks. He's like the others. It's . . . it's hideous."

She climbed down to the edge of the river, walked among the clumps of grass that grew just beside the water, then halted. Larousse pointed in the direction of the castle.

"He's there, can you see him?"

"Yes, quite clearly. Now get rid of those idiots who're trampling around all over the place. The forensics team will be here in a minute."

Larousse turned on his heels without replying. He made do with yelling at some onlookers.

"Daniel, call de Palma again. Tell him to get out here. We need him. Too bad if that prick Delpiano kicks up shit, we'll find an excuse. He and Marceau were friends, I think."

"O.K., I'll deal with it."

"Then we'll have to go and search his place. At once. In two minutes' time, I want there to be three officers turning over his house."

Marceau had been laid at the foot of the ramparts, on the rock often used by the kids of Tarascon as a diving board. It was a fisherman who had discovered him. His first thought was that it was someone who had fallen from the ramparts.

"Anne? Michel here. I'm not going out there. It's too late, anyway . . ."

"Up to you."

"I'm sorry, Anne, but it'll take me an hour to drive there. Do you see?"

She hung up and took a good look at the people who were watching what was going on. Way up in the ramparts, over 80 metres from the ground, there were several faces framed in the crenellations.

She noticed a brigadier from the local police section and asked him for some binoculars. He disappeared among the horde of police cars, then came back with a pair of 8×30s. She aimed them at the castle and made out some tourist heads, all of them fair, probably English or Dutch, out on a family excursion. Then she panned left and saw three little boys leaning over the wall and gesturing at the corpse.

"And their parents leave them to it," she said to herself.

She scanned along the walls of King René's Castle. There was no trace of blood or anything out of the ordinary. At last she reached Marceau's body, which shone in the sunshine like a pool of nail varnish.

"The first time, it was in front of the Tarasque," she muttered to herself. "The second in the crypt of Saint Martha, and now on this rock."

She was about to lower the binoculars, when a taller figure appeared behind the boys. She peered upwards and saw a man with a cap on his head. The outline remained for some time in her field of vision. Then she had the feeling that their eyes met. The figure disappeared, all at once.

She immediately grabbed Romero by the arm and whispered to him:

"There's a man up there acting suspiciously. I don't know if I'm imagining things or what, but I think we should take a look. And be quick about it."

"O.K., but no running otherwise he'll spot us."

In less than two minutes, they were both standing in front of the castle's postern. As they went through the door, Moracchini flashed her card at the janitor.

"Close the entrance and let nobody out, except for children."

The local official, who was bulky and half asleep, struck a pose of importance and carried out the order without a word.

"How many stairways lead up to the roof?"

"Today just one. The other one's closed."

She drew her Manurhin and entered the castle courtyard.

A few tourists stared at her and backed off whispering when they saw a revolver's black steel in the policewoman's hand. She stared at them one after the other. Mentally she compared each face and form with the capped silhouette on the ramparts. None of the men in the castle courtyard matched the image she had engraved on her memory a few minutes before.

Romero took up position on the far side of the courtyard and scrutinised the arrow slits and windows around him.

Some tourists in shorts and sandals emerged from the Gothic staircase, clearly surprised to see an armed man and woman looking at them. It was the family that Moracchini had spotted earlier, with the three little boys who had been leaning over the battlements.

Romero asked them if there was anybody left at the top, but no-one understood what he was saying. He moved them out of the courtyard and told the doorkeeper to hold on to them while they searched the castle.

"Shit, Anne, we don't have a radio."

"Too bad. We can't waste any time. Let's go up."

She dived into the half-lit stairwell, climbing fast and trying not to let her Converse shoes clack against the cold stone.

After two L turns to the right, the steps came out in a vast room hung with tapestries. Romero entered behind Moracchini, then ran across to the far side, before entering a second room and emerging again at once. To her right, Moracchini noticed a wooden arrow against the wall, indicating the route for the visitors in three different languages.

A staircase as broad as the first led to another room as vast as the previous one, but better lit. A tourist was reading an information display inside it. She aimed her gun at him, and he turned pale. He put his hands up and stammered something in German. She motioned to him to leave by the stairs. He did not need telling twice, but walked crabwise as far as the door without taking his eyes off the threatening gun.

A second arrow pointed to the upper floors of the castle. Moracchini saw that the staircase was a spiral one, narrower than the others. A real rat trap. She gestured to Romero to cover her, before starting upwards as quietly as possible, two steps at a time. He followed a metre behind.

The roof was deserted. She headed for the place where she had spotted the man in the cap and leaned out over the void. It certainly was the best vantage point for observing what was going on below. She could see the two forensic scientists who were busying them-selves around Marceau's body and, beside them on the riverbank, Larousse gesticulating wildly as he talked into his telephone.

Meanwhile, Romero was pacing around the roof.

"We've missed him, Anne. He must have gone down at top speed and we missed him."

"Shit, shit and shit!"

"Can you describe him?"

"He was quite tall, with a white cap over his eyes. Like half the population of this fucking town."

She leaned on the ramparts, trying to think out a strategy. Beneath her feet, the Rhône flowed peacefully on towards the delta of the Camargue. Its huge green curve seemed almost motionless in its bed.

"Let's go down and take a longer look. Then we'll see."

The room on the second floor told them nothing, nor did the next one down. King René's Castle was completely deserted. As they went down the second staircase, Romero stopped dead. He had heard something.

"Did you hear that?"

Moracchini shook her head.

A second rattle reached them. It came either from below them or from behind one of the walls. The two officers dashed down the stairs and stopped at the place where the stairs gave on to the court-yard, through a doorway carved with stone flowers.

More banging echoed through the silence of the castle.

"It's that way," Moracchini said. "On the river side."

They emerged from the stairwell and headed towards the possible source of the noise. At first, all was silent, then after twenty seconds that seemed like an eternity, a song rang out:

"*Lagadigadeu, la tarasco, lagadigadeu . . .*"

The voice was imprisoned inside a room of the castle. But it was impossible to say exactly where it might be coming from. Its owner must be somewhere behind the walls, in a place that communicated with the outside world by some such means as an arrow slit or narrow door.

"*Laïssa passa la vieio masco . . . Laïssa passa que vaï dansa . . .*"

There was a long silence. And then, plainly from further away:

"*La tarasco dou casteu, la tarasco dou casteu . . .*"

Moracchini searched in all directions. She almost glued her ear against the walls. On his side, Romero went back up to the large room on the first floor and leaned out of one of the windows. He saw nothing but the Rhône and, over to his right, Marceau's body drying in the sun. The voice had gone for good.

After twenty hours' work, the technicians came back with over two hundred samples. From some of these, the scientists sometimes removed a good twenty different specimens. In all, over eight hundred items were sent to the biology laboratory at Nantes.

The next day's *Provence* was headlined: 'Police Officer Brutally Murdered'. The national papers picked up the A.F.P. reports and added their own not always welcome comments. The Provence of Mistral was shown in a variety of unflattering lights. Not a single article refrained from mentioning Tartarin and the Tarasque. It was the headline story early in August. It lasted ten days, and no longer.

In mid-August, the first forensic results arrived on the desks of the police and of Marie-Paule Garcia, the investigating magistrate. The scientists had found dozens of unknown D.N.A. traces, but the only one that made any sense was the sample taken from Marceau's wounds, which matched those taken from Rey and Morini.

Moracchini, Romero and the other officers who had searched Marceau's house found photocopies of documents, letters, and plans from archaeological digs, some of them in German. Moracchini at once made the connection with the papers de Palma had seen in Steinert's office. She decided to place them under seal while waiting to see what else would turn up.

On Marceau's bedside table, next to the telephone, the police found an address book with the contact details of regional politicians and businessmen. In the wardrobe they collected another, thicker note-book with names and numbers. Once all of this information had been put together, what emerged was a huge network of illegal gambling machines organised by Marceau and Christian Rey on behalf of Morini. The policeman covered up the racket and got twenty per cent of the profits. Rey took thirty and Morini fifty, protec-tion included. This told potential competitors: "Lay off Le Grand's slot machines." Now that the notice was out of date, the one-arm bandit war was going to start all over again. The B.R.B. and illegal gambling boys were going to have their hands full.

But the most interesting discovery was made during the subse-quent search of Marceau's private parking lot. Several handguns turned up: two CZs, two Colt .45s and a 9 mm Beretta. Hidden above the control box for the opening mechanism of the garage door, they also found a box of 9 mm shells wrapped up in a chequered towel and a full SIG 29 clip. The gun itself was nowhere to be found.

The Timone forensics unit released Marceau's body after two weeks, like a beast letting go of its prey after feeding on it.

The Baron and Maistre attended the funeral alongside Marceau's elderly aunt. No-one else came. Their former team-mate was incinerated at the Tarascon crematorium at 9 o'clock on a Thursday morning.

As he watched the coffin disappear into the mouth of the furnace, Maistre crossed himself.

"I can still see him as he was the first time we met in Paris. He was looking for Boyer's office. He wasn't a bad guy."

"He could have killed me but didn't," the Baron said as he turned away.

Isabelle Mercier's name was not spoken.

Twenty days after the discovery at Tarascon Castle, things still stood as they were. The links between Rey, Morini and Marceau were known at last.

Moracchini had examined the police officer's career in great detail, and certain grey areas appeared, particularly in financial terms. Marceau had been fixing up a ruined family house in Baux-de-Provence, a property inherited from his mother. The work had cost around a million francs, a sum that was far beyond his means.

She noticed once again that their investigations were centred inside a perimeter that stretched between Baux and Mouries and between Eygalières and Maussane.

For a few days, the Baron distanced himself from their inquiries and from everybody else. He spent his days fishing, either on the burning pebbles of the Baie des Singes, just opposite Maïre, or at the far end of the snaking tarmac of Les Goudes, or else around the creeks of Morgiou and En Vau, snug in a hired Zodiac inflatable dinghy, alone and tiny on the waves that washed over the limestone's fantastic shapes.

The Baron had chosen this retreat so as to withdraw into himself, to delve inside his soul; his only companions in sadness were the great opera singers in the headphones of his Walkman: Renata Tebaldi, Carlo Bergonzi, Mario del Monaco, Montserrat Caballé . . . in well-worn versions of *Aïda, Turandot* and *I Pagliacci*. Real Italian opera full of heavy emotions and flawless melodies. His personal favourites, as a child of the sun.

He had not caught much, either on the languid sea or in the music of his fathers.

He only understood when he changed to Wagner and Strauss, to Melchior, Varnay, Rysanek and Flagstad. When he folded away his rods and returned the Zodiac. His other half was far away. For weeks now, Isabelle Mercier had not called on him from the far side of the known world.

Ingrid Steinert had gone back to Germany for an indefinite stay. Settling her inheritance from her husband was causing her endless problems. She was now the owner of a large stake in Klug-Steinert Metal, which raised the hackles of many of her in-laws. She telephoned the Baron several times. Late in the evening, after spending endless hours in the offices of lawyers and notaries in the four corners of Germany.

When de Palma emerged from his torpor, he immersed himself in books about the German occupation of Provence. He spent whole days at the Méjanes library in Aix-en-Provence, amid students about to retake failed exams in September, soaking up dissertations, theses and symposium papers.

Not once did he see the name of Steinert appear. On the other hand he learned how many of the region's powerful families had consorted themselves with the occupiers after 1942, the year of William Steinert's birth. But most of the studies remained extremely discreet about the names of those involved and the fortunes amassed during that period.

It was when he opened a dissertation about the region of Tarascon entitled *L'épuration en Provence: 1944–1946* that the Baron came across the names of Steinert and Maurel. The account had been written in 1966 by a Gilbert Sicard, and in his preface the author warned the reader that he would cite no names of witnesses or victims without the express permission of those concerned or of their families.

...In the months that followed the liberation of Provence, between August 1944 and January 1945, old scores were settled in the region of Les Baux, and in particular in Maussane and Eygalières.

According to the witnesses we have questioned, the most sordid event took place at a farmhouse called La Balme, where Emile, the eldest son of the Maurel family, was shot dead and his sister Simone had her head shaved...Yet from various statements it would appear that the Maurel family had never collaborated with the occupiers and that this was in fact a settling of differences between powerful inhabitants of the region, fed by old rivalries and jealousy...Etienne, Emile's younger brother, had even been part of the Vincent Group, a particularly active resistance network commanded by a farmer in Eygalières named Eugène Bérard.

Henri Bayle, the head of the F.F.I. in Tarascon, claimed that none of his men was mixed up in this affair. At least, this is what emerges from the statement he made to the gendarmerie of Tarascon during the investigations into the case that were carried out in 1952, after a complaint had been lodged by Simone Maurel's brother, Etienne...As often happened, the case was quickly closed and no charges were made. Cited in the statements and Maurel's accusation are the names of the region's most powerful landowners. Henri Bayle declared that he had never heard it said that resistance fighters had shot Emile Maurel. This is confirmed by the records of the F.F.I...

According to oral testimony, Simone Maurel's head was shaved in the village square of Eygalières, where she was then exposed to public condemnation. It is easy to imagine the degree of humiliation experienced by a young woman whom people spat upon (statement of a man who witnessed the scene)...

She was accused of having had a liaison with a German, a certain Karl Steinert, who was neither an army officer nor in the police . . . According to the same oral sources, nothing was proved, but it seems that Simone Maurel was judged by a kangaroo court made up of the same people who had had her brother shot . . .

De Palma made a few notes on his pad. At the foot of the page, he wrote in capital letters: REVENGE.

France Telecom came up with three Gilbert Sicards, one in Fontvieille, one in Arles and one in Tarascon. De Palma tried them all. The first two were dead ends. When he dialled the Tarascon number, he got an answering machine which informed him that Gilbert Sicard would be away until the beginning of September. He left a message.

He picked up Bérard's photo and examined it closely. Once again, he had the impression that a door was slowly closing. That hope was forbidden.

It was now late August.

The first of a new wave of gangland killings occurred in the centre of Aix: nine 11.43 bullets took the life of François Lomini, one of Morini's lieutenants. Three days later, it was the turn of Jérôme Lornec, shot down in front of the 421, the nightclub Morini had put him in charge of.

Jean-Luc Casetti was taken out by three bursts from an Uzi in a bar on avenue de la République, over a glass of pastis.

Gangland abhors a vacuum.

24.

It had been raining all morning. The flagstones leading to Saint-Blaise's church were gleaming with water and misery. It was twenty-two years to the day since de Palma had last been there.

And some years since he had returned to Paris.

He could still picture the white coffin carried by the undertaker's assistants from Porte de Bagnolet, and the hundreds of bouquets of flowers and naïve drawings from the neighbourhood children.

That day, he had parked his service car, an unmarked R8, in rue des Prairies. Maistre and Marceau were with him, stiff in their too-tight dark suits. Maistre's straight black hair fell down over the collar of his shirt, giving him the look of a romantic Napoleon. Marceau was curly-headed, his adolescent features marked with sadness and disgust.

De Palma walked slowly up the steps of Saint-Blaise's church then stopped in front of the door. He did not enter. A force held him outside. He angled to the left, and climbed the few steps that led to the local graveyard. An old woman was filling a green plastic watering can from a tap in the central alleyway.

He passed in front of Brasillach the Collaborator's tomb and was amazed to find it in perfect condition. Isabelle's sepulchre lay one lot further on. Some fresh flowers had been laid there, presumably that very morning. There was a plaque with the photo of the girl. She was smiling.

Beside her name, there were also the names of her parents: her father who had died eight years later, and her mother a year after that.

He put down the bunch of violets that he had bought at the

florist's on rue Belgrand. He wanted to say a prayer, but he did not know any for the dead. The old woman came over to him.

"Did you know her?"

"Yes, I did."

"She was a pretty little thing, wasn't she?"

De Palma bent down and straightened the violets, which had slipped down onto the granite.

"She always winked back when people looked at her," he said, standing up. "A little smile in the corner of her mouth and a wink."

"Are you a family member?"

"You could say that."

A few drops of rain splashed on the tombstone, making a dry slapping sound. De Palma looked up. Heavy clouds were advancing from the east ring road towards Porte de Bagnolet.

"And the police never caught the one who did it!"

"No, never."

"If you want my opinion, they can't have looked very hard."

"Do you think so?"

"Definitely."

"Maybe you're right."

"Are you really a family member?"

"No, not really."

"I see."

"Why do you ask?"

"Because that's where they should have looked. In her family."

In a flash, de Palma pictured again the long nights spent going through statements. Everything had gone through the mill. The slightest testimony. The smallest clue. All the forensic evidence had been gathered, but in those days the police scientists knew nothing about biological sampling.

"You're not from around here, are you?"

"No, I'm from Marseille."

"I didn't know they knew people from Marseille."

"You don't always know everything about everybody."

His face clouded over, and she realised that she was intruding. He was thinking about Marceau, his old team-mate in Paris who had ended up in trouble. He did not blame him. He alone knew that Marceau had been a decent man right up till the end, despite the corruption, despite the tortured soul. Marceau had been an excellent marksman; he had won prizes. He could have killed de Palma three times. But he had not done so, no doubt in memory of Isabelle and this tragedy which had bound them together for ever.

De Palma took a long look at Isabelle's face stuck there on the marble of her grave. She looked so like Ingrid that he felt shaken to his very roots. Isabelle and Ingrid, years apart. Almost a lifetime.

A violent pain shot across his forehead and spread out in his skull. He massaged his temples until the migraine abated.

Because that's where they should have looked. In her family. He repeated the sentence to himself several times.

The old woman had disappeared at the far side of the cemetery, towards rue des Prairies.

He turned on his heels and walked back down rue de Bagnolet.

At the Saint-Michel terminus, a few steps away from police headquarters, he ordered a beer and telephoned Judge Brivet. A secretary answered and told him to call back. He gave her his number, name and rank. She promised to pass on his message.

Nowadays, Gilbert Brivet worked in the financial section in Paris. Twenty years before he had had the duty – a crushing one for a young magistrate – of dealing with the Mercier investigation. De Palma wanted to have a word with him, one old hand to another. Brivet must have almost reached retirement age.

The Baron had just ordered a second beer when his mobile rang.

"Michel? Gilbert here. How are you?"

"Fine, fine, and you?"

"Up to my neck in it as usual. But I can't complain. Can we meet?"

"That's why I called you."

"Jesus, Michel, it's good to hear from you!"

"Same here."

"Let's meet up at Les Chauffeurs, how about that?"

"It still exists?"

"Etienne's gone. He doesn't run the restaurant any more, but it's still really nice. And, this evening, there shouldn't be too many people."

Gilbert Brivet still looked like a choirboy. At over fifty, he had kept his youthful features despite his greying hair and life's little dramas. He was neither married nor divorced: no woman would stay with this eternal adolescent caught in the corridors of power.

From his student past, he had retained the manner of a scholar who knows everything about anything, capable of listing all the records he had ever listened to and the hundred of detective novels he had devoured. Although the hard knocks of destiny had given him a rather weatherbeaten appearance, which only added to his charm. As a magistrate he was fearsome and feared, one of the few who could make the political microcosm tremble with his accusations and sly leaks to the press.

When the Baron appeared in the doorway of Les Chauffeurs, Brivet stood up, almost knocking over the bottle of red wine in front of him.

"Well, well, well, Michel. What a turn-up!"

"Good evening, Judge."

Brivet still had the same deep comma-shaped furrow that divided his forehead in half when he was happy or worried.

"While I was waiting, I did my sums. The two of us go back nearly twenty-five years now."

"The Americans were leaving Vietnam. I remember it as if it was yesterday. With Maistre, we introduced you to a certain Marcel Gouffé. It was 8.45 and the end of his time in custody. He had admitted everything, the murder of his wife and the rest. During his questioning, we also watched shots of the chopper over the American embassy in Saigon. Yes, just like yesterday, my man!"

"Back then, you, Maistre and Marceau were a team of aces. What's become of them?"

"You haven't heard?"

"Heard what?"

"Marceau is dead."

"Shit. But how was I supposed to know?"

"It was in all the papers. A month ago."

"Fuck. I was on holiday in Africa."

"It wasn't a happy end . . ."

The Baron took a menu from their waiter.

"He'd gone wrong, you know. He was up to his ears in dodgy deals. Not a pretty story."

"Jesus fucking Christ!"

"Yes, quite. They killed him. But not in a decent way. Very indecent, in fact."

Gilbert Brivet laid his pale eyes on the Baron, who was studying the menu. He weighed him up, as though trying to gauge the force of the knocks that his friend had received and those he had returned.

"What you're telling me is awful, Michel. He often used to come and see me. In fact, every time he came through Paris. He always called and we would meet up."

"He shot at me."

"What?"

"Three times. He shot at me three times."

The Baron pronounced this last sentence rather like a suspect in custody, releasing some of the guilt that was weighing down on him.

"Hang on there, you're telling me that Jean-Claude Marceau took a shot at you . . . But . . ."

"You heard right."

"Fuck."

The Baron ordered a veal cutlet in a cream sauce with fries, just as he had done during all his years with the Paris police. He raised his eyes, and could almost see Marceau and Maistre in front of him. Marceau with his long locks and moustache like the singer Georges Moustaki, his idol at the time. Marceau who had been a socialist despite it all, a master at stake-outs, and capable of orchestrating an interrogation as if it was a dialogue scripted by Godard.

"It's odd to see you again like this, Michel. You turn up out of the blue, with your news of death . . . It makes me . . ."

Brivet's eyes misted over with misery and nostalgia. He trembled on his seat, like a young tree bracing its strongest branches against the north wind.

"But now you're with the finance squad, you're out of all that!"

"Yes, I am. But sometimes I miss the old days. I'm sorry we don't see more of each other."

"That's my fault. I got married. Then I wanted to forget about Paris and my old life."

"I think we've all been running away from the same thing."

De Palma ordered two pastis.

"I visited her grave this afternoon."

Brivet placed his elbows on the table and laid his chin on his interlaced fingers.

"And I wondered if . . ."

"Stop, Michel. There's no point going back over that now. Life just played us one of its rotten tricks that evening. On you, Maistre, Marceau and me. And as rotten tricks go . . ."

Brivet closed his eyes.

"If you only knew how many times I've played that thing over in my mind: usually it's not me who's on duty that night, usually I don't deal with cases like that. Jesus, it's the first time, and I'm too young. And instead of calling in an old hand to help me out, I decide to play magistrate . . ."

He gulped his pastis, put his glass on the table and spun the ice around for a moment.

"That's all you can say about the matter. We were there when we should have been somewhere else."

"True. But the worst of it is that after that – well I've seen my share of cold meat, believe me. But, I don't know why, I've never been able to get her out of my head."

The Baron trained his eye on his friend, who kept his own eyes fixed on the ice cubes he was still swirling in his glass.

"I went to check out the exhibits."

"And?"

"They're still there. In the courts, they throw nothing away, odd as it might seem. I wondered if we might be able to get something out of the D.N.A."

The Baron gestured to the waiter for two more glasses of pastis.

"That will be difficult! Both for the tests and for the comparisons.

284

The boys in the genetic labs are a pain in the arse."

The magistrate's face was sad, his eyes humid.

"I don't know," he said. "I'm no longer involved in that kind of case and I never need them. In finance, all we deal with are figures."

"But I can ask for comparisons to be made."

"Even if you're not officially on the case any more?"

"Hang on, am I a cop or aren't I? All we have to do is justify opening the case again."

"But that's the problem. Plus there's the fact that the bastard probably isn't even on record."

"Who knows? More and more are getting caught like that."

"Hmm," said Brivet, sipping his pastis.

The magistrate concentrated on the menu for some time. The waiter came over. The Baron looked at his friend, who was hiding behind a list of dishes, prices and culinary descriptions.

"I'll have the same as you, the veal cutlet."

"It's funny. They haven't changed the menu."

"No, when the old boy left, they decided to keep the same style. And they were right. The place is packed every night."

"I have the impression that it's still the same tablecloths . . ."

"They repainted the walls once. But with the same colour. As for the tablecloths, I think it's nostalgia making you see things as before."

"After that we used to go to Le Bus . . ."

"If only they'd known about that at court!"

"They knew, of course they did."

"We once bumped into a lawyer there. Just once. Their sort didn't go to Le Bus because it was full of druggies. They preferred more upmarket joints."

"Yes, Le Bus was full of gangsters . . . And boys from your home town too."

The Baron turned his palms up towards the ceiling.

"And we didn't smoke only tobacco!"

The two cutlets arrived at the same time. The Baron stared at his fries swimming in cream.

"In fact, why on earth did we start eating here?" Brivet asked.

"It was my cousin who recommended the place. It was the last real wine and coal merchant in Paris. That's why."

"It's a shame Jean-Louis isn't here."

"He's a real Parisian, but you won't get him out of Marseille."

"What about you, Michel?"

"I've asked to be transferred back here."

Brivet put his knife and fork down on the wrong side of his plate, as though he was left-handed.

"You did what?"

"You heard me right! Last week, I asked to come back to the *Brigade Criminelle* in Paris. And I got Gégé to back up my request."

"He's the chief of police now."

"It helps to have friends."

Brivet picked up his knife and fork.

"You're still the craziest person I've ever met," he said, waving knife and fork in front of him.

25.

Moracchini put down the headphones beside her Toshiba, the service laptop.

She read back the sentence she had just typed, then she frowned and blinked.

The beast is coming . . . The old witch will dance . . .

The number dialled belonged to Chandeler, to his office line. And the call had been made from a telephone box in the centre of Tarascon.

The lawyer had absolutely insisted on his telephone being tapped and an investigation opened. The first call he had received was on Thursday, August 28, and the second on the 30th. The message which had just been recorded by the police computer was dated 3 September.

The three calls had been made from boxes located within the triangle formed by Maussane, Tarascon and Arles. Moracchini had turned everything there upside down and examined everyone who was on police records for even the slightest misdemeanour: nothing.

The receivers of the telephones used had been sent to the forensics lab in Marseille for D.N.A. sampling. In theory, she should get the results the next day.

She had then sent a tape of the man's voice on 3 September to be analysed by the scientific team in Ecully. The sound lab had taken its time before sending the following report:

The voice belongs to a person of male gender, aged from forty to fifty.

The individual in question does not present any vocal

particularities or difficulties of pronunciation which would indicate an alien or someone of foreign origin. French is thus his mother tongue.

The man tries to conceal his accent, but characteristics remain which would indicate that he speaks with a natural southern and more particularly Marseille accent; the manner of stressing the nasal consonants being typical of that region.

We add that this person proves to be particularly clever at concealing his voice . . .

She put down the report, chose a lock of her hair and started plaiting it without taking her eyes off her computer screen.

That morning, she had called up de Palma. He was still in Paris and had not said when he would be back. He had sounded cold on the telephone, which had made her both sad and furious with herself. So she had decided to distance herself from him as much as possible. It had become obvious that she missed de Palma, and this growing dependency scared her.

She went down to the surveillance centre and came back with another C.D. of tapped calls which she slipped into her computer. The three telephone boxes were not among the numbers used. There were a whole lot of mobiles, far too many for her mood that day. She decided to give Chandeler a call.

"Maître Chandeler?"

"Maître Chandeler didn't come to work this morning."

"Really?"

"And I must say I'm extremely worried. Usually he phones if he hasn't come in in the afternoon."

She looked at her watch. It was 3 p.m.

"If he doesn't phone in the next hour, call me back. Ask for Capitaine Anne Moracchini of the Marseille P.J."

She stared at the long list of mobile numbers and set to work. Romero was taking a day off.

The first thing she did was eliminate all the numbers that appeared more than three times, reasoning that the man would certainly not have used the same telephone that often. This removed over half of them, or thirty calls over a period of twenty-nine hours. Then she excluded all the female voices. This left a total of twenty-one calls.

Four of the remaining people had hung up at once. Eight of them were clients, but one of these drew her attention: the man on the telephone sounded panicked and was talking in a disjointed way about property investments. She decided to listen in more detail later.

The thirteenth call filled her with fright. The number used belonged to Bouygues Telecom.

First there was a long silence, during which just a few meaningless sounds could be heard. Apparently, the person on the telephone was in a very quiet place: there was no noise of traffic or passers-by. Then, ten seconds later, came the song:

Lagadigadeu, la tarasco, lagadigadeu . . .

The voice stopped.

A few seconds later, a second voice, as deep as a bass note from an organ, struck up the same melody. At the end of what Moracchini called the couplet, the first voice joined in:

Laïssa passa la vieio masco . . . Laïssa passa que vaï dansa . . .

She put down the headphones. Her hands were trembling. She called de Palma at once and got his voice mail. She hung up with a curse. Romero was unavailable too.

She had to know at once where this call had come from. There was a chance that one of the singers had used his personal telephone. The chance was a slim one, but it was worth chasing up. She tried Romero again, and he finally answered.

"O.K., Anne, I'll be there straight away."

Commissaire Delpiano was on holiday. His deputy advised her to apply to the investigating magistrate. She called him and summed up the situation.

"I think this recording should be analysed at once," he replied.

"We'd have to go to Lyon!"

"I think you'd better go yourself."

"I'll leave right now."

"Fine. I'll sort out the red tape and send a fax to Ecully. Speak to you later."

*

The north-bound motorway was gridlocked. She put the siren on the roof of her car and set off down the hard shoulder, passing by the line of cars that shimmered on the hot tarmac.

De Palma called.

"I'm on my way to Ecully. I should be there by seven this evening."

"Anything new?"

"You're a pain in the arse, Michel. That makes three times I've called you!"

She explained the situation.

"O.K., I'll try and join you there. I should be able to make it by about eight. We'll have dinner and talk this over."

"Hang on, I don't come from Lyon, you know!"

"Neither do I. We'll sort something out."

His words brought a smile to her lips. She looked at the passenger seat. There was only her shoulder bag and the file of tapped calls. She had not brought anything with her for the night . . .

At six p.m., most of the officers and staff who worked in the various departments of the scientific centre at Ecully were finishing their shift. Moracchini crossed the gardens and walked up the side of the large building that contained the national genetic fingerprint records and biological analysis laboratories.

She had driven like a creature possessed, at an average speed of over 160 kph, which meant peaks that topped 200. Her official Xsara was boiling by the time she stopped it in the visitors' car park.

It was the first time that she had been to this strange place, secluded from outside disturbances. Amid a park planted with cedars and pines, the police had set up some cutting-edge laboratories in Bauhaus-style buildings of two or three floors, all right angles, made of glass, metal and wood.

At the end of the main drive, she turned towards the computer, sound and video laboratories.

"The sound department, please?"

The doorkeeper, a blond lad immaculately dressed, looked up over the reception counter.

"You want to see Leila Hamdi?"

"That's right."

"Second floor. The lift's over there, to your left."

Hamdi was deep in the middle of a conversation between two mobsters. *On my mother's life*, one of them said. *You're dead, I swear*, yelled the other. Behind the voice that kept on repeating *On my mother's life*, she had identified the sound of a bus stopping and then pulling off again. One of the two men had called from somewhere close to a bus stop.

The scientist spun round on her chair when she saw Moracchini appear at the door and knock on the frame.

"Hello, Leila, I'm Anne Moracchini."

Hamdi stood up.

"Yes, I've heard a lot about you. We get news from all over France around here."

Moracchini shook her hand.

"So this is an emergency, you say? It's the same guy from the other day, I suppose."

"That's right. And it's red-hot!" she replied, handing her the C.D. "Did you get the fax from magistrate Laurence Modiano?"

"No, that's not my department," she replied, shrugging. "Anyway, I couldn't care less about all that red tape."

Along the wall behind her there was a row of recording equipment: a Revox with enormous tapes, a Nagra and a large number of machines with VU metres, ranging from the simplest mini-cassette player to the very latest digital model. To the left of the door, two large computer screens were displaying the curves and graphics of sound sequences.

"Impressive kit!"

"It's the best there is," the scientist replied, stroking her computer keyboard. "Most of the software comes from Russia . . . it was invented in K.G.B. times and perfected later. I've also got some programmes from the F.B.I., but they don't work so well. It always surprises visitors when I tell them."

Most police officers had problems understanding what she did. There was a world of difference between fieldwork and a doctor of physics capable of identifying the origin of a sound that was inaudible to their cloth ears. Yet Hamdi had worked on several famous cases and made vital contributions.

"Is it long?" she asked.

"No, just a couple of minutes."

"We'll proceed as usual. I'll listen to it first in my headphones, then we'll talk. You can go and get some coffee if you want, the machine's down the corridor, turn left then left again. Come back in five minutes."

On one side of the lab, big picture windows looked out over the adjacent corridor. Moracchini saw a commissaire pass by whom she had known for ages. She went outside while Hamdi slid the C.D. into her digital player.

Five minutes later, Moracchini was back. The scientist still had her headphones on and was thinking, her elbows on the desk, one index finger tapping on her mouth.

"This is weird," she said, taking off the headset. "Really weird."

"Why's that?"

"Was it picked up from a mobile?"

"Yes."

"What time?"

"At 20.34."

Hamdi looked at the computer screen and pointed at a window displaying some green clouds, denser in some places than in others.

"This is the sound spectrum of what we're about to listen to. It gives us the profile."

She clicked her mouse and the profile started to scroll. Moracchini heard a whole lot of new noises, sounds she hadn't heard in her office.

"That," the technician said, pointing with her finger, "is your caller's breathing. He thinks before he speaks. I'd say he was an anxious sort. Those little traces are the noises around him. They're barely audible because he's inside what I think is a car or a small room. The sounds are all muffled and there's no echo. But we can still clearly hear bird calls, and what you see there is a frog. If I isolate it, look what we get."

A couple of adjustments, and the sound of croaking became clear.

292

"But there are loads of them!"

"Your customer is next to a pond or a lake, anyway a place where there are plenty of frogs."

"How about a marsh?"

"Why not indeed!"

She let the sounds run on then paused on a spike in the profile.

"That's the call, or even the grunting, of a bird I don't recognise. There are several of them. Your guy could have been in a zoo. In any case, close to a bird I don't know. And I know quite a few!" she added with a grin.

Moracchini said nothing. She was completely fascinated by her colleague's equipment and know-how.

"Now, as for the voice, it's the same guy as last time. I told you he was clever, but now he really impresses me. I've only seen this once in my life. In Vietnam."

She peered at Moracchini, over her thick glasses.

"It's someone who can produce two voices at the same time."

"You mean that both voices on the tape belong to the same person?"

Hamdi nodded a big yes.

"Look, those are the A and the R of the high voice when it says *tarasco*, and here are the same letters pronounced by the deeper voice. They're identical. But it's practically impossible to find two people who have exactly the same A and R. The same goes for the other vowels. They're pronounced identically, but on different registers."

"That's amazing. How is it done?"

"The Vietnamese guy I met told me that he used his stomach, a kind of ventriloquism! I could hardly believe it, but he managed to produce two different sounds in that way. I can't tell you any more, except that your customer is a rare case. Extremely rare."

Moracchini's mobile rang.

"It's Michel. I'm at the train station in Lyon."

"Already?"

"It's nine o'clock!"

"Can you make it to Ecully?"

"No, there's no point. Tell me about it later. I'll try and find a couple of hotel rooms and I'll call you back."

"If you find just one, I wouldn't mind . . ."

Hamdi stared at her intensely.

"Was that a colleague?"

"De Palma. Do you know him?"

"Everyone knows de Palma. He was one of the first people to ask me for a voice analysis, and one of the first to trust me. Is he coming here?"

"No, he doesn't think he can make it. But if we go out for a bite to eat, do you want to come along?"

"Sorry, this evening I can't. I have a date. We'll work on for a while then stop before my head explodes."

She sat down in front of her computer and listened again to the same extract. Then she picked out a particular sound and clicked on several windows.

"I've got to identify this damn bird. It's the key to the whole thing. Can you hear it?"

It was like a slight grunt, at first in a middle register then deeper, like an "r" ending with a sort of "wou" then an "a". The call came back at frequent intervals: *rrwouaa, rrwouaa . . .*

"It's the sort of thing you don't pick up with your own ears. It was the software that identified and amplified it."

Rrwouaa, rrwouaa . . .

"I think you've already been a great help, Leila."

"No problem. That's my job!"

She turned towards a second computer and went online. Then she made two telephone calls.

"Shit, all I'm getting are answering machines," she said with a sigh.

She tried yet another number. In vain. Then she stood up, removed the C.D. from the player and replaced it in its box.

"Can you come back tomorrow, around ten?"

"Do you think that . . . ?"

"It's essential. I'll try to identify the bird and all the rest. Right now, I can't do anything more. Everyone's shut up shop. But tomorrow I'll contact some colleagues or scientists in France who may recognise this sound. This evening, it's not possible."

"O.K. I'll see you then."

"But I'll give it a go again later, in my place. If I find out anything, I'll give you a ring."

It was now 10 p.m.

De Palma had taken a room in the Hotel Ibis by the station. When they got back, it was past midnight and they tossed a coin to see who would sleep on the street side of the bed. The Baron won.

"Let's have a night cap. I've got a couple of things to tell you."

She took two individual bottles of vodka from the minibar and mixed them with orange juice. As she did so, she told him about the events of that day.

"A groaning bird?" he said, puzzled. "I'd never have thought that a bird could groan."

"But that's what comes out of the machine."

"Leila is almost never wrong. So this is big news. And if our friend Chandeler hadn't started shitting himself, we'd never have thought of birds."

"Chandeler hasn't been heard of since this morning."

"I'm afraid he'll end up like the others. It's the same rationale. And we can't do a damn thing about it!"

"This isn't the first time we've been in this kind of situation, and it won't be the last. In cases like this, it always takes several corpses before you find a pattern. This time, I think we've made good progress and I don't have a sense of feeling helpless."

The Baron was tense. He ran his fingers through his hair several times, blinking nervously as he did so.

"It's because I'm completely self-centred and reckon I should solve everything in record time! De Palma the protector of his fellow human beings . . . So when I fail, I blame myself and feel I should take on the universe. I've been thinking things through, Anne – life in general and myself in particular. And I realise that I'm arrogant and selfish. On this case, you've done as much as I have, you keep me up to date with what you do. I tell you hardly anything. I'm really sorry."

"Sorry isn't bad!"

He sipped at his screwdriver, running the sweet, cool liquid down his throat.

"Texeira also made a recording of the voice. I forget to tell you about that and I didn't even send it to the lab. Sometimes I think I'm the king of jerks. Wrapped up in myself."

She sat down next to him and massaged his neck.

"And I haven't told you about the Liberation either, and Steinert's connections with La Balme."

"You'll have time enough tomorrow, in the car."

"More and more often, I wonder what I'll do after leaving the force. Have you ever thought about that?"

"Don't take this badly, but I've got a good few years on you."

She caressed his cheek and drew him towards her, sliding a hand beneath his shirt. She kissed his chest, and drew his leg between her own. He felt her firm body, tense with desire, her breasts crushed against his torso. She undid his belt and laid him back.

Much later, in the middle of the night, he woke up. Moracchini was asleep. The red light from the street was coming through the cracks in the shutters. His mind was empty.

It was the first time in a long while.

Leila Hamdi was waiting for the two of them beside the coffee machine. She had tried to conceal the signs of a sleepless night under a thick layer of make-up, and had varnished her nails a bright red that stood out against the white plastic of the cup in her hand.

During the night, she had consulted two colleagues in the U.S.A. and one in Germany about the strange bird calls. The Americans had come up with answers that sounded implausible: the species they credited with the sound was a type of moorhen found only in the swamps of the Mississippi delta. The German had owned up his ignorance at once, but suggested an obvious lead: websites run by birdwatchers.

For hours, she had surfed the net looking for sites with sound recordings, and at around two in the morning, with eyes red from staring, she hit the jackpot: ornithopedia.com had one of the most extensive archives of bird-call recordings imaginable. All she had to do was to find the right one. It took her another couple of hours to download all the grunts that sounded more or less like the one on the tapped telephone call. In the early hours, she went to bed with a single name clear in her mind: the white spoonbill.

On arriving at the lab, she immediately compared the two profiles: they were identical. So when she saw Moracchini and de Palma arrive on the second floor, she threw herself at them.

"I've got good news for you," she said as she kissed them both. "It's a white spoonbill. And apparently, they're extremely rare."

De Palma said nothing until the lab door closed behind them.

"A white spoonbill, you say?"

"Stone-cold certain."

He telephoned Texeira at once.

"Have you got white spoonbills in your sector?"

"Of course, but they're rare. They're a sort of mythical bird for lovers of the Camargue."

"Mythical?"

"What I mean is that they're quite hard to observe. They're extremely picky migrators."

"Are there any here at the moment?"

"Theoretically speaking, yes. But I haven't seen any since the end of spring."

"Any chance you can clue yourself up?"

"Perhaps, but I don't see how."

"Neither do I, but you have to try, Christophe. And as fast as you can . . . right now, I mean! I can't explain why, but you have to."

"O.K., I'll get on it. I'll call up all my birdwatching friends."

Moracchini and de Palma left Ecully at about 10 a.m. Moracchini took the wheel. For a long while, until they had left the traffic jams around Lyon, the Baron kept his eyes pinned on the rear of the cars in front of them. It looked as if he was sailing in murky waters.

She did not even try to lift him out of this strange torpor. On the other side of the Lyon tollbooth, it was her mobile that broke the silence.

". . . the phone used to call Chandeler was reported stolen at the commissariat of Tarascon on July 19th at 10.15. That's all I can tell you."

"Thanks, Daniel . . ."

Chandeler gathered his strength. It had now been over a day since he had drunk or eaten anything. It felt as though his lips were coming off in shreds, and his tongue and throat were growing as rough as sandpaper.

He groped around in the darkness until his hands climbed a groove in the wall. At the top he found a right angle, a horizontal line, and another right angle. This must be a door. He was sure of it. He gauged its size and changed his mind. It was more like a trapdoor.

It was the only way out of the place where he now was.

Trying not to make a sound and holding his breath, he stuck his ear against the panel of the trapdoor and made out a noise on the other side of someone rummaging in what might be a drawer or a piece of furniture. Whatever it was, the movements sounded agitated and were accompanied by a deep voice that kept repeating, in a loop, as if chanting a mantra:

Lagadigadeu la tarasco, lagadigadeu dou casteu . . .
Lagadigadeu la tarasco, lagadigadeu dou casteu . . .

Suddenly, the voice moved away and he heard a door slam shut. His jailer had left. Feverishly, he felt around the panel and discovered, on the right-hand side, a hole. There was a lock but no handle. He put an eye to the hole. It was blocked, but a tiny ray of light came through it. This beam, as fine as a needle, brought him a joy such as he hadn't felt for ages. Small as it was, this hint of day gave him hope.

He sat down on the floor of his prison without taking his eyes off the source of light. After a moment the point was as large as the sun.

26.

Ingrid Steinert was standing in the shade of the mauve wisteria that spilled down over the patio, between the rambling roses which were back in bloom. She was wearing a tight cotton dress, stretched by her thighs and breasts and fastened with a knot behind her back.

When de Palma came over to her, she took a final drag of her cigarette before flicking it into the garden. She held a limp hand out.

She had cut her hair quite short, like a schoolgirl's from the 1940s. That gave her a curl over each ear and a straight fringe, which made her look extraordinarily young. De Palma remembered that Isabelle had exactly the same haircut in the last known photograph of her.

"How are you, Michel?"

"I must admit that I'm happy to see you again . . . and a little embarrassed too."

She gazed at him as if to examine his conscience. In the distance, a tractor could be heard coming and going across the fields. On the road from Eygalières, he had noticed a group of grape-pickers in a vineyard that must belong to La Balme. Because of the heat wave, the harvest was early that year.

He raised his eyes and peered at the hills of the Alpilles, looking for Bérard's sheep.

"What an awful way to go, don't you think so Michel?"

Weighed down by memories, he did not reply. He simply nodded and waved a hand in the air.

"So the grape-picking has started?"

"Not today. It rained last night, a heavy thunderstorm. The farmers have gone to inspect the vines to see if there hasn't been too much damage. We'll start in a few days' time when it's all dried out."

The noise of the tractor stopped. Everything turned calm again. A cool breeze, still charged with the vicious mood of the storm, caused the heavy leaves of the plane trees to flutter.

"I'll have to go back to my autumn collections," she said. "My life's in a terrible mess. I'll also have to deal with the olive trees. Nothing has been done for months."

Laura, the housekeeper, came out of the living room.

"I'll have to do some shopping in Arles, Madame. Do you mind being left on your own?"

"No, not at all."

The sky above the Alpilles was turning red, with blue flames piercing the clouds like blasts from a blowtorch.

"Are your husband's papers here?" De Palma asked.

She hesitated. Her eyes scanned his face.

"Quite a few of them. As a matter of fact, I was wondering when you'd ask if you could look at them."

"I think the time has come."

"What exactly are you looking for?"

"Everything."

"I've been through them and tried to sort them out. I've set all his letters aside, and what you call his papers in a big box. It's upstairs. If you want, we can go and take a look."

There were documents dating back over many years. De Palma tried to organise them chronologically. The oldest came from the Sixties and read like everyday thoughts in a diary kept by a foreign tourist in Provence. There were also some poems and a lot of notes about birds. De Palma read through them in detail. He had in mind the white spoonbill that the wiretap had revealed.

"Do you remember William ever talking about a bird called the white spoonbill?"

"Particular memories, no. He said it was very rare, and getting rarer. He was always very glad when he managed to photograph them. You know, he adored the birds of the Camargue."

De Palma dipped back into the ornithological notes. They included precise accounts of nesting locations and maps to show observation points, but none concerned the places he had already located. Steinert

300

had inserted photographs with descriptions written on the back: velvet scoter, red-breasted merganser, great skua, yellowhammer . . . William Steinert had been a gifted photographer.

She came over to him, he could almost hear her breathing. A second bundle included a notebook on recycled paper. On the first double spread, Steinert had jotted down a date, 1990, which was no doubt the start of its use. Overleaf, there was a picture of a water rail lurking in the quiet of the marshland, its red beak brilliant against the green and gold of the rushes. On the facing page, Steinert had written:

Water rail. Rallus aquaticus.
    One nest with 5 eggs on 23 March 1990. Samphire field north of Le Vigueirat, thirty metres from observation point 18.
    One nest and two chicks on 14 March 1997. Samphire field of La Sigoulette, 43°30/4°28.
    The chicks will not be flying in August.

On the fourth page, there were the same kind of notes about a common crane, taken the following year. De Palma flicked through the book rapidly, then stopped about halfway through.

White spoonbill. Platalea leucorodia.
    Two specimens. 17 August 1995. 07.30. Marshes of St Seren.
    One specimen in flight on 28 June 1999. 18.20. Redon salt marsh.
    In Delachaux: observed quite frequently. Around 51 sightings between 1957 and 1979. Quite common in July and August. Very few in winter.

There was something unreal about the photograph. It showed a white spoonbill gliding in the summer heat, borne up on the thermals, its snow-white wings spread wide in the sunlight.

"He also used to mention the black stork. He said that with the white spoonbill it was the most beautiful bird in the region. It's also very rare. Look at the next page."

There was a stylish shot of the big bird, strangely majestic in the middle of a meadow in the Camargue, where it seemed to have strayed. De Palma had never seen one before and found it magnificent.

Steinert had noted:

1 specimen. 19 May 1998.
   If Texeira is to be believed, this is the first photo taken since 1987! Anyway the only one known.

He leafed through the rest of the book but found nothing else of interest. The only thing that stuck in his mind was Texeira's name. He telephoned the biologist.

"Any news of white spoonbills?"

"No. Nobody's seen any for months. At the start of the summer, there was someone who sent me some shots he had taken. I must admit I was rather jealous."

"Do you know this person?"

"No, I'm afraid not. Why?"

De Palma let a moment's silence pass by, while he changed gear.

"Have you ever met this visitor?"

"Yes, in fact I have. We'd spoken together, a few days before I got the photos."

"Do you remember him?"

"Quite clearly. I'm observant."

"Go on."

"He's tall, about 1 m 85. Hair chestnut or black. Aged around fifty. With the look of an old globetrotter, if you see what I mean – scruffy trousers, and a combat jacket . . . A bit of a hippy, or a dreamer. There are quite a few people like that in the world of birdwatchers. They're often highly intelligent with it."

"Describe his clothes . . ."

He motioned to Ingrid to hand him a piece of paper and a pen.

"Jeans rather grubby, army jacket khaki, and sandals like the leftist militants used to wear in the Seventies."

"Viet Cong sandals?"

"That's right."

De Palma made a note.

"On the other hand his kit was terrific. You could say it was the classic photographer's kit, but at prices that only the keenest amateurs or professionals will pay. Also he had periscopic binoculars."

"What are they?"

"They're like a periscope . . . you know, as in a submarine: see without being seen. Not many people have those!"

He jotted down this detail in block capitals and underlined it twice.

"And have you seen him since?"

"No, but while we've been talking, I've been downstairs to check the observation log. The day was June 28th. I received the photos a few days later."

"And how does that fit with the voices?"

"Well . . . Jesus, it was practically the same day, or somewhere close. Do you think that . . ."

"I'm not thinking, Christophe. I'm observing! It could mean nothing."

"Hang on, you're starting to scare me!"

"Oh, you're in no danger. No danger at all!"

Ingrid had stood up and was staring intently at de Palma. Her cotton dress filtered her tall, firm figure in the morning light that slanted through the windows.

De Palma thought hard. All this was not really taking him anywhere, but it had him so excited that gusts of heat were rising inside him. He wanted to act and was desperate for the means to do so, or concrete lines of investigation. He had to admit the truth: he was standing on the threshold of a room in total darkness, and didn't know how to turn the light on. But another door had just opened.

Ingrid came over, sat down beside him and opened another notebook, which had cardboard covers and was bound like a real book. Their shoulders touched. He was hypnotised by her long fingers as they turned over the pages.

"I looked at this one yesterday," she murmured. "I think you should look at it, Michel."

She turned over another three pages and passed him the notebook. He felt her breast lie gently on his forearm for a second.

"When I found this last night, it really scared me."
She laid her hand on his shoulder.
"Read it, Michel."

It has been said that the Tarasque, half-human and half-reptile from the Jurassic, symbolises the Roman dominator settled in Provence over a long period.

For the Vokae who lived on the right bank of the Rhône and the Salluvii who were spread out between Monaco and Marseille, Rome could be symbolised by a monster. It is something one can easily imagine: a beast emerging straight out of the imagination of peoples subjected to the Pax Romana. This monster could symbolise this domineering Rome. But there is more to it than that.

The Tarasque is a reptile. Some have seen in it a representation of mankind's basest instincts (the reptilian brain), others have seen it as the gods of paganism tamed by Saint Martha.

But can it not also be viewed as the representation of a bane that really existed? Bérard says that the truth lies there and that tarasques existed. Back to Roman times: the Roman legion that occupied and administered the region of Tarascon was based in Nîmes. Its emblem was . . . a crocodile.

Bérard says that the Romans brought with them those huge reptiles captured in the Egyptian Nile. They are said to have used them as mascots. What is much more certain is that they used them in the arenas of Nîmes and Arles . . .

What is more, the crocodiles of the Nile could readily adapt to the climate and habitat of the Camargue, in many ways similar to that of the banks of the Nile.

From this point on, Steinert had written fast, his hand so fine and spidery that it was barely legible.

This could explain the spoor I saw yesterday in the marshland of La Capelière. I had never seen anything so big and so impressive. It was not made by an animal listed among the fauna of the

Camargue. I mentioned this to Bérard. He told me: "She's back, I called her and here she is." The look in his eyes was frightening . . .

I'm going back into the marshes tomorrow at nightfall to check these marks. I don't want anyone to spot me. After that, I'll show it all to Texeira.

NB: Bérard seemed out of his mind.

De Palma looked up from the notebook and let his mind wander through the maze of clues that now lay before him.

He had just read what must be William Steinert's last words. Ingrid had laid her hand on his arm.

"I don't know why, but I've made the connection with what I've been reading in the press. You know, those mutilated bodies. The crocodile, the Tarasque . . ."

"It's the presence of Bérard that worries me most. I think we're in great danger."

De Palma concentrated. He wanted to burst his head open, the ideas were hurting so much. He mumbled, pointing his index finger at some imaginary point on the table.

"Bérard, the Tarasque, William . . ."

He wanted to add: "and the Germans", but restrained himself.

"Bérard, the Tarasque, William, the birds . . . The Tarasque, the birds . . . Bérard and the Tarasque."

She put a hand on his shoulder and gently squeezed the muscle that bulged beneath his shirt.

"Bérard and the Tarasque . . ."

He looked for an unusual detail. Boyer, his father figure on the murder squad, had taught them that technique: an element that does not seem to fit into the jigsaw and that finally completes it. He rapped his hand on the table.

"Was the shepherd interested in the occult arts?"

She searched in his face.

"I think he was. William used to say that he was a bit of a *Zauberer* . . . a sorcerer! He nursed his sheep with plants that he alone knew about. Sometimes he told William about impossible things . . . William even told me that he had had some incredibly intense esoteric experiences with Bérard."

"Why haven't you told me this before?"

She moved even closer to him.

"I don't know. I never took it very seriously. William was a mystic about nature, I have trouble believing in God."

De Palma put his arm round her shoulder and hugged her hard. She let her body lean against his chest.

"I believe you, Ingrid."

He relaxed his embrace.

"Can I offer you something to drink?"

Through the window, he stared at the spectacle of trees under the sun. She smiled at him gently, then produced two glasses.

"I've opened another bottle of Muscat, Michel. I know how much you like it."

They drank the sweet white wine and spoke at length, first about William Steinert, then about the few notions of magic that de Palma possessed. Then the conversation drifted on for over an hour. She opened a second bottle. The wine came from the old vines alongside the Downlands.

They played at exposing their lives, taking care never to say everything, until their minds ran out and a strange sensation of joy arose between them.

She was standing beside the window, and it seemed that the forms of her body had suddenly been highlighted by a watercolourist's brush. Irresistibly he went over to her, and took her hands. She did not resist and offered him her lips. He lost himself in the warmth of her face. It was as if she had been born from the sun.

Her breasts were hard under the cotton of her dress. He raised his hands along her sides and then her back; her skin was bathed in her woman's heat.

27.

The sultry humidity had been rising for some time.

Chandeler reckoned that the sun must be approaching its zenith or possibly past it. The sounds of drawers and cupboard doors being opened and closed reached him through the wooden slats of the trapdoor.

Suddenly, he heard a door slam with a heavier noise, different from the others. The man who was keeping him prisoner must have just gone out. This was not the first time. On each occasion, the lawyer had noticed that his jailer returned after a period he reckoned at over an hour.

He went over to the trapdoor, guided by the tiny point of light that glinted through the shadows, then he started to bang on the wood, first with his shoulder, then with his heels. His keeper gave no sign of life, which gave him courage.

He braced his hands on the floor for maximum support, then drew his knees up to his chin and kicked out hard. A violent pain shot from the tips of his toes to his spine. He slipped his nails between the edges of the door and noticed that there was now a little give. He crouched back down and kicked, again and again.

The pain in his feet and legs was becoming unbearable.

He clenched his teeth. Tears were in his eyes.

Another blow.

The trapdoor gave way.

He threw himself at the aperture.

He was free. Blinded by light.

On a desk in front of the trapdoor was a huge computer with a screensaver showing large white birds. The cries of birds emerged from the loudspeakers. On the other side of the room, to either side of the window, stood two stuffed white birds the size of storks, the same as the ones on the monitor.

On the walls there were photographs pinned up. In snapshots taken with a zoom lens, Chandeler recognised Morini, his former client, taken at a three-quarters angle, sitting in his bar. In two other shots, a man was walking in the street. Above it a Post-it read: Jean-Claude Marceau.

Chandeler began to tremble. Thirst was constricting his throat, but he did not take the time to look for water. He gathered the little strength he had left and headed towards the door. It was locked from the outside. A huge bunch of keys hung from the door jamb. His fingers shaking, he tried the keys one after the other. Twice the bunch fell from his hands. His feet hurt as if they had been beaten by canes. About a dozen keys later, he found the one that turned.

The door opened out onto a narrow path that retreated through a reed bed. He walked as fast as he could, trying not to scream each time his feet touched the ground. Most of the rushes had to be over three metres high. He turned round and saw that his prison was no more than a tiny farmhouse, half engulfed by ivy, concealed in a grove of ash trees and reeds. It was absolutely invisible in its jungle sanctuary.

Father Favier's fingers were long and gnarled, as though one-euro coins had been slipped in between the phalanges. His hands were in constant motion, which Moracchini read as a sign of nerves.

"You're telling me that just before the death of Christian Rey you spoke to Gouirand in your church!"

"That's right, yes. But why are you asking me these questions again?"

She ignored the priest's reply, went over to him and tossed her hair back provocatively. Favier did not even notice her gesture.

"Never mind about your discussion. You then state that once Gouirand had left your church, you heard some noises, is that right?"

"As I've already explained several times: Gouirand had come to fetch the Tarasque to clean it. When he had gone, I closed the door behind him. Everything seemed quiet, then I heard those noises. I couldn't find out where they came from, but I'm sure I heard them! Someone was there, and then that someone left. I'm sure of it!"

"As if with the help of the Holy Ghost?"

The priest smiled with mild disdain.

"You could put it like that."

She stood up and stretched. She was wearing tight jeans and a T-shirt she had won at the police marksmanship competition.

"So what do you think about all this, Father?"

"I don't know what to reply. Of course, I don't believe all these stories that are going around in Tarascon! Just imagine it, only yesterday some more people came to ask me to say masses to fend off the evil spell. Masses to fight the Tarasque . . . Some people believe in a curse, others are asking for processions through the places of the legend of the Tarasque. Do you see me telling the bishop that I'm off on a procession to the castle of Tarascon or in the marshes of the Camargue? Not to mention what the journalists would have to say."

"Yes, I can quite understand!"

"Oh no you can't! I've had official requests addressed to me to go and bless the waters of the marshlands. It's as if the people in the town were possessed by this demon. Even the young lads from North Africa are talking about the Tarasque, can you believe that? I mean, it's not even part of their culture . . . My predecessor did warn me, but I never thought it would go this far."

She continued to stare at him, trying to catch his attention with female wiles, which had to be bothering him, but he did not show it.

"Each to his own monster. You have the Tarasque, we have the city football team."

She pointed at the window.

"And do you know where this Gouirand is right now?"

"No, honestly, I don't," he replied, turning his hands up towards the ceiling. "I think he may have simply gone away on holiday."

She turned back towards her computer and clicked on the criminal records file.

"O.K., I don't see any reason to detain you. Thanks for coming in."

"I have nothing to add except to say that this is the work of a madman!"

De Palma appeared in the doorway and tapped on the frame.

"Come in, Michel. I think you know Father Favier."

De Palma held out his hand. Moracchini placed herself between the two men.

"I just wanted to check a few details again with the priest of Saint Martha," she said. "But I'm through now."

The priest got to his feet and picked up an old battered leather briefcase, which he had placed on her desk.

"Your colleague in Tarascon also questioned me twice."

"The Tarasque ate him too!"

The priest stopped playing with his fingers and stared back at de Palma. He was wearing a curious expression, both eyebrows raised at a slant.

"It isn't funny to say that, sir, really not funny."

De Palma placed a hand on the priest's back and guided him gently to the door.

"You're absolutely right, it's no joke."

The man of God slipped out like a shadow and disappeared down the green corridor.

"We've got to lay hands on Gouirand. I'll have him brought in."

"Bérard too was a Knight of the Tarasque."

"Really? I'm going to end up wondering who wasn't."

He handed her a sheet of paper, on which he had made a series of notes:

White spoonbill (Platalea leucorodia).
Shape and size of a pure white heron. Long black bill, shaped like a spoon at the end. The adult has an orange strip on its chest and, in spring, a long orange/yellow head crest. Immature: no strip, black wing-tips, pink bill. Silent except during the breeding season when it produces a groaning call.

Shallow fresh and coastal waters, nests in colonies in trees, bushes and reed beds on marshy ground.

86 centimetres.

Can be observed in the Camargue in spring and autumn. Nests in North Africa. Groaning sound from nests (not in Camargue). Occasional clicking of bills.

Long neck, long feet. Flies with neck extended.

Feeds on aquatic invertebrates and small fish.

"Very interesting, Michel. But it doesn't tell us much."

"I copied it from a birdwatcher's guide for the Camargue. Take another look."

She read back through the notes, murmuring each word.

"Jesus, so it sings only when nesting, and that happens only in North Africa."

"So the recording was a sound montage. A very clever one, but a montage all the same. I think we really are up against a madman of a kind we've never imagined before."

"Any ideas?"

Moracchini had sat down on the edge of her desk; she was examining her nails and frowning.

"We'll have to investigate the ornithology freaks. All those obsessed with our little feathered friends. You never know . . ."

"Yeah, but in the meantime Chandeler is out there in the wilds, with the psycho."

"What can I say?"

"Nothing. Just say nothing."

As he emerged from the reed bed, the man knew at once that his prisoner had given him the slip. Without knowing why, he felt it, but he had had to prepare the beast. And that was not an easy thing to do. He had been making it fast for a while, and the storms that span in the sky above the delta had swamped the air with electricity.

The beast was more uptight and dangerous than ever before.

He took out his knife and ran inside the house. Inside it was quiet.

He stopped, his arms flailing in front of the staved-in trapdoor. In the late afternoon shadows, the white spoonbills were watching him with their glass eyes. They seemed to be laughing at the strange trick that fate had played on him.

He stayed still for some time. His mind was so clouded that he felt as if his cerebral convolutions were muddled together.

From the computer came the clicking of beaks and groaning. It was the spoonbills' song of love and grace during their nuptial display. He smiled as though emerging from his torpor. The recording was on a loop. It dated back to the days when he had worked for an Algerian oil company.

After a moment, it seemed to him that the stuffed birds were coming to life on their varnished wooden stands. He walked over to them on tiptoe, uttering little cries, like quiet groans.

Tears filled his eyes. He wiped the sweat that was running down his temples. His hands were trembling, his guts churning. He tried to get hold of himself, but shakes and painful spasms were knotting his entrails. He went closer to the birds, and stopped less than a metre away. With the tips of his fingers, he stroked their marvellously white plumage. He sank his fingertips into the down of their long graceful necks.

He asked the spoonbills to give him the strength to fight through the crisis that was now submerging him, but the trembling soon turned to convulsions, and he collapsed.

He came round some time later, unable to tell how long the attack had lasted. The spoonbills were still there, he could hear the dry clicking of their long, spoon-shaped beaks and the groaning of the males.

Mad with rage, he went outside and headed for a lean-to beside the house. He returned a few minutes later with a jerry-can of petrol. His eyes were red with fury, and saliva was dribbling from his lips, twisted downwards by an unknown pain.

He went inside the house and methodically spread fuel at strategic points. Then he nervily struck a match and rushed outside, pursued by the fire's hot breath.

He stopped running a long time later, when he found himself on

312

the road to Salins-de-Giraud. A column of smoke was rising in the distance, a huge exclamation mark above the marshes.

At that moment, he thought of the beast. Only at that moment did he realise that she would be furious and that nothing could stop her.

28.

Chandeler felt a bony hand shake him vigorously. He half-opened his eyes and saw a weather-beaten face with slanted eyes staring at him, its lips twisted upwards in a grin that revealed two rows of ivory teeth.

"Wake up, sir! . . . Wake up . . . Can't stay here."

Chandeler squinted and saw that two Asians were looking down at him nervously.

"Wake up, sir! . . . Not possible . . ."

He gathered the last of his energy to mumble a few words:

"Must . . . call . . . the police. I . . ."

"We not police, sir . . . We work in fields. Workers!"

Chandeler heard a torrent of onomatopoeias flooding his weakened mind. He thought for a moment that he was hallucinating again. Since being kidnapped, he had constantly been wandering between the real world and nightmare visions.

He tried to stand up, but immediately felt powerful arms catch hold of him and raise him from the ground to carry him to a trailer coupled to a vineyard tractor. All at once he found himself lying in the middle of some crates that smelled of raw earth and greenery, with the sun blazing in the sky up above him.

Four people sat beside him in the cart. Four Asians to whom he gave a smile of gratitude. Then the procession crossed a field that was out of his line of sight and turned down a sunken lane bordered by ash trees and poplars.

It must be quite late in the day, the blue sky was becoming tinged with pink and orange. A smell of diesel and smoke enveloped him, the tractor almost stopped and the engine shifted up a gear: now they were driving down a tarmac road.

He gradually recovered his spirits as he exchanged glances with his saviours. After escaping, he had walked for some time until, exhausted, he had found a stream, where he had drunk his fill of water, and a place in a curly bush, away from prying eyes. It was next to a field, maybe a vineyard, he could no longer remember. What did it matter? He had fallen asleep.

For some time, he observed the men who had rescued him, and realised that they must be illegal migrant workers. He had heard tell of this sort of workforce trafficking in the Camargue. Several big landowners had been caught red-handed using modern-day slaves. They generally came from Thailand or Cambodia, and worked like coolies for a handful of euros.

The man who greeted him in the farmyard of La Fraysse must be foreman, or something like that. The Asians vanished into the buildings.

"The workers found you just as they were finishing work. I am Fabrice Luciano, I'm the manager here."

"Chandeler, member of the bar in Marseille."

The foreman recoiled.

"How did you come to be in such a state, on the edge of a strawberry field?"

"I . . . I . . . it's too long and too crazy to explain. I must speak to the police."

"I can take you to Marseille if you like."

"No, no, I must call the police!"

"Listen, sir, I . . . how can I put it? The workers who brought you wouldn't like the police to know that they were working here . . . if you see what I mean."

"I must speak to the police. Let me call them."

"So long as you don't tell them what happened here. I don't want to see any policemen or gendarmes around here."

"O.K. I'll call a friend."

At 7.12 p.m. de Palma's mobile rang.

*

It all went very quickly. Less than an hour later, de Palma arrived at La Fraysse with Moracchini and Romero. Chandeler was sitting at the big dining-room table and finishing the meal he'd been given.

When he saw the police officers, he stood up and wrung their hands for some time.

"It's the first time in my life that I'm glad to see a policeman."

"There's a first time for everything," de Palma replied. "Now, tell us about it all."

Chandeler's expression changed abruptly, a veil of terror covered it. It was only after a long silence that he started the tale of his kidnapping: on leaving the court in Marseille, where he had been defending an industrialist accused of bribing civil servants, a man had approached him then discreetly stuck a gun in his belly.

"He was forty-five to fifty years old. A metre eighty, maybe more . . . He was about my height in fact, and I measure one metre eighty-five. Dark, shoulder-length hair, small blue eyes and bushy eyebrows. A thin nose . . . Unshaven. He was wearing a safari jacket, jeans and sandals."

Chandeler had not argued with this man's orders and had got into a nearly new Ford Scorpio. This detail had struck him: it must have been a hire car. Then they had driven towards Martigues, Fos and the Camargue.

De Palma produced a map of the Rhône delta and unfolded it on the table.

"Try hard to remember. We're on the long straight line of the R.N. 568. At some moment you turn left. Is it this road?"

"Yes, that's it. Beside it, there's an old caravan and a wrecked fridge."

"Then you drive on."

"We drive for quite a while down the same road. There are mown fields on both sides . . . I mean, there's nothing in them . . . We continue and arrive at a junction, there's a signpost pointing to Sambuc. We drive . . ."

Chandeler reflected, his eyes closed, rerunning the journey in his mind.

"On the right, there was a large expanse of water, and on the left reeds everywhere. And then . . ."

Chandeler plunged back into his memories. He frowned.

"I want to remember, but I can't."

"Did you drive for long in that direction?"

"No, not at all."

"How many minutes," Moracchini asked.

"No more than five."

She looked at de Palma.

"It sounds like it was near La Capelière."

"There's been a fire there!" the foreman said.

"A fire?"

"An old farmhouse has just burned down. It nearly set light to the entire region."

"Could you take us there?"

"No problem."

De Palma looked at Chandeler, he seemed completely wrecked.

"I suggest you stay here for the moment. We'll come back soon and drive you to Marseille. O.K.?"

Chandeler simply nodded in reply.

Astride the main branch of an old ash tree, he watched two cars pass by on the road to Sambuc. The first was a Japanese 4×4 of a make he didn't know, the second a Peugeot 406. Cops, he thought.

Previously, he had observed the dance of the fire engines and the vehicles of the gendarmerie converging on the blaze.

The sun, still heavy with light, was sinking into the silver of the Vaccarès. There were flamingos, non-migrants, pecking in the depths of the water before disappearing into their secret reed beds.

Cops won't find anything, he thought. Nothing. Except for Chandeler, who would no doubt give his description. And the lawyer would provide a host of useful details to the police. The second car, that was it: not gendarmes, but cops from Marseille, the P.J. and perhaps even that damned plainclothes detective he'd seen in Morini's bar and then spotted again in the lawyer's office the other evening. That one, he knew by instinct he had to beware of. The same type as Marceau, violent but gifted with sensitivity. That said, he had nothing against him and would do nothing as long as this officer did not interfere with the beast's designs.

He turned towards the fire. There was no more smoke, the firemen and gendarmes must now be combing through the house. But everything must have burned.

Why had he set it ablaze? Was it a fit of folly, as uncontrollable as it was unforeseeable?

In fact, he had no idea. It was not the first time that his nature had overcome him. He saw marvels and then all at once everything would collapse, at the slightest snag, the smallest detail that spoiled the whole. It was like a blot of pollution in the midst of nature. A flower of dishonour in the vastness of his pride. He had to destroy, even if it meant losing everything.

The memories of the past few months returned to him. He had the feeling of having accomplished a good part of his mission. The Tarasque had accomplished what was expected of it. The park would never exist. That was the main thing. He had eliminated one of the brains, Morini, and some of his best soldiers. A pity about Chandeler.

He sincerely regretted the death of Steinert. It had made him sad, truly: they had shared so many things together.

Steinert had wanted to see the beast.

And he, the Knight, had always refused to show it to him. It was Bérard who had made the decision. Steinert had not been initiated. Or not sufficiently.

But Simone's son had been more stubborn than a mule, he had wanted to see all the same. So he had looked for it. Until the day when he had found it. You always end up finding what you look for.

How had he done it? He didn't know. He supposed that Steinert must have followed him. And the beast would have eaten him if he had not run like a thing possessed.

Unfortunately, it was dark, and William had not seen the marsh. And he hadn't been able to save him, otherwise the beast would have escaped.

He had had trouble bringing it back into its lair, among the rushes. Several times, he had sung the song of the servants of the beast to calm it down and, finally, it had consented to follow him.

Sadness filled him. William would never know the end of the story. He would never know that everything had been achieved.

The Vaccarès was completely absorbing the sun. Like a tranquil monster that methodically swallows its prey before slowly digesting it. A light wind rustled the parched leaves of the tree. He sniffed the air like a wild animal gauging the danger. Just as Bérard had taught him, the old man, the chieftain.

Bérard the magician.

Wisps of charred wood and scorched tiles tickled his nostrils. The face of the old shepherd surged up again, as though his old master had returned across the river of death to give him strength.

He stayed in his tree until nightfall. Then he climbed down, as agile as a wild cat which decides that the hunting hour has arrived. It must have been past nine o'clock when he disappeared into the rushes, dry and sharp as sickle blades.

It smelled of burned grass and sugary wood. The heat of the blaze was still rising from the ground and from the stones fallen from the wall.

Moracchini was questioning a fireman from Le Sambuc, who was doing his best to explain, by pointing at the remains of the farmhouse, that the fire must have started inside the building.

De Palma wandered onto the path and walked for about a hundred metres. The reed bed had been caressed by the flames; close to the house, the tips of the canes were singed.

Along the path recent footprints could clearly be seen; some soft green herbs had been broken, what looked like a water hyacinth had been crushed.

He turned round. He was in the middle of the reed bed and the ruins of the house had vanished from sight. All that was left was the smell impregnating the heavy air.

For a hideout, you couldn't find better, he thought. Just a few paces from the road.

He took a few more steps and saw that the vegetation had been disturbed. Some young rushes, lower than the others, had been broken and prints were clearly visible in the sandy soil and in beds of moss. "This must be Chandeler's escape route," the Baron thought.

He retraced his steps and saw Moracchini searching in the ruins of the farmhouse.

"We need a forensics team," she said when de Palma reached her. "Try finding anything in this mess!"

She kicked out at the carcass of a half-melted computer.

"According to the firemen, he set fire to the place with petrol. He must have spread it around then lit a match."

"Simple and effective," de Palma replied, lifting up a still-smoking joist.

The fire brigade captain approached and handed them a black object: it was the bowl of a pipe that had resisted the flames. De Palma shifted it in the palm of his hand. He suddenly remembered that the first thing that he had noticed on entering Steinert's office was a strong smell of aromatic pipe tobacco.

He remembered too that Mme Steinert had assured him that her husband never smoked. De Palma was a man who believed in signs, and he sensed that the genie of the police had just sent him one. All that remained was to interpret it.

Moracchini came over.

"Interesting?"

"Maybe. Let's go on searching. This could be our lucky day."

Beneath a pile of stone which had fallen from the walls, they found a carbonised mass and, beside it, a singed white feather.

"A white spoonbill," the Baron said.

Digging deeper, he found a plaster base with wires sticking out of it. After a moment's reflection, he realised that it must be the framework of a stuffed bird.

They learned nothing from the rest of the house. A sea breeze had risen and blown the strong smell of the blaze away across the Vaccarès.

Because that's where they should have looked. In her family. That sentence, pronounced by an old woman in a Paris graveyard, suddenly struck his forehead like a rubber bullet. *Because that's where they should have looked. In her family.* He felt old, incapable of catching balls on the bounce, a washed-up player with a lousy backhand. He had not even asked for the old woman's name. Pain entered at the top of his skull and descended between his eyes.

A fireman raised his helmet. The black smoke had given him the face of a miner. He placed his axe against a section of the wall and lit a cigarette.

The next day, Gouirand reported to the offices of the *Brigade Criminelle* at ten o'clock exactly. Moracchini questioned him for over two hours and learned nothing new except for a few details about Morini's youth and some of his friends in the police force. She thus discovered that Morini had quite simply grown up with an important regional politician. Christian Rey had been part of the same network.

"What about Bérard, did you know him?"

"I often used to see him during the traditional festivals, at Christmas or the festivals of the Tarasque. He would come and recite poems and tell us legends in Provençal. People said that he was a member of the *Félibrige* and that he was a descendant of Frédéric Mistral."

"He was also a Knight of the Tarasque!"

"I know that he had been one once, but long before I started taking care of the Tarasque. I spoke to him about it a couple of times. He even gave me some advice when I wanted to make some new costumes."

"So you knew him?"

"Only vaguely."

"What about Steinert?"

"Never met him. Nor heard of him, till I read about him in the papers."

That morning, de Palma had debriefed Chandeler.

The lawyer explained that S.O.D.E.G.I.M. had been dissolved and Philippe Borland had dropped out of sight long ago. Shortly before dying, Morini had been busy starting up a second company, a kind of gasworks based in Monaco and Luxembourg, and whose capital consisted of cash coming in from every imaginable tax haven.

"Morini was with me when we went to see Bérard. We wanted to buy his stake in the Downlands, but he refused."

"What happened then?"

"He told us that he was going to see to it that we'd never be able to build on that land."

"And you threatened him!"

"That was Morini. He got annoyed and wanted to scare him. I guarantee you that I tried to intervene, but I couldn't do anything."

De Palma knew the rest of the story.

"When did you first receive the mark?"

"One or two days after we went to see Bérard."

"And did it arrive at your home?"

"Yes, it did. Why?"

"Because very few people know your personal address!"

Chandeler had started. He realised that he would never sleep in peace again until the police laid their hands on the man who had tried to murder him.

"Maybe it's time you told me everything."

"Yes, I think it is."

Chandeler had picked up his telephone and asked to be sent up a packet of cigarettes. Two minutes later, a young woman had opened the door and had placed on the occasional table a tray with a pack of filterless Craven-A, a box of matches and an ashtray.

"I need to think things through and get some sleep," he said. "Could you come back at the end of the afternoon?"

He had lit a Craven-A and drawn on it greedily. The lawyer was in such a state of agitation that de Palma could smell the rancid odour of his fear.

"We all knew each other . . . That's what you have to understand. I'm a local boy, too."

After four pulls on his cigarette, he stubbed it out and coughed slightly.

Gouirand glanced nervously at de Palma when he saw him enter Moracchini's office. He had never come across him before, and he read such determination on the officer's face that he instinctively recoiled.

"We're getting to know all the family at last, Michel. I get the impression that everyone knows everyone else!"

"More than you think," the Baron said.

Gouirand's gaze kept on shifting from one officer to the other. Moracchini noticed this and sat down behind him to unnerve him.

"M. Gouirand, I have the impression that the Tarasque is bringing bad luck all round."

"I don't see what you mean."

"Rey and Morini were Knights of the Tarasque, weren't they?"

"It's true, I knew them back in the days when they were part of the team. I've already told that to your colleague."

De Palma massaged his wounded shoulder. He stared at the chief Knight intently.

"And what about Marceau?"

Gouirand's expression changed, his lower lip drooping slightly. It made him look suddenly old and pathetic.

"I don't know what you mean . . . I've already answered all your questions."

The Baron's face relaxed, and his eyes sparkled.

"You see, M. Gouirand, in crime there is always a logic. People kill one another for thousands of reasons, and it often happens that these reasons have no apparent logic. Yet that logic is always there, in front of us. Our job is to understand it. Always, do you understand? It's a duty. I knew Marceau for years. We were colleagues at police headquarters in Paris . . . They were the best years of my life. Then I came back to Marseille, and Marceau to Tarascon."

De Palma stood up and passed his hand over his forehead.

"For months, I've been telling myself that Marceau was in Tarascon because the force had sidelined him and that he wanted to return home, just as I wanted to come back to Marseille. Quite simply. Then I learned that he'd been topping up his pay by doing odd jobs for the mob. Quite simply. So far, so logical."

Moracchini stared at the Baron. She noticed that the muscles of his face were stiffening and the veins in his arms standing out.

"And then Marceau gets eaten by your cursed animal: there, there is no more logic. Why?"

He suddenly turned his back to Gouirand.

"Because there are certain things I don't know ... and what can I possibly not know about a friend of twenty-five years' standing?"

He spun round and darted his feverish gaze into Gouirand's eyes.

"M. Gouirand, I've spent all night thinking about this. And I've noticed something stupid. Really stupid. Marceau was born in Tarascon. He came from an old-established family. Just like you, like Rey, like Morini, like most of the knights. It's as stupid as that. Except for this: you and Marceau are from Tarascon. But not your parents, who were born in one of those dismal surrounding villages, like hundreds of the town's inhabitants. Logic, do you understand me? As for the rest, I must say that I used my imagination a little and I think I've got it right."

The Baron picked up a chair and sat down in front of Gouirand. He sized him up for a few seconds.

"Why didn't you say that you'd known Marceau for ages and that he too was a Knight of the Tarasque ... Why?"

"I don't know ..."

Gouirand hid his face in his hands. De Palma observed him.

"Did you also receive the warning?"

The Knight's head sank even lower.

The Baron stood up and motioned to Moracchini to come aside and talk to him. They spoke in whispers.

"The best thing for him is to go into hiding, and straight away. We haven't caught our psycho yet, and he could well change his M.O. and start blowing away whoever's left before we can get to him."

"We could even put him behind bars if we want to. We've got enough on him. All I'll have to do is phone up the magistrate."

"Good idea. Put him in custody. We'll see clearer tomorrow."

"How did you work that out about Marceau?"

"I was bluffing. Chandeler told me that they all knew each other, so I improvised from there. I'll have to go back and see him soon. Ask our friend the same questions now. He'll wind up thinking we know everything."

They went back to Gouirand. De Palma resumed his place in front of him.

"I think you can tell us his name," said Moracchini harshly. "I think it's time! Enough people have died. Do you realise what your silence can cost you in court?"

"If I knew his name, I'd have told you a long time ago. But I don't."

She pursed her lips and tried to make eye contact with the Baron.

"I believe you," de Palma said. "But, I only half believe you . . . I think you're hesitating between several people. Am I mistaken?"

"No, sir."

"What if I tell you that he's a keen birdwatcher, crazy about our feathered friends, and spends most of his time in the Camargue? A metre eighty-five tall, looks a bit like a hippy . . ."

Gouirand stiffened on his chair. He wiped away the drops of sweat that were beading on his forehead.

"It's Vincent Soubeyrand," he murmured. "It can only be him."

"He was Steinert's best friend, wasn't he?"

"That's right. Soubeyrand from the Clary domain."

"Does he still live there?"

"No, there's only his mother, Mireille, and some farm workers."

Moracchini jotted down the address and summoned an officer to take Gouirand down to the cells. De Palma looked at the road maps. Clary lay beside the road between Maussane and Eygalières, just a few kilometres away from La Balme.

"There's a telephone, shall we try?"

"Why not?"

She plugged the loudspeaker into the telephone and entered the number, without taking her eyes off the keyboard. A man answered. She frowned.

"Am I speaking to Monsieur Lebel?"

"You've got the wrong number."

"Sorry, I must have made a mistake."

They looked at each other in mutual thought: a man's voice in a house where a woman was supposed to be living alone. It might mean nothing, but it had to be checked.

"How funny," said de Palma. "Vincent and Mireille."

"What's so funny about that?"

"They're the heroes of Mistral's masterpiece."

"Right. And then there's an unhappy ending in the Camargue."

An hour later, de Palma and Moracchini drew up in their police Xsara in a sunken track bordered by oak trees, a few metres from the turning that led to the Clary farmhouse. From a distance, the unmarked car was quite invisible.

De Palma drew his Bodyguard and walked into the copse beside the road. The baking air buzzed with the song of the cicadas. At each footstep, scraps of dead wood and dried grass crackled beneath his feet. After fifty metres, he stopped in a sweat. The Clary farmhouse was in front of him, on the other side of a vineyard that still smelled of ripe grapes.

Moracchini came to a halt beside him and took out her binoculars.

"There's nobody outside the building."

"Let's go."

"The only problem is the dog. There's always a damn dog in this kind of place."

The Baron mopped his forehead.

"There's a chance in a thousand that he's here," she said. "That's all. And if we do anything stupid, we get ourselves demolished by our learned friends."

Moracchini's hair was full of long pine needles. She drew her Manurhin and hefted it in her hands.

"You're probably right, Anne, there's very little chance that he's here. But we still have to go. No two ways about it."

"If you say so," she replied, watching him push forward under cover of the vines.

She let him go on for a few metres and headed for the drive so as to block any possible escape route.

She had not reached her objective when a first shot rang out. The bullet ricocheted in front of her, raising a clod of earth. She dived down onto the dusty path, and rolled over to take cover behind a row of vines.

"Are you O.K., Anne?" De Palma cried out.

She just had time to reply before a second shot hit the drive at random. She realised that the sniper could not see her and concluded that he must be in the house and firing from a first-floor window, just behind the pine tree that must be blocking his line of sight.

The Baron had crawled towards the farmhouse, flattened to the ground. A breeze blew sour stenches that came from the pens, and the smell of oil from the farming machinery. Black flies danced in the air around him, and mocked his jeopardy. There was dust in the sweat of his forehead and his clothes were covered with dirt.

When he was no more than ten metres from the buildings, he stood up and studied the windows. Everything was still. Despite Moracchini's fears, there was no dog. He concluded that the herd had gone out and that the dogs were guarding the animals.

He decided to move on to where he could flatten himself against the wall, when he heard the characteristic sound of a motorcycle starting up. It was coming from the garage he had noticed when he was at the far end of the drive.

"The car, Anne!" he shouted. "Get to the car!"

The double doors of the garage banged against its walls and a big motorbike rocketed out. De Palma stood up and fired. The driver bent down over the handlebars and started weaving to right and left. De Palma fired again and again, fanning his shots. When the clip was empty, he threw down his gun, drew his Colt .45 and ran after the bike. A single bullet hit the motorcyclist, who jerked in his saddle.

Thirty metres further on, Moracchini braced herself in firing position and aimed at the motorcyclist. Three shots rang out. None of them hit their moving target. The bike slalomed once more, then swerved left into a field and disappeared.

When de Palma came over to her, fury was still gleaming on his face. She said nothing, but flicked open the cylinder of her Manurhin, removed the still-warm casings and filled the empty chambers with three new .38 shells.

"We have to search the house," she said, frowning.

"Forget it. I think we'd better go and see Chandeler. He's expecting me."

Chandeler was sitting in his chair, a glass of Islay, his favourite whisky, in his hand.

Moracchini and de Palma walked towards him. Both of them had seen enough dead men to know that the killer had been there just before them. A trickle of blood still glistened on the grey-veined marble of the living room, sketching its Chinese calligraphy as far as the lawyer's luxurious Persian rug.

Chandeler had looked death in the face. He had probably even talked with his executioner. Vincent Soubeyrand had put a bullet in his head, a hollow-point which had left a neat round hole in his forehead and blown apart the back of his skull. Pieces of brain were stuck to the armchair.

She put a hand on the corpse's forehead.

"This happened less than an hour ago," said de Palma, leaning over the body.

"It was a nine-millimetre, for sure. And I'll eat my hat if it wasn't a SIG that killed him."

Chandeler's murderer had folded his victim's hands over his stomach and placed a white feather between his fingers.

"Jesus, all of this really gives me the creeps," Moracchini said, taking a step backwards.

De Palma picked up the feather and took a long look at it.

"The signature hasn't varied from the start; but he can't take them to the Camargue any more for the creature to eat them. He's panicking, Anne. He no longer knows where to turn and he's going to start shooting in all directions."

"Do you have any idea of the place where he's hiding?"

"No. Chandeler was our last chance to find out. He's crafty and he's been observing us for some time now. He knows how we operate. He's always at least one move ahead of us."

"And we can't even give out his description."

29.

Saint Joseph's was a private secondary school whose surrounding wall took up a large part of one side of rue de Beaucaire, just a few metres away from Tarascon town hall.

It was 5 p.m.

In front of the gates, children were running in all directions, excited by their first day back at school.

The Baron spotted Gilbert Sicard, who was watching them come out. Two days before, Sicard had replied to the message de Palma had left on his answering machine. The former history student had become a teacher and was now headmaster of a Catholic school.

"Good evening, M. de Palma. Come into my office."

They crossed a concrete playground planted with three ancient plane trees. The classroom windows looked out over a shadowy courtyard, and a grey door led to the headmaster's office at the far end.

"This is all very sad . . ." Sicard said, weighing in his hands a copy of his dissertation, before putting it down on his desk.

"You're just about the last chance I've got."

Sicard had an odd-looking face: round, with eyes like marbles and thick oval glasses perched on an aquiline nose.

"I must tell you that I myself come from those very same villages. My mother was born in Maussane and my father came from Fontvieille."

Sicard opened his thesis and riffled through the pages with his thumb.

"There are things missing from my version," he said. "But you must understand that I wrote it in 1966. I was very young at the time."

He knew the history of his native village thoroughly. He spoke at length about the period of the Occupation, and named one after the other the families that had collaborated with the Nazis. The Reys had been the most involved. One of their sons, Christian's uncle, had died in Pomerania in the SS uniform of the Charlemagne Division. The Reys had consolidated their fortune and had not been among the families investigated during the subsequent purge. Christian Rey's grandmother had even been part of the kangaroo court that had judged Simone Maurel.

"These are very painful stories," he said, closing the cover.

He then spoke of the bogus resistance fighters who had shot Simone Maurel's brother. De Palma noted the names of Gabriel Morini and Sébastien Marceau. Emile Maurel had been shot down without any semblance of justice. Gabriel Morini and Sébastien Marceau had gone to La Balme and had killed him in the guise of belonging to the resistance.

"Why do you think they did that?"

"For money, Monsieur! Or rather, for land. The Maurel family was the richest in the region and it has to be said that Simone's parents hadn't always been very straight when they bought land. Just before the war, they had got their hands on the Downlands by paying off old Morini, an Italian lumberjack who had married a girl from Eygalières, a girl called Bérard . . . Justine Bérard. He was an old drunk who had sold the land to Maurel for a song. The Maurels wanted it all, and for that the younger members of the Morini family could never forgive them! That transaction ruined them in fact, do you see?"

De Palma saw the jigsaw coming together. *Because that's where they should have looked. In the family.* He opened his bag and took out the photograph he had found in Bérard's house. Sicard took it and stared at it for some time, as though running a magnifying glass over each person in the shot.

"Where did you find this picture?" he asked with a frown.

"I'd rather not say."

Sicard put the photograph down and folded his hands. A glint of bitterness turned his eyes cold.

"It's the Tarasque," he said, still staring at the picture. "The Knights of the Tarasque who are standing round the monster are descended from the most powerful families of Tarascon and its vicinity. You can see Bérard, Émile Maurel, Lucien Soubeyrand . . . At the end of the fifteenth century, King René codified the brotherhood of the Tarasque in such a way that the sons of the great families of the region came together instead of fighting duels. In those days, it was only the sons of the powerful who had the right to serve the monster. Before the war, this tradition was still in force and that must have made a lot of jealous people. Especially because these families are very traditional. The Bérards descended from one of Mistral's daughters, and I think that the Soubeyrands were connected with Roumanille. In this part of Provence, let me tell you that is quite something!

"Let me tell you also that during the war they had quite a problem choosing a side, because most of them were Catholic fascists. But they were also patriots, Bérard and Soubeyrand above all. Etienne Maurel, too. They formed the Vincent network and were in the resistance right from the start. They were also members of the *Félibrige*, that famous literary circle . . . Bérard was even its laureate once."

Sicard opened his hand and pointed a thumb towards the ceiling.

"So here we have tradition, jealousy, revenge . . . In the series of murders that happened last summer you can find all of that. According to what you told me earlier, it was a conflict between two conceptions of Provence: traditionalists and those who wanted to use its folklore for more commercial ends. It's more complex than that. I know nothing about the plans for the leisure park that you mentioned. I do know that the real motive was revenge."

Control of the Tarasque had changed hands, and Vincent Soubeyrand, the heir to an epoch, could not bear that fact. In the middle, there was Bérard, the former head of the Knights and the master of them all. Old man Soubeyrand had died in the 1950s after his fall from fortune, and his son Vincent was badly unbalanced. He was notoriously violent, and from what Moracchini had managed to unearth so far, he had been jailed several times for assault and wounding during village dances and election campaigns.

"What about Steinert?"

"As a matter of fact, I don't know much about him. I always thought it odd that he bought the La Balme farmhouse. I don't know why, but I said to myself that there was a secret behind all that."

"He was the son of Simone Maurel and Karl Steinert."

Sicard stared at the photograph. His eyes were wide, and shone like a mirror reflecting flames from a fire.

"If there is anyone who should have been out for revenge, it was him. And he didn't do it. That will be the final truth of this tragedy."

He uttered this last remark in a murmur that lost itself in the silence of the empty school.

30.

It appeared on the front page of *La Provence*.

Giant Crocodile Shot in the Camargue

After the panther of the creeks, this might have sounded like another hoax, if the farmers of the Camargue had not been finding the carcasses of bull calves and colts in the swamps of the delta . . . Completely devoured by jaws of an exceptional size . . .

. . . According to the first examinations carried out by specialists from the Natural History Museum of Marseille, the creature was a Nile crocodile, a species increasingly rare. It is now extinct in Egypt itself, where the animal once symbolised the god Sobek. Only a few specimens of this formidable predator have been identified recently, but further upstream, in the region of the great African lakes.

This crocodile had already ravaged flocks of sheep and had devoured a wild colt. It was the local farmers who decided to organise hunts which resulted in the finding of the reptile . . .

How did such a creature come to be living wild in the Camargue? That is the question which the gendarmerie of Tarascon are now looking into . . .

Moracchini put down the newspaper and rubbed her eyes.

Daniel Romero arrived in the office, three parallel wrinkles marking his forehead. His gestures were nervous. The day before, he had been given a dressing-down by a magistrate and he was worried already about the appointment he had at 11 a.m. with Delpiano, the head of the squad.

"Have you seen the news?"

Romero shrugged his shoulders without even glancing at the paper.

"Have we got the D.N.A. results?"

"Yes, they arrived not an hour ago."

"And?"

"It's certainly the monster they killed yesterday. It devoured the bodies of Christian Rey and the others. We're on the right track."

Romero muttered something then looked at his watch.

"Have you called Michel?"

"I've been trying for an hour, he can't be found. Neither on his home number nor on his mobile."

"Yesterday, he told me that he was going to take a trip to the Camargue. He wanted to check a few things out."

Moracchini picked up *La Provence* again and crumpled its pages as she turned them.

It was the end of October. Over the delta, clouds had gathered and were weighing on the sky still red from the sun.

The Baron was alone, barefoot, on the long beach of Beauduc.

All day long he had been searching the reed beds around the observation hut once again, with rage in his heart. He had found precisely nothing.

Texeira had joined him late that morning and had told him about the black stork he had spotted, not far from the buildings of La Capelière. They had then called up the memory of William Steinert, and the hunt which the farmers had organised since the previous week to find the crocodile.

The sea breeze was shifting the sand across the surface of the beach. It made his ankles itch. He sat on the ground and leaned back against a breakwater. In front of him, the grey black trunk of a poplar lay like a huge carcass on the golden sand. The next storm would probably roll it out to sea, or deposit it further along the delta.

He closed his eyes and breathed deeply. The air that came from

334

the vastness of the sea made him feel better and unknotted his stomach.

The day before, he had received in his letterbox a light envelope marked 'By Air'. The postmark showed that it had been sent from the central post office of Annaba, Algeria, on 26 October.

The letter it contained was brief; it was a man's handwriting, fine and harmonious.

Michel

I shall keep, as a memory of you, a pistol bullet. The odd farewell gift that you gave me on our last meeting at the farmhouse of Clary. A surgeon friend of mine told me that it was an 11.43 shell and that I was lucky to be still alive.

You nearly killed me, Michel. And I'm almost sorry that you did not succeed. But that is the way things go. Do you know that, at William's funeral, I was standing behind Ingrid and our eyes met?

I know that you have been seeking your truth for some time by investigating the murky world of real estate in Provence. That was a good idea, but it made no sense, even if it might have seemed to . . .

The story reads differently.

There were twelve who served the Tarasque. Twelve who seemed to form a single person and whom the war was to separate. Some did their duty as men, others were like crows on carrion. I saw my lands change hands, my lands burn. My father destroyed.

Ai jamai descata lou plat davans moun paire* . . . As we say in Provençal. And my father died of grief and misery descended upon us.

When the smallest parcel of our Provence began to cost millions, I saw yesterday's swine sell the land of the immortals. After the death of my father, I was compelled to sell the fields that my family had tilled for ever so as to pay the death duty. On the death of my mother, our house will be sold for the same reason. Thus does our eternity change hands.

---

* I never looked at my food before my father.

William was my friend, the best I had. Perhaps you remember the poem that Ingrid read over his grave:

Ich hatt' einen Kameraden,
Einen bessern findst du nit,
Er ging an meiner Seite
In gleichem Schritt und Tritt . . .

William did not want that vengeance. Not like that. He never knew about what I was planning. What I did, I did for the honour of our two families and that of my master Bérard.

I owed you this fragment of confessions. The rest has no importance and I have trust in your intelligence.

The first white spoonbills arrived yesterday. They are magnificent, aren't they?

Vincent

Soubeyrand had enclosed with his letter two photographs of spoonbills taken during a mating display. The big birds had their wings spread and their necks were intertwined.

The Baron stood up, crumpled the letter into a ball and threw it to the wind that lurked between the hillocks. He thought of Isabelle Mercier and looked for her image of innocence. Beyond the dunes, there was only the blur of the foam that the sea was stirring.